THE CONSORT

⅃᙭ᕁⅬᙠᙠᕁᙏ ᙏᕁᔕⅬ

Ariel MacArran

The Consort
By Ariel MacArran

Cover Design: Steven James Catizone

Published by Here Be Dragons
ISBN-13: 978-0692226766
ISBN-10: 0692226761

Also available in eBook publication

PRINTED IN THE UNITED STATES OF AMERICA

1

ᛂᚤᚨᛖᚢᛂᚢᛉᚤ
Precipice

"*Please...*"

Alari slid her hands across the chill marble toward the goddess, the aged stone rough beneath her palms as she pressed her forehead to the floor.

The warm, golden light of morning streaming in from the high arching crystal windows set the colors and jewels of the sanctuary ablaze but the floor where she lay prostrate was as cold as the knot in her stomach. For three days now Alari had secluded herself here in Lashima's innermost sanctuary of the Imperial Palace, praying from the time the sun rose over the Empress' city until long after it set. Her words had long since crumbled from elaborate invocations in the ancient tongue to simple pleas. Only the priestesses who served the goddess were permitted this most sacred space—priestesses and the Imperial family.

As First Imperial Daughter of the Az-kye Empire, Alari could enter this sanctuary.

And her betrothed, Jazan of the Az'rayah, could not.

Alari raised a tear-stained face to meet Lashima's gentle gaze. The goddess' dark hair was loose around her lush figure, one hand holding her cloak of stars and the other reaching outward, her long graceful fingers slightly spread to alter lives through her touch.

"Help me..."

Alari had never been particularly devout. She celebrated the festivals of the gods and goddesses for the fun to be had, attended religious ceremonies as required of a princess of the Imperial House, but she had not prayed since childhood—and certainly never like this.

Today she would be mated to Jazan.

Pleading had not swayed her mother, the empress, from this course. Jazan was of excellent lineage, a powerful warrior and a handsome one as well. This marriage would strengthen the Imperial House in a time when it very much needed strengthening. No intervention from the god of Fate these many months had interrupted the myriad forms and rituals of the formal courtship required for a royal marriage.

Certainly the mere fact she did not love him and did not wish to be bound to him had not dissuaded Jazan. He would be mate to—and someday father of—an empress; Jazan, ambitious son of an ambitious clan, would not let something as inconsequential as his betrothed's happiness stand in his way.

The courtship rituals were completed, every tradition observed, and the High Priestess of Lashima, goddess of Love, had given her benediction. The ceremony would take place at midday and by this time tomorrow she and Jazan would be bound to one another.

There was no escape.

Unless Lashima herself intervened.

Alari had little hope that the goddess would. But there was nothing left to do now save pray. She pressed her cheek to the floor, wetting the marble with her tears.

"Please . . ."

"How long are we supposed to wait here?" Kyndan asked Nisara, barely moving his mouth. He shifted his weight slightly, still facing the elaborately carved double doors to the reception room. The minutes had ticked by as they stood in the polished hallway of the Az'anti clanhouse and still the doors hadn't opened to admit them. For this mission Kyndan had undergone neuro-accelerant linguistic training to supplement the Az-kye he'd learned during his captivity here. He was fluent in that language but he spoke now in Tellaran.

"Until the Az'anti clan leader formally welcomes us," Nisara murmured.

Kyndan allowed himself a very quiet—very annoyed— sigh.

He was a Commander in the Tellaran Fleet, not a diplomat. Certainly he should not be the one attending the opening ceremony of the peace talks on the Az-kye homeworld. He'd spent almost a year enslaved on this fucking planet and gods knew he had no desire to ever set foot on it again.

Except that his father, Admiral Maere, had requested he represent the Realm at the opening ceremony.

As had his sister, Kinara, who through her marriage to an Az-kye was now leader—*Ti'antah*—of the Az'anti clan, as well as the architect of the peace talks between the Tellaran Realm and the Az-kye Empire.

Kyndan had some choice words for both of them.

Not the least of which involved being kept waiting here at attention, stifling in his dark blue and white dress uniform, to see his own sister. That same little sister whom, after their mother died when she was eight and he eleven, he'd coached to throw a darshball, comforted when she awoke from nightmares all that first year, taught how to fire a blaster.

Hell, whose *nose* he used to wipe.

At his side, Lieutenant Nisara de'Cator adjusted the set of her shoulders, her own blue and white dress uniform spotless and her pale blond hair worn in a restrained up-knot. Nisara, of course, couldn't *wait* to return to Az-kye.

Despite once having been her bed companion, Kyndan bore her no ill will for falling in love with another; their relationship had years ago transformed to a warm friendship. Nisara had cared enough for him, so treasured their friendship she'd joined his sister months ago in breaching Az-kye space on the most poorly thought out act of revenge ever attempted by a Tellaran crew. Nisara hadn't learned he still lived until long after she'd been enslaved herself and fallen very much in love with an Az-kye warrior, Dael.

Personally, Kyndan didn't get the attraction.

Usually the Az-kye were dark-haired with eyes so black the pupil was nearly impossible to see. The women had pale to warm golden skin and tended toward the delicate with some genuinely distracting curves. But the men of the warrior class could only be described as savage, animal skin–wearing clods.

Two such brutes flanked either side of the double doors where Kyndan and Nisara stood at attention. Both men had sword hilts visible over their right shoulders and the beading marking them as warriors of his sister's clan over their left.

Tall for a Tellaran, Kyndan himself was a scant inch shorter than one and a bit taller than the other warrior but he had no desire to tangle with either. Especially since it had been impressed upon him by the Fleet brass that his task was to play nice on this mission. He could still see Admiral Henlon, his bushy mustache silver against his dark-skinned face as he delivered the lecture.

"This is the first time they're treating Tellarans as equals, Commander. You're going to their homeworld to represent all of us. I expect you to comport yourself with the utmost dignity."

Kyndan extended his neck a millimeter against the pinch of the dress jacket's collar.

Why does "dignity" always mean such godsdamned uncomfortable clothes?

"You know," Kyndan murmured, his eyes never leaving the shut doors in front of them, "when Kinara was nine, she decided to give herself a haircut. I have holos."

Nisara gave a choked laugh. She barely had time to stifle her smile as the doors finally opened and an Az-kye woman, her hair streaked with gray, emerged.

Kyndan recognized Laric, one of his sister's attendants, from his time as a slave in that household. Unlike then, Laric now met his eye respectfully.

Maybe there is an upside to this mission after all.

Nisara straightened smartly. "Commander Kyndan Maere of the Tellaran Fleet to see the honored clan leader of the Az'anti."

Laric inclined her head. "You are welcome to this house. Know that the empress' peace is upon you and you shall draw no sword within."

"Shouldn't be a problem." Kyndan smirked. "Since we don't have swords."

Laric blinked, her mouth working for a moment. Az-kye honored tradition above all else and she was completely thrown when he deviated from the ritual greeting.

"Oh, for gods' sake, Kyndan," came his sister's impatient call from inside the room. "Leave poor Laric alone and get in here!"

Huffing a sigh the maid stepped aside to allow them entrance. Kyndan gave her a grin as he passed and her nostrils flared in disapproval. Az-kye warriors may need to be stoic in public but Kyndan was happy to remind her—and anyone else—that those rules didn't apply to Tellaran men.

Now nearly seven months pregnant and cutely cumbersome, Kinara was helped to her feet by Aidar, her Az-kye mate. While they shared their father's height, his sister had their mother's straight red hair while he favored his father's warm brown waves. Kinara's hair had grown longer since he'd seen her, her face chubbier, but her blue eyes, so like his own, were bright with welcome.

"How's my little sister?" Kyndan asked.

"Not so little anymore." Kinara laid her hand on the curve of her abdomen, a little out of breath from crossing the room.

"Wow, Kinna," Kyndan said with a mock frown at her rounded belly. "You're *huge*."

She punched his arm. "I'm happy to see you too," she grumbled.

"Ow," he complained, rubbing his bicep. "I hope that kid inherits your right cross."

"Don't beat him up, Kinna," Nisara said, with a sidelong look at Kyndan as Kinara hugged her in welcome. "You'd be the second mommy-to-be to do it this week and it's getting embarrassing for the crew."

Aidar frowned and Kyndan held up a hand toward the warrior in protest. "Hey, that first one got me with a sucker punch."

Aidar blew his breath out, his blond hair, so unusual for his people, gold in this light. "You are joking."

Kyndan snorted. "You don't understand humor, Az-kye."

"I do not understand *Tellaran* humor." Aidar gave a solemn nod. "It is agreeable to see you, Kyndan Maere."

Kyndan blinked. His and his brother-in-law's first meeting involved trying to blast each other's ships to hell at the Az-kye–Tellaran border. His capture and enslavement by Aidar hadn't done much in the way of forging a friendship either but regaining his freedom and seeing how much his sister loved this warrior had at least mitigated the worst of his aversion.

And it was hard to hate someone who loved Kinara so much.

"It's agreeable to see you as well," Kyndan said, not missing how his sister's face lit up. "I'm being polite," he muttered at Kinara.

"And with the peace accords," Nisara said, "that makes *two* historic events this week."

Aidar gave a short, deep laugh.

"See?" Kinara threw a smile at Aidar. "He gets *good* Tellaran jokes."

"Maybe my humor will improve now that I'm not standing at attention in the hall," he said with a pointed look at his sister.

Kinara winced. "I'm sorry. I really didn't intend to keep you waiting out there so long. I was having a last-minute consult with a Servant of the Empress. To kick off the Festival of Ren'thar Her Imperial Majesty will be giving her official sanction to allow peace talks to begin." Kinara shifted her weight. "There was a question about—uh, protocol."

Kyndan's brow creased. "What kind of question?"

Kinara's face flushed. "About whether you would be permitted to stand with me when Empress Azara gives her benediction for the talks."

"I'm here as the Tellaran representative. Where am I supposed to stand? At the back door?" Kyndan's nostrils flared. "Is that 'Tellarans have no honor' thing still an issue?" he asked sharply. "They don't think we're good enough even to *speak* to?"

"No, it's just they're having a little trouble—"

"I hope they at least have the decency not to enslave my crew," Kyndan bit out with a sharp look at Aidar. "This time."

"Kyndan, try to understand what a huge shift in thinking this is for them," Kinara urged. "They have trouble accepting that even though Tellarans don't have clans like they do, the same traditions they do, they still have honor."

Kyndan's lip curled. "Sorry, it's just been so long since I heard 'clanless Tellaran' that I guess I just got used to not being *property*." He took a step back. "But hey, I'm happy to spare them my offensive presence by getting the hell off this godsdamned planet!"

"Kyndan Maere," Aidar said, stepping forward before he could leave. "Some Az-kye have learned that Tellarans have honor. Different than ours, certainly, but just as strong and vital."

Kyndan stopped short. It was such a reversal for this warrior and so sincerely—so *respectfully*—said that he began to feel a little regret for his outburst.

"To prove it so to the Empire you must not leave." A ghost of a smile touched Aidar's mouth. "Perhaps the Az-kye are slow to change. But we are capable of it."

"Okay," Kyndan muttered, throwing a grudging look at Kinara. "I can see *a little* of what you like about him."

Kinara put her hand on Kyndan's arm. "I know it's going to be rough for everyone at first. But think of what peace between the Tellarans and the Az-kye will mean, what good cultural exchange and trade will do—for all of us. I really need you to give this a chance."

"All right, fine, you can stop making with the 'please, big brother' eyes." Kyndan looked at Aidar. "And a brother-in-law—or friend—would just call me 'Kyndan.' Like you do with Tedah. Wait, where's Tedah? And Bebti?" He hadn't seen his best friend since Tedah had resigned his commission to return to his Az-kye wife, and Kyndan was looking forward to seeing his nephew again. "I thought they were going to be here too."

Kinara gave a warm, maternal smile at the mention of the boy's name. A street child that she'd adopted—to Aidar's initial horror—Bebti was now as loved as their own son could be. It was hard not to love that kid and, clan traditions be damned, Kyndan thought of him as family.

"Bebti's swordmaster's got his hands full trying to keep a nine-year-old focused already," Kinara said. "He's not about to excuse Bebti one second before the official start of the holiday, but you'll see him tonight. And Tedah will be at the Imperial Palace with Lianna for the start of the festival so we'll see him soon. Oh," Kinara added brightly, "and the First Imperial Daughter is getting married today."

"We're going to a royal wedding?" Kyndan asked, exchanging a worried glance with Nisara. "Kinna, we haven't been briefed on that protocol and we sure didn't bring a gift fit for a princess."

"Oh—uh, no." Kinara's cheeks flushed again. "You won't be attending the ceremony but they've agreed to do you the honor of letting you be there when the princess goes into the sanctuary to be married."

"You should let me sit down for that kind of news," Kyndan deadpanned. "I may faint from all this honor."

Aidar folded his arms. "He jokes again?"

2

Surrender

Too highborn to wear any color but black, Alari held her arms out to allow the maids to dress her. The gown was heavy; glittering with thousands of tiny jewels in the midmorning sunlight of the First Daughter's living quarters, it was reminiscent of Lashima's cloak of stars. A gown to honor the goddess of Love.

The gown she would soon take her final vows to Jazan in.

"Why look you as if Meithea will drag you to the underworld at any moment, Alari?" her sister Saria, Second Imperial Daughter, asked. "You have everything."

"Everything?" Alari echoed.

"You are First. You will rule all with the finest warrior in the Empire as your mate. You have always wanted to leave the homeworld and in a few days you will travel to Az-litha to represent the empress, with Jazan at your side."

The weight and volume of the elaborate gown brought a dizzying wave of claustrophobia as the maids fastened her into it.

Alari's nails bit into her palms as she struggled to draw breath. "Things are not always as they appear."

"What is *that* supposed to mean?" Saria demanded.

Her sister did love her, but at only nineteen she had not the patience nor experience to understand. Someday soon their mother would choose a mate for Saria too.

May the gods spare her a mate like Jazan.

"Sister, what is it, really?" asked Saria, her dark eyes worried as she came to stand behind her. Saria's black court gown too was elaborate with embroidery. Taller than she, her sister had yet to grow into the maturity of her form. "Do you still fear being bound to him?"

"To never again feel desire for another, to find arousal only with Jazan my whole life long?" Alari shuddered. "I can think of no worse thing."

"But *why*?" her sister asked. "You told me he was mannerly."

"He was," Alari murmured as the maids worked, adjusting her skirt, refreshing her cosmetics.

Saria shook her head. "He has visited your bed for weeks. You cannot fear joining with him *still*."

Despite how her attendants, teachers, and mother had instilled restraint into her, Alari's eyes stung. "Perhaps someday you will understand."

Though I pray you never do.

"You should not have waited till you were betrothed to take a man to your bed," Saria determined shortly. "You should have chosen men to join with you before you were promised, as other women do. *I* will not be bound so inexperienced."

Alari flinched inwardly at her sister's unintentional cruelty.

When I was nineteen summers I might have thought life so simply remedied, heartache easily sidestepped by those clever enough to avoid it. It does not seem possible that I should have lost all hope in the span of three years . . .

Perhaps though, Saria was afraid too—afraid of an arranged marriage when other women could choose a mate for love alone.

"I have chosen a lover." Saria's cheeks flushed becomingly. She had always been the pretty one and Alari the serious sister. "Naret of the Az'larna. He is very handsome."

"Mind that you will someday be mated to one Mother and her advisors select," Alari warned quietly as her maid added jewels to her hair. "Do not become too attached to this warrior."

"I do not think I will love him. In any case, she has already agreed he may visit me." Saria took her hand as she had when they were children, when they'd hidden beneath the quilts and whispered secrets. "I will tell you all about it," her sister promised. "And you will tell me what it is like to be bound."

Alari closed her eyes briefly and let go of her sister's hand so the maids could slide rings onto her fingers. "Can we not speak of something else?"

Saria considered. "Tellarans are come to the Empress' city to seek peace. Naret says some of their warriors are women. Perhaps we will see one."

Alari's brow creased. "A woman warrior? Does she dress in black and carry a sword?"

"He says she wears trousers like a man," her sister said. "But carries no sword."

Alari's frown deepened. "How are they marked as warriors if they do not have swords?"

Her sister shrugged. "They are Tellarans."

"I wish I could talk with one of them," Alari murmured. To speak to one must be like conversing with a creature so foreign as to seem otherworldly, the wildness of their ways, the strange, unimaginable landscapes of faraway planets . . .

"A barbarian?" Her sister gave a short laugh. "You might as well wish for wings to fly away from the palace." Saria met her eyes in the mirror's reflection. "Will you not tell me what troubles you, Alari? You used to tell me everything."

Her attendant placed the final jewel in Alari's hair and stepped back.

Looking back at her from the mirror was the very image of an Imperial bride.

Alari turned away. "There is nothing to tell." Her throat tightened to see how high the sun had climbed. "And it is time to go."

It took a half hour to get from Kinara's clanhouse to the palace entrance and two hours for their party to get from the arched, colorfully carved Gate of the Blessed inside the Imperial palace itself.

Kyndan was gritting his teeth before they made it halfway across the tiled courtyard. It seemed like every ten feet an Imperial Servant or another clan leader would bow or nod to Kinara with a message or a question or just to pass the time with a chat. Nisara had been disappointed to hear that only one Tellaran would be permitted to attend today's ceremony; Kyndan would have happily swapped places with her if he could have.

The palace grounds were the size of a small city. Enclosed within its walls were the empress' residence, the House of the Imperial Children, and many other buildings including theaters, soaring banquet halls where thousands of guests were served at a time, and religious sanctuaries dedicated to each of the Az-kye gods and goddesses. The grounds also held enclosed parks with fountains and gardens where jaha birds proudly strutted, their iridescent feathers shimmering in the sun as they spread their wings in display. The Imperial palace was a riot of color and carving but every person from highest clan leader to servant was dressed in black.

Warriors wore black anyway and there were so many of them about that Kyndan almost didn't notice the one warrior who looked back at him with amused green eyes.

"Tedah!" he said, smiling.

His friend caught himself before smiling back— warriors didn't smile in public—but his hand clasped Kyndan's warmly.

"Gods, it's good to see you, Kyn," Tedah said.

"You too," Kyndan said. He turned his attention to the pretty young woman at Tedah's side. "This must be Lianna."

"Yes," Tedah said with a loving look at her.

"I am pleased to meet you, Commander Maere," she said.

"Call me Kyndan," he said. "Believe me, Tedah talked about you *nonstop* for months. I might know you better than I know him."

Lianna smiled. "I was very pleased when he came home."

The idea of Tedah considering Az-kye *home* after being enslaved here was ludicrous but Kyndan gave a nod anyway. "He sure missed you."

"How's everyone on Rusco?" Tedah asked as they followed Kinara and Aidar into the palace.

"Your father says he'll never forgive you. Your mother says not to listen to your father." Kyndan paused. "But she also says a grandchild will do a lot to swing things back in your favor."

Tedah's mouth twitched. "She said that?"

"She made me write it down," Kyndan said, then more seriously added, "They miss you."

"I miss them too," Tedah said quietly. "But," he said, cheering, "once you get this treaty done I'll be able to take Lianna for a visit."

"And they will be able to come here," Lianna said.

Tedah seemed to suck his upper lip inward a little and Kyndan realized he'd done it to keep from laughing.

"What are you thinking, my mate?" Lianna asked, with amused suspicion.

Tedah's mouth twitched a bit again. "I'm just *very much* looking forward to introducing my father to your mother."

When Lianna walked ahead to have a word with Kinara, Tedah looked at Kyndan. "How are the Tellarans taking the idea of peace with the Az-kye?"

Kyndan gave a half shrug. "Politicians are for it, so's most of the populace."

"The Fleet?"

In a palace hallway filled with black-clad courtiers, his blue and white dress uniform was gathering a lot of curious glances. "A little more cautious, but that's to be expected."

Tedah gave him a level look. "What about you?"

Kyndan looked away. "Peace is always best," he said. "Isn't it?"

"Kyn, I know you might still have some—"

"Not the time," Kyndan broke in shortly. "Or the place."

"Right," Tedah said, then after a moment continued, "So isn't the palace amazing? Being here is like being transported back in time to the court of the Tellaran king."

"Yeah, still, just one person with that kind of power . . . It's a little, uh, narrow."

"It's sure more efficient than the republic. The empress wants something done, she just does it. No debate, no motions voted on by a room of representatives. Her word is law."

Kyndan glanced ahead at his sister. She'd made a name for herself among the Az-kye by getting a seat on the Council for Trade. "What about the Councils?"

"Yeah, there's some bureaucracy," Tedah admitted. "There's certainly the opportunity to move up in influence if you're ambitious."

"And belong to the warrior caste," Kyndan returned in a low voice, glancing around at the black-clad warriors and their ladies.

"The Realm had princes and kings," Tedah said with a shrug. "The Az-kye have clan leaders and an empress."

Surrounded by so many of their people—and headed to meet the ruler these people worshipped as second only to their gods—was not the time to give his opinion on their backward, barbaric ways.

"So, what's that?" Kyndan asked with a nod at the scrolling artwork that took a third of the upper edge of the wall. It was elaborate, detailed work, accented with gold leaf and jewels that sparkled in the sunlight streaming through the high windows.

"Well, this is the hall that leads to Lashima's sanctuary and *that*," Tedah said, "is a depiction of *The Thousand Nights*."

"Oh." He should never have let Kinara and his father talk him into coming back here. Being surrounded by Az-kye again, hearing the buzz of their language, set his teeth on edge. Just the *smell* of this world brought back ugly memories of defeat and brutal beatings—

"You know, the story of Ren'thar and Lashima?" prompted Tedah.

"I kind of skimmed their spiritual beliefs," Kyndan admitted in Tellaran. Switching languages earned him a couple of disapproving looks but better that than say in Az-kye that he barely knew a festering thing about their gods.

Tedah lowered his voice to answer in the same language. "It's the story of how Ren'thar, the warrior god, took a thousand nights to seduce the goddess Lashima."

"Patient guy," Kyndan said wryly.

Tedah didn't laugh of course—he had to control his expressions like any other Az-kye warrior now—but his mouth quirked upward a bit and his eyes flashed with amusement. "Yeah, well some of that legend is very, uh, detailed."

Kyndan glanced at the artwork again but this stuff seemed tame enough—the mighty god offering his lady goddess fruits, summoning birds to sing for her, turning a river to fill a cup of water for her. "Az-kye erotica?"

"You should get a copy," Tedah said. "You know, in the interests of cultural understanding."

Kyndan shot him a disbelieving look. Ancient Az-kye religious texts weren't going to have anything he hadn't heard of before. "Yeah, maybe."

One of the Az-kye ladies looked him over as she passed, a small smile on her mouth and her gaze speculative over her fan.

"Besides," Tedah said, "before marriage, women here are very . . . open to experience."

"Absolutely not," Kyndan said flatly.

Tedah raised his eyebrows. "You don't think they're attractive?"

"Look, Tedah, I only agreed to come because it was my last chance to see Kinna before the baby arrives. In a week I head back to Tellaran space then I ship out for a four-month patrol. I was out of the game for a year," he reminded. "We both know I'm damned lucky to get a command again at all." Kyndan threw a disdainful glance at the image of Ren'thar kneeling adoringly at Lashima's feet, the god's powerful arms bending a rainbow as an offering to her. "The last thing I need in my life right now is some kind of romantic complication."

Kinara caught his eye. She, Lianna, and Aidar were standing beside a snowy-haired woman and it was clear from his sister's urgent glance that she wanted him over there.

"Elder," she said as he joined them, "allow me to present the Tellaran representative, Commander Kyndan Maere. Commander, this is Sechon, Leader of the Council of Elders."

Kyndan inclined his head. Sechon was sturdily built with a strong proud carriage despite her snowy hair. "A pleasure, Elder."

"And a pleasure to meet you as well, Commander," Sechon said warmly, her dark eyes sharp and intelligent. "You are the first Tellaran I have met."

Kyndan kept himself from glancing at Kinara or Tedah, both who, despite being obviously of Tellaran birth, were reckoned Az-kye through their marriages. His sister was an Az-kye lady; *he* was a no-account Tellaran.

The sooner he got back home where things made sense, the better.

"I hope I'm the first of many," he said. "Maybe someday you'll visit Tellaran space."

"Do you know, such never occurred to me." The elder looked delighted. "Perhaps someday, Commander, I shall."

"Sechon has been a great supporter of the peace talks," Kinara said.

"Well, then, my people owe you a debt of gratitude for your efforts on our behalf," Kyndan said.

"The Lady of the Az'anti gives me too much credit," Sechon said with a laugh. "It is she who made the talks possible, but I was pleased to have offered what assistance I could. It is a time of hope for all of us. But," she said, with a regretful smile, "I have one or two things to see to before Her Majesty bestows her official sanction. If you will excuse me?"

"Of course," Kinara said.

"I look forward to speaking with you more at another time, Commander," Sechon said.

"She seems nice," Kyndan said when the elder was out of earshot.

"*She* is Leader of the Council of Elders," Aidar said. "And as the empress' most trusted advisor Sechon has the ear of the empress."

"Well, then I'm glad she's on our side," Kyndan said.

There was a stir at the end of the hall, a murmur.

"The First Imperial Daughter," Aidar said quietly.

Kinara threw a worried glance at him. "Okay, remember—"

"Princess. Bow," Kyndan muttered. "I got it, Kinna."

In perfect civility, the center of the hall cleared as the Az-kye drew toward the walls to make way for the princess and her retinue to pass.

Two warriors preceded her and around her walked no fewer than eight women. The princess was surrounded but her attendants kept respectful distance, leaving a circle of isolation around her. The women were older, their heads held proudly, dressed all in the black and gold of Servants of the Empress.

She was young, slender, far too delicate looking to be heiress to the throne of such a vast empire. She seemed to be swallowed in her formal black gown and her elaborately dressed dark hair shone like ribbons in this light. Her skin was smooth and pale, her full pink mouth drawn as if she held back a deep inner hurt by will alone.

She was pretty enough, he supposed, but Kyndan had never been one for the fragile type.

Sighing inwardly, Kyndan moved back with the others, impatient for the princess to pass, impatient for this mission to be over. He wondered if he would have to stay the whole week on Az-kye or if he could manage to bow out of some of the festivities his sister planned for his visit and get back to Tellaran space early. He would be taking command of the cruiser *Sertarian* shortly after his return; he still hadn't met with his first officer and he had a dozen personnel postings to approve.

The princess and her attendants were a scant few paces away now and everyone in the area dropped their eyes, bowing respectfully at her approach.

Except Kyndan.

He knew he was supposed to. Certainly Kinara had impressed the vital importance of observing royal protocol upon him.

He just couldn't.

Because in that moment she looked right at him. Velvety, soft black, her eyes were haunted by a sadness that speared him to his core.

And suddenly there was no Fleet, no Tellaran Realm, no Empire, no palace.

Just her . . .

3

⅃ⅎᚲ ᚹᚫᛚᛚᚪᚿᛂ ⅎᚿᛂᛂᚲᛒᚷᛂ
The Goddess Whispers

Alari dragged her feet but the press of Imperial attendants around her propelled her forward. At the eastern end of the palace lay the doors to Lashima's sanctuary where she and Jazan would make their vows. The distance was far too short. Along her path, every person stood with eyes downcast and heads bent in acknowledgment of the First Imperial Daughter.

Save one.

One man looked boldly at her. He was tall as a warrior and broad through the shoulders but his hair was short as no warrior would wear it. Warm brown was a hair color sometimes seen among the Az-kye but wavy like his, never. In a sea of black, his clothes of dark blue and white tied with a yellow sash set him apart and he wore no sword at his back.

Tellaran.

She had seen only a very few of them and always from a distance. Tellarans had been kept as slaves until the red-haired clan leader at the man's side had returned them all to their own space. Certainly none of them had ever been permitted within a dozen paces of an Imperial princess before.

Alari never expected to see one of them so close and she passed within an arm's length of him. The color of the sky in summer, the Tellaran's intelligent eyes held echoes of both deep pain and humor, the skin around them greater creased with care than should be at his age. His handsome, square-jawed face was more expressive than any warrior's would be and as she met his gaze, his brow creased ever so slightly, his full mouth parting.

She had the sudden impulse to reach out, to thrust her hand around those who stood between them for him to clasp. Alari could almost feel the warmth and strength of his fingers wrapping around hers.

And then they were past him and she was in the sea of black, of downcast eyes and bent heads again.

Tedah nudged him. "Hey, you okay?"

Kyndan blinked. "Yeah." He cleared his throat. "Yeah, I'm fine."

"You were supposed to bow," Tedah reminded with a quick worried glance around them. No one else seemed to have noticed his breech of protocol. "In fact, you looked dazed for a minute there."

Kyndan looked down the hall. He couldn't see her any longer. The murmur of conversation resumed, the buzz of the Az-kye language humming in his ears again as the courtiers and servants crowded back into the center of the aisle and blocked his view.

She was on her way to get *married,* for fuck's sake.

"I'm fine," Kyndan repeated.

Tedah was frowning at him.

He gave a short laugh to shake off the last of his bemusement, drawing scandalized looks from the nearby Az-kye.

Right, no laughing.

"So," Kyndan said. "I guess we should get over to the sanctuary so the empress can give her blessing or whatever."

"Actually," Kinara began brightly, "the elder said that to show her favor for the treaty, the empress will be acknowledging us at the end, right before the princess and her betrothed make their formal declaration."

"Ah," Kyndan said.

"It is a great honor," Aidar said.

"In the Tellaran culture, most important usually goes first," Kyndan said.

He read surprise in Lianna and Aidar's dark eyes.

"Because otherwise you have people standing around waiting," he explained.

They looked at him blankly.

"It shows you think their time is important." He said this last bit a little too sharply.

"That's not how the Az-kye see it," Kinara put in quickly. "They see it as not rushing you out of the way to get to someone with more status."

"So what you're saying is to make us happy they make us go last?"

"Well," Kinara said with a half-shrug. "*Second* to last."

"I guess today's just full of honors for me," Kyndan sighed.

He was *definitely* going to figure out a way to leave early.

The empress stood before the jeweled doors of Lashima's sanctum as Alari took her position on her mother's right. Jazan gave a small smirk when he saw her, then took up his own place to the left of the empress, all of them waiting as the court assembled. Alari wished they might take forever, that the closed sanctuary doors might never open.

In the last hours before the festival of Ren'thar would begin her mother made the traditional gestures of generosity. The empress presented gifts to a number of children, some of whom, dressed in their ragged best, had clearly been brought from the lower city for the ceremony. A few young boys selected by talent, or more likely the influence of powerful relatives of the merchant class, were elevated to the warrior caste and sent to homes to be fostered.

The empress granted gifts to the temples, of course, and announced that the winner of the contests this year would be permitted to formally court the Princess Saria.

Alari saw her sister blink and a rush of worry clouded her sweet face.

In a magnanimous gesture Empress Azara allowed the Tellaran to approach her along with the red-haired clan leader.

The Tellaran man walked with grace and a pride that was surprising. He had a boldness to his gaze when he looked at the empress that bordered on the insolent and, just for an instant, Alari saw his blue eyes glance her way.

He and the red-haired *Ti'antah,* impeded by the size of her belly, bowed to the empress.

"*Ti'antah* of the Az'anti," the empress said. "It is agreeable to see you."

"Thank you, Imperial Majesty," the clan leader replied. "It is an honor to be in your presence again. And I thank you again for granting my request to serve you and the Az-kye people in these peace talks."

Alari knew Kinara of the Az'anti by sight. All the Empire knew the woman whose mother had sent her to confront the attacking Tellaran Fleet months ago, how she had succeeded beyond all expectations. Although Kinara had been welcomed home by the empress herself, gifted honors and rewards beyond measure, neither Alari nor her sister had ever been permitted to meet her.

Her mother hated this woman.

Alari knew, but had never so much as whispered to any, even Saria, that her mother feared the Az'anti clan leader's growing renown as well.   Kinara was even whispered to be a *Cy'atta*—a Stardancer—emissary of the goddess Lashima and therefore a grave threat to her mother's rule.

"After such service as yours to the Empire," the empress said with a beneficent smile, "it is I who must claim the honor of our acquaintance and offer thanks for your efforts in this matter."

Kinara bowed again, as far she was able. "You are too kind, Imperial Majesty. Please allow me to present to you the Tellaran Realm's representative for the peace talks commencement, Commander Kyndan Maere of the Tellaran Fleet."

"Of course," Azara said graciously. "All of Az-kye welcomes you, Commander."

"The honor is mine, Imperial Majesty." The Tellaran's voice was deep and warm, his Az-kye perfect, but the way he formed the words was smoother, imparting a soothing hum to their tone. "I bring you greetings from the Tellaran Council and their hopes for a new era of peace between our peoples."

"With your permission I will begin talks for a peace treaty with the Tellaran Realm immediately," the red-haired clan leader said.

"Certainly." Azara held her hand out; an attendant gave her a datapad. "I have chosen the names of clan leaders to assist you in these efforts, Kinara of the Az'anti."

The red-haired clan leader blinked but recovered quickly to take the datapad. "Thank you, Imperial Majesty." She glanced at the list, her brow furrowing slightly. "Would Your Majesty wish all of these clan leaders to take part in the talks?"

The empress raised her eyebrows. "The talks will be involved. A great deal needs to be decided."

"Imperial Majesty," Kinara of the Az'anti began hesitantly and even from here Alari could see the clan leader's dismay and disappointment. "To involve all these clan leaders—it will take months just to *begin* the talks."

"My Lady of the Az'anti," the empress said, slightly reproving now. "This must be done properly. If the Tellarans are to be our allies we must know it to be a *lasting* peace." The empress smiled again. "I look forward to the peace and security these talks will bring my Empire."

She gave them a nod of dismissal; the pair bowed again and withdrew.

Alari's stomach knotted.

No more official duties, no more delays . . .

The High Priestess of Lashima started forward. Jazan, along with members of his clan, proudly stepped into position and Alari willed her feet to move as the court readjusted to take their proper places for the declaration.

Sparkling with gemstones placed to recreate the night sky as it appeared over the city at the time of the spring equinox, the doors of the sanctuary remained closed before her. The court stood arrayed before the entrance to the goddess's sacred space; reflected in the stones there, Alari could see the black of the courtiers' clothing, the bright garb of the ancient and bent High Priestess of Lashima as she hobbled forward on her cane, and a single jewel of blue and white.

Alari took up her place next to Jazan, the position of her attendants forcing her even closer to him. Alari's hands pressed against the gems embroidered into her skirt, the stones' edges rough against her damp palms.

Saria sent her a worried look and the empress gave her a brief, rare nod of approval. Alari sought the comfort of the goddess' gaze but Lashima's kindly face was concealed behind the doors of the sanctuary.

They had now only to declare publicly for each other and the doors to the sanctuary would be opened. She and Jazan would walk inside with the High Priestess to stand before the goddess, they would clasp hands, and the last words that would unite them would be spoken.

High Priestess Celara's hair was snowy, her back bent with age, a thousand creases on her papery skin, but her smile was kindly, her eyes bright and joyous as befitting one who represented the goddess of Love.

"If you would enter Lashima's sanctuary to be mated, speak now to your intent," High Priestess Celara intoned. "Jazan of the Az'rayah, do you choose the First Imperial Daughter Alari?"

Her heart pounded so hard she suddenly feared she would be ill.

Please . . .

"I do choose her," Jazan said proudly.

"First Imperial Daughter, do you choose Jazan of the Az'rayah?"

Alari opened her mouth to reply with the ritual words of declaration to name him in return but then, as if another spoke through her, she cried: "No!"

She saw the astonishment of the court, felt the sudden stillness in Jazan beside her, saw the High Priestess blink.

Alari turned her head to meet his sky blue gaze.

"I choose Commander Kyndan Maere of the Tellaran Fleet!"

4

The Challenge

There was an instant of shocked silence then the eyes of everyone—the empress, the priestesses, the court, the warrior at the princess' side—turned toward him.

"What?" Kyndan blurted.

He sought Kinara's gaze and Aidar's as well only to find his sister and brother-in-law equally stunned.

"Daughter," the empress hissed. "Answer High Priestess Celara proper—"

The High Priestess, possibly the only one in all the Empire with the power to do so, held up her hand to silence the empress.

"Princess Alari has declared for this"—Celara glanced at Kyndan—"man." The High Priestess tilted her head to regard the scowling Jazan. "Jazan of the Az'rayah, do you cede your claim?"

"*He* is no warrior! He is not even *Az-kye!*" Jazan spat. "I see what game you play at," he snarled at Alari and her lips went white. "You think I will not meet this Tellaran filth in the Circle." He addressed the High Priestess. "I do *not* cede!"

"*Filth?*" Kyndan stepped forward, no doubt blowing all those weeks of nicey-nice diplomatic talks to dust. Kinara tried unsuccessfully to pull him back but he shook off her hold. "What the hell is going on?"

The eyes of the court were on him but right now he didn't give a damn about their stupid protocols.

He glared at them. "Is one of you going to festering *answer* me?"

The empress' black eyes narrowed at him then she gave Aidar a short nod.

Aidar stepped forward. "Commander Kyndan Maere of the Tellaran Fleet," he said. "First Imperial Daughter Alari has chosen you."

"Chosen me?" Kyndan demanded. "What do you mean, chosen me?"

Aidar looked at him levelly. "To be her mate."

Kyndan's gaze snapped to Alari. "She did *what*?"

Her dark eyes met his, her mouth parted but she didn't speak.

"Kyndan Maere," Aidar said, wresting his attention back. "Jazan of the Az'rayah has not relinquished his claim."

"Yeah," Kyndan said impatiently, tearing his eyes away from Alari. "I heard that. What does it *mean*?"

"He will take challenge for her."

Kyndan felt his face heating with annoyance.

"He will fight for her," Aidar clarified.

"Fight *me* for her, you mean."

The guy was as big as a sular that'd fed on nothing but growth stims. Then Alari's dark eyes met his again and Kyndan struggled against the urge to shove past them all, to stand between her and that hulking brute.

Kyndan held Alari's gaze for a long moment.

"So what you're saying is that if we fight and I win," Kyndan said finally, "she marries me instead."

"Yes," Aidar answered.

Kyndan addressed the empress. "If I lose, will it affect the peace talks with the Tellarans?"

"Kyndan," Kinara whispered frantically. "Oh, gods, don't do this! Please, you don't—"

Empress Azara shot his sister a look and she fell silent.

"No, it will not," Azara said. "But as Jazan of the Az'rayah has said, you are not Az-kye. *You* are not a warrior." She gave him a smile that didn't touch her eyes. "A Tellaran is not capable of acting as a warrior would and we do not expect such of you."

Kyndan's nostrils flared. All those months being regarded as less than an insect, all the abuse, the humiliations he'd suffered as slave on this world because the festering *Az-kye* thought themselves superior to Tellarans. The burning frustration of seeing his crew treated the same, the powerless rage of that year, seared through his mind in a flash of red.

The empress addressed the High Priestess. "This man is unworthy. Continue with—"

Kyndan's fists clenched. *"The fuck I am!"*

His crude shout echoed through the arched hall of the Az-kye palace. Kyndan saw Aidar go pale; he heard the scandalized gasps of the court but he was past caring about any of that.

"I am a *Tellaran* warrior. She chose *me*," Kyndan said, jerking his chin at Alari. "You want a fight, Az-kye?" he demanded, narrowing his gaze at Jazan and bared his teeth. "I'll *give* you one!"

Jazan's eyes went cold and cruel. "Then I will take challenge now."

Aidar addressed the High Priestess urgently. "Commander Maere does not know the rules of the Circle. He must be allowed time to prepare. You must allow a month at minimum."

"A month?" Jazan exclaimed, then turned his eyes to the High Priestess. "You cannot allow such!"

The High Priestess addressed Kyndan, her eyes regretful. "If you would claim yourself worthy, Tellaran warrior, then you must be worthy now. I will allow you an hour to prepare yourself."

"You deem *him* worthy to be mated to an Imperial Daughter?" the empress demanded with an outraged gesture at Kyndan.

"I do not have to." Celara raised her eyebrows. "Your daughter did when she named him, Imperial Majesty." The High Priestess touched Alari's arm. "You will be under my protection until challenge is decided, child."

Alari's face had blanched and she sent him a pleading gaze, shaking her head ever so slightly.

He wet his lips. Was she regretting her hasty choice, then?

"Hold on," Kyndan said. "She and I need to talk alone first."

Jazan moved between them like an eclipse, a wall of black animal skins and muscle.

"You will *never* speak to her alone, Tellaran," Jazan snarled. "And in an hour I will kill you in the Circle."

The Az-kye warrior stalked off. With a final look of distaste in his direction, the empress whirled on her heel to stride away, her attendants flying after her. The High Priestess drew the princess along as the court exchanged shocked, excited whispers.

Alari looked over her shoulder at him, her dark eyes wide with horror.

"Oh, fuck me," Kyndan managed. "It's a fight to the death?"

5

ᚠᚴᛏᚴᚾᚢᛃ
Paladin

A little less than an hour later Kyndan stood barefoot and dressed in only a loincloth, awkwardly gripping the Az-kye sword Aidar had found for him.

So much for dignified . . .

"You could have spoken up," he said to Aidar.

Aidar looked at him impatiently. "We did *all* speak up for you! Why did you not refuse? Why did you not listen when my mate begged you not do this? The Empress Azara-behn the Heart of Heaven's Children *herself* excused you. And did you insist to undertake this fool thing I sought to give you time to train and you did not even plead for that!"

Kyndan looked at the wicked sharp blade in his hand, flashing in the light of the warrior's prep room as he turned it this way and that. "So I have to kill him?"

"Or he will kill you."

"Actually kill him?"

"Or *he* will kill *you*!"

Kyndan shook his head. "Why the hell did she do it anyway? Why choose *me*? Why not an Az-kye warrior? Gods, there were dozens there."

"It was a scandal, an affront to Jazan and his clan, that she should name another just before the final vows," Aidar said. "It is generations since such was done but the First Imperial Daughter has the right to name any man not already mated or betrothed." His head came up, his dark eyes suddenly hopeful. "Are you betrothed, Kyndan?"

"Sorry, no."

Aidar sighed. "A shame. But any warrior the princess could name, Jazan of the Az'rayah could fight and defeat. I cannot but believe she thought he would not agree to the Challenge. Truly, it is unseemly that he has."

"Because it's beneath him to fight me," Kyndan said tightly. "Because it shames him to have to fight a Tellaran."

"Yes," Aidar said bluntly.

"So she names me because she thinks it's a solid out for her and no one has to fight. At least she wasn't trying to get me killed when she did it." Kyndan tried a practice swipe with the blade. "Well, that'll make marrying her a smidge less awkward for me."

"I hope you survive to do so," Aidar said solemnly.

Kyndan's brow creased. "Have you ever thought of becoming a Fleet Counselor? You have a real talent for inspiring positive thinking."

Aidar gave a nod. "It lifts my heart that your humor has not left you."

"Aidar," Kyndan said, lowering the sword. "Why don't you use this time to tell me how I *can* win, rather than tell how sorry you are that I'm not going to?"

Aidar shifted his weight.

Kyndan blew his breath out. "Okay, how about this? How would *you* win, if you had to fight him?"

Aidar considered. "He is taller, his reach longer, and he is extremely well trained. Jazan is a warrior mighty enough to be the empress' choice to sire a ruler . . ."

"Okay," Kyndan gritted out as Aidar trailed off. "He can beat the snot out of me. We *know* that. Does he have any weaknesses?"

Aidar looked grim. "Jazan is intelligent and well versed in strategy. He is renowned to be fearless in combat and his clan is an ancient and mighty one."

"The perfect warrior," Kyndan murmured. "And the perfect mate for an Az-kye princess . . ."

Maybe he should get out of this. He probably still could. Go to the High Priestess, complain that he didn't know it would be a death match, say he had reconsidered. Claim that *he*, a lowly Tellaran, could never be worthy of being the mate of the First Imperial Daughter.

But then she'd marry Jazan.

And she's terrified of him.

It was in the way she looked at Jazan, the way she tried to make her delicate form even smaller as soon as she took her place beside him.

The Az-kye had strict gender roles but it was essentially a matriarchal society. She was a woman where women had the advantage. She was an Imperial princess. For gods' sake, she was heiress to the Az-kye throne itself. What could *she* have to fear?

None of this was his problem anyway. The whole thing was an internal Az-kye matter. She'd tried to get out of an arranged marriage she didn't want and it didn't work. She'd figure something out. And if she had to marry this guy, she really had the upper hand here, didn't she?

He should hand over the sword and get the hell out of here. Put the dress uniform—which was uncomfortable but at least covered his ass—back on and walk away from this fight. The peace talks would go forward with the empress' blessing and Princess Alari would get the ideal Az-kye mate.

Alari.

He hadn't even known her name when her eyes first met his.

Eyes as dark, deep and soft as a summer night . . .

Kyndan tightened his grip on the sword.

"Okay, he's Ren'thar in mortal form," Kyndan said with a dry reference to the Az-kye's warrior god. "What's Ren'thar's weakness?"

Aidar's brow creased. "His mate, Lashima."

"Goddess of Love." Kyndan studied Aidar. "You know Az-kyes a hell of a lot better than I do. You saw them together. Do you think Jazan loves Alari?"

Aidar gave a snort. "I think Jazan a warrior who loves himself alone. He would not force a woman to be his mate if she named another, did he love her."

"Did you love Kinara when you married her?" Kyndan asked suddenly. Kinara had agreed to be Aidar's mate to win freedom for her enslaved crew, Nisara and Tedah among them. But Kyndan had never really thought about why Aidar had married a Tellaran slave.

Aidar's dark eyes were lit from within. "With such depth I cannot even speak to it."

"That's good," Kyndan said quietly. He tilted his head. "So if I marry Alari I'll become part of the Imperial family, right?"

"Yes."

"And once I'm the princess' consort you'll have to bow to me, won't you?"

Aidar's face mouth twitched in amusement. "I would."

"Don't worry, Aidar." Kyndan grinned. "I'll make sure you're front and center for the wedding."

"First rule of combat is to know you are going to win."

Kyndan recalled hearing Lieutenant Deril say that on his first day at the academy. The man was a windbag but he knew his stuff.

"Have confidence that, no matter what," he'd said to the class, his Leman accent giving his words a clipped, harsh tone, *"you will prevail."*

Kyndan stepped into the arena, his heart hammering in his chest. He'd learned long ago at the academy how to get out of his own way, to go beyond the fear, how to trust himself and his training to handle anything he came up against.

I will win.

I just need to figure out how . . .

The circular arena had a dirt floor and was surrounded on all sides with stands for an audience. In the center, brightly lit from above and marked with stones to show the boundary, was the Circle. He couldn't cross the stone boundary by more than a step; to do so meant being cut down by warriors who waited outside in case of such an occurrence.

Run, you shame your clan and they kill you anyway.

Once Kyndan stepped inside the Circle he would win or he would die.

At least it's a nice turnout.

The stands were more dimly lit, filled to capacity and then some. There were many more outside who pressed forward at the arched exits, peering in from the corridors outside. The empress was easy to pick out; she commanded the very center of the stands and sat surrounded by her advisors and attendants.

He spotted Kinara and Aidar on the right. Tedah was there with them, Lianna at his side. The three looked grim but Kinara looked sick with fear. He'd asked Aidar to keep Kinara outside. In her condition she didn't need to be watching this, but clearly his brother-in-law had lost that argument.

Knowing Kinara, Aidar probably lost a lot of arguments.

A single other light burned as brightly as the one lighting the Circle. Directed down it illuminated an observation balcony over the space.

Alari stood there, alone.

Her posture was straight, her head held high, but she gripped the rails so tightly even from here Kyndan could see the tension.

Jazan entered at the same time from the other side of the arena. Dressed as Kyndan was, in loincloth alone, the man was a mass of muscle and scars.

With Kyndan her chosen, Jazan was the challenger. As such, Jazan went first to stand in front of Alari. She said something to him but from where Kyndan stood he could not make it out.

Whatever it was, made the warrior's lip curl and he stalked away to take up his place in the Circle opposite from where Alari stood.

As her chosen, Kyndan went second to stand before her. He would start the fight from this position, standing in front of her, standing as her protector.

She looked so fragile up there, so alone. It wasn't right that Alari should have to watch this with no one to comfort her. She deserved better care.

Kyndan gave a bemused half smile as he took up position beneath her. *When did I start thinking of her as mine?*

"Tell them," she said hoarsely. Her dark eyes were wide as she looked down at him, her lower lip trembling. "Tell them you do not wish for this challenge. He will let you go. He will let you live."

Kyndan had been in battle. He'd been in simulations at the academy where they messed with your brain so bad that you didn't even realize it wasn't real, just to test you. And when he'd entered the Fleet he'd accepted the possibility that he might die but he wasn't really willing to.

He'd always held something back.

But this wasn't a fight for ideals or territory or because he was ordered by some data pusher back at Central Command. If he lost here Alari was going to spend her life with that brute.

This was for *her*.

And he wasn't going to hold anything back this time.

"I'll be a good mate," he said simply then he turned to face Jazan.

6

The Circle

He really is a beast.

Half a head taller and with biceps the size of Kyndan's thigh, the man was massive.

He's got height, strength, weight and reach on me. He's been training with a sword since he was eight and this is my first time even holding *one.*

What are my advantages here?

Kyndan drew his breath in and let it out slowly.

Right, none. How can I win anyway?

That Aidar had asked to have a month for him to teach him the rules was ludicrous. Kyndan hadn't even needed the whole hour to get them. Basically they were: step into the Circle, don't step out, kill the other guy.

Well, I've managed two so far.

At some unknown signal Jazan suddenly broke from his position opposite. Kyndan tensed, gripping his sword in the en garde position, but the Az-kye didn't rush him.

Instead Jazan slowly arced toward him. He moved back and forth, pacing like a Leman mountain cougar, his brows drawn low over his angry dark gaze.

One swing of that starblasted sword and this is over. Why is he waiting to attack?

Kyndan's eyes narrowed, sizing up the warrior as Jazan paced toward him. Jazan held his sword like it was an extension of his arm, graceful despite his bulk, wielding the blade as if the thing weighed nothing at all.

Jazan was a heartbeat from pinning him against the boundary stones right beneath Alari. Kyndan darted quickly to the right to get some space between them.

Damn it, he's got to have a weakness somewhere!

"I'm surprised you agreed to fight me at all," Kyndan threw out.

Jazan's lip curled in disgust. "I should not have to."

"You don't," Kyndan pointed out. "I'll let you walk out of here right now. All you have to do is give up Alari."

"Think you I would let you take *my* place as consort?" Jazan jeered. "You are stupid as well as honorless, Tellaran."

"You don't know anything about Tellarans," Kyndan snapped.

Quick as a coiled snake Jazan struck and with the very tip of his sword cut Kyndan's face.

It happened so fast Kyndan scarcely had time to blink.

He stumbled back, his cheek stinging, and Jazan took up pacing in front of him again.

He could have taken my eye. Gods, he could have cut my throat before I even had time to block!

"You are weak," Jazan scoffed. "You are nothing."

"And *you're* losing," Kyndan threw back, adjusting his grip on the sword.

Jazan's blade suddenly sliced his right forearm like a hot knife through tararoot mousse. Kyndan drew his breath in sharply at the pain. He risked a quick, foolish glance to see that it was a flesh wound and not deep at all.

What the hell is he doing?

"Am I losing, Tellaran?" Jazan mocked.

"It's true," Kyndan gasped. "You—all the Az-kye— are losing to the Tellarans. *That's* why your empress is finally willing to talk peace. Your ships are too slow, your society based on stagnating, outdated rules. We outgun you now. In a few generations the Az-kye Empire will fall to dust."

"It is the Tellarans that will fall," Jazan snarled. "You are barbarians. You are like animals."

"Maybe that's why Alari wants me instead." Kyndan smirked. "Because some Tellaran seed is exactly what your royal line needs."

With a casual flick of the blade Jazan cut his left thigh open.

Kyndan let out a howl of pain as his leg collapsed under him. Face down in the dirt, curled in agony, he barely kept hold of the sword.

Nausea roiled his stomach and Kyndan was coughing against the powdery dirt. Only pure survival instinct got him halfway up. Dimly he was aware of the audience getting to their feet and Kinara screaming his name. Blind with pain, he was crawling away when his hand hit against a black stone.

Something about that stone was important.

Certain-death-like important but he couldn't remember what the hell it was.

Right. Second rule. Don't cross the boundary.

But now he was trapped against the stones. He pressed his palm on the cool black surface of the boundary, willing the coldness, the hard solidity of the rock, to steady his mind and let him think.

Somehow it penetrated through the pain and fear fogging his brain that Jazan hadn't killed him yet.

Why the fuck not?

Gritting his teeth, Kyndan pushed against the stone, using it to help him get to his feet. Sweat was running into his eyes and Kyndan hefted the sword out into a weak en garde position but Jazan wasn't anywhere near him.

Az-kye warriors didn't smile or show emotion except in private and in the company of those they were closest to. The Circle was one place that social rule didn't apply.

But considering the sadistic smile on Jazan's face now, Kyndan really wished it did.

Jazan waited on the other side of the Circle, apparently content to let Kyndan get to his feet before the warrior finished filleting him.

Hey, I'll take whatever I can get . . .

Kyndan couldn't keep from groaning in pain as he staggered away from the edge of the Circle towards Jazan. He hadn't landed a single hit or even blocked an attack but he raised his sword anyway.

"You know, I didn't get a chance to ask," Kyndan got out between teeth clenched in pain. "Will I have any official duties as consort or is bedding the princess my main responsibility?"

Jazan knocked Kyndan's sword downward, hitting so fast and hard it sent a jarring shock up Kyndan's arms when the blade met the ground. Kyndan's sword hit the dirt, then Jazan lifted his massive arm and clipped Kyndan with an upper cut under the jaw with the hilt of his sword.

Kyndan slammed to the dirt floor hard enough that he saw stars. His face went briefly, blessedly numb.

Jazan gave him a contemptuous look and stepped back.

Kyndan blinked rapidly, the arena spinning around him.

Okay, I get it now. He's taking the time to humiliate me before he kills me.

Kyndan suddenly wondered if Aidar would act like this and decided that his brother-in-law wouldn't.

This guy's supposed to be the very best but an honorable warrior wouldn't do what he's doing.

Jazan threw a narrow, gloating look up at Alari. Under the bright light tears shimmered in her velvety eyes.

Gods, this isn't about humiliating me at all. This is about humiliating her*! He wants her to suffer.*

The numbness was gone far too quickly. His jaw felt like it had been hit with a tarasteel block. His lip throbbed fiercely and he had a hell of a time getting back on his feet. His legs were shaky and he had to use the sword as a lever to get up at all.

He doesn't love her. All he cares about is being consort. But he can have that without hurting her.

What am I missing here?

He was filthy now. Between the sweat and dirt and blood he was a mess. His leg was throbbing but Kyndan guessed Jazan had deliberately missed the artery so he wouldn't bleed out.

Now he just needed to survive long enough so he could enjoy worrying about his wounds getting infected.

"The palace seems nice." Kyndan limped toward Jazan. He was shaking with fatigue and pain, his leg bleeding freely as he hefted the sword again. "Good place for Alari and me to raise a family."

"I could cut out your tongue but I would have her hear you beg to end it, Tellaran," Jazan spat.

"Hey, I'm happy to end it right now," Kyndan said amiably. "Put down your sword and I'll let you walk out."

"You are an unworthy opponent," Jazan growled. "I will have not even a scar for this."

A scar? He hasn't even broken a godsdamned sweat!

"Giving up?" Kyndan got out through his throbbing lip. "I knew you were a coward."

"*Coward?*" Something showed for an instant in the Az-kye's gaze then Jazan's face hardened. "I will enjoy killing you slowly."

Fucking hell, that's it! You did something you know a warrior shouldn'*t do. And so now you're not bothering to act like a warrior at all.*

The look in Alari's eyes when they met Jazan's—

"Only a coward hurts a woman," Kyndan hissed, pitching his voice so only Jazan should hear. "Like you hurt her."

Suddenly there was fear in Jazan's eyes. There was shame.

It didn't matter that Kyndan didn't know exactly what the warrior had done to Alari; he could guess. More importantly *Jazan* knew what he'd done.

Kyndan's teeth bared in disgust. "That you dare call yourself a warrior after what you did tells me that your honor isn't—and never was—worth a *damn.*"

Jazan's face spasmed.

"It doesn't matter who walks out of here. You've already lost," Kyndan taunted. "Because I still have *my* honor while you have *none!*"

Jazan roared and rushed him, swinging his sword to deliver a blow that would cut a man in half.

An Az-kye warrior would stand tall and accept the end of his life, knowing it the honorable way to die.

But Kyndan wasn't an Az-kye.

At the last instant he sidestepped and dropped. Pain shot through his leg like fire at the movement and he threw all his focus onto bringing the sword across his body. Taken off guard, Jazan tried to stop short and Kyndan swung outward just as the warrior came parallel. And—while it was as clumsy swordsmanship as likely ever seen in any

Circle—a cut that deep through the tendons at the back of the ankle would cripple even a huge, hulking beast of an Az-kye.

And did.

Howling, Jazan stumbled then fell face first into the dirt.

Kyndan pushed the tip of his sword into the dirt to heave himself up. He was on his feet in the next moment, heavily favoring his left leg but at least he could hobble. Jazan's leg was deformed where the bulky calf muscle jumped up behind his knee. He was also losing a lot of blood.

Jazan arched, his teeth bared and the cords standing out on his neck as he struggled to his knees. The powdery dirt made the air burn in Kyndan's lungs as he hefted his sword. All he had to do was bring the blade down hard enough now and he'd take Jazan's head off.

An Az-kye would.

Lucky for you I'm Tellaran.

With a sharp movement Kyndan brought the sword down and struck the back of Jazan's head with the hilt, knocking the Az-kye out cold.

Gasping, Kyndan took stumbling steps back. He shakily pushed some of the sweat-soaked hair off his forehead with his forearm and spat to get the taste of dirt out of his mouth.

The arena was silent around him. Every person in the place was standing, staring down at him.

Kinara had her hand against her mouth, her other hand gripping her mate's. Aidar's face was slack with astonishment. Tedah and Lianna wore expressions of shocked disbelief.

His breath was coming hard and with slow, painful progress Kyndan limped across the Circle toward Alari.

He was panting, blood roaring in his ears and only halfway across the Circle when his gaze met Alari's. She had her hands to her mouth and she was shaking her head a little.

Damn it, isn't anyone *happy I won?*

Alari's dark eyes went wide.

And she wasn't looking at *him*—

Kyndan spun and brought up the sword a spare instant before Jazan, his face savage with hatred and his leg dragging, skewered him. He knocked Jazan's blade aside and on the back swing caught the warrior across the throat.

Jazan collapsed at Kyndan's feet. He twisted in the dirt, making gurgling choking sounds that echoed in the quiet arena, then finally went still.

The crowd stared down at him in silence. Tedah caught his eye, his expression urgent. Kyndan, shaking with reaction and blood loss, frowned as his friend held a fist out, moved it up a bit, then repeated the action.

Oh, yeah. I forgot.

He turned toward Alari and met her wide-eyed gaze.

Swaying on his feet, Kyndan hefted his sword high in an Az-kye warrior's declaration of victory.

Alari gave a sob as the arena erupted into cheers.

7

"That festering *hurts*!"

Aidar shook his head, a smile playing at his mouth as he worked to clamp closed the wound on Kyndan's leg. "A warrior bears pain uncomplainingly."

"Screw that!" Kyndan snarled, still annoyed that while he'd made it out of the arena on his own, Aidar had to half carry him back to the warrior's prep room. "Give me a godsdamn pain killer!"

"I am almost finished," Aidar said, unperturbed. "You would show yourself a worthy warrior, would you not?"

"A worthy *Tellaran* warrior!" Kyndan bit out. "Tellaran warriors get analgesics! Have you even *thought* about finding me a medtech?"

Aidar gave a short laugh. "There. The last is placed." He wiped the area clean and smeared ointment on the wound then started bandaging the leg. "The ointment will ease the pain and heal you quickly. It will be a fine scar indeed." He glanced at Kyndan's cheek approvingly. "As will that one."

"A scar on my *face*?" Kyndan exclaimed, his hand flying to the bandage there. "I'll look like a fucking holodrama villain!"

Aidar raised blond brows, the old scar that ran the length of his left cheek pulling a bit.

"No offense," Kyndan gritted out. "But I'd prefer not to have any scars at all, thank you."

"Our healers are very skilled. Do you wish not such trophies, I will fetch you a healer to treat you now so you will bear no mark. I thought you intended to honor Alari, but since you do not . . ." Aidar shrugged as he finished covering the cut on Kyndan's arm.

Kyndan blinked. "You guys purposely scar? I thought your medicine was just not advanced enough to prevent them."

Aidar gave a snort. "Our women do not bear scars, nor do those not of our caste, Kyndan."

"*Our* caste? So now I'm part of the warrior class?"

"Of course." Aidar said, surprised. "Only a warrior can take Challenge. You became one when you stepped into the Circle. You bore yourself bravely and would be counted one of us even if you had died there. And to turn your back on a warrior such as Jazan . . ." He shook his head admiringly as he finished the bandaging. "I have never seen such mad courage."

Kyndan shifted. "I only wanted to knock him out."

Aidar looked startled. "Why would you do such?"

"Because I didn't want to have to kill him!"

Aidar's gaze became hooded. "You did not hesitate to kill Az-kye before."

"I was under orders to open fire on your ship," Kyndan fairly spat. "My duty, my *honor*, requires me to follow the orders I am given—whatever they are. I will not apologize."

"So you *have* come to regret it."

Kyndan's head came up. "I didn't say that."

"No," Aidar said mildly. "But you wouldn't think to apologize at all if you did not."

Kyndan looked away. "Do warriors get antibiotics?"

In response, Aidar pulled an injector from the medkit. "We are proud, not stupid."

Fortunately the injection didn't hurt at all. Of course that was about the only thing on him that didn't. He was going to have a bunch of bruises, his lip was split, his face and arm were sore, but his leg was the worst of it. Despite the ointment slowly easing away the discomfort, his thigh still throbbed enough to make him queasy. Aidar had sent to arrange a litter to carry him back to the Az'anti clanhouse and he sure wasn't looking forward to that trip. Sore, shaky with pain, and exhausted, Kyndan let his eyes fall shut.

The door banged open. Kyndan started badly, hissing against the shooting pain in his leg when he moved.

"How is he?" Kinara demanded, sweeping into the room, Tedah at her heels. Then she was at his bedside, peering down at him anxiously. She didn't wait for Aidar's response. "How are you?"

He gave them a smile and from their horrified expressions he was glad he hadn't gotten a look in the mirror yet.

"I'm glad you killed him!" Kinara spat. "Saves me from having to do it myself!"

She was round bellied as a gourd, pudgy-cheeked from pregnancy, and dressed from head-to-toe in the glittering ensemble of an Az-kye lady. She looked about as menacing as a wide-whiskered baby snouse.

Still, knowing Kinara, she probably would have taken Jazan on. From the look on Aidar's face his brother-in-law likely thought so too.

"I'm okay." Kyndan sent a nod toward Aidar. "Apparently I'm a warrior now. And hey, I'll have some nice scars to prove it."

"Well," Tedah said, "you're a couple ahead of me but I'll catch up."

Kinara's brow creased a little and he laughed inwardly at what must be going through her mind. Az-kye warriors bore their scars with pride but that didn't mean she thought her brother should have them. Not that she'd want to say something to that effect in front of her Az-kye mate of course . . .

"But you're Tellaran," she said finally.

"Well," Kyndan said. "I wouldn't want to pass up an opportunity to honor my princess."

Kinara exchanged glances with Aidar.

"What?" Kyndan asked.

Kinara wet her lips. "About that. You have a decision to make and not a lot of time to make it."

Kyndan raised his eyebrows. "What decision?"

"Well," Tedah said, shifting his weight. "If you want to be Alari's mate or not."

Kyndan frowned. "I fought for her. Don't I *have* to marry her?"

"Alari declared publicly for you," Aidar said. "You accepted Challenge and won but *you* have not declared for *her*."

"In fact, honor is completely satisfied so you can back out," Kinara assured quickly.

"You mean she has to show up for the wedding but I don't?"

Aidar gave a nod.

"Hold on." Kyndan's eyes narrowed. "What aren't you telling me here?"

"Alari is the First Imperial Daughter but she is not the only child of our empress," Aidar said. "She has a younger sister. Do you become Alari's mate, the empress must make you part of the Imperial family but she will not tolerate a Tellaran consort on the Az-kye throne. Alari will be an

Imperial Daughter but she will no longer be heiress to the crown does she take you as mate."

"Okay," Kyndan said, swallowing back the unexpected crush of disappointment. *What was I thinking anyway? Me, marrying a princess . . .* "So it's in Alari's best interest if I *don't* show up?"

Tedah's face was grim. "There's something else."

"The empress cannot permit such willful disobedience in her heiress," Aidar said. "Your victory in the Circle is unquestioned and witnessed by many. Her Imperial Majesty is honor bound to permit the princess to take you as mate but the choice is now yours. Do you choose not to . . ."

Kinara put her hand on his arm. "Then the empress has decreed that Alari will wear the white."

Kyndan was left speechless for a moment. "She's going to disown her and make her clanless?" he got out. "Make her own daughter a slave?"

Aidar gave a nod and Kinara looked glum.

"Slavery or life bound to a barbarian, huh?" Kyndan gave a short, bitter laugh. "So Alari suffers either way and everyone sees what happens if you cross the line. That's some empress you guys have."

"The empress must first cleave to the throne or she cannot rule," Aidar said grimly. "Such demands a certain ruthlessness."

"Ruthless?" Kyndan's lip curled. "The woman has the warmth of a Utavian desert serpent. Did you see the way she looked at me when I agreed to fight? You'd think she'd be flattered I was willing to die for her daughter."

"She'd prefer you had," Kinara said bluntly. "You defeated her handpicked choice for Alari *and* you're Tellaran. And right now everyone is talking about how you took Jazan down. You did more to raise regard for Tellarans in these people's eyes in a few hours than a hundred years of peace could." She shook her head. "The empress is not going to make it easy if you become her daughter's mate."

"And what was that little game with the list of clan leaders?" Kyndan asked. "Why would the empress agree to let talks go forward with us then throw something like that out?"

Kinara chewed her lip for a moment. "I'm not sure. She might have really been concerned about seeing everything done right or she could just be playing this to delay the talks."

Kyndan sighed. "Well, I didn't go through all that to have Alari to wind up a slave. I'll marry her."

Kinara's brow creased. "Oh, Kyndan, are you sure?"

He gave a shrug. "Yeah, I mean, if it doesn't work out between us, at least we tried."

"Uh," Tedah put in. "That's not how Az-kye marriages work. They mate for life."

Kyndan frowned. "Well, Tellaran marriages are meant to be lifelong too, remember? But people do split up."

Kinara looked at Aidar and Tedah. "He has to be told."

"I don't think he wants you here for this, Kinna," Tedah said quickly. "We'll tell him."

Kyndan's queasiness racketed up another notch. "Tell me *what*?"

8

ᚦᚱᚨᚢᚲᚾᚨᚱ

Plangent

What have I done?

Once First Imperial Daughter, now in disgrace, Alari knelt on the floor, her arms wrapped tightly around herself. She had long ago learned to hide her true feelings, knowing her tutors and maids were also her mother's spies.

But for the first time in her memory, Alari was completely alone.

Alari's chest felt hollow. Her father, dead eight summers now, had been a powerful warrior with a kindly heart and great love for his mate and children. *He* would have not have hesitated to intervene, even with his beloved mate, on their daughter's behalf. He alone had the strength of heart and power to protect her from her mother's wrath, but now there was none who would dare.

Bereft, rocking herself on the cold floor of her room, Alari again felt the scalding pain and aching sorrow of his loss.

The setting sun made harsh shadows in her silent, spacious apartments. Her attendants—even those who had been with her since babyhood—fled after her mother named her punishment. The fortunate among them would serve Saria now.

Her sister now was First Imperial Daughter and their mother's heiress.

Outside the Empress' city erupted into the joyous noise of the first night of the festival of Ren'thar. In the coming days young warriors would seek to prove themselves in the contests and win renown enough to attract a highly placed mate. The opera houses would be packed to bursting as troupes performed tales of the god, his battles, his courtship of Lashima. Public entertainments provided free to all as the empress' gift to the city would bring joy even to the poorest of her people. Families threw open their doors, thousands of lanterns spilled light into the streets as clans gathered for lavish feasts.

The court would be feted for days on end with banquets, plays, musical performances, and parties as the city celebrated. Alari would know none of those pleasures.

Her mother had been livid at her defiance. She would not have escaped entirely unscathed even if Jazan had won but now . . .

"You would have this Tellaran?" her mother had demanded coldly as Alari knelt, her forehead pressed to the floor at the empress' feet. "You would be mated to one who is not even Az-kye? So be it. Only pray, Daughter, that this barbarian bothers to claim you at all!"

Tomorrow Alari would be publicly disowned by her clan, thrown into the street to be sold as a slave in the Empire she had been raised to rule.

Or she would be mated to the Tellaran.

Jazan had been an Az-kye warrior, subject to an ancient code of honor, and that had not stopped him from—

The last daylight slipped away, plunging the rooms into darkness. Alari pressed her hands hard against her mouth, her whimpers echoing through the empty rooms.

Kyndan looked between Tedah and Aidar.

"Fucking hell," he managed. "I can't tell if you're joking."

Aidar folded his arms. "We are not joking."

Kyndan turned to his best friend. "Tedah, we've known each other since primary and I'm telling you right now, my leg is godsdamn *killing* me so—"

"*Not* joking," Tedah interrupted.

Kyndan shook his head a little. "So you're saying we make our vows then we go someplace private—"

"Yeah," Tedah put in. "Believe me, you're going to want *private*."

"Then Alari and I drink this binding wine stuff and . . ." Kyndan shook his head.

"Look, I'm sorry, you just can't—It's not physically *possible* to have sex, *nonstop*, for a whole *day*—"

"Or more," Aidar said.

"—is it?" Kyndan finished.

Aidar and Tedah both gave a nod.

"I really can't tell if you're joking!"

"We are not," Aidar said firmly.

"Uh, there's more," Tedah said, shifting his weight. "After that, well . . ."

"After that *what?*" Kyndan demanded.

"You're not going to be able to have sex with anyone else."

Kyndan let his shoulders fall. "Right. We'll be married."

"No." Tedah cleared his throat. "Because you won't be *able* to."

"Wait, what?" Kyndan breathed.

They looked back at him solemnly.

"Ever?" he asked weakly. "With *anyone?*"

"Not as long as your mate lives," Tedah said. "That's why before people take vows here, sex is pretty casual. Once you make that commitment, well . . . it's a lifelong one."

"What about *her?* Will she be able, I mean, with someone else—?"

"Nope."

Kyndan looked between them. "And . . . and you did this when you got married?"

They both nodded.

Gods knew he wasn't *about* to ask Aidar but Kyndan gave Tedah a questioning look.

Tedah gave a laugh, clearly reading what he wanted to know from his expression. "Kyndan, better than you can *even* imagine. And it stays that way between you two but . . ." He sobered. "This is a very serious decision. You can't just walk away. I loved Lianna and I knew what I was doing. I can't imagine the hell it must be to be bound to someone you hate."

"Or fear," Kyndan murmured.

Gods, no wonder she did it.

Kyndan wet his lips. "Look, I don't know anything about Alari and I've spoken to her all of *once.* I thought at worst we could try it and if didn't work out we would have our marriage dissolved but now—" He ran his hand through his hair. "I just don't know if I can do this."

9

The Sanctuary's Entrance

He is not coming.

Alari had declared publicly for him and there was no recanting. By her mother's decree the Tellaran had until midday to claim her. She stood alone at the door to Lashima's sanctuary now, shunned by the court gathered on the opposite side of the hall, her hands clasped together to hide their trembling as she waited.

Late into the night she wept in the dark emptiness of her apartments. Her whole life she had been attended to, cared for, waited upon. Alari had never had to fetch her own breakfast or dress herself but none wished to serve a princess who might see the next sunset as a slave.

He had fought so bravely for her yesterday and left the Circle on his own two feet after facing the fiercest warrior to be found within the Empire.

His sky eyes were so earnest when he had promised to be a good mate . . .

His kindly gaze when she'd passed him in the hall yesterday, her one shining hope that he would keep his vow in the Circle, gave Alari the courage to face the court this morning. Without maids to help her enhance what few charms she possessed, she wore her hair simply; she did not know how to arrange it herself. She intended to wear the gown she had worn here yesterday with its many jewels and elaborate beading, hoping to please his eye so that he might find her worthy still, despite her disgrace.

She dissolved into tears to discover she could not fasten that dress, or any of her other fine gowns, unassisted. In the painful silence of her rooms, wiping at her face, Alari searched for even one dress in her wardrobe with fastenings at the side and front she could manage to put on unassisted. The gown of Imperial black she wore now was far too plain for the occasion, her hair unadorned, her cosmetics scant. She felt ashamed that he would see her attired so poorly.

But she had labored, weeping, for nothing. He would not see her at all.

She held herself proudly as she had been taught; her features schooled to conceal her true feelings, to hide how fear churned her stomach.

By the empress' order the court would bear witness to her humiliation and many were eager to be on hand to view the fall of one so high. The bows at Alari's approach had been shallow this morning and few dropped their eyes. Most had not even bothered to acknowledge her until she was a handbreadth from them.

And none spoke to her.

In whispers that carried through the arched hall to where Alari stood alone, some of the courtiers cast wagers on if he would appear, and the odds offered that he would were long. Alari's face flushed when one courtier— correctly— noted that the princess was so badly outfitted she had even forgotten her hand fan on her *supposed* mating day.

High Priestess Celara had been granted, due to her advanced age and status, the privilege of a chair to sit upon but no other had.

The empress waited with her courtiers, on the opposite side of the sanctuary doors from where Alari stood, alone. Her Imperial Majesty's back remained unbowed as the morning wore on, her head held high, showing neither sorrow nor regret for the punishment she lay upon her eldest. The Empire she ruled was her true heart's child and she would do anything to protect it.

Its needs would always come first.

Saria, First Imperial Daughter, stood at the empress' side, nearly as sumptuously arrayed as Her Majesty. She shamefacedly avoided Alari's gaze, wise to fear their mother's anger if she were caught sympathizing and helpless to save her. Alari knew her sister well, saw the drawn, frightened look on her face, and knew she was not alone in not sleeping the night before.

Saria was heiress to the Imperial throne now but that came with its own dangers, its own sacrifices.

The sun climbed higher and still he did not come.

Perhaps the Tellaran had risked his life only in hopes of being mated to the First Daughter or, at the very least, an Imperial heiress, and now she was neither . . .

But no Az-kye warrior would have come to claim her now either. To be mated to a disgraced daughter who had lost her inheritance—even a princess—was a fate not to be envied and her mate would share her shame. Alari would be held up as an example of how the empress would strike back if crossed. She would stand as a lesson for heiresses throughout the Empire and future Imperial Daughters of the dangers of defiance.

But it was only when the High Priestess stood, her aged face drawn and sad, did Alari surrender all hope.

High Priestess Celara, leaning heavily on her jeweled cane, slowly crossed the polished floor and her eyes showed nothing but sympathy. She made her way to where Alari stood alone, the first to speak to her that day.

"I am so, so sorry, my child," she said softly.

Tears stung Alari's eyes.

High Priestess Celara laid a gentle hand on her arm. "May Lashima's gaze always rest kindly upon you."

Alari's throat closed and she could do no more than give a shaky nod of thanks. Trembling she turned toward the empress for the pronouncement that would cast her out of her clan, her home, and take even her name from her, forever.

There was an annoyed muttering from the court at the far end of the hall. The grumbling grew nearer and in the next moment the Tellaran, spitting a curse, pushed his way through the crowd of courtiers.

His face was flushed, his blue eyes all the more striking for it, and he was dressed again in the Tellaran warrior clothes of blue and white with the yellow sash. He limped toward her heavily favoring his left leg and the waves of his hair clung damply at his temples. He still bore fading bruises on his face, his lip still a bit swollen from the challenge yesterday. The cut Jazan had left on his cheek had healed over, the mark still red and angry, and Alari blinked in admiration of the scar he had earned in her name.

He was much taller than she remembered and she had to tilt her head to meet his gaze. He was broad of shoulder as well, his eyes bright with intelligence.

"Sorry," he said with a chagrined smile. "They don't make way for Tellarans like they do for princesses."

"You—you are here," Alari managed.

"I didn't mean to keep you waiting," he said, his blue eyes anxious. "My leg's hurting like a—it's, uh, slowing me down and it took forever to get through the crowd."

"Oh," she murmured.

He addressed the High Priestess. "I'm new at Az-kye weddings. I may need a little guidance, Your Eminence."

High Priestess Celara looked amused but her gaze was kindly as always. "You shall have it, Commander Kyndan Maere of the Tellaran Fleet."

He cleared his throat. "Listen, for the actual wedding vows, you can just call me 'Kyndan Maere.'"

Smiling, the High Priestess inclined her head then turned to make her way to the sanctuary doors.

He gave Alari a nod. "I'm ready if you are."

She had an urge to reach out and touch his broad chest, to run her fingers over the dark blue fabric of his coat, to trace the scar on his cheek with her fingertips.

To assure herself he had truly come for her . . .

Kyndan leaned forward, humor crinkling the skin around his eyes. "Don't worry," he whispered. "It looks pretty easy in the training holos."

Many of the court wore expressions of disappointment that they would not bear witness to her enslavement. Her gaze went to the High Priestess, the doors of Lashima's sanctuary sparkling behind her.

He touched her elbow. "Come on," he urged gently, taking a step toward the doors. "It'll be all right."

Tears blurred her vision. "I am glad you are here, Kyndan Maere."

Unexpectedly, and as no Az-kye warrior would ever do in public, he reached up to gently cup her cheek in his warm, broad palm. "You call me just 'Kyndan,' okay?"

"Kyndan," she agreed softly and let him lead her to stand before the High Priestess.

Unlike yesterday, Alari and her intended had no one at their sides. He was Tellaran and she in disgrace.

Kyndan threw a glance over his shoulder. "My sister and friends should be here in just a minute or two," he said apologetically to the High Priestess. "We just need to wait till they're here. Then we can start."

High Priestess Celara, leaning heavily on her jeweled cane, raised white eyebrows. "Tellaran matings must be very different."

His face colored. "Yeah, they sure are."

"You have a sister?" Alari knew nothing of Tellaran clans. "She is your clan leader?"

"She is *a* clan leader," Kyndan said. "You probably saw her yesterday. The red-haired woman."

Alari's brow creased. "You are of the Az'anti clan?"

"No . . . Look, Tellaran families are different. Now she's Kinara of the Az'anti, but she's still my sister, even though we don't have the same name anymore."

Alari's glance darted to the crowd and she saw the Az'anti *Ti'antah* arrive with her mate. A woman dressed in blue and white like Kyndan's joined them and a warrior of the Az'yan clan stood protectively by the blond Tellaran. Another warrior, one plainly born Tellaran but bearing the bead markings of the Otan clan, came too and an Az-kye woman, clearly his mate.

"She comes to protest our mating?" Alari asked worriedly.

He gave her a surprised look. "Of course not. She just wants to see us get married. You'll be her sister-in-law. Because you've married her brother, you become her sister," he explained at her questioning look. "But that's confusing for people so we say sister-in-law to show that you married into the family."

An Az-kye warrior became part of his wife's family and took her clan name as his own. Alari's glance went to her mother. The empress looked back at her with cold eyes.

"Do we become mates now, you will be of the Imperial family, Kyndan."

"I know things are a little different for the Az-kye. When Tellarans marry we make a new family. So maybe that's what our family can be, Alari—one that's both Az-kye *and* Tellaran. I know I'll be part of the Imperial family but to the Tellarans you'll be Alari Maere." He searched her face. "Is that all right?"

"Yes," she said after a moment. "I will be Alari Maere."

Warriors did not smile in public but he showed no hint of hesitation or shame, giving her a wide grin despite his swollen lip.

He gave the High Priestess a nod. "Okay, we're ready."

10

𝕏𝕃𝟽𝕙𝕩
Mated

Their footsteps echoed in the emptiness of her apartments. Traditionally a feast followed the final promises but when Alari and Kyndan emerged from the sanctuary, their vows spoken, the court had departed. The hall was empty save for those who had accompanied Kyndan.

The clan leader of the Az'anti had embraced Kyndan as had the other Tellaran-born warrior and the Tellaran woman. They all—Az-kye and Tellaran—offered surprisingly warm wishes to her as well. Kyndan grinned when the Lord of Az'anti bowed his head as befitting the tribute due an Imperial Daughter's mate.

"Wow," Kyndan said, taking in the brocades, the carved works, the sweeping balcony overlooking the city. "This is where you live?"

"I have resided here since I took my first steps but Her Imperial Majesty may direct us to other quarters now that I—" She swallowed. "I am no longer First Daughter."

"I'm sorry about that."

Her brow furrowed. "*You* are sorry?"

Kyndan gave her a rueful smile. "Marrying me means you aren't even an Imperial heiress any more."

"I would not have been in any case." Her hands pressed against her skirt. "Did you know what would have happened if you did not come to claim me?"

"Yes," Kyndan said quietly. "I spent a year enslaved on Az-kye."

Her mouth parted. "*You* were clanless? How is it possible that you—you—?"

"Got my name back? Reclaimed my honor?" he asked, his eyebrows raised. "Well, in my opinion, I never lost it. Tellarans don't do that, Alari. Strip people of their families and their names, send them into everlasting servitude and forbid them to wear anything but white. So when I got home the whole clanless thing didn't apply."

Alari stepped closer to whisper: "*You* were one of the slaves returned to Tellaran space?"

His full mouth curved and for an instant her eyes were drawn there.

"It's not a secret, Alari. Yes, I was. In fact," he continued, his smile fading, "I considered that. Waiting till you were declared clanless and then taking you to Tellaran space instead."

Her throat tightened with hurt. "You wished me your slave?"

"No, of course not," he said quickly, waving his hand. "I meant, take you to Tellaran space where you would be free."

"But *why*?"

He looked surprised. "So you wouldn't have to marry me."

Did he think that so much the better? To be stripped of name and honor, to be invisible to all those she held dear and forced to live among the barbarians?

But he did, she realized, looking into that steady sky-blue gaze. It was his home and they his people. Clearly he esteemed their ways.

"That—that was kind," she said at last.

The skin around his eyes crinkled with humor. "Well, hopefully you'll still feel that way tomorrow."

Alari suddenly found it hard to look at him.

"This is some view you've got," he said abruptly, walking out onto the balcony. "I bet you can see the whole city from here."

The sky was pink and orange with the light of late afternoon and already the second night of the celebration was starting. Even from here they could see the bustle of the Empress' city as lanterns were lit and last-minute preparations were attended to. From here too they could see the spray from the falls, its droplets sparkling in ever-changing rainbows by the light of the sun.

He nodded at the city below. "So how long does this Ren'thar festival go on?"

She knew so little of his culture; her keepers would have thought it contaminating to expose her to such barbarous ways and sheltered her from it all they could.

"Tellarans—they do not have festivals then?" Alari asked, coming to stand beside him.

He gave a laugh. "Many, but I suppose the closest god we have to Ren'thar is Jadan, the god of War."

"What of Lashima?"

"Arrena is the Tellaran goddess of Love. Jaden's wife Bathena may be goddess of Peace, but even so, she wouldn't put up with any messing around."

"Oh." It was hard to imagine a place the Queen of the Heavens did not watch over. "Ren'thar's festival lasts six days. This is the second night."

"Looks like fun. Anything you want to do? I'm game for anything we can sit down for," he said, wincing as he shifted his weight.

Her hands clenched. "It—it is our binding time."

"Yeah, listen, Alari, about that . . ." He turned to face her. "I'm not an Az-kye warrior so I'm not embarrassed to admit that my leg is really bothering me. From what I understand of the whole binding thing I don't even want to attempt it till my leg is fully healed. And I really—I want to get to know you," he said, his voice soft. "I want to make sure we're both ready to be, uh, *bound*. I want to join with you before we're bound and I know it might be a while before that happens too." His eyes were rueful. "Right now you're probably pretty afraid of me."

Startled, Alari met his gaze.

"I know Jazan hurt you," Kyndan said quietly. "I know how he hurt you."

Alari froze. *How could he—?*

"But *I'm* not going to hurt you like that, Alari." Kyndan traced her cheek with his fingertips. "Not ever."

Her mouth parted but she managed only a weak choked sound. Her hands opened and closed helplessly.

Kyndan held her gaze and eased closer to her. After a moment his arms went around her, his hold light, easily broken should she but step back. Despite his gentleness she tensed, half expecting his embrace to tighten to a cruel grip, his strong arms to push her down and hold her no matter how she cried—

But Kyndan's touch was gentle. His body radiated heat, his scent male, foreign, and at the same time so appealing. The warmth of him was too tempting. Shy, Alari slid her trembling arms around his waist.

He cradled her against his shoulder. Had anyone soothed her so since childhood? She closed her eyes and drew the comfort of it into herself, ashamed of her desperate, ravenous need of it as he rocked her.

"It's all right," he murmured, and she felt him press a kiss against her hair.

"I am so sorry," she whispered.

"You don't have anything to be sorry for. Whatever happened, whatever he did, the blame belongs to him alone. And when—*if*—you ever want to talk to me about any of it, I promise, I'll be there to listen."

She did not deserve such care, such kindness from him of all, and she drew away. "I should not have named you."

He sighed deeply, his expression resigned. "We're not bound yet, so undoing this should be possible. Let me talk to my sister."

"No, I . . ." She put her hand on his chest, feeling his heartbeat under her palm. "He could have killed you."

"Wait," Kyndan's brow furrowed. "*That's* what you're sorry about? Because you named me and I had to fight?"

"I still cannot believe I did such." She dropped her gaze. "The words were spoken before I knew it myself. And even then I thought he would not face challenge from—from—"

"A Tellaran," he finished for her. "I'm just sorry I didn't get a chance to tell him I was wearing white a few months ago."

She looked up at him in horror. "He would have been enraged by the dishonor of having to fight such a one!"

His mouth was upturned a little at the corners, his eyes crinkled again.

Her brow creased. "You are joking."

He gave a short laugh. "Wow, I really *am* going to have to work on that."

He took both her hands in his—a gentle, courtly gesture—and suddenly she thought of how Ren'thar seduced Lashima with a thousand days of tenderness.

"I know you thought I wouldn't have to fight at all," he said. "But would it take the shine off my victory if you knew I had no idea it was a fight to the death?"

Her eyes widened. "You should have told them you did not understand!"

"Well, I was pretty well committed to it by then and I knew I couldn't lose."

His confidence surprised her. She thought it certain he would not survive the fight; even now she could scarcely believe that he *had*. "You could not?"

"'Course not!" he scoffed. "You're my girl. I wasn't about to let someone *else* marry you."

"Your girl." She searched his face. "You say this to honor me."

He gave her a quick smile. "That was the idea, yeah."

"Have you had many other girls, Kyndan?" she asked suddenly.

His color rose. "Nothing serious."

"But you joined with them? You mounted them?"

He gave an embarrassed laugh. "Whoa, how'd we wind up in this area of space?" He shifted his weight, wincing again. "You know, maybe if I'm going be this uncomfortable, I could be a little more comfortable?"

He looked at her expectantly but his words left her at a loss.

"I mean," he said after a moment, "maybe if you want to continue this, I could sit down?"

"Oh! Yes, of course."

Alari drew him into the main chamber and he settled himself on one of the couches, his face tight.

He extended his leg and closed his eyes; his brow was still furrowed but he let his breath out. "Okay, that's a little better."

"Will you take wine, my mate?" she asked, then remembered that she had no one to serve him.

His eyes snapped open, his blue gaze a little alarmed. "Uh, how about just some cold water?"

She would have to get it for him herself. Her apartments contained a well-appointed kitchen but she had never cooked. She couldn't recall the last time she had even entered that room. She went down the hall, her footfalls echoing eerily in the hallway, and pushed open the door to the kitchen.

She stood in the doorway for a moment at a loss; surely there must be a glass or cup somewhere in here. The room had been left tidy but she had to open a number of cabinets to find which one held the cups. Standing on tiptoe, she lifted down a wine goblet made of astuk crystal and carefully filled it with chilled water. Alari kept her eyes on the cup as she walked to keep from spilling.

Kyndan gave her a nod of thanks when she handed it over and he drank thirstily.

She stood shyly at his side. She should offer him a meal but she had never prepared one herself. Considering how long it had taken for her to bring the water she knew it was hopeless even to attempt it. She feared too that the Imperial servants would not obey her and bring food from the palace kitchens if she directed them to.

"I regret I have no attendants to serve you as I should, my mate."

"That's okay," he said with a casual wave. "It's not like I ever had servants before."

"You are poor, then?"

He gave a startled laugh. "Not particularly. My commander's salary can support a family and I'm even entitled to a housing allowance to live off base. But servants are a bit above my pay rate, I'm afraid."

"I have always had servants, tutors, attendants around me." Her eyes went uneasily about the chamber, the echoing rooms beyond. "I have never been alone."

"Did your mother take them away?"

"Oh, no. They did not wish to share my fate. Some now will serve my sister, others will seek another posting within the palace."

"Wait." He frowned. "They *wanted* to go?"

"I am in disgrace," she reminded, shifting her feet.

A flush spread up his neck. "So they just took off and left you here all alone?"

Alari dropped her gaze. "Yes."

"What a bunch of festering—! Gods know I was in no shape to come for you myself yesterday," he said, his voice rough. "But if I'd known, I would have sent someone—Aidar or Tedah, even—to bring you to me."

A lump formed in her throat at how he rallied to her, how angry he was for her sake. And she had so little to offer him . . .

"Your leg," Alari said suddenly. "I should attend to it."

"Oh." He shifted on the couch. "Uh, no, you don't have to do that."

"I am your mate, it is for me to do." She hurried to fetch the beautifully carved wooden box of supplies from its display.

She returned to Kyndan then stopped short, embarrassed. "It was a gift from the Priests of Behur." His brow creased and Alari raised the box a little. "A betrothal gift."

Understanding lit his face. "You mean when you got betrothed to—Listen, you really don't have to—"

"You prefer I not use this because it was intended for another?" She wasn't even sure where she could fetch another medkit. She would have to go in search of one.

"No, that's—no, I'm sure it's fine. I just—"

Alari put the box on the table and sat beside him to reach for his trouser fastenings. "Here, I will help you—"

Kyndan jumped away, on his feet in an instant. "*Okay*, you know what? We should get out to that festival while it's still early."

"I have been taught to treat your wounds as a proper mate should," Alari protested. "It is my duty to tend you."

"No, really." Kyndan cleared his throat. "I'm fine."

But he wasn't and his leg obviously pained him. But why would he not let her attend to it? Did he think her disgrace left her utterly unfit to carry out even the least of her responsibilities?

Her shoulders fell. "As you will, my mate."

"All right, look, I'm—" He passed his hand over his eyes. "Okay, but I can take my pants off by myself. Do you have a blanket or something?"

She nodded and went to her bedchamber to fetch a quilt. It took some hard tugging to pull it free of the wide bed. Alari found the quilt heavy and unwieldy and she wondered how the maids managed their tasks so effortlessly. She returned to find he had still not undressed. Perhaps Tellaran climes were warmer.

"You are cold?" she asked, glancing at the fireplace. She had never lit a fire before and she was suddenly annoyed at herself for not, in all her life, having watched closely enough to even attempt trying it now.

"No," he said, taking the blanket from her. "I need this to cover up."

"Cover up what?" she asked, then realized what he meant. She glanced down with frank curiosity. "Are Tellaran men's staffs different than Az-kye's then?"

"You know," Kyndan said, pinching the bridge of his nose. "That's a question I've never had cause to ponder before."

Alari waited and finally Kyndan threw her a frustrated look.

"Oh!" Alari turned her back to allow him privacy to undress, wondering if all Tellarans were so bashful and now very curious if he were indeed different than Az-kye men.

Behind her there came rustles of fabric, then a creak of the chaise as he sat.

"Okay," he said. "I'm ready."

The quilt was arranged over his lap but he had left his left leg bare. She had to bite the inside of her cheek not to giggle at how carefully Kyndan had tucked in the edges around his hips, very sure to cover himself fully.

His leg was well muscled but beneath the dark hair his skin was much paler than that of his hands or face.

Very bashful indeed if the skin there has seen so little sun . . .

Alari sat beside him and drew the table a little closer so that she might reach easier. He craned his neck to see inside the box when she lifted the lid. Alari rubbed the sanitizing solution over her hands, then eased the bandage on his leg away.

"Who did such?" she asked, with a nod at the nearly mended flesh of his thigh.

"Aidar. My sister's hus—uh, mate." He was staring at his leg. "Wow, whatever he used on me, it worked fast. I mean it's aching but it looks a lot better than I thought it would."

"He did not use enough," Alari said disapprovingly. "It should not pain you so much."

"I thought part of my job was to bear pain without complaint."

"Even so," Alari returned shortly, deftly rubbing the ointment in, "you are deserving of better care than he has given."

"I guess Aidar will never be a proper Az-kye lady after all. He'll be crushed," Kyndan said. "Let me tell him, okay?"

Alari looked up, her brow creased. "Why would he want—? Oh."

"Yeah," Kyndan agreed. "Joking again." He nodded at his leg. "So, what do you think?"

"It will be a fine scar," she said solemnly.

"Actually I meant, how is it healing?"

"Oh." She examined the wound carefully. "It shall be fully healed in a day or so. Is the pain less now?"

"Yeah," he said, sounding surprised. "Actually it's much better. What *is* that stuff anyway?"

"Eshi ointment?" She wiped her hands clean and offered the jar to him. "A gift from the God Behur. His priestesses produce and distribute it in the healing god's name."

"Maybe we should talk about setting up some kind of trade for it."

"Trade?"

"Yeah, you know, trade it to the Tellarans. When the peace treaty is completed."

Alari reached for a fresh bandage. "Yes, perhaps when the treaty is made." She dressed the wound to the keep the ointment against it. "You must tell me if the bandage comes free. I will treat the wound and cover it again."

"I will." He gestured at his leg. "Thanks."

"There is no need to thank me. I am your mate."

She held his gaze, her hands lightly resting on either side of his thigh, his skin warm under her palms. Jazan's intent had been to torment this kind, brave man, to humiliate and shame him, to draw out his suffering for hours, if he could.

She had not thought she should ever feel safe alone with a man again but she did now, with him.

"I am pleased you won me, Kyndan," she said softly.

"Yeah," he murmured. "Me too." He tore his gaze away. "Let me get dressed and we'll head out to the festival."

"I have no attendants to accompany us," she reminded, her shoulders slumping. "I cannot even summon a litter to carry me."

"Well, that's okay. We can just go on our own and walk around."

"*Walk* through the city?"

"Sure, why not? Kinara says there's lots going on in the temple district. It'll be fun." His blue eyes reflected puzzlement. "What's the matter?"

"I have never done such," Alari said, struggling even to *imagine* herself doing it. "Gone outside without being concealed within a litter. Ventured out without my maids and guards. It is rare that I am allowed off the palace grounds at all. I have never left the Az-kye homeworld."

His brow furrowed. "Really?"

"I am—was—First Imperial Daughter and as such considered too valuable to risk."

"Oh," he said. "Well, I guess the *up* side to not being Imperial heiress is that doesn't apply anymore. There's no reason you can't go now. I mean, if you're already in disgrace, who's going to care?"

She blinked. Could she really do such? Walk through the streets at his side; see the capital without the gauze of the Imperial litter's curtains obscuring her vision?

He indicated the empty apartments. "It's not like there's anyone here to tell us no."

With a tingle of excitement, Alari realized she had not been ordered by the empress to confine herself to her quarters. She had not been given any orders at all. She was not First Daughter now; perhaps the unyielding boundaries and sharp confines of the life she had known were not longer in place . . .

"Do you—is your leg well enough to do such?" she asked, her words coming out in a rush.

"Uh, sure. It's sore but stretching should help that. I can always hire a litter for us if it gets worse. Kinara made sure I had plenty of Az-kye currency for the mission."

Her heart was hammering. "I might be recognized,"

"Well, if you didn't go out much and were concealed most of the time you did—" He studied her for a moment, then gave a quick smile. "I have an idea, but we *will* need to hire a litter or we'll miss most of the festival tonight."

"But how will we leave the palace grounds?"

He shrugged. "We'll just walk out. They're going to be a lot more interested in keeping people from getting in than worrying about who's leaving. Besides, I'm the Tellaran representative and you're my wife. Keeping us here against our will is going make for one very ugly response from my government."

"All right," she breathed, leaning toward him, her hands resting on his thigh again. "Yes. Yes, I want to walk through the city."

"Uh, okay." He avoided her gaze. "Just let me get dressed."

Her brow creased at how he was suddenly, acutely disconcerted.

"What is it?" She glanced down and her mouth twitched a bit seeing the cause of his shyness. "Truly, Kyndan, you are worried I will see your member is standing?"

Alari had never seen any man blush so deeply. He looked so utterly and charmingly discomfited that, for the first time in nearly a year, Alari gave a full and openhearted smile.

He went still and his blue eyes widened.

"Gods," he murmured hoarsely. "You're beautiful, Alari."

She ducked her head; she was not dressed to her best advantage by any means. She looked at him sidelong, surprised to realize she hoped he found her posture flirtatious. "It pleases me that you call me such."

For a spare instant he glanced at her mouth then met her eyes again. "Call you what?"

"Alari."

His brow furrowed a bit. "That's your name, isn't it?"

"After I reached womanhood and was named First I was addressed only by one of my titles, even by my mother and father. Only you, and Saria, call me 'Alari.'"

"Saria?"

"My sister. She who is now First Imperial Daughter. She was in attendance today to Her Imperial Majesty when you came to claim me."

"I might have been a little distracted just then. Maybe you can point her out later."

The very idea of having to "point out" the Imperial heiress made Alari smile again. "I have never met anyone like you, Kyndan."

"Well, you're my first princess." He passed his hand over his eyes. "Man," he muttered, "did *that* come out wrong."

Alari gave a startled giggle.

She could not even think when she had last laughed . . .

"I will let you dress now, Kyndan," she said, and stood, turning her back. Smiling, she clasped her hands in front of her as she waited, fighting against the impulse to peek.

11

The Festival of Ren'thar

"Well?" Kyndan asked, his voice muffled by the dull green curtain between them. "Is it okay?"

"I do not know," Alari answered honestly, regarding her reflection. "I have never worn any color but Imperial black."

"Come out," he urged. "Let me see."

She brushed aside the rough fabric and shyly stepped out from the curtained dressing area. The shopkeeper and her mate remained at their place near the shop's entrance but they craned their necks to watch as she emerged. She was unused to having people of the merchant class meet her eyes at all and, as neither had bowed to her, it was plain they did not know who she was.

But they seemed agog at having a Tellaran in their establishment.

Kyndan smiled. "You look great."

Alari smoothed the skirt of the dress, flushing at his appreciative look. She, too, thought the pale pink gown with threads of gold shot through it—a color scandalous on an Imperial Daughter—very pretty. Free of the heavy beading and embroidery that enriched her court gowns, this dress was both light and comfortable to wear and she very much liked the way his eyes lingered on her body.

"It's perfect," Kyndan said. "Let's settle up and have some fun."

"What about you?" Alari asked with a nod at his blue and white clothes.

"I think I'm going to look Tellaran no matter what I wear," he said, his blue eyes amused.

Alari glanced through the shop window at the pedestrians strolling in the lower city. "But it will soon be dark," she pointed out. "And even by lights of the festival none will be able to make out your eye color until they draw very close but—"

"But my uniform will be spotted a half-kilometer off," Kyndan finished, then gave a nod. "All right, I'll get something too. I can probably pass for a merchant."

Alari blinked. "But you are a warrior! You should dress so."

"And last time I checked," Kyndan reminded in a conspiring whisper, "*you're* a princess."

"So we shall both be disguised?" Alari asked, smiling as she touched the soft fabric of her gown.

Kyndan winked. "Our secret."

While Kyndan found clothing Alari looked hungrily around the shop. She had never been anywhere so crammed with delightfully jumbled things. There were clothes, shoes, statues of the gods, sweets, and garishly bright bead necklaces. One of the shopkeepers' little daughters smiled at her, her bright clothing and missing front teeth giving her grin an impish look. Alari smiled back at the child.

"Well?" Kyndan asked.

He had changed into loose, dark clothing, not too different from what the shopkeeper's mate was wearing. Despite his wavy hair he did indeed look very like one of their class—save his sky-color eyes, of course.

Alari gave an approving nod. "You are perfect, Kyndan."

The shopkeeper was pleased to have the sale. She also readily accepted additional payment to have one of her older children deliver the bundle containing his uniform and Alari's dress to a house in the upper city.

"Where did you send our things?" Alari asked as they stepped out into the paved street. The stones were uneven and broken in places; she had to step carefully in the gathering darkness of early evening.

"My sister's clanhouse," Kyndan said. "I wanted to get quarters for myself at one of the inns for the stay planetside but she wasn't having it. I'm kind of glad I gave in now and made her happy. I've been a lot of trouble to her on this trip already."

"Because of me," Alari said, her voice quiet.

"Nah," he replied airily. "I'm usually a lot of trouble."

Seeing the humorous glint in his eyes, Alari laughed.

"Hey, I'm getting better at this!" he enthused and, as if were the most natural of things, took her hand in his.

She flushed at the feel of his skin against hers, acutely aware of the radiating heat his big body against her side.

Kyndan's warm blue eyes met hers and her heartbeat sped up.

Perhaps, if he were to go very slowly, perhaps we could—

"Come on," he said with a gentle tug on her hand. "The temple district's only a couple streets over."

"There are many rituals I attended as First Daughter in the temples." She was suddenly anxious to safeguard their adventure, their time alone. "Perhaps we should go somewhere else."

"No one's going to recognize you. Not dressed in pink with your hair loose down your back." He threw her a grin.

"Not walking around with some no-account ruffian like me."

Alari bit the inside of her cheek as they joined others walking in the direction of the temples but he was likely right. She wondered if even Saria would recognize her like this.

And what would any of them do in any case? He was right, she was already in disgrace.

"Oh," she exclaimed as they entered the boulevard near Lashima's temple. "It looks so different!"

The air was fragrant with the smell of warm confections and cooking meat. Many booths, some garishly decorated, lined the district for the selling of food, drink, and trinkets. Brightly colored lanterns were strung everywhere for the festival and there were a number of small, temporary stages set up beside the temples to provide music or plays in tribute to Ren'thar. Tumblers and jugglers moved through the square to entertain and people moved about with an air of happy anticipation.

It was so odd to simply *walk*, to be able to move without the half-dozen maids that had always accompanied her everywhere, hemming her in. The freedom of it was exhilarating—to be relieved of keepers and tutors and courtiers eager to befriend the Imperial heiress for the power she would someday wield.

It made her wonder too. How much could she truly have understood of her own people when she had been so sheltered she had even never walked among them?

"You haven't been down here for the festival?" Kyndan asked. "Kinna said this is the place to be."

"No, I have always been kept to the pal—" She broke off, suddenly conscious of the crowd around them. "Home," she finished.

Kyndan nodded toward a grouping of food sellers. "I'm hungry. How about you?"

Many stood about, enjoying offerings from the food stands, some even ate as they walked.

"Yes," she admitted.

"Any preference? I don't know much about Az-kye festival food."

Freed from the isolation of the court and its stifling protocols, she suddenly felt giddy, almost like a child again and eager to explore.

Alari glanced around then nodded at a nearby booth. "That one."

"What are they selling?"

"I do not know."

Kyndan looked puzzled. "Then why do you want what they're serving?"

"Because whatever it is, I know I have never had it before," she said, pulling on his hand to urge him that way.

"Okay, Princess," he said with a surprised laugh. "A— whatever it is—coming right up."

At the booth Kyndan gave the proprietor a friendly nod. "Two."

The merchant inclined his head and provided two pastries, each wrapped in festive iridescent paper. The man stopped short as he was handing back Kyndan's change, astonished at find himself looking at a blue-eyed Az-kye.

"I—" the man began.

"Enjoy the festival," Kyndan said cheerfully, dropping a few coins in the tip bowl.

He handed Alari one of the pastries, heading off before the man could get another word out.

"Now *that*," Kyndan confided once they were out of the man's earshot, "was funny."

She laughed.

Kyndan bit into the pastry. "Not bad," he said around a mouthful.

Alari took a careful bite, surprised by the meat-filled dough. It was spicier than the cuisine she was accustomed to and very greasy. It was like nothing she'd ever had before.

It was like nothing she'd ever *done* before—standing in a happy throng of brightly garbed people, her gown as light as a jaha feather, eating in the middle of the street under a good-humored blue gaze.

Standing so close to Kyndan, her skin tingled and Alari felt a rush of attraction that she had thought long since razed by pain and humiliation.

"This is wonderful," she said softly.

"Where we should really go is Winter Carnival on Xeltan," Kyndan said as they walked and ate. "They have some of the best street food in the quadrant there. The Xeltani create a whole city from ice and snow right at the base of the Hupan Mountains. It's amazing—real shops and working restaurants made of snow. You can even stay in the inns they carve, if you don't mind sleeping on a bed as comfortable as only a big block of ice can be."

Alari stopped eating. "Xeltan?"

"One of the Tellaran worlds. On the farthest side of Tellaran space from the Empire, actually."

Alari blinked up at him.

"What?" he asked. "You don't like snow?"

"I have never left Az-kye, Kyndan."

"Well, yeah." He gave a short laugh. "But that doesn't mean you can't *ever* leave. I mean, especially now."

Leave the homeworld? Alari regarded him wide-eyed, her heart hammering.

"Of course," he said stiffly after a long moment. "Maybe you don't have any interest in seeing *Tellaran* worlds."

"Oh, no," she breathed. "I would love to see the city made of snow."

His brow furrowed. "I'll take you if you want to go. It's in a few months."

Alari's gaze was drawn to the distant spires of the Imperial Palace. "I do not know if the empress will give me leave to do such."

"All due respect to Her Imperial Majesty," Kyndan began a little sharply, "you're married to a Tellaran citizen now. She'll *have* to let you go."

For a moment Alari imagined herself exploring worlds she had only heard whispers of. Tellarans were known throughout the Empire to be brutes, barbarians with no sense of culture or civility, but Kyndan had shown her more kindness, more warmth, in a few short hours than she had ever known from—

A whole city made of ice! What other sights, what other wonders, might those distant worlds hold?

"Perhaps." She wet her lips. "Perhaps you are right."

He gave a nod. "It's settled then. Next Winter Carnival on Xeltan."

Alari hesitated then she, too, gave a nod. "Xeltan."

They joined the crowd to watch one of the performances depicting Ren'thar and Lashima's courtship. The tenors sang out Ren'thar's praise of the goddess, while the divine pair was acted out by two masked performers.

Alari nipped her lip to keep from giggling at Kyndan's shocked expression when the performer playing the god bared his impressive erection as he and the woman representing Lashima reenacted the gods' first coupling.

"That was very, uh, interesting," Kyndan got out when the performance ended to enthusiastic applause.

She looked up at him, genuinely curious. "Tellarans are not so open with love play then?"

"Well, I've certainly seen some raunchy—I'm in the Fleet, after all," he muttered. "But they just—I mean, right in front of *everyone*!" He passed his hand over his eyes. "I'm not sure you could get away with it on Nima, and that's saying something."

"I thought the timing superbly done," she commented. "Ren'thar and Lashima were both very well acted."

"Yeah, that wasn't *acting*!"

"You did look quite scandalized." Her mouth twitched. "Especially at the conclusion."

His glance darted her way.

"Ah. It is because I was with you."

"You're a princess," he grumbled. "I'm trying to be a gentleman."

"So gentlemen do not relish the sexual pleasures?" she asked, inwardly astonished by her own audacity. She was usually not so bold and never so flirtatious but it was a thrill to see him so startled—so *interested*—by her daring. "I think they do not have much to recommend them, then."

His mouth was curved up a bit, his lips working as if he intended a rejoinder but his mind could not form one.

She tilted her head. "Perhaps you should reconsider being such a gentleman, Kyndan."

Heat flashed in his blue eyes and his glance went to her mouth for an instant.

Then he wrenched his gaze away and nodded toward another of the temporary stages. "That one's just starting. Looks like we can still get a good spot."

This performance was no less explicit than the last and the performers astonishingly limber. Alari couldn't help her smile at how Kyndan kept shifting his weight.

"Is the *whole* festival like this?" he asked in an aggravated whisper, his face reddened to the hairline.

"I do not know how the pairing of Ren'thar and Lashima is usually celebrated in the city," Alari admitted. She craned her neck to see. "But I should think not. There should be performances of their early courtship the farther we go from Lashima's temple."

"Yeah, let's try that," he agreed hastily and with one final wide-eyed look at the stage indicated she precede him out of the crowd.

They took their time, pausing to watch the tumblers, weaving their way toward the outer edges of the celebration. Kyndan looked relieved that this area was devoted to recounting Ren'thar's many gifts to his lady goddess: how he bargained with Azis, goddess of the rainbow, to fill the worlds with color to please his lady's eye and how he himself wove the cloak of stars to place upon her shoulders.

Kyndan was careful of her, shielding her when the crowd was dense, keeping himself between her and the rowdy ones who had consumed too much drink.

At a stand near the temple of Meithea he purchased quen'dila pastries for them. These Alari had sampled before, and their sweet, nutty flavor was a favorite of hers. He hadn't complained about his leg being sore but spying a few empty benches in the grove beside the temple, she suggested they go there to eat.

With so many drawn to the center of the temple district and the entertainments there, this small grove had little of interest to offer. Its location farther back from the main thoroughfare and the little wall blocking it from the street made the little park an island of quiet.

Kyndan indicated the bench. "Princesses first."

"Tellarans had a king once," she said as he settled beside her. She knew that much of them at least. "Do they have princesses still?"

Kyndan laughed. "No princesses, not for about five hundred years or so. There was an attempt once to restore the monarchy. They even had a new king. It's a pretty good ghost story actually."

Many operas, and the legends they were based upon, featured restless shades but she was surprised to hear the Tellarans had such tales too. "Tell me this story."

"Well, a couple hundred years back when the republic triumphed the king escaped but before he vanished from Tellaran space he paused long enough, of course, to vow revenge. His ghost is always lurking about, ready to seize an unsuspecting vessel at the border to carry him back to claim his lost throne. There's any number of holodramas about it. You know—intrepid crew ignores the locals' warnings and enters forbidden space, the ship's engines go out, one by one the crew vanish," Kyndan said a with mock theatric timbre. "The last brave ensign defeats the evil royal specter at the cost of his own life. Months later the ship is found adrift at the edge of the badlands, with no survivors and a mysteriously damaged log . . ."

Alari's brow creased. "*Bad*lands?"

"That's what Tellarans call the area between your space and ours."

"We call it 'Ren'thar's sword.'"

"His blade at the ready to fight the enemies of the Az-kye?" he said with a raised eyebrow.

She offered a smile. "To defend us."

"Well, those ion fronts might be hard to navigate but apparently, that's exactly the kind of inhospitable environment angry spirits prefer. On my first tour, the commander—Hiren, that was his name—he was superstitious as hell. Anyway, middle of the night shift and *he* thinks he hears—"

Alari startled as the man came upon them and immediately Kyndan was on his feet, moving to shield her.

It took a moment for Alari take in the dirty white smock, realize what it represented.

Clanless.

She had never been so close to one of them; they were not permitted on the palace grounds. None were ever allowed to be in her vicinity at all, if it could be helped. She had seen only a handful in her lifetime on the rare occasions she had been given leave to enter the city proper and they not were cleared from her sight.

This man was as tall as Kyndan—the height of a warrior—but was far thinner than any should be. His face was drawn, his dark eyes held the lackluster look of hopelessness before he lowered them.

"Forgive my offense," he mumbled. "I sought only to avoid the crowd—"

"There's nothing to forgive," Kyndan said, the tension in his posture easing. He jerked his chin at the man. "What's your name?"

The man flinched, his head drooping further. "I have none."

"The hell you don't," Kyndan replied, his voice low and angry.

The man did not raise his eyes and after a moment, Kyndan spoke again, his voice gentler this time. "What did it used to be?"

Alari did not think the man would answer but finally very, very softly he said, "Utar."

"Utar," Kyndan repeated. "What's your clan, Utar?"

The man swallowed, his eyes on the ground.

"What *was* your clan, Utar?" Kyndan asked.

"Az'shu," he murmured and in that whisper was such longing that Alari's throat tightened. "Utar of the Az'shu."

She recognized the clan name. The clan leader, Helia of the Az'shu, was powerful in the Council for Trade.

"Are you hungry, Utar?" Kyndan asked. "Stupid question, of course you are. Here," he said and held out his pastry. After a moment Alari gave hers to Kyndan too. Kyndan gave her a grateful look then offered both to the man. "Take them."

The man sent a guarded glance at Kyndan then dropped his eyes again.

"They're yours," Kyndan assured. "It's not a trick. I won't take them away at the last moment or throw them in the dirt." He extended them further. "Take them."

After a moment the man hesitantly reached out, the scars on his arm showing white.

A disgraced warrior then. His dark hair was roughly chopped, only a few inches longer than Kyndan's, but warriors wore theirs long. Someone had decided to humiliate him further by cutting his hair off.

The man held the pastries gingerly in his dirty hands, his mouth working then he inclined his head in thanks.

"Who owns you now?"

The man shook his head and Alari frowned. He had not even been sold but cast out into the streets to starve? His crime must have been grave indeed for Helia to do so.

"Do you know where the Az'anti clanhouse is?" Kyndan asked.

The man's brow furrowed but he gave a spare nod.

"I want you to go there now," Kyndan said. "Tell the guards that the clan leader's brother, Kyndan Maere, sent you to her. Tell Kinara—that's her name—that I said to take you in." He put his hand on the man's shoulder. "I promise you'll be treated well at the Az'anti clanhouse, Utar."

The former warrior sent Kyndan a quick glance, his brow knitted. For an instant hesitant hope showed in his eyes and then he bowed again.

The man wolfed down one of the pastries before he'd gone a half-dozen paces.

Kyndan watched him go, his face taut.

"You were very kind to him," Alari said.

"I *was* him," he said bitterly. "A few months ago it was *me* walking barefoot with bleeding feet and an empty belly, getting my supper yanked away by Az-kye who thought it was funny. They brought me planetside in a festering cage and I spent the good part of a year confined to the Az'quen clanhouse grounds." His lip curled. "The Az'quen clan, my *owners*. I didn't even speak Az-kye then. Most of the time I didn't know what the hell they were telling me to do. 'Course I learned the coarse words quick; they're the ones I'd hear right before the blow landed."

His face was clouded with anger and pain. "You don't know what it's like. You feel like a bug getting crushed and there's *nothing* you can do. You just have to *take* it because there's no getting away and fighting makes it worse—"

Her gaze met his then and Kyndan broke off, his expression stricken.

"I'm sorry," he said hoarsely. "I didn't—Look, just tell me to shut up when I'm saying something stupid like that."

"You have every right to your anger, Kyndan." She closed her eyes briefly. "To hate those that caused you such suffering."

"Did you ever tell anyone, Alari?" he asked quietly. "Tell anyone what he did?"

Her throat tightened and for a long moment she searched his face, half in shadow, half lit by the lanterns of the festival beyond.

"Our courtship had come to the time when we were to be left to ourselves at night," she began finally, her voice low, reluctant. "The first few times when my attendants withdrew he was respectful, mannerly, gentle, but I did not grow to care for him as a mate should. I sought the advice of High Priestess Celara. I even spoke to one of my mother's advisors of it. Both strongly counseled me to wait, that my feelings might change. But one morning I followed my heart and told Jazan I did not want to be bound to him, did not wish to be his mate. He was disappointed, yet I thought him agreeable to the break. But that night—he—" Her nails bit into the skin of her palm as she clenched her fist. "I could scarcely believe it had happened! As soon as he—I ran from him and locked myself in the bathing chamber till my maids came the next morning. I went to her Imperial Majesty and knelt before her, begging to be released from the betrothal." Her lip trembled. "The empress said that as heiress there were things that I must bear. That to rule I must accept I could not have things always as I liked them. She ordered the marriage to go forward."

"Gods, Alari." His face was ragged. "I'm so sorry."

"I hated him," she whispered tightly. "Perhaps the hate is still there but I cannot feel it now. To see him yesterday—I felt such horror at it. And such relief to know him dead. For the first time, in so very long, I felt safe." She met his gaze. "And you? Do you still hate the Az-kye, Kyndan?"

His face turned toward the celebrants strolling beneath the cheerfully colored lanterns. The warriors with their black animal skin clothes and swords, their ladies brightly dressed as exotic birds, the merchants, the beggars, the men and women of the companion life offering their sexual favors for sale; the street children, barefooted in their tattered clothing, enjoying the openhandedness of the festival patrons, their faces sticky with quen'dila candy.

"I wake up sometimes, shaking so hard I feel sick and I can't—" he said finally, his voice low and rough. "It was so godsdamned hard to come *back* here. I didn't want to. I didn't even know if I could without—without—"

His eyes were unseeing, haunted. She touched his arm and his gaze focused on her.

"If you had not returned to Az-kye, had you not fought for me, I would be Jazan's mate now."

His face was tight. "I know."

"Thank you for claiming me today." Tears stung her eyes. "I would have been clanless too, had you not come for me."

"No." His eyes flashed blue fire and his hands came up to clasp her shoulders. "It *never* would have been you, Alari!"

His fevered glance went over her face and he pulled her against him bending his head toward her. She could feel the rise and fall of his quickened breath, how his heart pounded under her palm. Kyndan's mouth poised a hairsbreadth from hers, his body trembling. In a rush of nervousness and excitement and courage Alari lifted her mouth toward his—

He let her go and she stumbled a bit at the sudden release.

Had she done something wrong? If Tellaran men were so bashful perhaps their women were equally demure. Had she been too forward?

He was avoiding her gaze now and her body suddenly went cold.

Kyndan knew what had been done to her.

Was that it? Her heart hammered with hurt. Did knowing what Jazan had done so disgust him that he could not even kiss her?

"Listen, I—" Kyndan took a step back. "Come on. I'll get you another one of those pastries."

12

The Welcoming

Kyndan climbed out as soon as the litter stopped at the Az'anti estate and offered his hand to Alari. Kinara's house too was strung with lanterns for the festival and they were still lit. It was late in the evening but the sounds of celebration in the city could still be heard.

"Are you certain the clan leader will not mind?" Alari leaned forward in her seat, looking anxiously at the clanhouse. "That I have come to visit unannounced?"

"You're family," Kyndan reminded. "You don't have to be *announced*. Besides it's this or back to the palace." He looked pointedly at her dress. "You probably aren't going to want to head back there wearing that anyway."

"No," Alari agreed quickly.

Kyndan took her hand. "Come on. Even if we don't wind up staying, your other dress is inside, remember?"

Reluctantly she stepped down and stood with her hands clasped before her as Kyndan paid the litter bearers.

"It's all right," he assured when she turned worried eyes to him. He touched her back to draw her along with him. "Really."

The guards tensed at his approach, clearly not recognizing him in the Az-kye clothing.

Kyndan raised his hand to them in greeting. "Is Kinara here?"

Their stances eased at the sound of his voice but they regarded his clothing, and Alari, with unquestioned curiosity.

One of the warriors gave him a nod. "The *Ti'antah* is within."

"'Kay, thanks!" Kyndan returned as he and Alari crossed the courtyard to the clanhouse.

One of the little housemaids opened the door. She looked about thirteen, her clothes plain but neat, her braided hair worn up. Kyndan didn't recognize her but the clanhouse required a large staff to run and there were always servants coming and going between his sister's holdings.

"Do you wish to speak to the head of housekeeping, you must go around to the back door and ask at the kitchens," the girl said primly, plainly mistaking him for the merchant he was dressed like and ready to shut the door in his face.

Kyndan gave Alari a wry look. "So, am I impressing you yet?"

Just then Laric, Kinara's maid, crossed the hall and spied him in the doorway.

"Metara, that is the Tellaran ambassador! He is an honored guest here," she admonished and waved her hand impatiently. "Foolish child. Step aside and allow him enter!"

Her face flushed, the girl scurried out of the way and Kyndan gave her a reassuring smile as they passed to show he wasn't offended.

"Is Kinara still up?" he asked Laric and glanced up the stairway. "I thought we could say hi."

Laric glanced between them then, her expression so puzzled that Kyndan wondered for a moment if he had slipped back into speaking Tellaran.

Laric's gaze rested on Alari and her brow creased. Suddenly her eyes went wide. Her mouth opened and closed and in that moment Kyndan had the unkind thought that his sister's most trusted attendant looked very like a mohu fish.

"Imperial Daughter," she gasped and bowed low.

Alari's cheeks pinkened becomingly but her eyes flickered her discomfort to Kyndan. "Rise."

Laric straightened, her throat working. "Imperial Daughter, my lady is—" The little housemaid was staring openmouthed at Alari; Laric put a hand to the girl's back and pushed her toward the stairs. "Tell your lady to come at once!" she hissed at the girl. Laric looked back at Alari as the girl ran up the stairs. "My lady is—I—we did not *expect* Your Highness."

"No, I—please forgive the intrusion," Alari said quickly.

Laric's hand went to her chest. "Your Highness could *never* intrude! Oh, but our clanhouse is shamefully unprepared for—!"

"Laric, it's fine," Kyndan interrupted. "I'm sure she doesn't mind."

The sound of running footsteps could be heard on the second floor and in the next moment the little maid, Aidar—looking hastily dressed—and Kinara, her sleeping robe tied over her rounded belly, were coming down the stairs.

Aidar bowed as soon as he got to the bottom of the stairs and Kinara threw Kyndan a look that was both wide-eyed and aggravated; then she too bowed.

"Imperial Daughter," she intoned, sounding out of breath as she bowed, her red hair hanging loose around her face.

"Lady of the Az'anti," Alari returned, her cheeks reddened now.

"We, uh, we weren't expecting you," Kinara said, straightening. "We haven't prepared the household for—" Looking utterly flustered, Kinara turned to her maid. "Laric?"

"I will—" the attendant broke off and whirled, urging the young housemaid ahead of her. "Tell the kitchens!" she said in fierce whisper. "Find Lerita!"

Kinara watched her maid go as if dismayed to find herself abandoned so and she and Aidar exchanged looks.

"Your Highness, I beg forgiveness for our poor welcome." Kinara shifted her weight. "Uh, to our shame—"

"Okay," Kyndan broke in. "Enough! Just *stop!*" He ran his hand through his hair. "Look, we're tired and we just wanted to say a quick hello before we went to our room."

Kinara blinked. "Your room. Oh. Okay."

She exchanged another glance with Aidar.

"Okay," she said again. "Look, Kyn, I mean Kyndan— I mean *Imperial mate,* I thought, we *all* thought, that—We weren't *expecting*—Oh, man." She closed her eyes for a moment and threw her hands out. "How about some tea?"

"Yeah, sure, perfect," Kyndan said, relieved his sister was finally remembering her manners. "Tea sounds great. What do you think, Alari? Tea?"

She nodded quickly and it was hard to tell really which one of the three was the most uncomfortable.

"How about—" Kinara's glance darted about. "Okay, let's—sitting room! Everybody into the front sitting room."

His sister turned that way and Kyndan noticed that Kinara had recently picked up tiny bit of a waddle to her walk. Aidar strode ahead to open the doors for her.

Alari looked up at him, her dark eyes filled with agonized embarrassment.

"See? I told you." Kyndan said dryly. "That went just fine."

An hour later Alari walked with Kyndan to the quarters he'd been given at the uppermost floor of the clanhouse. She looked around curiously as he closed the door behind them.

"I know it's not what you're used to," Kyndan said, extending his hand and inviting her to explore. "But it's pretty comfortable."

The rooms were done in soothing greens and blues. The bed was charmingly tucked into an alcove and the fire in the small sitting area already lit. There was a bathing chamber with a bathing pool, sweeping balconies on either side of the suite, and windows all around.

The suite was pleasant but revealed little of her new mate's personality and held only scant evidence that he resided here at all. A datapad was left tossed casually on the table; she could just see a bag on the floor of the dressing area off the bathing chamber, and the closet appeared empty but for a few folded things.

The doors to the balcony off the sitting area were open and Alari stepped out to breathe in the sweet evening air. Festive lanterns dotted the city like thousands of twinkle bugs and in the distance she could see the shining spires of the palace.

"Pretty good view, huh?" His face flushed. "Not as good as what you're used to, I know . . ."

"It is lovely," Alari said softly.

Kyndan cleared his throat. "I asked Kinara to send some things up for you to use tonight. They should be in the dressing room."

"She is kind," Alari said. "Our sister."

"Yeah, Kinara's got a big heart." He smiled fondly. "Almost as big as her mouth. That means," he explained when Alari gave him a puzzled look, "she sometimes talks before she thinks things through."

"She is well thought of," Alari offered. "Some say she is a Stardancer."

He gave a careless shrug. "I don't know much about the legend. Tellarans don't have anything like that. But if anyone could turn out to be a goddess' favorite human it's Kinna."

Alari gave him a smile. "I think so too of Saria."

She went back inside. She brushed her hand along the back of the carved chairs, the polished wood floor smooth beneath her slippers. The fire gave off the warm scent of fragranced wood and someone had left light refreshments in the small dining area.

"Is this okay? I mean, we can still head back to the palace."

"No, I would we stay here, Kyndan." Experimentally Alari touched the mattress then sat down on it. "A fine bed."

He cleared his throat again. "Yeah, it's pretty comfortable."

Impulsively she toed her slippers off and swung her legs up to lie down. It was a wide bed with many pillows, the bed linens fine and soft beneath her fingers. Not nearly as large as the intricately carved bed with its brocade hangings that she had known as First Daughter yet this bed seemed warmer, more welcoming somehow.

In a rush of fear and excitement she realized that Kyndan had lain here, in this bed, last night.

That shortly he would lie beside her.

"It is so," she agreed, a little breathless. She studied the ceiling above the bed and gave him a quick, shy smile. "It will be curious to wake somewhere else."

"Wake somewhere else?"

"Than the quarters of the First Daughter."

He came to the foot of the bed, leaning against the carved hitiwood bedpost. "You've never slept anywhere outside the palace?"

"Nowhere but my chambers." She sat up. "When we were children Saria would sometimes sleep in my room. We would hide beneath the covers and tell secrets."

"Kinara and I were close when we were kids." He smiled faintly as he too sat on the bed. "You and your sister—are you still friends?"

"She is my only friend," Alari said.

"Princesses aren't allowed to have friends?"

She clasped her hands in her lap. "Allowed, yes. But no one offers friendship to the First Daughter without the anticipation of reward."

"So they were your friends because you were going to be empress?" His brow furrowed. "Is that why no one was standing with you today when we made our declarations? Because you were disinherited?"

"Yes."

"What about your sister?" he asked sharply. "She didn't stand with you either."

"Saria is First now. My mother's heiress. She cannot risk displeasing her or . . ."

He raised his eyebrows. "She'll be married off to a barbarian?"

"No, Saria is now the only heiress. She will be someday take the throne and must have a proper Az-kye mate." Alari wet her lips. "Her Imperial Majesty intended our mating to be my punishment, Kyndan." She looked at her hands and her voice was very soft. "But I do not find it so."

"I'm glad," he said hoarsely.

Through the open balcony doors came the faint sounds of those celebrating into the night, while inside, the crackle of the fire and her own quickening breath filled her ears. They were alone, sitting side by side on the bed they would share tonight, and she saw in his eyes that he realized it too.

Trembling, her heart hammering, Alari moved closer. Her hand slid over the bed linens, resting just beside his. He had been so gentle with her today. The specter of Jazan's ugliness still hovered at the edge of her mind but if Kyndan were gentle with her now perhaps—

He stood. "Well, you're probably pretty tired. I'll let you get some sleep."

"Will you not be sleeping now too, Kyndan?" Alari asked, her heart sinking.

"I've actually got some work I should do. I didn't get a chance to write my report to the Council about the status of the peace talks. They'll be expecting it."

"I will wait for you," she offered.

"No. I might be up for hours," he said with a wave of his hand. "Go ahead and get some rest. We don't have anything planned till midday so you'll be able to sleep in.

They've arranged some such thing or other tomorrow. Tour of the city, that kind of stuff."

"Oh," she murmured. She had been so relieved today when he said it would be long before they joined, let alone were bound. Now she did not know what to think and she blinked back tears before he should see them.

"I'll see you in the morning." He hesitated then gently cupping her cheek he pressed the lightest of kisses to her forehead. "Sleep well, Alari."

She nodded, willing herself not to cry until the door shut behind him.

13

ꝆꞀꝆꝆꝆꝆꝆꝆ Ꝇ Ꝓ
Tellaran Ways

"You're lucky I *didn't* use my right cross, Kyn," Kinara said the next morning, her rounded cheeks pink with anger. His sister had waylaid him on his way down to the kitchens and grabbed his arm to pull him into her apartments. "How the hell could you embarrass me like that?"

Kyndan scrubbed his face with his hands. "Maybe you could let me have a cup of caf before you lay into me? I didn't get much sleep."

She glared at him for a moment then snapped off an order to one of her maids while he and Aidar exchanged nods. Morning light streamed through the windows and while her attendants had laid out breakfast, that particular Tellaran beverage wasn't usually one of the offerings. He'd brought some for his visit and a bunch more for Kinara to enjoy after he left.

He took the cup Sella offered and nodded his thanks. Sella was a pretty thing, especially when she smiled in return, but he couldn't forget how she hadn't even bothered acknowledging his existence when he'd been a slave here. One of the many things he didn't miss about Az-kye.

"You should have sent me a fucking message, given me some warning—*something*!"

Kyndan took a seat at the table and took a grateful swallow of caf. "I didn't think it was going to be such an issue."

"An *issue*?" Kinara threw an outraged look at Aidar. "He shows up on our doorstep an hour before midnight—unannounced—with an Imperial Daughter and he didn't think it would be an *issue!*"

"I still don't understand what the problem is," Kyndan grumbled, rubbing at his eyes. "She's my wife, she's your sister-in-law. Are we going to need an engraved invitation every time we visit?"

"Look, Kyn, there are very strict rules of etiquette that have to be followed in Az-kye society. You can't just run around doing whatever you want!" She sent a narrow gaze at her mate. "Not one word, Aidar. I *mean* it."

Aidar's mouth twitched then his face smoothed to warrior impassivity. "I do not think to speak of such."

His sister's eyes flashed dangerously and Kyndan held up a hand before Kinara's temper went critical. "Look we had to go *somewhere* and believe me we weren't welcome at the palace."

Kinara's brow creased as she eased herself into a chair. "Why do you say that?"

"Uh, well, let's see," Kyndan said, pretending to frown. "None of the courtiers—including her sister—were speaking to her, her own mother didn't hang around to wish us well after the wedding, and all of Alari's attendants had already taken off for better prospects. In fact, the only way we could have felt any *less* welcome is if the Imperial guard had thrown us out on our asses."

Kinara exchanged a look with Aidar. "I didn't know it was like that for her."

Kyndan lifted his cup again. "In case you've forgotten, marrying me was supposed to be as bad as being cast out of the clan."

Kinara glanced at the doorway. "Speaking of which—"

"Utar," Kyndan said in greeting at seeing who it was. "You're looking better."

The disgraced warrior gave him a spare glance then lowered his eyes again. He did look much better than he had the night before. Still very thin, of course, but he no longer had that desperate look of hunger in his eyes. He'd bathed and his clothes, still white, were clean and new.

"He's all set for you," Kinara said.

Kyndan's gaze snapped to his sister. "For me? What are you talking about?"

"Your servant," she said with a nod at Utar. "My clan has fed and clothed him. He's been given a bed on our estate so he'll be nearby to serve you. Oh, don't worry, I deducted the cost from the funds you've been provided for the mission for your slave's keeping."

"My—?" Kyndan broke off and threw a look at the one-time warrior. "Hey, do me a favor, Utar—Go to the kitchens and tell them to brew more caf, okay?"

The man bent his head in acknowledgment and when Kyndan was sure Utar was out of earshot, he gave Kinara a sharp look. "My *what*?"

"Your slave," Kinara repeated. "You told me to house him for you. I did."

"I told you to take him in for *you*."

"The Az'anti clan doesn't own any slaves, Kyndan," she said coolly. "I'm pretty sure you remember why."

"Only the Az-kye practice slavery, I'm Tellaran," he reminded tightly. "I can't own a slave, Kinna. He has to stay with you."

"Oh, hell, no, Kyn. He's yours, all right."

Kyndan held her gaze but Kinara met him look for look.

"Okay, fine," he gritted out. "I want him freed anyway."

"Free a slave in Az-kye space. Great plan." Kinara raised her eyebrows, her expression politely interested. "How are you going to do that again?"

"I'll just free him," Kyndan snapped.

"Again, how? I mean if it were that easy I would have freed *you*, right? I wouldn't have had to gather all the Tellarans and return them to Tellaran space, I could have just—" she made a flinging gesture "—freed them all."

"Okay, you're the expert on Az-kye society. How do I free him?"

Kinara considered. "Well, he could marry into a clan with the clan leaders' permission. That is, if anyone wanted to marry someone clanless which no *sane*"—she glanced at Aidar, who grinned at her—"person would do. Once every two or three hundred years or so one of them is freed by Imperial decree. You have an in at the palace, maybe you could try that."

"That's *it*?" Kyndan demanded. "*Those* are the options?"

"Or Tellaran space," Aidar offered.

"But in the meantime . . ." Kinara took a sip from her cup. "Hey, this *is* good caf, Kyn. Thanks for bringing it."

Kyndan passed his hand over his eyes. "Well, I'm really looking forward to making my report to Admiral Henon *now*." He stood, took up an at-ease stance and gave a nod to the imaginary admiral. "'No, Sir, no treaty, but I married an Az-kye princess, accidently acquired a slave, and—oh, I forgot to mention—the empress *hates* my Tellaran ass. That's right, Sir, all in the first forty-eight hours of the mission.'"

"Commander Maere!" Laric said sharply from the doorway.

"I don't think Admiral Henon is the worst of your problems right now, Kyn," his sister said, looking at him over her cup.

Laric's nostrils were flared, her skirts billowing out as she barreled his way.

Sighing, Kyndan turned to face the maid.

He had slept beside her.

There was an indentation on the other pillow and very faint scent of him in the bedclothes. Alari reached across the bed to rest her hand where his body had lain.

Despite his urging that she should not wait for his return, she had tried to remain awake but the day had been very long. At some point she had fallen asleep and he had come and gone again before she awoke.

For the first time in her life, she had awakened in an unfamiliar place. For a moment she just lay luxuriating in the newness, in the astonishment of finding her life, the path of which had been determined from the moment she had drawn her first breath, now so radically altered.

Alari's fingers traced the smooth linen where Kyndan had slept.

Her experience with Jazan had been so painful that she, who used to giggle and whisper with Saria over men who set her breath quickening, who had been brought up to think of coupling as a joyous gift from the gods, had felt not a flicker of desire at the sight of any man for nearly a year.

Until yesterday.

And she had never longed for any man's touch as she did now for Kyndan's.

She scooted over to his side, brushing her check against his pillow, breathing in the warm scent of him. He had joined with other women. Certainly he was handsome enough that he would have his choice.

Perhaps he simply does not want me . . .

And yet there had been hunger in his eyes last night, his body taut and trembling, when he had pulled her against him. Her palm on his thigh had brought him to standing.

Was it the way of Tellarans to be so reticent in bedding? But even so, surely he could have *kissed* her . . .

What Jazan had done was so appalling that at times even now it seemed unreal. He should have lost all honor, all status and been cast from his clan but her mother's order that the marriage go forward effectively silenced any outcry she might have made about his crimes.

But she did not know how Tellarans viewed such things. Did Kyndan think she should have called out to her guards instead of stifling her pain, denounced Jazan publicly in defiance of her mother's order, that she had not fought hard enough?

Her throat tightened. Was it, then, what Jazan had done to her? Did the idea of it so repulse Kyndan that he could not see beyond it?

The door opened and, embarrassed to be caught on his side of the bed, she quickly sat up as Kyndan came into the suite.

"You're awake." His smile was instant upon seeing her and encouraged by his bright look she smiled back.

Kyndan came to the bedside. He was dressed again in the clothes of a Tellaran warrior, the dark blue of the tunic bringing out the color of his eyes. "Did you sleep okay?"

She nodded. "Yes, very well, my mate."

"Do you feel like going out into the city? Kinara's invited a few friends of ours for dinner tonight but Nisara arranged a tour of the city."

"Nisara?"

"Lieutenant Nisara de'Cator. She's a pilot really but she's acting as my attaché for the mission." He sat on the bed. "She met someone—a warrior—when we were captives here. She probably would have volunteered to carry my luggage if it got her back to Az-kye." Kyndan tilted his head, searching her face. "How are you feeling? I know it must be frightening, to have your whole life turned upside down like this."

"I am well."

"I'm not a courtier, Alari," he reminded gently. "I'm not pretending friendship to get something from you. It's okay to tell me how you are really."

Kyndan's blue gaze warmed her center and suddenly she did not know where to look. She took in the bright, cheerful suite, the sunlight streaming in from the windows, the sweet fresh air from the open balcony doors.

"Truly, I am well, Kyndan." she assured and gave a shy shrug. "And hungry."

His smile widened. "Well, that's easily fixed. Two of Kinara's women will be bringing breakfast up any minute. They're going to act as your maids while we're here and Laric will supervise them."

"You will share the morning meal with me?" she asked hopefully.

"I think it's my only option now. I got an earful from Laric this morning for not sending ahead to let them know you were coming. I'm afraid she'll poison breakfast unless she thinks you'll be eating it too."

She folded her hands in her lap, smiling. "You must tell her I thought myself well greeted and honorably welcomed to the clanhouse."

"Yeah, something tells me that she's not going to be assured by anything *I* say to her. I wasn't her favorite person when I lived here before and showing up unannounced with an Imperial princess in tow might have me now officially counted among the enemy."

"You lived here as a . . . a—?"

"'Slave' is the word I think you're looking for. Kinara—well, Aidar really—rescued me. You know, I never thanked him," Kyndan said thoughtfully. "'Course he punched me in the face to do it. It's going to be hard for me to think of a way to say 'thank you' that won't involve an elbow strike of some kind."

Alari's brow creased. "How did *hitting you* rescue you?"

"I was with Unata, the Az'quen heiress, in the Council of Elders chambers, I turned my head and found myself looking right at Kinara." He shook his head. "I couldn't believe it. I didn't even think; I just headed right for her. Aidar knocked me down—*twice*, dammit—and claimed I was trying to attack his mate. Unata had to hand me over to the Az'anti clan. So after that, I lived with the Az'anti till I went home. Hey, breakfast," he said as the door opened. Seeing that Laric had accompanied the maids, Kyndan leaned over to whisper: "You don't mind if I eat off your plate too, do you? Just in case?"

She laughed. The women came in to bow to her. She gave them leave to rise and Laric indicated that the maids should set the table.

"Here," Kyndan said, standing. Her new sister had sent a robe that matched the nightdress she wore and he took it from the nearby chair.

Alari pulled away the bedclothes and stood as he took a step toward her holding out the robe. His gaze dipped to her breasts outlined in the light fabric of the nightdress then he flinched and snapped his eyes away. He extended the robe a little further toward her, turning his face.

Her smile faded. She slipped her arms into the robe.

He was attentive and talkative at the morning meal, taking particular delight in shocking Laric with the jokes he made to an Imperial Daughter. He did not after all eat off her plate as she half expected he would, but his manner of dining was very different. He did not signal to the maids to fill his plate or seem to expect her to direct them as his mate. He picked up the dishes and served himself—and her—with scarcely a pause in conversation.

He sipped on a Tellaran beverage then offered it to her, his eyebrows raised. She tried not to make a face at the bitter taste but he laughed at her reaction.

"Caf is kind of an acquired taste," he said as she handed back the cup of disconcertingly muddy liquid. "Nisara will be here in about an hour to take us on the tour. I'm sure she'll understand if you want to skip it though. We could stay here instead so you can rest."

"No, it would please me to go," Alari said and took a swallow of her own—much more palatably sweet—spiced tea. He could not begin to imagine how exciting it was to her to go about the city with him again.

Then a maid came in carrying her court gown and Alari's mood dimmed.

"What's the matter?" Kyndan followed her gaze. "Is it the dress?" He gave her a questioning look. "Do you want to wear the pink one?"

"It is *traditional* for an Imperial Daughter to wear Imperial black, Commander," Laric said shortly.

"She's married to a Tellaran now. She can wear whatever she *wants*," he said impatiently, then looked at Alari and softened his tone. "You know Tellaran custom is to wear black for funerals."

Alari blinked. Az-kye donned white for mourning. "It is?"

"Yeah. I mean, you can wear the black if you like. But if you wanted to wear another color, doing so would acknowledge Tellaran tradition."

"Blue. I want to wear blue," Alari said quickly, then her cheeks warmed.

He smiled. "Blue, it is." Kyndan looked at Laric. "The princess would like a *blue* dress."

Laric's mouth turned downward in disapproval.

"I'll be happy to go out and buy her one if you don't want to do it," Kyndan offered.

Laric shot him a narrow look that said volumes of what she thought of that idea. "Well," she huffed. "What *shade* of blue?"

14

Three hours later, dressed in a gown of deep sky blue only a bit darker than the color of Kyndan's eyes, Alari stepped out into the sunshine of the lower city marketplace and smiled over her shoulder at him.

"You could have warned me," he grumbled to Nisara as the door to the café closed behind them.

"The proprietor *said* it was spicy."

"Spicy?" he echoed. "I think it actually took the top layer off my tongue."

"Well, you should know better to take a big chomp like that," Nisara said, frowning at him.

"*That's* your response as my cultural attaché? I should have known better?"

Nisara threw him an impatient look. "Yours was okay, wasn't it, Al—Your Highness?"

"It was delightful," Alari said honestly.

The casual good humor of her companions, sitting in a room of strangers, trying dishes considered too common to be offered at the palace, and all of it new to her. The tiny wizened owner talked and joked and flirted outrageously with her male customers while she served. She fussed over the Tellarans, and Alari too. News had already spread through the Empire of her scandalous marriage, but dressed as she was in blue, and with other Tellarans from Kyndan's crew visiting the city, no one recognized her as an Imperial Daughter—or Kyndan as her mate.

"I think she piled on the spice on purpose as a joke," Kyndan said good-naturedly. "The owner was something else, though, wasn't she? I'm surprised she can fit a restaurant and customers *and* that much personality into such a small space. So what's next?"

"I thought we could head out and see the shrine of Azis," Nisara said. "She's their goddess of the—"

"Rainbow," Alari finished, her heart picking up speed. "Yes, please, I should very much like to go."

Kyndan's smile was puzzled but he shrugged. "Azis' shrine it is."

Kyndan craned his neck following the spiraling galleries of the building. "So it's an art museum?"

"It's a sanctuary," Nisara corrected. "Azis is also patron goddess of the visual arts."

"Well, that makes sense," Kyndan said.

Alari looked around hungrily. It seemed an age since she had last been here. She spied one painting that she knew well, and two more that she had never seen just here on the first floor. That brushwork was the kind done during the Xar dynasty and the canvas revealed Pelnarah's hand—

"The Day of the Red Falls," Alari breathed.

"Alari?"

She could scarce tear her eyes from the work long enough to glance at him. "It is from the time of the great divide of Empress Yi'ara's reign."

"Uh, do you want to take a closer look at it?"

She nodded, her quick footsteps already taking her in that direction. The brushstrokes were so short, so precise!

The colors were dark without a hint of muddiness; it almost thrummed with intensity of the coming conflict.

"And you . . . like this?" Kyndan asked.

"It is sublime," Alari murmured, clasping her hands together against the urge to touch it, to feel connection to one who possessed such mastery. But that would be sacrilege, an offense to both Azis and to the artist's genius.

"I guess I just didn't think battle scenes would be your thing."

"This is not a battle scene," Alari argued. "It is the complete story of an age. Look you on the way the shapes of darkness—in the water there, in the shield that one carries—form the image of Ren'thar? Do you not see it?"

He frowned. "Not really . . ."

"Here," she cried, seizing his wrist to urge him farther back, and Nisara followed. "See you now?" Holding her arm out she traced the pattern. "See you how the god's hand hovers over the victors? How his head is bent in sorrow over those that fall?"

"Yeah," Kyndan murmured. "I didn't even notice it. You're right, that is pretty amazing."

"Look you now from here," Alari said, moving them to the right. "See you how the fallen are led from the city by the goddess of the Underworld?"

"Wait, the painting changes depending on where you stand?" Kyndan asked.

"How do they do that?" Nisara asked.

"Different shadings of paint are done at various depths but the lighting must be perfectly set to bring out all the scenes within," Alari said. "I have never seen this work before. In Pelnarah's earlier paintings the strokes are far more smooth and long. There used to be a painting on a level above of the falls. If you stood just so, you would see

Azis as both woman and rainbow bursting from the spray simultaneously."

Kyndan sent her a curious glance. "Why didn't you tell me you were such an art lover?"

Alari flushed. Even Saria would only listen to her babbling on about it for so long.

"Well, come on," Kyndan urged, taking her hand. "You can't stop now. Take us around and tell me and Nisara what we're looking at."

Her heart hammered at the feel of his long fingers intertwined with hers, his blue eyes smiling down on her. She wished very much that Nisara were not with them, that they were alone here.

Alari nodded to a level above. "That one is called *Flight of the Jen'tala*. It dates from the Li'thar dynasty of the First Empire but the colors are still remarkably vibrant. We could start there."

"Sounds good."

Alari basked in his encouragement as they went through the sanctuary despite having to share his attention with Nisara, delighting in the opportunity to spend the afternoon so.

It was late in the day when Nisara parted company with them to attend a party with Dael's family. Friends were also to attend dinner at the Az'anti clanhouse and Kyndan went to hire a litter to carry them back.

Alari waited just inside the gate of the sanctuary grounds for his return when she spied a familiar face walking along the boulevard.

"Elder," Alari said, surprised.

Sechon blinked. "Imperial Daughter. I am very pleased to see you!"

Her fear that the elder would shun her evaporated but Alari's face warmed as Sechon took in her blue gown. "It is good to see you too, Elder."

"And you as well, Princess," Sechon's mouth quirked upward. "I have never seen you in colors before."

"Ladies not of the court wear bright shades in honor of Azis and Lashima." Alari lifted her chin. "And my mate is Tellaran; they consider black the color of mourning."

"I see," the elder said, her white eyebrows raised. "Well, blue looks very fine on you, Your Highness."

Alari's hand went to the skirt of the gown, a little embarrassed for her sharp tone to an elderly woman who had only ever shown her kindness. "I am sure Her Imperial Majesty would not approve . . ."

The elder gave a faint smile. "I do recall another Imperial Daughter who—when she was young, mind you, did once or twice scandalize the court by wearing a bright color to turn the eyes of a handsome warrior her way."

Alari blinked. "The empress—?"

Sechon shrugged, her eyes crinkled with humor. "I am old now and my memory could be failing. But I do recall such at least one such occurrence. Perhaps Her Imperial Majesty would not be so shocked as you imagine."

In Alari's mind her mother loomed as such a powerful figure, the very embodiment of Az-kye tradition. It was hard to imagine her as a young woman—let alone one infatuated enough to flaunt tradition within the very walls of the palace.

The elder's gaze turned serious. "I spoke to First Daughter Saria yesterday. She—*we*—have been very worried for you. We none of us knew where you had gone. We none of us expected you to leave the palace."

"Her Imperial Majesty did not restrict me to the palace grounds," Alari said defensively. "I did not disobey the empress. And I am in disgrace, none should care *where* I am."

"Even in disgrace there are those who care for you. I certainly am pleased to look on you." Sechon tilted her head. "Perhaps you might disregard Tellaran sensibilities for a few hours to don a gown of Imperial black and visit the First Daughter?"

Alari hesitated.

"I will be at the palace tonight and tomorrow as well," Sechon offered. "Perhaps, if needed, my memory could recall other Imperial Daughters who have disregarded convention . . . when they were young."

Alari smiled and touched the elder's arm. "Tell my sister I will come in the morning."

The elder inclined her head. "I will. And, Princess, if you ever have need of me . . ."

"Thank you," Alari said quietly.

Kyndan arrived just as the elder's litter was being lifted up.

"Our ride's coming down the street now. That was Sechon, the Leader of the Council of Elders, wasn't it? Everything okay?" he asked, his brow slightly furrowed, glancing toward the departing litter.

"It is so," Alari assured. "I am to visit my sister in the morning."

"At the palace."

She tilted her head. "This troubles you?"

"No." He folded his arms. "Okay, yes, to be honest, Alari, I'm not exactly happy about how they treated you. I'd feel a whole lot better if I went with you tomorrow."

"Of course you will go," she said, surprised. "You are my protector."

"Oh." he said, his expression a little bemused. "Right." He gave a short laugh. "I probably need to get Aidar or Tedah to run through all that with me."

"Tellaran men do not act as their mates' protectors then?"

"Well, they're certainly protective *of* them, but how that plays out on a practical level is a little different. A bit less sword swinging and a bit more 'call me when you get there.'" He nodded in response to the litter bearer's bow and, taking Alari's hand in a suddenly protective grasp, led her that way. "I'll be sticking with the sword concept tomorrow."

15

ꟿ ᑕꞀ ᚷᐸᏟ Ⴤ ᛘᎩᎶᏟᐳᏟᎶᐟ
Cultural Exchange

Alari had spent her life surrounded by the finest warriors in the Empire but had never met anyone with as much courage as Lianna of the Otan.

"You and Tedah were bound while he was still wearing the white?" she asked astonished and put down her teacup.

Lianna nodded and threw a fond glance at her mate, now warrior but born Tellaran, Tedah. After the evening meal they gathered to continue their conversation in a less formal sitting room at the back of the Az'anti clanhouse. Seated comfortably together on the couches and chairs, they enjoyed their tea and wine before the open garden doors. The warm night air blew into the sitting room and the sounds of celebrations drifted in on the breeze.

Clearly Kinara and Aidar of the Az'anti, as well as Kyndan, already knew the story but Alari could scare believe it.

"Were you not even a little . . .?" She could not think of a word that would encompass the act of a clan heiress sneaking off to take a slave as a mate.

"Insane?" Tedah asked over his wine cup, drawing laughter from Lianna.

"Did you not fear the clan leader would cast you out?" she asked Lianna.

Lianna smiled but there was an echo of pain in her eyes. "To be parted from him would have been a worse fate."

"Still," Aidar said. "Her Highness does well to think you mad for such."

"You married Kinara," Tedah reminded.

"I was clan leader then," Aidar returned. "And faced no punishment."

"Beyond having me for a mate," Kinara said, smiling.

He took her hand, his dark eyes shining. "I would have no other."

"But was your mother not angry?" Alari asked.

"Furious," Lianna confided with a laugh. "She took me to Lashima's temple and demanded the High Priestess unbind us."

"But no one is ever unbound!" Alari had heard of perhaps a handful of such happenings in the history of the Empire. "You cannot tell me High Priestess Celara considered it?"

Lianna shook her head. "I cannot think it was ever a possibility but Her Eminence intervenes kindly when she can, I think. She took me into the inner sanctuary and asked me what *I* wished. I said that it did not matter if I were unbound or not. I would still be Tedah's mate and he mine. She went to my mother and said that while she might have the power to undo our mating only Lashima could truly unbind a pair and clearly She had not made it so in my heart." Lianna giggled. "I think it the only time my mother was ever left speechless."

"So her Eminence outright refused?" asked Alari. "What did your mother do?"

Lianna shrugged. "What could my mother do then but welcome Tedah to our clan?"

"And as graciously as you can imagine," Tedah put in dryly.

"My mother is very fond of you," Lianna protested.

"Your mother is fond of my engineering skills. I overhauled half her cargo vessels and upgraded the other half."

"*And* made her very fond of you."

"She even addresses me by name now."

"What did she call you before?" Kyndan asked then grinned. "Or don't I want to know?"

"'My daughter's mate,'" Tedah supplied.

Kyndan raised an eyebrow. "That's not so bad."

"Yeah, right. 'Good morning, my daughter's mate,' 'Will you take tea, my daughter's mate'—really, try it for an *hour*."

Kyndan laughed. "Father tried to convince Fleet Security to drag Aidar away in tarasteel cuffs when he came to bring Kinara home."

"He did?" Tedah exclaimed. "Why?"

"Because I wouldn't let Father have the pulse rifle back," Kyndan said. "Speaking of warm welcomes, Alari and I are going to the palace tomorrow. I'm probably not any more welcome there now but you won't have to get permission for me to go this time," he said to Kinara.

One of the house guards came to the doorway, and Aidar gave the man a nod. "I must see to the patrols." He put down his wine cup and stood. "Do you wish, Kyndan, I will find you a sword to carry tomorrow."

Kyndan gave him a thoughtful look. "I think I'll stick with my blaster and be a *Tellaran* protector."

"Sechon will be there," Alari said as Aidar left. "She has offered her support."

"I like her. The elder always been very kind to me." Kinara took a sip of the spice tea Sechon had sent that afternoon for the princess' stay. "And she sends thoughtful gifts."

"She has been my mother's chief advisor as long as I can remember," Alari said. "She offered to intervene on my behalf if ever I had need of it."

"Perhaps in the spirit of the festival Her Imperial Majesty will welcome you home," Lianna said. Alari imagined that she often looked for the brightest of outcomes; the heiress of the Otan reminded her very much of Saria. "What do you think of the festival?" she asked Kyndan. "Tedah says Tellarans have a similar celebration."

"It *is* a bit like carnival on Rusco but this one hasn't required me to do any dancing yet. You know?" Kyndan said at Alari's questioning look. "Dancing?"

"You are a dancer, Kyndan?" She had seen many performances by the Imperial dancers but they were reared to that art from childhood and devoted their lives to it. A First Daughter would never make a public dance performance but as a young girl she had lessons intended to make her appreciative of the Imperial dancers' skill.

"Actually I don't think I've ever seen Az-kye couples dancing together like Tellarans do." He stood suddenly. "I bet there's enough room in here if we move some of this stuff out of the way. Help me out, Tedah."

The women stood and the two men lifted chairs and tables and pushed the couches aside.

"Come on." Kyndan offered his hand to her when they had cleared a large space in the room. "It's all right," he said, smiling at her hesitation. "I'm not *that* bad at it. Oh, wait a sec, I forgot to ask." Kyndan looked to the Az'anti clan leader. "Do you have any music for this, Kinna?"

"For slow dancing, I'm guessing?" Kinara asked.

Alari looked between them. "Tellarans do fast dancing?"

"Yeah, but we're not going to be doing that," Kyndan said. "This is easier for me to teach."

She gave a hasty nod. "I, too, think it best for us to start slowly."

He took her hand and her cheeks warmed when he drew her closer. "Slowly it is."

He placed her hand on his shoulder, put his hand on her waist and held her other hand with their elbows bent.

"This is how we will dance?" Alari's brow creased. "There is not room for us both to move do we stand so close."

"We move together and mostly you'll go backwards. No," he said when she turned her head. "You look at me."

"Do I look at you, Kyndan, I cannot see behind me." She would not care to attempt this blindly. "I will not know where to step."

"No, I'll be looking behind you."

"But *I* will not know where to step."

Kyndan gave a short laugh. "I'm really not explaining this very well, am I?"

She tried not to let her disappointment show when he let her go.

"Come here, Kinna," he said as the music started playing. "Help me show her."

Kinara gave him a disbelieving look. "I'm not exactly at my most graceful," she said resting a hand on her rounded belly for emphasis. "And it's been a long while since I danced."

"You don't have to win the carnival ball dance competition here. We just need to give Alari an idea of what it looks like. Come on," he said, waving her forward. "You're the only other one here who can dance."

"Hey, I can dance," Tedah protested.

"Tedah," Kyndan threw over his shoulder, "for the last time, I'm not dancing with you."

Alari and Lianna gave a startled giggles but Kinna blew her breath out.

"He might be a better choice," she warned. "I'm going to have to stand so far away we might as well have a boloball between us."

"Does your mate dance so?" Alari asked curiously.

"Yeah, we're still working on that," Kinara grumbled good-naturedly as she took up position with Kyndan. "It's not something I want to try again without clearing all the breakables from the area."

Alari moved back to watch and to her surprise the two moved in tandem, Kyndan stepping forward while Kinara stepped back. They moved in time with the music and despite the clan leader's concern she seemed, to Alari's eyes, to glide effortlessly about the room.

Alari had never seen anything like it. It looked strange. It looked exotic.

It looked *fun*.

"You can do such, Tedah?" Lianna asked, surprised. "Why did you not tell me?"

"Hey, I'm an Az-kye warrior now. Warriors aren't big on dancing."

Kyndan stopped and Kinara's face was flushed, tendrils of her hair sticking to her temples.

"What to you think?" Kyndan asked Alari as he released Kinara. "Ready to try?"

Nervous and excited, Alari took up her position with Kyndan.

"Dancing," Aidar said, stopping short in the doorway and looking very much as if he wished to flee the room. He sent a guarded glance at Kinara. "Are we to dance as well, my mate?"

"I'd say you're off the hook till after the baby comes." Kinara sat then took up her jaha fan to wave at her face and lifted her fiery hair to cool her neck. "Five minutes and I feel like I'm sitting on top of a crystal manifold with a busted coolant unit."

"Okay, now," Kyndan placed Alari's hand on his broad shoulder and her hand held in his, his other at the curve of her waist again. "On the beat I step forward with my left foot and you step back with your right. We'll just do that a couple times so you can get used to it and then we'll add on, all right?"

Alari wet her lips. "All right."

He got her to move her feet the right way till they were able to move together, their steps forming a square. It was unnerving at first to move backward without looking where she was going but Kyndan directed her so effortlessly, so confidently, she soon relaxed in his arms. Over the next hour he progressed to moving her around the room and then turns.

As she got better he held her even closer. The two of them moving in rhythm together like this, while not lewd in the least, echoed the act of joining and she wondered if he would move with such smooth confidence inside her. The sudden longing for it made her face hot and embarrassed she cast about something to say.

"Do all Tellarans do this?" she asked a little breathlessly as they swayed and turned to the music.

"I don't know about *all* but you'd be surprised how many formal dances, official functions, and such that a Fleet officer is expected to attend. My father sent me for lessons at the base social club so I wouldn't embarrass myself.

Gods, I *hated* it—a clumsy kid tripping over my big feet with a dance teacher four times my age. I can still hear my friends snickering."

"Were they not also clumsy?"

"Oh, no danger," he said cheerfully. "I snickered when it was their turn."

She suddenly worried that he thought her so inept. "I am grateful for your patience in teaching me."

"No, you're good at this." He smiled down at her. "You must be a natural."

She found herself looking at the full curve of his lip. She glanced away, startled to see that the others had left the room and she hadn't even noticed them going.

Kyndan followed her gaze. "I guess we scared them off," he said with a laugh and stopped. "I thought we were doing pretty well."

"It was well done," Alari agreed. "I very much like to dance with you, Kyndan."

His hand was still at her waist and hers on his shoulder, their hands still clasped. His smile faded, his hold softened, became warmer now.

Her heart sped up, her gaze on his mouth again.

But suddenly something changed between them. Kyndan let go and took a step back.

"Well," he said with a brightness that seemed forced. "That's a starter lesson anyway."

She swallowed back her disappointment. "Thank you."

"Sure." He glanced toward the garden doors; the moons had long since risen. "It's actually getting pretty late. We should probably turn in if you want to make an early visit to the palace."

Alari waited in their bed for him, plucking at the bedclothes with her fingers. When Kyndan finally came from the bathing chamber, he wore only loose sleeping trousers. He took the time to extinguish the lights as he came and he avoided her gaze.

Drawing the covers down he climbed in to bed. She could feel the warmth of him beside her, remembered how it felt to have him pull her against him in the temple district, remembered the tremble of hunger in his body as his mouth hovered over hers.

After a long moment he met her eyes. "We should probably get some sleep."

Her throat tightened against disappointed tears.

Kyndan hesitated then caught her chin to press a kiss so light and soft he barely brushed her mouth. "Good night, Alari."

Suddenly the frustration, the *unfairness* of it, was too much and her hands curled into fists.

"Do not do such," she said hoarsely.

He pulled away instantly. "Sorry, I didn't mean to—"

"Do not treat me as if I am broken!" she said, her voice low and fierce. "Think you I am so despoiled by *him*?"

"What?" He reared back. "Alari, I don't think that at all. I just—"

"I want to be like your other girls, Kyndan!" she cried, gripping the sheets. "I want you to *see* me the same! I want you to *treat* me the same as you did them—not as if I am damaged!"

He shook his head. "That's not what I was—"

"I know you are thinking of that—of what *he* did!"

"No! Actually I've been thinking of—well, Lashima."

She stopped short. "What?"

"You know, how Ren'thar won over Lashima. Because he was so gentle and, uh—" His face colored. "Patient."

Alari's brow furrowed. "I do not understand."

"*The Thousand Nights of Tenderness*." He gave a frustrated gesture. "Well, gods, you're *Az-kye*, Alari! I thought—I mean, I figured that's what you'd *want*."

"You read *The Thousand Nights*?" She blinked at him. "To learn how to rouse me?"

"Well, not *all* of it. It's pretty long. After the Circle I asked Tedah to get me a copy but I didn't have a lot of time so I kind of skimmed till"—he gave a sheepish half shrug—"I got to the good parts."

She searched his reddened face. "*That* is why you have not—?"

Surprised, touched, and giddy with relief, Alari burst out laughing.

He slumped back against the carved headboard, his color high. "Not exactly the ecstatic response I was going for."

"Oh, Kyndan," she said, smiling and shaking her head. "You are so pleasing to me I cannot even speak to it!"

Alari moved so she was on her knees facing him. She nipped her lip and studied him for a moment. His face was flushed, his blue eyes chagrined, his warm brown hair charmingly rumpled.

Alari drew a deep breath and seized her courage, lightly brushing his full lower lip with her fingers. He blinked and she traced the scar he had earned for her then the line of his jaw, feeling the roughness of tiny stubble. She rested her fingers at the hollow of his throat for a moment before skimming the warm lightly furred skin of his chest.

His eyes widened when her touch trailed lower still, the muscles of his stomach tightening under her fingers. She watched his breath quicken; he was fully roused now, tenting the soft fabric of his sleeping trousers. His mouth parted in a shaking breath as her hand ran over his hardened length.

Her fingers went to either side of his waist, edging the waistband lower. He held her gaze searchingly and after a moment lifted his hips so she could pull the fabric down. She watched as his shaft sprang free and found that he was different from men she had seen only in how beautifully he was formed. He made a soft strangled sound as she closed her hand around him, marveling in the velvety smoothness of his skin. Her fingers, wrapped around his staff, didn't quite meet as she caressed him.

"Gods . . ." His mouth parted, his breath ragged, his eyes half-shut as he watched her stroke him and pressed his hips toward her. His large shaft grew still more taut in her hand. A bead of moisture appeared at the tip and she rubbed over the slickness with the pad of her thumb.

"This is what I want, Kyndan," she said huskily. "I want you so roused you are wild for me."

His hand came up swiftly to cup her cheek then, his blue gaze fevered.

"If you want me to stop," he said hoarsely, "*any time* you tell me to stop, I will. You just tell me. All right?"

She nodded and in the next moment his mouth was on hers, hot and demanding, his palm at the back of her neck to press her closer.

Alari caught her breath at the heat of it and if she thought his earlier hesitation due to inexperience or reluctance she was completely mistaken. Kyndan was confident and skilled, his tongue just tracing the inside so her upper lip for a moment before he deepened the kiss.

Her center tightened at the heat in his eyes as his fingers traced along the sides of her neck, to her shoulders to slide down the straps of her nightdress. The linen fell away easily and she swallowed at the anxiety at being so exposed to him.

His gaze went to her breasts, his eyes softening. "You're so beautiful . . ."

He wet his lips, his hand warm and gentle as he cupped the fullness of her breasts. The lightest touch of his thumb over her nipples sent a shock of tightening pleasure through her. In a quick, startling movement he caught her by the waist. He swung her around and she thrilled at the forcefulness, rejoicing at how unafraid she was of his eagerness. Then the softness of the bed was against her back and he was kneeling between her legs.

His fingers trembled a little as they hooked the edges of her underwear and Alari felt a cool rush of air over her center as he pulled away the last of her garments. She was naked now, his eyes hot and hungry as his palms against the inside of her thighs eased her wider. His shaft jerked a bit as his gaze went to her folds and it roused her more to be so open and exposed to him.

"Gods," he said raggedly. "I've wanted this so much."

Alari wanted to ask if he was as pleased by what he saw as she was but the light caress of his fingers starting at her knee and sliding up her inner thigh took her breath from her.

"Just to be able to *touch* you . . ."

Her center tightened sharply as his fingers brushed there and she closed her eyes briefly, lifting her hips toward him slightly. His smile was almost feral as he took in her reaction.

"Oh, no. I've wanted this too much to rush, Princess," he whispered huskily, his touch skimming over where she was most sensitive. "That was just a taste."

His touch went up over the dark hair curled between her legs, over her belly and between her breasts. He leaned forward then, his hand bracing the bed next to her as he lowered his body to hers.

Her mouth parted at the wonderful shock of skin against skin. His body was very warm, beautifully muscled, and Alari's hands went to his back as he settled over her, the heat of his shaft against her center as he brought his mouth to hers.

He caged her body with his arms, lazily kissing her, and his hard body over hers, the tantalizing touch of his hardness against her center, made her lift her hips to rub against him.

He made a soft sound then, between a laugh and a groan.

"You're not making it easy to go slow," he said thickly.

His legs were hard with muscle against the inside of her thighs; a quick lift of his hips and his hot hardness would be plunging inside her.

"So do not go slow," Alari urged breathlessly. "You have given me enough of a taste now."

"A taste. . . *there's* an idea . . ." His head bent to catch the tip of her breast, the moist heat of his tongue on her nipple making her lips part. Her fingers ran through the soft waves of his hair as he drew the tip into his mouth with gentle suction.

He turned his attention to her other breast and he shifted a bit so, while his shaft was still heavy at her thigh, there was space between their bodies. His palm smoothed over her ribs, waist, and lower belly to her center, lightly tracing the folds there.

"Hmm," he murmured approvingly at the sound of her moan. "I like that. Be even better when I bring you to your pleasure . . ."

It was maddening how his fingers barely skimmed over her nub, his touch sending every nerve through her belly, thighs, center, and buttocks tingling. She clasped the flesh of his broad shoulders to press him closer, to urge him on.

"So impatient," he scolded hoarsely and grasping the dark hair there, gave a gentle, possessive tug that sent her arousal soaring. "You don't know what it's taking for me not to spread you wide, not to be inside you right now."

She rocked herself against his hand. "Kyndan, please . . ."

"My sweet, impatient princess." His touch changed to circle where she was most sensitive, taking her between his thumb and finger. Her eyes shut, her mouth parting at the waves of sensation as he stroked her.

Keeping his thumb circling against her, he slid a finger, then two, into her slickness.

"Gods, so wet . . ." he groaned against her mouth.

He was above her now, one elbow braced beside her head, the hot tip of his shaft positioned between her lips. His blue gaze met hers and then he was entering her, clasping her hip to hold her still.

He was thick, stretching her fully, and he searched her face, the question in his eyes.

"Gods," she cried, her hands going to his hips to urge him on, trying to move against him. "Do not stop!"

A hot smile flitted across his face then his gaze dropped to watch himself as he filled her. His shaft hit her most sensitive spot with every movement as he pulled back and again as he filled her.

Kyndan held her steady, his fingers pressing into the flesh of her buttock, every thrust driving her higher, bringing her nearly to the brink. He was rock hard inside her now, his body taut, curled toward her, the muscles of his stomach trembling as he drove into her. She was so close and Alari's hands went to his hips to press him deeper. She cried out as her climax hit, contracting hard around him.

Kyndan made a strangled sound at her release and his rhythm changed, his strokes faster and harder now. He thrust deep, then again and it was a thrill to sense him at the end of his control. He stiffened, shuddering, and she felt the throbs of his shaft as his seed burst deep within her.

Gasping at his release he collapsed against her, their bodies slick with sweat, His head came to rest at her shoulder, his mouth parted against her throat, his breath hot and moist against her skin.

Still trembling, Alari wrapped her arms around him, the waves of his hair soft against her cheek.

As if his body felt too heavy for movement, he lifted his head to meet her gaze. He quickly searched her eyes, the slightest crease in his brow, but whatever he saw in her gaze instantly melted his concern away. He gave her a quick smile.

"I must be crushing you," he mumbled, sounding chagrined and still a bit breathless as he slid away from her.

"I do not mind," she protested, but he was already collapsing beside her on the bed.

Her flash of disappointment at the loss of contact only lasted a heartbeat; in the next moment he gathered her against him. He cradled her, one arm around her, his hand holding hers at his chest.

He gave a soft laugh. "Sorry, looks like Ren'thar's got me completely beat on patience."

Alari rubbed her cheek lightly against his shoulder. "I thought perhaps you did not want me."

He gave a disbelieving look. "You had me stiff and throbbing just by taking enough pity on me to change my bandage."

"I did not mean to embarrass you then."

"I thought you must know I kept hoping, just *hoping*, your hand would slide up just a little more and . . . Gods," he said, his voice taking on a note of astonishment. "I'm getting hard again just thinking about it."

She glanced down and his shaft was at half-stand again.

"Besides *wanting* you was embarrassingly obvious," he said with a meaningful glance downward. "But I was trying to give you time to want me back, to do things right." His gaze was rueful. "I really was doing my best to court you like an Az-kye would. At least like I *thought* an Az-kye would. I don't know, maybe I missed a lot by skipping the beginning of *The Thousand Nights*."

"I would not know. I never read the beginning," she confided with a playful smirk "I, too, was more interested in getting to the 'good stuff.'"

His face flushed a bit, his eyes alight with interest. "Really? What was your favorite part?" he asked, his voice husky.

"Hmm . . ." His eyes widened when Alari wet her palm with her tongue and slid her hand over him. With two strokes she had him groaning and at full stand. "Perhaps, Kyndan, it is best I show you . . ."

16

Homecoming

Smiling and looking a little sleepy the next morning, Kyndan helped her step down from the litter onto the tile of the palace's inner courtyard. "I just can't get over the size of this place."

Alari looked at the familiar grounds and smoothed her black court dress. As a girl she had walked here beside her father, she holding one of his hands and Saria the other. She and her sister had run as children across these very stones, giggling, long before they grew to the age when they were expected to walk with sedate decorum.

"It seems small to me," Alari said softly.

"You're kidding, right?" Kyndan asked with a glance around the palace grounds, at the empress' residence, the house of the Imperial children, the theaters and ballrooms, the parks and banquet halls.

Alari gave a quick smile. "There is a city beyond these walls, a world, many worlds that I have never seen. You have been to worlds light years away."

"Yeah, but when I got there my room was the size of a snouse nest," he said. "And sometimes about as well furnished."

"Imperial Daughter . . ." Alari recognized Urenna; the woman had been one of her attendants a spare few days ago. "The First Daughter has consented to see you."

Alari nodded but Kyndan looked annoyed on their walk to the House of the Imperial Children. They garnered wide-eyed looks, and most did not bow to Alari until the very last moment, skirting the very edge of offense. Whispers followed in their wake.

"Nothing like being gawked at," Kyndan muttered. "You know, I could set this blaster to a wide beam. Stun them in big groups. That'd teach 'em to stare."

In a burst of daring she threaded her arm through his, a posture completely inappropriate for an Imperial Daughter, and grinned up at him. "Let them stare."

He gave her a surprised smile but his smile faded as he recognized where the attendant had brought them. "These are your quarters."

"These are the quarters of the First Daughter," Alari corrected. "I do not mind," she assured when she saw his frown. "Truly, my mate."

Saria, her clothing and jewels now more elaborate and fitting for the Imperial heiress, rose from her seat when they were shown into the sitting room. Alari was pleased to see that Sechon was present as well.

Alari bent her head to her sister and Kyndan bowed.

"First Daughter," Alari said.

"You are welcome here, Imperial Daughter," Saria said, and in her tone Alari could hear her discomfiture at welcoming her to what had recently been her home.

"Imperial Daughter," Sechon said, inclining her head.

"Elder," Alari said. "I am pleased to look on you."

"As I am to look on you," the elder returned. She turned her attention to Kyndan. "And you as well, Imperial mate." She tilted her head. "Or should I call you 'Commander'?"

Kyndan cleared his throat. "I'm actually on Az-kye as the Tellaran representative so 'Commander' is really more appropriate, I think."

"As you like," she said warmly. "But my age has gotten the better of me, I'm afraid. I have sat too long and I must walk for a bit or I will grow too stiff to move. I was just going to enjoy a walk in the gallery. Perhaps you will join me, Commander?"

Kyndan glanced at Alari. "Maybe another time."

"Certainly," the elder said. She looked at Saria. "If you will excuse me."

Saria nodded and when the elder had gone she addressed her attendants. "Leave us." They hesitated and she threw them a cold look. "Obey me or I will find others to serve who *will*."

They hurried from the room and as soon as the last had left Saria embraced her.

"You should not have gone without telling me," Saria scolded, hugging her tightly. "I was so worried for you, Alari."

"There was no need to be," Alari assured, drawing back and throwing a fond glance at Kyndan. "Truly he is an exquisite lover." Alari smiled at how his cheeks flushed then turned back to Saria. "But you must tell me—did Naret of the Az'larna visit you?"

Her sister's cheeks pinkened, her face alight. "It was wonderful, Sister, to be opened so."

"Opened?" Kyndan wondered.

"Opened," Alari repeated. "The first time a man enters a woman—"

"*Okay!*" Kyndan said taking a step back. "I think this ship just arrived in the area of space where the men are advised to disembark."

Alari met Saria's puzzled look. "Tellarans are shy about such things."

"How curious." Saria looked at Kyndan. "But not when he mounts you, Alari?"

"*Urgently* advised to disembark." Kyndan took another step back, reddened to the hairline. "I think I'll see if I can catch the elder and take her up on the offer of that tour after all."

The moment the door was shut behind him the sisters' eyes met and both laughed.

"You are fond of him," Saria said. "Tell me quickly— what is it like to be bound?"

"We are not yet so." Saria looked surprised and Alari drew her to sit down. "But tell me more of Naret. Will you keep him as your lover?"

Saria laughed. "Of course! But I have even better news," her sister enthused. "It has been decided that I am to represent the empress at the dedication of Lashima's new temple on Az-litha!"

Alari felt a shock of envy. She had never been permitted to go offworld, to travel anywhere, as First; only after taking Jazan as mate would she have been allowed to go. "You are?"

"I leave tomorrow." Saria's smile widened. "And Naret will go with me."

"How exciting for you."

"Sometimes I did not think I should *ever* leave the homeworld. And to do something so important and—" Saria's face colored. "I am sorry."

"Were you envious of me?" Alari asked softly. She often wondered before but it had always been a silent agreement between them not to speak of the succession. "Because I was First?"

Saria looked away. "It is not easy to be Second," she said finally. "To know that I do not truly matter, that my mate will forever be disappointed that I will never be First, never be empress. And now—" She shook her head. "Forgive me, Alari. I would never have wished this for you."

"No, "Alari said softly, covering her sister's hand with her own. "I would have it this way, Saria. I would have you First and have freedom for myself."

Saria blinked. "Freedom?"

Alari shook her head, smiling. "I envied *you*, Saria. You would be free to do as your heart wished once I was mated and bore a child. You would be able to travel, to go as you wished. You would be an Imperial Daughter and far freer than I ever would be."

"So—" Saria searched her eyes. "You do not hate me now that I am First? You are not angry that you are not even Second?"

Alari laughed. "No. I would have you First and happy Saria. I have my freedom and Kyndan as mate. I am happy not to be an heiress at all."

"Alari says this place seems small to her," Kyndan said. Lined with windows made of actual astuk crystal not plexisteel, the galley alone was the length of four boloball fields. "But I'd need a geo-locator just to find my way out of the 'fresher."

The elder gave a startled, delightedly scandalized laugh. "You are unlike any Imperial mate this palace has ever seen."

Kyndan gave her a grin. "I'm going to take that as a compliment."

Sechon inclined her head. "As well you should, Commander."

He knew he was likely the only Tellaran—since Kinara and Tedah counted as Az-kye—ever to be allowed within these halls. The palace was a marvel of soaring ceilings and stone floors so highly polished they shone like mirrors. Carved and painted arches linked one gallery to the next and through the windows of crystal the fountains and gardens of the Imperial parks were bursts of color below. Seeing all this was an amazing, once-in-a-lifetime opportunity but the stares were annoying.

"Looks like you aren't the only one who thinks so."

"You are Tellaran," Sechon said. "And yet a member of the Imperial family. Such has never been done, never been *imagined*. They are curious and," she said heavily, "the Princess Alari was much loved."

Kyndan's mouth tightened. "But she isn't now."

Sechon waved her hand. "No, no, you misunderstand. I meant, loved as First. Loved as she who would be empress. Now the Princess Saria will rule and the Az-kye do not like change." She shook her head. "It has been a difficult transition for everyone."

"Yeah," he said a little sharply. "Sure looks like little sister lost no time moving into Alari's spot."

"Princess Saria is now First; she must assume that role, no matter how much she loves her sister. Do not judge Princess Saria too harshly. She has had little joy in being Second. To be an Imperial Daughter but not to have hope of inheriting is not an easy fate, Commander. I was one such."

"You're an Imperial Daughter?" Kyndan asked, though why he should be surprised he didn't know. He knew hardly anything at all about the royal family.

The elder nodded. "I, too, was once Second. High Priestess Celara and I were both sisters of Empress Teshir, our present empress' mother. Though my sister Celara's calling was never to rule."

Kyndan frowned. "You and Celara are the empress' aunts?"

"Of course. In fact, Empress Azara and my daughter, Helia of the Az'shu, were born the same year."

"So, doesn't that make you an Imperial heiress too?"

Sechon raised white eyebrows and Kyndan had the feeling he'd just asked a really stupid question.

"No, I gave up my right to inherit upon being named an elder, Commander," she said, gracious despite his ignorance. "In order that I may advise Her Majesty with an unfettered heart. As the gods may grant that I shall serve Princess Saria, when she is crowned."

Kyndan sighed. "And if it weren't for me, Alari would have been empress. Of course," he added, "she'd also be married to Jazan now."

The elder flinched.

Kyndan frowned. "Did I say something to, uh, offend, Elder?"

She closed her eyes briefly. "Jazan was son of my son."

Kyndan blinked. "Jazan was your grandson?"

"No," the Elder corrected. "Only my daughter, Helia, bears grandsons."

Uh, okay. Wait, Jazan was Alari's second cousin? Then he pushed aside the bewildering machinations of Az-kye Imperial familial relationships as the horrified realization snapped into place.

"Oh. Elder," he stammered. "I'm sorry—"

She shook her head and touched his arm lightly. "Jazan died as a warrior. But while his father joined another clan he was still my child's child." She sighed. "I hoped he would make Princess Alari a pleasing mate."

He glanced away. "I'm not sure that was going to happen anyway."

"What do you mean?"

He had pitched his voice low enough when goading Jazan in the Circle that only the warrior had heard his words and he already wasn't feeling good about this conversation now. Revealing to this elderly lady, who seemed as fond of Alari as Alari was of her, that her grandson was guilty of criminal acts when it wasn't even his secret to tell was out of the question. But he wasn't very happy about having to lie about it either.

"I don't know. Just a feeling, I guess."

She looked at him a bit puzzled then offered him a half-smile. "Do encourage the princess to consider returning to reside at the palace. Her sister misses her terribly and they were always dear to one another."

He was due to return to take command of the *Sertarian* shortly and while he'd had ideas about their future living arrangements, Alari remaining behind in Az-kye space never even occurred to him.

Looking along the length of the galley, the ceiling of brilliant colors and carving soaring above, the crystal windows and the falls that kicked up spray of shifting, sparkling rainbows a half-kilometer high, Kyndan felt his stomach sink.

What did he have to offer Alari that could possibly compare to *this*?

"Yeah," he said quietly. "I'll talk to her about it."

17

ᏉᎲᏗᏤᏗᏗᏤᎾ ᏠᏫᏗ ᏃᎲᏗᏤᎲᎪ
Bending the Rainbow

Alari looked up from her seat on the chaise where she had been looking at some of the sketches Saria had left for her and smiled at Kyndan.

He glanced around Saria's living quarters. "Where's your sister?"

"Responsibilities of the First Daughter have called her away." She indicated the low table before her. "But she had refreshments brought for us. Are you hungry?"

"Yeah," he said and she smiled inwardly that despite being the mate of an Imperial Daughter he did not think to look for another to serve him. He filled his own plate from the offerings. Waving away the attendants Saria had left for them, Alari poured the tea for him herself.

He nodded at the drawings next to her. "What's all this?"

"My things were moved to other quarters," Alari said. "But these Saria kept back to give me herself."

"Can I see?" Kyndan put down his plate and leafed through a few of the sketches. "Wow, these are beautiful. Hold on," he said suddenly, looking intently at one rendering of the falls. "Alari, did you do these?"

Alari's face warmed. "Yes."

"Gods, you aren't just an art lover," he said, his blue eyes alight. "You're an artist."

She gave a quick, embarrassed laugh. "No, I shall never be such."

"Are you kidding? *Look* at these." She was touched to see how carefully he handled her work. "They're amazing."

She ducked her head. "Think you so?"

"Everybody must think so! Why, what have other people said?"

She busied herself with her teacup. "Only you and Saria have seen them."

"You haven't shown these to anyone?" he asked, frowning. "Didn't you have a teacher?"

"When I was a girl Saria and I both were given instruction in art as we were in dance and music, so that we might appreciate the work of those artists." She took a quick sip of tea. "Not so that we should become such ourselves."

"They *discouraged* you?" he asked, his tone disbelieving. He went still. "How much did they discourage you, Alari? Gods, *that's* why you were so interested in going to Azis' sanctuary, why you looked at the paintings like a starving man would look at food . . ." A flush ran up his neck. "They wouldn't even let you go to a museum?"

Alari looked away. "An heiress must attend to her duties, not her interests."

"I can guess who told you that. 'Course you aren't First Daughter anymore, you can draw all you want now."

"What?" Alari blinked up at him, her cup halfway to her mouth. "What?"

"Sure, why not? You're not even the Second."

Alari shook her head a little. "I am still an Imperial Daughter."

"So?"

"But—but it would be . . . unseemly to apply myself so."

He gave a short laugh. "Gods, it couldn't possibly be worse than being married to a Tellaran."

She put her cup down, the china clinking from the tremble in her hand. "Would you not be shamed to have your mate do so? To apply myself to an endeavor so beneath my birth?"

"Alari," he said softly, "I would be proud of you. I *am* proud of you." He gently laid the drawings down. "You love doing this. You're great at it. Of course you should do it."

Alari looked at the sketches she'd done. She could spare so little time for them that some had taken her weeks to complete. There were days filled with her responsibilities as Imperial Heiress where she lived for the few stolen minutes late in the evening where she could draw again. Saria sometimes bribed one of her own maids to purchase colors in the city and secreted them to her so she could sketch at all.

Looking up at Kyndan now, her eyes stung. "I would very much like a peridot colorstick," she said thickly. "It has been months since I had one."

He smiled. "Well, let's gather all these up, get ourselves a litter, and go shopping for peridot. Come on, Alari." He offered his hand. "We're going to buy you every color they've got."

At first Alari was careful to put her colorsticks, papers, and sketches neatly away. They were left tucked into a cabinet when Kyndan took her to the artists' quarter where she could view new paintings or explore the shops bursting with foils, paints, colorsticks, paper, and canvas. They ate the midday meal in tiny establishments where apprentices of the artist caste, their nails stained with pigment, gathered.

The older ones were about her own age and Alari, dressed in brightly colored dresses, sipping spiced tea from the mismatched china and surrounded by their lively talk on the techniques of aquarelle or tempera, almost felt she were one of them.

The next night as she drew Kyndan brushed aside her hair to kiss her neck, his arms going round her. She leaned back as his hands cupped her breasts, turning to meet his hot mouth with her own. He'd kissed her to bed, his hand beneath her gown sliding up her thigh, so roused his fingers trembled when they reached her cleft, the sketch and colors utterly forgotten.

But when she'd awoken in the morning her things were as she had left them on the table. She brushed a kiss against Kyndan's hair as he slept then crept to her place and lifted the colorstick, joyfully picking up again where she had left off.

Except for coaxing her with kisses to the bed for lovemaking or urging her to dinner in the dining room below stairs he seemed completely content letting her draw. He played the Tellaran game of darshball with Bebti and the other children, praising Bebti's emerging sword skills as the boy demonstrated with his wooden practice sword while she sketched the garden of the Az'anti estate.

He sat beside her in their rooms doing his own work and included her in the sitting room conversation with his sister and her mate or Tedah and Lianna when they visited, without ever implying she should put her colorstick down.

After two days Kyndan had a new table brought and set in the middle of their room for her use. She had so many colorsticks, so many sketches, on the dining table that they could no longer eat breakfast there and her nails too were now stained with pigment.

She smiled up at him from her place at the new table as he came in. Alari glanced at the balcony, surprised to see it was growing dark.

He dropped a kiss to her head. "You smile while you draw."

She blinked. "I do?"

He brushed a tendril of her hair away from her face. She wore her hair loose down her back as she'd not done since childhood; her dress was the same spring green shade as the colorstick in her hand.

"You even smile sometimes in your sleep."

Through the open balcony doors she could see the lanterns were lit. She put her colorstick down, wiping at her hands with a dampened cloth.

"It is the last night of the festival," she said. "Do you want to go to the final celebration by the falls?"

"If you like," Kyndan said, sitting beside her. "I've gotten some news from the Fleet. Good news actually. They've decided to upgrade the *Sertarian*. That's the ship I was taking command of," he explained at her questioning look. "Anyway, they've offered me the *Crystal Fall*."

"And that is a better vessel?"

"A *much* better ship," Kyndan said. "And I won't take command for another six months. I'll be on desk duty till then and I can pick the base." He took her hand. "That means we'll have six months together, Alari, before I have to do another rotation. And letting me select the base means we have some choices."

"Choices?"

He cleared his throat. "We could live on Rusco, of course, if you like. My father's there. Or we could choose another world. They're a bit stuffy on Zartan but Nima's a lot more open-minded. Admittedly not quite *Az-kye* open-minded but still, you might really like it there. And there's the Dethara Academy in Laku-Nima. It's one of the best art schools in the Realm. I checked and the new term starts in three months. They're pretty selective but my father's Niman and he knows a lot of important people there. Of course, once you got in you'd be on your own to succeed but with your talent. . . "

"I could—" She wet her lips, her heart hammering. "I could apprentice as an artist?"

"Why not? You're great at it. And Nima's a really beautiful world." He looked at her hand in his. "I just—I was thinking that we might buy a home there."

She blinked. "Purchase a dwelling?"

"Yeah, I'm sure we could find something you like."

"*I* could choose our home?"

He gave a short laugh. "Alari, you were raised to rule an empire. I don't think you'll have any problem picking a *house*."

"I was raised to rule," she said softly. "But where I would live, *how* I would live, even where my bones would someday rest, was decided the moment I was born. I have never had the life I would choose for myself, Kyndan."

"You can now." His blue eyes were rueful, his faint smile self-mocking. "Do you want to stay on Az-kye? Maybe return to the palace?"

Her brow creased. "You break your word to me, my mate?"

He shook his head a little. "Break my word?"

"You made a solemn vow. Or do you deny me the best street food in the quadrant?"

"The best—? You mean winter carnival on Xeltan? Alari, I'm not sure I would call it a solemn—Hold on," he said suddenly. "That was a joke, wasn't it?"

"Clearly Tellarans do not take the culinary arts as seriously as they should."

"Yeah." His smile was cautious, hopeful. "Maybe you could help me with that."

"Well, not from here I cannot." She looked at him as imperiously as only an Az-kye princess could. "I will have to return with you to Tellaran space."

He nodded gravely. "Probably the only way I'll ever learn."

Alari laughed. "I will have to learn to speak Tellaran. I will have to learn Tellaran ways."

"Well, neuro-linguistics will help with the language part." He thought for a moment. "Let me talk to Nisara. The only other one better versed in Az-kye–Tellaran cultural differences is my sister and I know she'll help." He searched her face. "You want to, though? Come back with me to Tellaran space to live?"

"Yes, my mate. The city made of ice, and friends and *dancing* and painting and a home we choose. And I will be Alari Maere." She wrapped her fingers around his, her heart lighter and more joyous than she had ever known. "I am ready now, Kyndan. If you are."

"Ready?" he asked, his eyes puzzled.

"To be bound to you."

He went still but she couldn't miss how his breath quickened. "Are you sure?"

"Yes." She smiled. "Are you?"

"Yeah! Gods, from what I've heard—" A flush warmed his cheeks. "Yes." He cleared his throat with endearing hopefulness. "So . . . now?"

18

ᏇᎪ ᎷᎪ
Bound

Kyndan closed and locked the door to their suite behind him, his face still burning.

Alari came forward to meet him. "Kyndan?"

In response he held up the small bottle of amber liquid in its tiny, delicate bottle and a goblet crafted of the same fine crystal.

"By the way, my estimation of my brother-in-law just went way the hell up," Kyndan said. "He got these for me without so much as a snicker *and* he's just taken my sister and nephew away for a surprise two-day outing to the southern continent. He said he'd 'take care of everything.' I'm hoping that means he's just transmitted the 'comm silence' code for us to the rest of the clanhouse. "

"They will not disturb us," she promised softly. "To do so would be sacrilege."

"Yeah, well, from what I've heard this is not something I want to stop in the middle of."

Alari covered the hand that held the bottle with her own. "We will not be able to stop."

"Oh." His breathing sped up and a current of heat jumped down his body to his groin at her words and her nearness. The tingle that ran through his buttocks at her light touch on his hand already had him standing.

"You are blushing," Alari said, smiling up at him.

"I'm more nervous now than I was my very first time," he said with an embarrassed laugh.

Gently she took the bottle from him and he followed her to the sitting area of their suite. She opened the flask and he held the goblet with slightly trembling hands as she poured.

"Okay," he said as she closed the bottle and put it down. "Okay. Now what?"

"Now you will drink some and I will drink and we will do so until it is all gone. Then we will kiss."

"You're nervous too," he said, looking into her beautiful eyes. "Aren't you?"

She smiled. "Nervous, excited, but certain." She gave a nod at the goblet he held. "Do you want me to go first?"

He took a swallow. It was strong, sweet, and instantly warming his mouth and throat as he drank.

He licked his lips. "Actually it tastes pretty good."

She laughed, taking the cup from him. "The nectar of Ren'thar and Lashima? Yes, it would."

He watched as she drank too, her dark eyes smiling at him over the rim before handing it back.

In the end he was the one who got the final drops. She took the cup from him and put it beside the flask then straightened, waiting.

He took her hands in his for a moment then drew her close and kissed her gently, her unique sweetness and warmth melding with the taste of nectar as he deepened the kiss.

He rested his forehead against hers. "Before any of this starts I want you to know, Alari," he murmured, "I love you."

She caught her breath and the sheen of happy tears in her dark eyes. "I love you too, Kyndan."

He kissed her again and she drew him toward the bed. Her hands were already undoing the fastenings of his tunic and pushing it off his shoulders.

He was nervous, and excited, and aroused but . . .

"Uh, Alari?" He cleared his throat. "I don't feel any different."

"Now who is impatient?" she teased. "Hurry, though, I do not think you wish to have your boots on for this."

He blinked and as he removed his boots she toed off her slippers.

"Hey," he protested as she started on her dress. "I wanted to do that."

Though why I'm complaining . . .

She'd already stepped out of the gown. Her underthings quickly followed, and his mouth went dry at the sight of her smooth, light golden skin, slender waist, and full pink-tipped breasts.

She glanced down. "Trousers," she prompted.

He had them off and his undershorts in an instant, already at full stand. A rush of heat hit him and a thin layer of sweat broke out all over his body followed by a tightening heavy throb through his already taut staff.

"Uh, wait, I think—*Gods*!" he got out as her cool fingers closed around his shaft. Every nerve in his body flashed with a fiery burst of pleasure just from that one feathery touch. She stroked him twice more and suddenly Kyndan was shuddering with the strongest climax of his life.

Gasping, his legs shaking, he had to grab the bedpost to stay upright. It took a moment for his head to clear even the tiniest bit.

"Sorry," he panted, utterly dismayed to have had it over so quickly. "I'm sorry—"

She silenced his mortified protests with a kiss and just the brush of her breasts against made his chest made him rock hard again.

The heat rose up to scorch him this time. Groaning and clumsy with need he pushed her back onto the bed to find her slick and blissfully open and buried himself inside her in one stroke. He arched over her thrusting fast and deep, spurred on by her cries as she quickly found her pleasure.

He couldn't help crying out, this climax was even more intense than the last.

Alari was already moving against him, roused again, and her slick wetness brought him searingly back to standing.

"Love—you," he managed with his last truly conscious thought then she drew him into a universe of unending arousal and pleasure and nothing mattered but her . . .

Kyndan stirred and feeling Alari nestled beside him, smiled before he even opened his eyes. Her glossy dark hair was spread across the pillow, its softness over his shoulder, her full pink mouth parted in sleep.

In the faint light of the Az-kye morning sun, she was the most beautiful thing he'd ever seen.

He brushed a tendril away from the soft curve of her cheek, content just to look at her. Their binding had ended sometime last night, leaving him more blissfully exhausted then he'd ever been. He couldn't say when he'd fallen asleep. What they'd shared came back to him in flashes, and his groin tightened just to think of it.

But it was more than sex. He grinned. Hell, it was more than amazing, not-to-be-believed mind-*blowing* sex.

She was so much a part of him now he could almost feel her heart beating, feel the peacefulness of her mind as she slept. He'd felt protective of her before but it was nothing compared to now. He understood—he *respected*—the willingness of warriors to fight to the last breath for their mates, why they would never retreat or surrender.

He wouldn't either.

An understanding of that bond completely reframed the whole Az-kye societal structure for him. Where before it was a ridiculous bunch of barbaric sword swingers and baffling archaic rituals now showed itself the socially functional expression of the bonding between mates. Just imagining a threat against Alari brought raging protectiveness. He understood now why the Az-kye sought to channel and contain it to the limits of the Circle. The elaborate rituals intended to prevent offense so those challenges wouldn't occur in the first place suddenly weren't archaic or stupid.

Somehow through fate or Lashima's blessing or plain dumb luck he'd stumbled into the life of this astonishing, precious creature. This gifted, beautiful princess who radiated joy just to hold his hand and look at a painting.

And she was *his*. His to care for, to protect, and he was so grateful that tears stung his eyes.

Her inky lashes fluttered like the wings of gossamerflies and then Alari looked at him with her dark, velvety eyes.

And she smiled back.

19

The Course Plotted

Breathing in the sweet fragrance of the blooming tashi tree she sat beneath in the Az'anti garden, Alari accepted the teacup from Kinara's maid. "I have requested an audience with her Imperial Majesty tomorrow to ask her blessing to leave Az-kye space."

"What will you do if she says no?" Kinara asked with a quick glance at Kyndan where he sat at Alari's side.

"I hope she will not," Alari said honestly. "But I will go no matter what her answer."

"Wow." Kinara waved the jaha fan to cool herself. "Then I hope she gives her blessing."

"I hope she takes it well," Kyndan said. "With the *Dauntless* due to break orbit in less than two days it doesn't leave a lot of time for her to come to terms with Alari leaving."

"If she does not consent then it is not likely I will be permitted to speak to Saria before I go. She will return to the Imperial homeworld tomorrow. I was hoping," Alari continued tentatively, "that I might entrust a letter to the Az'anti for her."

What she asked placed them at great risk of the empress' displeasure. Though tradition counted Kinara an Az-kye, it was common knowledge that Kyndan was her brother. Alari's mating to him, and their choosing to reside here instead of the palace, already put the Az'anti clan in an awkward position.

"Of course," Kinara said even as Aidar inclined his head.

Her throat tightened at how neither even hesitated. "Thank you."

"So, Nima, huh?" Kinara asked, smiling. "You know, Apovia is renowned for its artists. You should think about going to school there."

"You ruined my surprise," Kyndan grumbled good-naturedly then looked at Alari. "I have accommodations reserved for us in Galt-Apovia and made an appointment for you to tour the Sulun Institute. I thought you might want to consider that school too."

"Oh," Alari murmured then smiled widely at him. "Oh, that would be wonderful!"

"Don't decide till you've seen Nima," Kinara warned, holding up a palm.

"Have you been there, my mate?" Aidar asked.

"Father took us a couple times," Kinara said. "It's a paradise—white sand, waterfalls, rainforests." She nodded at Alari's yellow gown. "What's very casual on Az-kye is formal wear on Nima. For day, most Niman women wear less than what you'd consider a skimpy nightgown and a pair of sandals that they kick off half the time."

"They go barefooted?" Alari asked. Only the very poorest of the Az-kye and the slaves did that. "They *wish* to?"

"You've never done that?" Kyndan asked. "Kicked off your shoes and run barefoot through the grass?"

Alari raised her eyebrows. "Have you?"

Kyndan gave her a sly smile and knelt at her feet. She gave a startled yelp of amusement when he caught her by the ankle and pulled the slipper from her foot.

He put her foot down on the soft grass and had the next one off in an instant. He stood, handing her cup over to the wide-eyed maid, Sella, and caught Alari's hands to pull her to her feet.

"Come on," he urged with a grin and gently tugged, pulling her along to walk on the lawn.

"I did not think it to be so soft," Alari said surprised, delighting in the feel of the grass between her toes, the sunlight on her feet. "And warm."

Suddenly he caught her hand, his other hand at her waist, and spun her around, then stepped and swayed, leading her in the Tellaran style of dancing.

Laughing, caught by Kyndan's smile and sky eyes, the grass beneath her feet and the sun on her face as they danced, Alari did not notice anything wrong at all until the Lady of the Az'anti stood.

Kyndan stopped short. Alari followed his tense gaze and her mouth parted. The Imperial messenger crossed the garden, his eyes on her.

Kyndan let her go as the man stopped before her, his black armor and helmet gleamed darkly in the sunlight.

"Imperial Daughter Alari!"

Alari's stomach clenched. Her mother's majordomo, Jelara, should have sent a note to instruct her when to present herself tomorrow, not an Imperial messenger.

"I am Imperial Daughter Alari."

"The empress commands your presence."

"I do accept this summons and will come with all honor," Alari replied, the ritual words sounding strangled. "When am I to attend upon Her Imperial Majesty?"

"A litter awaits you," the messenger said.

Alari blinked. "You mean *now*?"

"Yes, Your Highness."

Alari's hand went to the skirt of her pale yellow gown. "I will change—"

"Our empress commands your presence immediately, Your Highness," the messenger said sharply.

Alari quickly put her feet into her slippers and, behind her, she heard Kyndan address Kinara.

"Get ahold of Nisara," he whispered tightly. "Tell her to get back to the *Dauntless* and be ready to contact the Tellaran Council."

His government was light years away, it was madness to set his one ship against the might of the Empire's forces, her mother might even command he not live long enough to leave the planet's surface—

"Her Imperial Majesty has not summoned you, Kyndan," Alari said quickly, meeting his gaze. "Perhaps it is best you remain here and await my return."

Kyndan's jaw hardened. "Oh, no fucking way. I'm coming with you, Alari."

Alari looked at the messenger. "My mate . . .?"

The messenger sent a spare glance his way and gave a nod. "We must leave, Your Highness."

Kyndan climbed into the litter beside her. One of his hands held hers and the other came to rest on the blaster he wore at his hip.

20

Royal Summons

Her unbound hair and yellow gown garnered
scandalized stares from the black clad courtiers and servants
as she and Kyndan hurried through the palace halls. Two
servants of the empress had met them upon their arrival on
the palace grounds, their pace quick and tense.

Instead of being taken to the throne room, the servants
led them to the floor above, to another of her mother's
official but less formal reception rooms. One of the servants
opened the door for her, the other preceded them inside.

"The Princess Alari," the servant announced. "Imperial
mate, Commander Kyndan Maere."

Inside were a few of the more powerful clan leaders.
Alari saw Pellena of the Trade Council and Mezera, Leader
of the Council for War and other Council leaders as well.

She recognized High Priestess Celara and Sechon the
Elder, standing beside the throne but for an instant she did
not know the figure slumped in it.

Alari's mouth parted. "Imperial Majesty?"

The empress raised her head and Alari drew her breath
sharply at her wan face, her drawn mouth.

She took a step toward the throne. "Mother?"

Mezera, the War Council leader, regarded her gravely.
"The elder and I have been keeping the empress' illness
secret for some time. But her health has worsened so that
we can no longer conceal it, First Daughter."

Alari froze. "First—?" Her heart sped up. "What of Saria?"

Her glance swept the room going from her mother to the Imperial advisors, the healers and clan leaders, blinking at their taut mouths and pallid complexions.

In Kyndan's face she saw shock collapse into grim understanding.

"What of Saria?" she asked again. "Where is my sister?" Alari's gaze darted from one stiff face to another and her voice rose. "*Where is my sister?*"

"The princess' vessel never arrived at Az-litha," the War Leader said. "Ships were sent in search of the *Ty'har* but when they arrived Princess Saria's ship was . . ." Mezera dropped her eyes, her voice tight. "There were no survivors."

"No." Alari shook her head again. "No. You are wrong. You are *lying!*"

"Alari." Kyndan caught her hand gently, his hand cupping her face to look into her eyes and in his face she saw the truth. He gathered her against him and her arms went around his waist, too stunned for tears.

"What happened?" Kyndan asked.

"We received a distress signal from the *Ty'har* stating their location at the edge of Ren'thar's sword. Assistance was sent—"

"How the hell did they wind up that close to the Badlands?" Kyndan interrupted the War Leader sharply. "That's light years from Az-litha."

"It appears that the *Ty'har* suffered a navigation malfunction," Mezera continued. "Before assistance could reach them the ship was hit by an ionic front. When the rescue ship arrived—"

"A *malfunction*? On the princess' flagship?" Kyndan echoed, disbelieving. "You don't think it might have been sabotage? That someone did this on purpose?"

"We do not know what happened to the *Ty'har*, the investigation into its destruction is just beginning." Mezera's shoulders sagged. "As is our grieving. The loss of Princess Saria is a terrible blow—for all of us."

The empress met her gaze, her face drawn with pain and grief. "As Mezera says, I am ill. The healers have not been able to help me and," her mouth trembled, "now with Saria . . ."

She reached out to Alari. Kyndan's embrace tightened comfortingly for an instant then he let her go. Alari hurried to close the space between them, to take her mother's hand in her own, shocked at how weak her mother had become.

"Alari." The empress' eyes were sunken and shadowed but they were steady. "I name you Regent."

"Regent?" Alari shook her head quickly. "No! I am not ready to—"

"We are none of us ready, Daughter. But you are prepared. Your whole life has been in preparation of this moment."

Sechon stepped forward imploringly. "First Daughter—Imperial Regent—the Empire, your *people* need you. Your mother is . . ." The elder trailed off, her eyes pained. "There is no other choice. The Az-kye must have a ruler. You *must* take the throne."

Frantically she sought Kyndan's gaze only to find his face closed and set.

She swallowed hard. There would be no parties or friends or dancing at the Rusco ball now. She would never see the Tellaran worlds, apprentice as an artist, choose their home . . .

Alari closed her eyes for a moment against the bitter shattering of her dreams then forced a nod.

Sechon let her breath out in relief and bowed low. "A blessed and long rule, Imperial Regent."

"Imperial Regent," echoed the advisors, the healers, the Council leaders as they bowed.

Kyndan held her gaze for a moment, his blue eyes stormy.

"Imperial Regent," Kyndan said hoarsely.

Her vision blurred with tears as he, too, bowed to her.

21

The palace was draped in white as the Empire began its month-long period of mourning for First Imperial Daughter Saria.

The next day Alari, dressed in pure snowy white, oversaw the rites for Saria at the temple of Meithea, making offerings to the goddess of the Underworld to guide her sister kindly. Kyndan stood at her side, proud and handsome in his blue and white Tellaran uniform, and she did not think that she could have remained upright without his strength beside her. No one spoke to her directly of it but Alari knew the courtiers whispered over his attire although, like the black-clad warriors, Kyndan too wore an armband of white in honor of Saria.

The empress had become so infirm her white-draped litter had to be carried into the temple and Azara reclined throughout the rites. It was doubtful her mother would ever recover enough to resume her place as ruler and the court, possibly the whole Empire, knew it.

The three days since Alari had become regent had been filled with meetings with her advisors, petitions to hear, decisions to make. Her grief would not excuse her. Kyndan accompanied her everywhere, a source of strength at her side at all times.

He rose with her before dawn and despite the scandalized glances of her maids remained as they dressed her. As regent her mourning court dress sometimes required fourteen layers of white silk, the last being heavily beaded. Her face, including her mouth, neck, and hands too were brushed with white makeup and a single finger-wide red line of face paint split her lower lip. They outlined her eyes in black and the area below her eyes from lower lid to mid cheekbone were rouged. Her dark hair was twisted up, ready for the crown.

"Leave us," Alari said before her maid, Tilanna, could place the cornet of regent on her head.

Her reflection was ghostly, frightening in its severity, and she remembered all too well when her mother appeared thus after the death of her father.

Now it is I who am the image of mourning.

"Why do they do that?" Kyndan asked quietly, meeting her eyes in the mirror's reflection. "Make you up like that?"

"The white is to show how the shock has altered me. The rouge to show my eyes reddened with weeping."

"And the red line on your lip?" he asked, glancing at her mouth.

"That by my own bite I will draw the blood of any who would harm me and mine. I must look fearsome, intimidating, vicious with grief as I take the throne." Hesitantly she sought his gaze. "Do you find me ugly?"

He gave a rueful smile. "I find you astonishing. I'm embarrassed to admit how much I'd like to pull those nine thousand layers right back off you and see you spread wide for me."

In all of this he was her comfort and her strength and she craved his touch, the feel of him hot and hard inside her. "I too wish for it." She glanced at her reflection dispiritedly. "But like this you cannot even kiss me."

"Well, I can't just wreck an hour of their hard work."

Her breath caught as he clasped her around the waist and lifted her effortlessly onto the bed. He gave her a hot smile as he flung her skirts up and slid her underwear down. He gently urged her legs open further and his eyes softened as they rested on her center.

"But you know," he murmured and leaned down to bring his mouth against the inside of her thigh. Her eyes fell shut as she arched toward him, already aching. His tongue trailed toward her center and his voice grew hoarse. "I have an idea that won't mess up your makeup . . ."

Alari sat upon the Az-kye throne, empress in all but name, clasping her fan in her lap as the petitioners squabbled.

"The Council for Trade has caused chaos in the markets," Telyn, Leader of the Council for Food, said heatedly. "Merchants everywhere are crying out to Your Majesty for justice! The Council for Trade's grab for power should alarm you as much it does us!"

Benne, the Trade Council Leader, countered, "Your alarm only stems from seeing your greed thwarted."

"*You* speak to me of greed?" Telyn cried. "When your Council has grabbed power for itself at the behest of a grasping, opportunistic Tel—"

At Alari's side, Kyndan tensed. Telyn broke off, clearly realizing she was delivering a challenge-worthy insult to one born the Imperial Consort's sister.

"*Newcomer,*" she finished then addressed Alari again. "We ask that the dispensation to the Council for Food be increased again."

"Imperial Regent," Benne countered, "prices offered by Trade and Food are comparable."

"But the profits are not! You levy fees for the landing and departure of all cargo shuttles but you do not impose those same fees on vessels owned by your own members— or on vessels owned by those whom you favor!" Telyn's face flushed red with anger. "In the few short months since Kinara of the Az'anti seized power for the Trade Council, their members have lined their pockets and built a network of lackeys throughout Az-kye space! There are those that say that Your Majesty no longer cares for traditional Az-kye ways." Telyn threw a narrow glance at Kyndan, standing beside her, clad still in his Tellaran uniform. "You may find your rule the weaker for it."

Kyndan took a half step forward. "Is that supposed to be a threat?"

Telyn met his glare. "A terrifying prediction of what will come if the Imperial Regent does not exercise her power wisely—and soon." Telyn looked at Alari. "This is your opportunity to reaffirm your adherence to the old ways, to restore the balance between the Councils!"

Sechon held up her hand. "If I may, Imperial Regent?"

"You are hardly objective in this matter, Elder!" Telyn scoffed.

"It is well known that though I relinquished the mantle of clan leader when I joined the Council of Elders, my daughter Helia also sits on the Council for Trade," Sechon said mildly. "But my vow was to administer to the Empire and to offer guidance that would reflect the highest good of all Her Imperial Majesty's subjects, despite former clan loyalties. The . . ." The elder glanced at Kyndan, "*achievements* of Kinara of the Az'anti are well known. While I applaud such resourcefulness, I regard a few of the

Council's policies as reflective of an unbecoming self-interest in those sworn to serve the Az-kye."

Benne stepped toward Sechon. "How can you possibly—"

Alari flicked her fan and that one small gesture was enough to silence them all.

"The request for further dispensation is denied," she said, forcing strength into her voice. "But all cargo vessels will pay equal fees, no matter their owner or the friendship they have garnered. Any vessel not paying export and import fees will be seized."

Telyn's face lit with triumph, Benne's dark eyes flashed with displeasure, and then they bowed.

"Mezera, Leader for the Council for War—" the majordomo, Jelara, began.

"I will retire now." Alari stood, signaling an end to the audience. She descended the dais, Kyndan a step behind her. The Council leaders, clan *Ti'antahs,* and courtiers bowed to her as she swept past them.

Her attendants hurriedly took up their places around them as she turned in the direction of the regent's apartments.

Upon entering her dressing room Alari handed her fan over and stood still, her shoulders heavy with exhaustion as the maids worked around her to remove her white mourning ensemble, to take the jewels and pins from her hair.

Kyndan folded his arms. "Why did you decide against Trade?"

"I did not," Alari said tiredly. "I did not grant Food the dispensation they requested."

"Did you decide against Kinara because she's my sister?"

Alari shut her eyes briefly in relief as she was freed from the heavy, beaded court ensemble, putting her arms out so that one maid, Tilanna, could settle the lighter white dressing gown around her shoulders, another attendant knotting the sash at her waist.

"I did not decide against Kinara, my mate. The Trade Council has used their power unfairly to enrich themselves for months."

"It looks like you'd rather make it harder for the poor to get a decent meal than look like you're favoring a Tellaran."

"Kinara is not Tellaran," Alari said as the maids finished wiping the ghostly makeup from her face and hands.

"But I *am*. Would you have made the same decision if I weren't here?"

"Were you not here, I would have been mated to Jazan and it would have been me on the *Ty'har*," she said brittlely. "It would have been *me* that died, not—not—"

A sob cut off her words and quickly she covered her mouth with her hands.

"Alari . . ." Kyndan caught her in his arms, cradling her against him.

"Give us a minute," he said to the maids. They hesitated and his nostrils flared. "That means, get *out*!"

The door shut behind them and Alari shook her head against his chest.

"I cannot believe she is gone," she sobbed. "I cannot!"

"I know." He cradled her head. "I know."

He held her a long time, rocking her as she cried before he led her to one of the couches in the room. He went into the bathing chamber and came back with a folded damp cloth, wiping her face with it. Then he held the cool cloth over her eyes.

Alari leaned her swollen eyes into the soothing dampness.

"This is nice," Alari hiccupped.

Kyndan held the cloth against her forehead. "My mom used to do this when I was a kid."

"She was kind, then, like our sister." Alari could not even imagine her mother doing such.

"She was," he agreed, with a faint smile. "It's funny, there were a couple times when we were at the clanhouse and I'd look at Kinna and think, gods, she looks so much like our mother."

"How old were you when—?"

"Eleven, almost twelve. But Kinna had only just turned eight." He brushed her damp hair back from her forehead. "It's stupid but when I was a kid I used to pretend she was just in the next room, that it was okay, she was only out of sight and quiet 'cause she was reading or something. That I could just walk into that room and tell her about my day or ask her something if I wanted to."

"I do not think that stupid," Alari said thickly. "On every turn of the palace halls I think I will see Saria. That I will come around a corner and see the honor guard of the Second, then she will smile and disdain protocol to hurry over to me. That she will take my hand, and smile and whisper in my ear what the courtiers are gossiping about today."

"I'm sorry I didn't get a chance to know her."

Alari's vision blurred with tears again. "I am grateful to have had such as she for a sister, but I wished many times that she had been the elder and I the younger. She longed to be empress and I . . . ." Her tears overflowed, guilt and shame tightening her throat that not all her grief was for Saria. "I very much wanted the life that we planned."

"Yeah, me too," he said quietly. "But I sure can't complain about the quarters." Kyndan sent a dry glance back at the apartments they were now occupied as regent and consort. "They're a hell of a lot nicer than anything I could offer you."

"Oh, Kyndan, I am—"

He caught her chin to look into her eyes. "Don't you dare say you're sorry."

Tears stung Alari's eyes. "I wish—if my sister—"

"I know." He drew her against him. "I do too."

22

View from the Top of the Falls

"Regent," Mezera, Leader of the War Council began the next morning, her voice chilly as the audience chamber around them, "I have come to discuss matters of Imperial defense, matters that *must* remain concealed from our enemies."

"I take it by 'enemies,' you mean me," Kyndan said sharply.

Mezera threw a narrow look at him. "Truly, Majesty, think you it wise to discuss our defenses in the presence of a *Tellaran?*"

"This is my mate of whom you speak," Alari reminded quietly.

Mezera's mouth tightened. "I mean no disrespect to you, Regent."

But the Tellaran can go fuck himself.

Kyndan's gaze narrowed and he fought the urge to throw Mezera out. The hostility of the courtiers and clan leaders toward him was escalating with every passing day and making Alari's task all the harder. Between the strain of taking on the monumental task of regent and fending off the razor sharp teeth of these sercats harping about *him* instead of doing their godsdamned *jobs*, she was getting exhausted.

"We're not at war," Kyndan bit out. "And in case you've forgotten, *honored* Council leader, my whole purpose in coming to Az-kye was to open peace talks."

"Those talks are inconsequential now," she retorted.

Kyndan folded his arms. "Who are *you* to make that decision?"

"I am Leader of the War Council," Mezera returned coldly. "And in the absence of an Imperial Warlord to command our forces, such decisions fall to me."

"Well, then maybe what we need is an Imperial Warlord!" Kyndan snapped.

There was a moment of awkward silence. Alari's glance flicked away and Kyndan nearly groaned as it snapped into place.

Oh, festering hell, it's supposed to be me!

That's why only the best warriors are considered to become consort. That's why Jazan was the top pick, why he wanted to marry Alari when he didn't love her. He would have been Imperial Warlord with power and influence to rival hers.

His face heated as he realized that not only had he blundered but that in doing it in front of the Council leader and Imperial advisors he'd embarrassed Alari as well.

"But since we do not *have* an Imperial Warlord," Mezera continued acidly. "It is my place to see to the defenses of our empire. The stabilization and protection of our territory takes precedence over any accords the *Tellarans* want."

"Accords *we* want?" Kyndan began furiously. "Because the Az-kye don't—"

"This audience is concluded," Alari broke in sharply. "Leave us. All of you."

Tight mouthed, the War Leader and her assistants quickly gathered their things and bowed. The majordomo and courtiers bowed too and left, shutting the door of the audience chamber behind them.

"I let her get to me," Kyndan said, annoyed. "I shouldn't have let her get to me like that."

"The War Leader was ever sharp spoken. And she is cunning."

"And she sure as hell doesn't want her ass out of that leader's chair." He met her gaze. "The Imperial Consort is supposed to command the Az-kye military forces."

"Yes."

Kyndan wiped his hand over his face. "I didn't know."

"There has not been an Imperial Warlord since my father died. I have no brother, Her Imperial Majesty did not wish to take another mate, and so the War Council was convened. They were to serve until . . ."

"Until you took a mate," he finished. "But you married me instead of Jazan and the Az-kye forces are not about to obey a Tellaran."

"Yes." Alari sighed. "And, my mate, you speak truly— Mezera wishes to keep her *ass* where it is."

Kyndan gave a choked chuckle and Alari joined him, their laughter filling the audience chamber.

After their laughter faded, Kyndan asked: "Are the peace accords really being put on hold?"

She sighed again. "As Mezera said, my rule has just begun. To make such a treaty now . . ."

"You can't look weak to the Tellarans."

She gave a short, humorless laugh. "I cannot look weak to the Az-kye! Empress Yi'saya, last ruler of the Xar dynasty was pulled from the very chair now in the Imperial throne room and thrown from the falls to the rocks below. After ten years of war and putting her three half-sisters to death, Empress Ilyn clawed her way to the throne and founded the Second Empire."

"I didn't know that," he said hoarsely. The Az-kye worshipped their ruler so fanatically it never occurred to him that they might ever have risen up against one. That there had been women who held this throne, possibly as young as Alari, who worked as hard as she did, who hadn't survived an uprising or their own family's infighting.

Gods, that's what Aidar meant when he said the empress had to first keep the throne. That's why her consort becomes warlord; the empress' military forces have to be controlled by someone she can trust completely.

Alari shook her head. "My mother is ill, my sister is dead. It is whispered that the gods have withdrawn their favor from me. Even now I know some claim my rule cursed, the Empire doomed if I remain on the throne."

Her dark eyes were haunted and Kyndan realized it was these fears most of all that kept her from her rest when she tossed and turned beside him.

He swallowed hard. He'd hardly helped matters. She had a consort who was not just Tellaran but wearing one of their uniforms. She had to rely on others because the one who was supposed to be her sword and shield wasn't even Az-kye.

"I must always show strength," Alari said. "I dare not give them further cause to doubt me. My mother has ruled long and well but what she could do I cannot yet. I cannot risk pushing the treaty now. The War Council must remain convened and their leader's counsel followed. There is no other choice."

Kyndan traced the curve of her cheek.

Yeah, there is.

23

Alari ordered her attendants to remain outside and entered the empress' residence alone to find the High Priestess of Lashima resting in the outer sitting room. High Priestess Celara offered her a kind smile, her hands interlaced over her jeweled cane.

"How does she?" Alari asked, glancing up the grand marble staircase to where the empress lay above. Even this sitting room was thick with the smell of incense; red powder had been scattered in the corners of the room by the priests of Meithea to misdirect spirits drawn by the empress' illness as a gateway to the living.

The High Priestess gave a half-shrug. "A bit better today, I think. We had tea together, she ate a little. We talked of the coming summer."

That the empress might not live long enough to feel the summer sun on her face made Alari's throat tighten.

"The High Priest of Behur is with her now. They make offerings daily to the god of Healing. As I do for the empress' sake." Celara's dark eyes shone. "As I do for you."

"What of my mate?" Alari asked suddenly. "Do you also make offerings for him?"

The High Priestess looked amused. "I do not think I offend the gods of the Tellarans do I ask Lashima to bless his seed, do you?"

"No," Alari murmured. "I suppose not." Kyndan himself might find it embarrassing that this devout, aged lady placed white flowers at the feet of the Queen of the Heavens, entreating the goddess to make him potent enough to get his mate with child quickly.

One of her mother's maids came then to bring her to the empress' presence. The priest of Behur was just finishing his incantation, the room thick with incense and chanting from the blue-cloaked priests.

Alari studied her mother, reclining here in the dim room, the curtains drawn as the empress' complained of sensitivity to light. If there were any improvement in the Empress' health, it was slight and Alari schooled her features so that her concern would not show.

She did not bow now that she was regent as she came beside her mother's sickbed but she inclined her head respectfully. The empress waved her servants out and the door shut behind them, leaving them in privacy.

"I have heard talk," the empress rasped without preamble. Her face was wan but her eyes were sharp as ever.

"There is always talk," Alari returned. "Always whispers and rumors circling the court. You taught me that to give them too much attention is to help them take seed and grow."

"They have never had such fertile soil as a Tellaran acting as Imperial Consort!"

"He is not acting as Imperial Consort. He *is* Imperial Consort."

"He walks the palace in the garb of a Tellaran warrior. He is not Az-kye. He has not taken his place within our clan."

"It was for you to welcome him to our clan and you did not," Alari reminded sharply.

Azara shifted on her pillows, her mouth tight. "Neither of you were to be found in the palace for me to do such."

"We are in the palace now," Alari pointed out. "Shall I have him brought here so that you can offer him your welcome? Give him your name as his own?"

"Had you taken Jazan as you should have—"

"But I did not," Alari flared. "I took Kyndan as mate."

Azara's eyes flashed. "You never spoke so to your empress before."

"I was never my empress' equal before," Alari said, clasping her hands to conceal their shaking. "I am regent now."

The empress seemed to sink into herself, as if that burst of anger had cost her much. "Perhaps you are angry. Hurt still by the punishment I named for you."

"You mean when you would have made me slave and thrown me out into the street?" Alari asked with raised eyebrows. "Truly, I never think on it, Imperial Majesty."

"I was too harsh, too rash in my pronouncement." The empress' eyes fell shut. "My illness and pain clouded my judgment. Let my mistake be your lesson, Alari."

Alari shifted her weight, wondering how sincere her mother was. Surely she had been suffering then. She suffered so greatly now Alari could hear the wheeze of her breath.

"I shall, Mother," she said quietly.

Azara opened her eyes, a glimmer of warmth in her gaze. "What has been done can be undone. Speak to High Priestess Celara. With the fate of the Az-kye at stake, she will agree. You can be unbound, able to seek a proper warrior, a proper consort, without delay."

"Never," Alari said hoarsely. "Kyndan is mine, and I his."

The empress' face fell. "You love him."

Tears burned her eyes, recalling how Kyndan risked his life to save her from Jazan's cruelty, his warm blue eyes, his tender lovemaking, his smiles. "Yes, I love him. I could love no other more."

"You are regent; you cannot put this man above the needs of the Az-kye," Azara said sharply. "This love is a weakness you cannot afford!"

"Did you love my father?" Alari asked, stung.

Suddenly the empress' eyes softened and her lower lip curved. Alari remembered then Sechon's story of how her mother had once donned colors against tradition to draw a certain warrior's eye . . .

"Beyond word or reason," she murmured; then her cheeks were drawn again. "And when he was lost to me, my heart shattered. I would not have you know such pain and even less so for one unworthy of you." The empress suddenly gripped her hand. "I do not trust this man. Your heart is his, but his heart is Tellaran."

Alari remembered Kyndan's spinning her in his embrace in the sunlight, the pride in his blue eyes when she showed him her drawings, his smile and, too, how he had argued for his sister, for the peace accords his people wanted . . .

Alari drew breath to cry out that her mother was wrong, that they were all wrong, that when the time came that Kyndan must choose he would choose *her*.

But when her lips parted to do so, she found she could not.

When Alari emerged from the Empress' quarters she was disappointed to see that although her honor guard was present, Kyndan was not. She wanted very much the reassurance of his smile, his blue eyes crinkled with humor, the warmth of his fingers wrapped around hers.

It was beneath the dignity of a regent and future empress but she could not help glancing this way and that in hopes of spying his tall form in the corridor.

"Regent?"

Alari turned at the sound of Sechon's voice. "Elder."

"Whom do you seek?" Then Sechon smiled faintly. "Or need I ask?"

"I thought that my mate would be awaiting me here," Alari admitted.

"I have not seen him yet this day, Imperial Majesty," said Sechon, falling into step beside her. The elder sent a glance in the direction from which Alari had come and lowered her voice. "May I hope she is better?"

"She is not," Alari said quietly.

Sechon's face fell then she lifted her chin. "I understand the healers have begun a new treatment," she said, her tone brighter. "They have great hopes of its effectiveness."

"So I have heard."

Sechon tilted her head. "There is more, I think, that weighs upon you, Regent."

Alari took in the attendants around them and the elder gave her an understanding look.

"Perhaps in deference to my age, Regent, we might sit a moment?" She nodded toward the door of a small, unoccupied reception room. "I would be grateful."

Alari inclined her head and directed her attendants to wait outside.

Once the door was shut Sechon joined her at the windows. The reception room overlooked one of the Imperial parks; it was late spring now and the garden was in full bloom. Grass just the color of peridot spread like a lush carpet under the golden light.

Alari pressed her hand against the crystal window.

I will never again feel the grass beneath my bare feet . . .

"I cannot but think you have many burdens upon you, Regent, but that one above all makes your heart heavy."

"I miss Saria," she murmured. "I weep for her, but I—I wish—"

"Ah." Sechon nodded. "So you had embraced being Imperial Daughter as Saria had embraced being Imperial Heiress. You feel some guilt for grieving that you will not have the life you wished when Saria has lost hers?"

Tears stung her eyes. "I know it shameful to feel so."

"No," Sechon said gently. "You do not dishonor your sister by other griefs that you know. Both are losses that must be acknowledged."

"And Kyndan . . ."

"What of him?"

"I . . . I fear he will never be happy here. Never happy among the Az-kye." Alari met the elder's kindly gaze. "My mother says—he will not be loyal." The flicker of dismay that crossed the elder's face sent jolt of fear ran through Alari's chest. "What is it?" Alari pressed her hands against her skirt to hide their tremble, the beads of her court dress rough against her palms. "What have you heard? Is it of Kyndan?"

The elder waved her hand. "It is nothing."

"Do you, like my mother, think his loyalty—his heart not mine but his people's?"

The elder drew herself up. "No," she said stoutly. "To be certain you chose your mate well. I am sure when the test comes he will not fail you."

Alari's stomach knotted. Though clearly Sechon did not wish to hurt her, she too doubted him.

As so many did . . .

Sechon laid her hand on Alari's arm. "This is a difficult time. And, if I may be frank, a dangerous one. But I have no doubt that you will find the strength to lead and protect your people, Regent. Whatever it is you need to do, you will not fail the Az-kye."

Alari turned her face toward the window, seeing the lawn of soft grass, just the verdant shade of the first colorstick he had bought her . . .

"No," Alari said thickly. "I will not fail you."

24

Old Friends

"There's my girl!"

Kyndan's warm declaration brought startled looks and a number of mouths turned downward in disapproval from the courtiers around them. He did not incline his head to her as he ought; he strode right past her honor guard and maids to kiss her forehead. It was far too familiar behavior in so public a place as the palace hallways, even for her mate, but Alari didn't care.

"Kyndan," Alari said, smiling up at him, feeling her doubts and fears wisp away under his blue gaze. "I was wondering where you were."

"I have a surprise for you," he said, taking her hand.

"What kind of surprise?"

Kyndan tugged on her hand to lead her along. "Come on."

"What is it?"

His only response was a warm smile, and her servants were disconcerted and flustered at the sudden change in direction and the utter disregard for protocol.

He opened the door to their quarters himself and Alari blinked to see his sister and her mate, Lianna and Tedah, as well as Nisara and an unfamiliar warrior waiting in the sitting room.

The women, and Tedah, threw her smiles then all bowed.

"What is this?" Alari asked.

"I thought it would nice if we had friends over for dinner."

Just looking at these people reminded her how happy she had been just a short time ago. The happiest she had ever been . . .

Alari smiled around at them. "I am pleased to look on all of you."

Nisara was closest and though no Az-kye would ever simply walk up and embrace the Imperial Regent, the Tellaran woman caught her in a hug. "I'm sorry about your sister."

Alari's throat tightened at mention of Saria, but Nisara's words were a comfort too. "Yes, her loss was great."

"How're you holding up?" Nisara asked.

Her maids' expressions were equal parts shocked and offended that a barbarian should show such familiar behavior.

Kyndan took Alari's fan from her hand and gave it to Tilanna. "I think we're okay for a while." When she and the other servants did not move, he continued sharply, "That means clear out."

When the door shut behind her unhappy attendants, Alari looked back at Nisara. "I miss her. I miss her greatly."

Nisara nodded, her hand on Alari's shoulder. "If you ever want to talk . . ."

The offer took Alari by surprise but she nodded. "I will remember." Her gaze went to the warrior at Nisara's side. "This is Dael?"

"He's never been inside the palace before," Nisara confided. "He was like a little kid on his first trip to the activity center."

The warrior flushed and inclined his head. "I am Dael of the Az'yan, Imperial Regent."

"I am pleased to know you, Dael of the Az'yan," she said smiling. "And you are very welcome to our palace."

"The honor is mine," Dael mumbled, and Alari noticed even the tips of his ears had gone red.

Kinara hugged Alari. "I'm here too," she murmured into Alari's ear, "if you need me."

"I thank you," Alari said thickly. Was this warmth common to all Tellarans? If so, they were a fortunate people indeed.

Tedah embraced her as well but Aidar and Lianna offered restrained nods and formal words to acknowledge her loss.

Kyndan pressed a kiss to her hair. "Are you hungry? Because not only are half the guests Tellaran, half the food is too." He nodded toward the dining room. "I asked Nisara to have supplies brought down from the *Dauntless* so you could try some Tellaran dishes. We have spring medallions, sular steak, fried hoss . . ."

"Fried hoss?" Alari wondered.

"It's a vegetable, breaded and fried," Kyndan said. "I really like it."

"He *loves* it," Nisara said with an eye roll. "He keeps the serving dish at his elbow and snarls at anyone who tries to get some."

"No, I don't." He looked at Alari. "I don't."

"Yeah," Kinara said, "he does."

He threw his sister an aggravated look. "Whose side are you on?"

"Nisara's," Kinara said as if it were obvious and hooked her arm with Alari's to lead her to the table. "And the rest of us are content to let you scarf the hoss—*after* you've let Alari try some."

Dael was a bit diffident but those who had known her for a time as simply Alari, with her colorful dresses, unbound hair and fingernails stained by colorsticks, were at ease with her during the meal.

They sat around the table serving themselves, laughing and talking. Kyndan, Nisara, and Tedah relayed stories of their academy days and even their time enslaved on Az-kye with a humorous tilt and an utter lack of shame.

Dinner turned to dessert, and dessert to wine and finally tea.

"They are so free with their thoughts," Lianna said to Alari as they sat together, sipping spiced tea. "So free with their hearts." Her gaze lingered on Tedah. "So open with their smiles. The first time I saw Tedah, he was in a cage in the middle of the street in daylight yet he refused to be shamed. He met my eye as if we had been introduced in full honors." Her mouth curved. "And he smiled."

"You were so brave."

"The heart longs for what it will," Lianna said with a shrug. "My mother was appalled but I knew eventually there would be a new scandal to wag tongues." She glanced at Kyndan and gave Alari a reassuring smile. "And someday soon people will move on to gossip about the next one and your heart will be left happy."

"And Tedah is now Az-kye," Alari said.

"I think Nisara will soon be counted among us too," Lianna murmured, nodding toward her and Dael speaking with Kyndan.

"I hope so. I like Nisara. And she is dear to Kyndan."

"He must be pleased you do not mind." Lianna shook her head. "I do not think I could be so contented if my mate cared so for his former paramour."

"His—?"Alari froze the teacup halfway to her mouth. "Nisara and my mate were lovers?"

Lianna's face flushed. "Tedah and Kinara spoke freely of—I thought you knew."

"No," Alari said faintly, her heart hammering as Kyndan laughed at some comment Nisara made, their heads close together. "I did not."

25

The Vow

Kyndan caught her from behind, wrapping his arms around her waist and pressing a kiss to the side of her neck. "Did you have fun tonight?"

She gave a spare nod.

"It was good to see everyone," he said. "Did you hear? Nisara's going to stay on Az-kye."

"That must please you," Alari mumbled.

"Makes me feel a little less outnumbered. Hey." Kyndan let go and threw her a smile as his servant came in. "I have something for you." His servant put the parcel down on the table. "Thank you, Utar."

The former warrior inclined his head.

"What is this?" Alari asked as Kyndan's servant left.

"Well, with everything that's been going on, we didn't do a very good job packing when we left the clanhouse so I sent Utar over today to finish up for us."

He opened the parcel and her breath caught when she saw what it contained.

"What's the matter?" he asked with a gesture at the colorsticks and papers. "Everything's here."

She took a step back. "Take it away."

"What?" Kyndan exclaimed. "*Why?*"

"Because I do not wish to see such again! Take it away!"

She turned then and fled the room.

"Alari!" Kyndan caught her in the sitting room. "What's the matter? I thought you'd be happy—?"

"Think you I wish to be reminded of what I cannot be?" she cried.

He stared. "Hold on, are you saying you aren't going to draw at all anymore?"

"I am Regent!"

"Yeah, I remember hearing something about that," he said tersely. "It doesn't mean you can't sketch anymore."

"Think you I would risk the throne for such?" she demanded, pointing toward where her colorsticks and sketches lay. "Will you have me give them *more* to gossip about? To whisper that I waste my time pursuing such foolishness?"

"Doing something you enjoy isn't foolishness," he retorted. "It's called being happy."

"We cannot all take and do as we please, Kyndan! We cannot all have everything we once took pleasure in!"

His brow furrowed. "Why am I getting the feeling we aren't talking about drawing anymore?" He searched her face. "Alari, what's the matter?"

"Nisara was your lover!" she threw at him.

"Yeah, and?"

"You did not tell me." Alari swallowed against a rush of hurt that he had not immediately offered comfort or contrition or sought to make her laugh. "Why did you not?"

"I don't know. I didn't think it mattered." He blinked. "Wait, you're not worried that I'm still interested in Nisara? We're bound, remember?"

To be bound to one would not keep you from loving another . . .

"She was your lover," Alari repeated instead. "But you did not tell me."

"That was a long time ago. Nisara and I are just friends now. Alari, it was nothing. It was over in a few weeks."

"Then why did you not tell me?"

A flush ran up his neck. "Hold on, you're perfectly okay with your sister taking a lover, or ten for that matter, and public demonstrations of—Sex here isn't just casual it's *recreational* and you're upset over something I did six—no, *seven*—years ago?"

"You still care for her!"

"Of course I do," he said impatiently. "She's a good friend. She really knows me."

Alari caught her breath. "As I do not?" she asked, her heart hammering with hurt. "Because I am Az-kye and she is Tellaran? Because she makes you feel less *outnumbered*?"

"No! That's not—Alari, I love *you*." His frown deepened. "Is this really about some brief relationship I had as a cadet?" He searched her eyes. "Alari, what's going on? There's something you aren't telling me."

"I think there is much *you* have not told *me*!"

He caught her hand. "Okay," he said quietly, holding her gaze. "Ask me. Whatever you want to know. Whatever is worrying you. Ask me and I promise you the truth."

There were so many whispers, so many trying to draw her this way or that for their own gain, casting doubt on his loyalties, casting doubt on his motives . . .

But only one thing clouded her heart now.

"Do—" She wet her lips. "Did you love her?"

"No," he said instantly. "I've never loved anyone but you, Alari."

"Did she love you?"

"I'm sure she didn't and I was fine with that," he said. "We were friends and it was a fun couple of weeks but we both knew quickly that it was never going to be anything more. She loves Dael and I'm glad she's happy."

Tears stung her eyes. Something about the utter absence of jealousy in his voice, in his face, when he spoke of Nisara's lover reassured her as nothing could have.

"All right," she said, finally feeling that she could breathe again. "All right, Kyndan."

"Tell me what else is going on."

She hesitated. "There is talk about—you. If you can be trusted. If you should be my mate at all. That it is unseemly that you are consort."

"Because I'm a Fleet officer." He nodded. "Well, can't blame them for that. I've already contacted Central Command; they've sent a new ambassador to take over. When he arrives, I'll resign my commission."

Alari blinked. "You are going to resign?"

"Tomorrow actually. It would have been sooner but I can't just walk in the middle of a mission." He gave a faint smile. "No matter how insanely wrong it's gone. I'm the Tellaran representative until my replacement arrives, but as soon as he does I'll be handing off my responsibilities to him." He raised his eyebrows. "Well, you wouldn't put much stock in my word if I broke it to someone else, would you?"

"And when you are no longer a Fleet officer?"

"I'll step up as Imperial Consort, as Imperial Warlord." He cupped her cheek in his palm. "And I'll bring my best to it, I promise."

Tears stung her eyes.

"That's what's been worrying you, hasn't it? That I wouldn't leave the Fleet for you." He took her hands in his. "Alari, I would do anything for you."

"This is not the life you would have chosen. It is not the life *I* would have chosen."

"Whatever life we build here will be good because we'll build it together. I love you, Alari. You've been so strong," he said softly, "through all of this. You may have to keep being strong but you won't ever have to do this alone." He pulled her closer. "And I promise, things are going to get better."

26

A Matter of Honor

"Of all the stubborn, impulsive, *stupid*—!"

"Sir—" Kyndan began.

"You were supposed represent the Tellaran Realm!" the admiral boomed out.

Behind him, through the window of the admiral's flagship *The Sundragon,* Kyndan could see the peaceful blue and green of the Az-kye homeworld. It made him uneasy to be so far away from her. It would be mid-afternoon at the palace now, Alari would be seated in one of the smaller audience chambers and he could almost feel her tension as her advisors and courtiers circled around her for another round of sniping and backstabbing.

"You were supposed to act with restraint, with decorum." The admiral had been at this for a while but his face was getting redder by the moment now. "With some godsdamned *sense* for once!"

Kyndan kept his eyes front, willing himself to keep his breath even. "Sir, respectfully, the situation—"

"What you have *done*, Commander, is create a diplomatic disaster!" the admiral fumed. "Do you have any idea how serious this is? There are Council members who are calling for your head! There has been talk of leveling charges of treason against you! For what? Some Az-kye tart that—"

"Father!" Kyndan barked meeting the admiral's blue eyes, so like his own. "You're talking about my wife."

"I couldn't believe it when I saw your report." Ryndar Maere shook his head. "I *can't* believe it. You, and your sister, both married to festering *Az-kye*."

"Father." Kyndan's voice dropped to a growl. "I'm not going to warn you again. You *will* speak of Alari with the respect my wife is due."

"Godsdamn it, *both* my children have married . . . married—"

"The enemy?" Kyndan supplied. "The Az-kye aren't our enemies anymore." He closed his eyes for a moment. "I'm not sure they ever were."

Ryndar gave him a disbelieving look. "They raided our ships, they destroyed your cruiser—"

"You sent me out to do a weapons test on their ships!" Kyndan broke in sharply. "Remember my orders? To blow whatever ships I could find straight to hell? To gather enough data to help make our new cannons even more lethal?" Kyndan could feel the familiar cold knot in his belly. "Your orders forbid me to even *warn* them! You wouldn't even allow them to surrender!"

Ryndar stopped short. "Is that what this is about?" he demanded. "Because you were ordered to carry out a military operation against our enemies?"

"There was no honor in what I did," Kyndan bit out. "In the orders you gave me."

"I ordered you to defend our people!"

"Your orders made me a murderer!" Kyndan hands clenched into fists. "Do you know how much it made me hate them? How much it made me hate *myself*?"

Ryndar's lips went white and Kyndan's breath was burning in his lungs. With a conscious effort he slowed his breathing and relaxed his hands.

"No," Ryndar said hoarsely. "You bear no responsibility here, Kyndan. You had no choice but to follow orders. Any responsibility—any guilt—is mine to bear."

Kyndan's eyes stung. "I had a choice. I just made the wrong one."

"Son—"

"No," he said roughly. "It's too easy to do that. To hide behind orders, to shift the blame to someone else."

A warrior and his honor. Ah, fuck, I am *turning into one of them.*

Kyndan passed his hand over his face. "But no, that's *not* what this is about. And as for marrying Alari, I had to."

Ryndar froze. "Wait . . . did they threaten you somehow? If they—"

"No. In fact, everyone—" He gave a short laugh. "And I mean *everyone*, tried to get me out of it."

"Then *why*?"

Kyndan shifted his weight.

"Son?"

"I just . . . *knew.* Like you knew with Mom." Ryndar stared at him and Kyndan offered an embarrassed shrug. "I think I liked it better when you were yelling at me."

"You'd known her what—a day?"

"You asked Mom to marry you an hour after you met her."

"I was crazy," Ryndar said shortly.

Kyndan gave a quick grin. "Well, now we know where I get it from." He searched his father's face, his smile fading. "It's not just me they're blaming here, is it? They came down on you too."

Ryndar looked away. "Get yourself to the medcenter," his father said shortly. "Get that taken care of, then we can talk."

"Get—? Oh," Kyndan said, touching the scar that Jazan had left on his cheek. "I'm, uh, actually keeping it."

His father's brow creased. "Keeping it? Gods, *why*?"

"It honors Alari and—" *This is going to go over really festering well.* "Because I'm an Az-kye warrior now and warriors are proud of their scars."

Kyndan could count on one hand how many times in his life he'd seen his father speechless but the look on the elder Maere's face said volumes.

"Alari is Regent of the Az-kye Empire," Kyndan reminded. "She has to be married to a warrior. So that means—"

Ryndar held up a hand. "Stop. Just stop."

"I can't," Kyndan said. "And as of now I'm officially resigning my commission."

"You're *what*?"

"Resigning," Kyndan repeated.

"No," his father said flatly.

"Father, you don't get a vote. I *have* to resign."

His father took up position at his desk, his arms on the surface, his fingers interlaced. He was the very image of a reasonable officer and had Kyndan been anyone else he would have believed this man a superior willing to listen, one he could win to his way of thinking.

But Kyndan had seen that same posture many times growing up. He knew that, while his father wanted to give the appearance of fairness, he had already made up his mind and a thousand pulse cannons couldn't dislodge him from his position.

"Explain this decision to me," his father said. "Help me understand where you're coming from on this, Son."

"Okay, how about this? Being consort to the Az-kye regent is going to make it a bit tricky to hit my objectives for the next promotion in rank."

His father's mouth tightened. "I wish you would treat this with the seriousness it deserves, Kyndan."

"I *am* taking this seriously. There are no options here. I have to resign." He took a deep breath. "I'm not just Imperial Consort now, I'm Imperial Warlord. I'll be commanding the Empire's armed forces."

"What?" Ryndar breathed.

"Imperial Warlord. Commander of the Az-kye military."

Ryndar was on his feet instantly. "This makes you a traitor!"

"I'm not a traitor," Kyndan said tightly. "We're not at war."

"What if we were?" Ryndar demanded. "What would you do, Son?"

Kyndan closed his eyes briefly. "Let's just make sure this peace treaty happens. You work on your end and I'll work on mine."

His father held his gaze for a long moment then sat and picked up a datapad.

"Commander Maere," Ryndar began with cold formality. "Your resignation is refused."

Kyndan passed his hand over his eyes. "You can't do that."

"The hell I can't."

"Fine, you've refused." Kyndan threw his arms wide. "Now what, *Sir*? Order me to Central Command to answer for the crime of getting married? Keep me from returning to

Az-kye by force and hold the Imperial Consort hostage? Take away my holo privileges and send me to my room? What's the plan here, Papa?"

Ryndar's nostrils flared. "There's still the brig, Commander."

"There are all of *two* Tellaran ships in Az-kye space," Kyndan said sharply. "And believe me, if you force a confrontation they'll blow me to pieces along with this ship. A warrior who dies in battle dies honorably. They'll think they're doing me a favor."

"Damn it!" Ryndar burst out. "I didn't raise you—or your sister either—to be festering Az-kye!"

"I'm just going to pretend you didn't say that." Kyndan blew his breath out. "She's looking forward to meeting you, by the way."

"Your wife."

"Her Imperial Majesty, Regent and Heiress to the Az-kye Empire, Princess Alari." Kyndan folded his arms. "Yeah, my wife."

Ryndar leaned back in his chair. "When?"

"Accept my resignation and assume the duties as Tellaran representative and—*maybe*—we'll ask you to the house for dinner tomorrow."

Ryndar lifted the datapad again, already tapping the screen. "I'm placing you on inactive status—"

"No," Kyndan groaned. "Father—!"

"For six months," his father continued. "If, at the end of that time, you have not presented yourself for service, your status will automatically be listed as 'separated.'"

"I'm not coming back. I *can't*. And six months to think about it isn't going to make any difference. You should just accept my resignation now."

"Well, this way your retirement benefits will be worth an extra fifty creds a month," Ryndar muttered, tossing the datapad onto the desk. "What time is dinner?"

Alari's head came up as soon as she heard his footstep in their quarters. She put down the war leader's report and hurriedly waved the servants out. Kyndan came into the sitting room then and her heart sank to see that he still wore his Tellaran uniform.

He gave her a smile as she stood up from the sitting room couch to greet him. "Well, I'm all yours."

She blinked. "You resigned? You are no longer Tellaran?"

"Well, I resigned. I'm afraid you're stuck with the blue eyes."

"So"—she clasped her hands—"you—will be Az-kye?"

"Az-kye as I can manage. My father is looking forward to meeting you tomorrow."

She nodded to the low table where a pot of steaming tea and an assortment of the Az-kye foods he favored waited. "Are you hungry, my mate?"

He shook his head. He looked tired, as if the experience had been a great deal more trying than he wished her to know.

"He was angry?" she asked quietly. "Your father?"

Kyndan's smile was rueful. "I'd like to say I've seen him angrier, but I haven't." He sighed. "And angry I could handle but he was . . ."

Alari searched his face, the resignation in his gaze, the slight downturn at the corner of his mouth.

Disappointed. His sire was disappointed and this hurts him deeply.

She swallowed hard. The Az-kye were a proud race and she had been raised to revere the traditions of her people. To be counted among the Children of Heaven was to be blessed and protected by the gods.

But to his sire—and to Kyndan—to be considered Az-kye was to be shamed.

Then Kyndan shook off his melancholy and gave her a quick grin. "Never mind. Anyway, it's a prestigious assignment so there's some squabbling back at the capital about who will be posted to the role of Tellaran ambassador but my father will be standing in at least for a few weeks. He pulled some serious strings to get here."

"Does he distrust us so that he must see to this task himself?" she asked, hurt.

"Yeah, I think the grandbaby he's expecting might have more to do with his visit. You know," he said at her frown, "Kinna's baby? His grandchild?"

Alari drew breath to point out that Kinara was of the Az'anti clan and therefore would bear no grandchild to him but then she closed her mouth.

The Lady of the Az'anti would think it his grandchild. Kyndan, the Imperial Consort, still reckoned Kinara his sister although she was of another clan.

Kinara, Tedah, and now Kyndan as well, each had a Tellaran core with only the thinnest veneer of Az-kye over it . . .

"Did he ask you to return to home with him?" she asked tightly. "To return to Tellaran space?"

"If you knew him you wouldn't wonder about that." Kyndan gave a short laugh. "Believe me, my father doesn't *ask*, Alari. But no, the idea of me returning with him was never really broached." He gave a firm nod. "It's done, though. I know I've got a lot to learn so I think it's best if the war leader stays where she is for a while."

Unexpectedly, he cupped her cheek. "I know you're worried. I can see it in your eyes. I know what people are saying about me, about us. But I'm going to make this work, I promise you."

"They will not make it easy," she warned. "They will test you constantly, as they do me."

His jaw hardened. "Let them. I'll remind whoever needs reminding that I'm consort, that I'm Imperial warlord."

She glanced away.

His brow furrowed. "What is it?"

"You say such but you still wear the uniform of a Tellaran officer."

He looked down at himself. "Huh." He gave her a slow grin that made her center heat and her fears fade to nothing. "Maybe you could help me out with that?"

27

There was ugly, there was hulking. And then there was the ultimate melding of the two—also known as Nuhar, Kyndan's new swordmaster.

Reputed to be the finest swordmaster in the Empire, Nuhar was a warrior in his middle years, heavily muscled and just as heavily scarred. As a young man Nuhar had won the contests an unprecedented three years in a row and had gone on to train dozens of young men of the best families. He was very particular about whom he took on as a student but he agreed, grudgingly, to teach Kyndan.

So the following morning before dawn, Kyndan rose and, careful not to wake her, pressed a kiss to Alari's hair. In the earliest light of day he folded away his Commander's uniform and donned the funereal black and utterly revolting *animal skins* of an Az-kye warrior to begin cramming to acquire skills warriors began learning at the age of eight.

"Did no one ever teach you how to wield your sword?" Nuhar demanded as Kyndan demonstrated of his current skill with the blade.

"Not in public," Kyndan muttered wryly.

The swordmaster's mouth flattened into a thin line.

Ugly, hulking, *and* entirely lacking in humor, Kyndan corrected.

The warrior took the sword, placed it on the floor and directed Kyndan to kneel before it as a show of his respect and humility to the blade. Kyndan shot a disbelieving look at Utar, who stood nearby, but the former warrior's expression didn't betray any disapproval or surprise at the swordmaster's order so Kyndan, sighing, obeyed.

Then leaving Kyndan, bare except for the loincloth, on his knees to show reverence to an obsolescent piece of metal, Nuhar talked feelingly about how the Az-kye sword was more than a weapon, more than a training tool, how in the hands of a true warrior it became a link through which one could touch the spirit of Ren'thar.

It sounded like utter nonsense and what any of this had to do with learning how to fight was beyond him. Kyndan spent most of Nuhar's rhapsodizing alternatively stifling yawns and wondering if he could get away with sending Utar to the palace kitchens to get him some caf.

"No offense to Ren'thar or to the, uh, sanctity of the blade," Kyndan broke in at a rare instant when the swordmaster paused long enough to draw breath. "But I don't have the usual ten years that warriors get to train. Maybe we could skip ahead to the part where I actually get to *pick up* the sword?"

Nuhar's expression remained one of warrior impassivity but his eyes narrowed, just a touch. "Stand you, and demonstrate the grip you will use to wield it."

Kyndan got to his feet and wrapped his hand around the hilt.

"Too loose," Nuhar said disdainfully. "A babe could strike it from you, do you hold it thus."

Kyndan's nostrils flared. "'Kay," he grumbled and adjusted his grip.

"Too tight, you will be rigid, clumsy, easily beaten do you hold it so."

"Why don't you—" Kyndan began angrily then caught himself. "*Honored* swordmaster, maybe *you* could show me how to hold the sword?"

"You must learn this for yourself."

Kyndan shot him a glare. "If I'm learning it by myself, what are you doing here?"

"*I* am the guide who will lead you to be the warrior that lives in your heart."

"Well, maybe you could check your guide map and find us a more direct route?"

In retaliation Nuhar took his metal blade away and handed him a child's practice sword like the kind Kinara and Aidar's adopted son Bebti used.

"Are you kidding?" Kyndan demanded, holding up the short, wooden blade.

"If you will have the seriousness of child I will treat you so," Nuhar returned.

"I don't have time for this! I have a hell of a lot to learn and I need to learn it by roughly *yesterday*. Give me back the real sword and let's get started."

Nuhar's dark eyes narrowed. "You will get a warrior's sword when you can act as a warrior."

"Give me back the other godsdamned sword!"

"I am the swordmaster." Nuhar folded his massive arms. "You are the student."

Kyndan flung the child's sword to the other side of the practice room, the wooden blade bouncing and skidding across the floor.

"No," he snarled. "*I* am the Imperial Warlord."

"An unworthy one," Nuhar spat and turned on his heel.

"Festering son of a—! *Get back here!*" Kyndan shouted.

Nuhar didn't even glance around, pushing his way out of the practice room reserved for use by men of the Imperial family.

Kyndan was furious enough that it took him a few moments to recognize the two warriors who entered the room shortly after.

"How's it, uh, going?" Tedah asked.

"Couldn't be better," Kyndan bit out. "I turned down a dream command in the Fleet to take up playing with obsolete weapons, my people think I'm a traitor, *her* people think I'm worthless, and even the palace gardener feels perfectly comfortable asking me when I'll be getting Alari pregnant. How are *you*?"

"I'm okay," Tedah said, frowning.

"I am well, Consort," Aidar said, inclining his head.

"That was my famous swordmaster, Nuhar of the Oron, quitting by the way," Kyndan said with a wave at the door the warrior had exited through. "In case you want to run after and get his autograph or something."

"I was fortunate to speak to him in the hall," Aidar said. "It was an honor."

Kyndan jerked his chin at his brother-in-law. "Any chance you could get him to come back? I didn't even make it through the first lesson."

Aidar folded his arms. "The swordmaster said he found you irreverent, disrespectful, and undisciplined."

Kyndan's brow furrowed. "What did you say?"

Aidar's dark gaze didn't waver.

"Oh, for fuck's—!" Kyndan threw his arm out. "Perfect," he bit out. "Hey, thanks for the visit, drop by the palace any time. What are you two doing here, anyway?"

"The ceremony to welcome the new Tellaran ambassador is at midday," Tedah said. "We thought we'd come early and catch you alone"—he glanced at Utar— "well, in private, first and see how things are."

"Okay." Kyndan studied him for a moment. "Why did you want to catch me alone, exactly?"

Tedah gave a half-shrug, his expression chagrined. "Lianna and Alari were talking and the subject of well . . . old times came up."

"*Lianna* told Alari about me and Nisara." He ran his hand through his hair. "Well, that explains how she knew."

"Lianna feels terrible." Tedah shifted his weight. "Did it cause a problem?"

"Yes, but I think I reassured Alari that what happened in the past is *in* the past." Kyndan looked between them. "I'm not the only one this caused a problem for, am I?"

"Dael was . . . taken unawares," Aidar said.

Kyndan sighed. He suspected Dael and Alari both worried that, lacking the tradition of being bound, casual sex between Tellarans might not be so casual after all. Or maybe they just had the same jealousies as Tellarans did but kept them buried deep under Az-kye mores. "Should I talk to him?"

Aidar looked surprised. "To what purpose?"

"Uh, to reassure *him* too."

Tedah and Aidar exchanged a glance. "I don't think that's the best idea," Tedah said. "You probably want to let him cool off."

"Or practice you more with the sword first," Aidar suggested dryly.

Kyndan gave a short, startled laugh. "Ah, fuck, I've been on Az-kye too long," he said, passing his hand over his face. "I'm starting to get your jokes, warrior."

The door to the practice arena opened and one of the Imperial servants came in. She wore the sash of a personal attendant but he didn't know this one, which meant she wasn't one of Alari's maids.

The woman offered a bow with cool self-possession as if he weren't standing in the middle of the room wearing nothing but a loincloth. "Consort, the empress commands your presence."

He bit back an acerbic reply. He'd already mouthed off to enough people for one morning.

"Tell her Imperial Majesty I'll be there shortly."

The woman bowed again and turned to go but not before Kyndan caught the flash of contempt in her eyes, and his nostrils flared.

Maybe I could have mouthed off to just one more . . .

His and Alari's lavish living space was located in the same building as her mother's, known as the empress' residence. But, although they might share a structure, Kyndan had never even been invited to step foot in this wing.

Kyndan's nose wrinkled as he entered the empress' chambers. The place smelled of medicines, too many incenses, and fading hope. He dressed again before he came, still unused to the feel of animal skins, still uncomfortable in the garb of a warrior. His clothing was distinctive in that it lacked the beading over the left shoulder that proclaimed his clan.

The empress had never welcomed him into it.

He didn't mind for himself so much but it bothered him for Alari's sake. He needed to figure out a way to get these people to respect him. And the empress' disapproval literally on his shoulder for all to see wasn't going to make it any easier.

Kyndan followed the servant into the empress' bedroom. The space, larger than the first floor of the house he had grown up in, was sumptuously done in red and gold brocades. It was less like a private sanctuary and much more in keeping with a place designed for public view. There were no quirky knickknacks or souvenirs as one might find in a Tellaran's most personal space. There were no family portraits or personal touches. This was not the private retreat of a mother or a woman—it was the bedroom of a monarch.

An enormous bed dominated the space, its elaborate carvings and great height making it more throne than sleeping place. On it Azara lay propped on pillows, healers, priests, and priestesses at her bedside. She looked weaker than when he'd last seen her at Saria's funeral rites. Her skin had sickly yellow tinge to it now and her cheeks were sunken as if the life were being drained right out of her.

But Azara still retained enough strength to look at him with intense dislike burning in her dark eyes.

He held her gaze for a moment, then bowed. "Imperial Majesty."

She let him stay that way for a few heartbeats and he gritted his teeth in annoyance.

"Consort," she said at last.

He straightened. "How are you, Majesty?"

"Dying," she said shortly.

"I'm sorry."

Azara's lip curled. "I almost believe you mean that."

"I *do* mean it," he said sharply. "Even if I were so petty as to wish you to the spirit world, Alari's already lost a sister. She doesn't need any more grief right now."

"I know something of grief, Consort," the empress said tightly. "I lost a daughter."

Kyndan shifted his weight. He tried to see her as a grieving mother, not as a woman who would have inflicted a lifetime of cruel servitude on her own child, who let Jazan continue to assault Alari for her own twisted reasons.

"I only met her once but Saria was a sweet girl. Alari loved her very much." He met her gaze solemnly. "I am sorry for your loss, Your Majesty."

A sheen of tears suddenly showed in Azara's dark eyes. "She was . . . a sweet child." Then the empress tore her gaze away. "Leave us!"

The attendants hurried out and Kyndan raised an eyebrow when the door shut behind them. "Well, everyone's gone. I guess you can tell me what you really think of me now."

"You seem clever for a barbarian," she returned coldly. "I do not think I need tell you."

He inclined his head. "Then I guess I don't really need to tell *you* either."

The empress' gaze narrowed. "You took my daughter from the palace without my permission."

"Alari is an adult and we don't need your permission to do anything." Kyndan raised an eyebrow. "Is that really why you brought me here? To scold me for taking my wife to the temple district so she could have some fun at the festival? Because I took her to visit my sister?"

Azara's eyebrows rose. "Is *that* where you took her?"

"Where did you think I took her? A damned cave? Besides, *you* disinherited her. Why the hell should you care where she was?"

"Just because Alari was no longer First Daughter, did not mean she was no longer *my* daughter. Did it not occur to you that I might have been worried for her?"

"No, I really can't say that it did. But the whole condemning her into slavery thing might have thrown me a bit."

Azara's nostrils flared. "You do not understand what it is to rule. You do not understand the sacrifice it demands. You will never understand why I did what I did."

"Because it's dangerous—for everyone—for a ruler to look weak."

"Yes," she said after a moment as if she were reluctant to acknowledge any intelligence in him at all. "That is precisely why." Azara looked at him hard. "Alari's rule is tenuous. She needs a strong warrior at her side, one who can help her hold the throne. You cannot."

"You might be surprised what I'm capable of, Your Majesty."

"You are not the equal of a warrior."

Kyndan's lip curled. "I think Jazan would disagree with you on that."

"Alari cannot hope to hold the throne with such as you for a consort. I only pray she sees that you are a danger to her," the empress hissed. "Before you are removed."

"Be careful, Majesty, you might discover how much of a danger I am."

The empress' eyes narrowed. "Is that a threat?"

"A warning," Kyndan corrected. "I'm not sure how much peace you'll ever have if your Tellaran son-in-law—a former Commander in the Tellaran Fleet *and* the son of a Fleet Admiral—turns up dead." He folded his arms. "Tellarans aren't Az-kye. They consider me one of their own; some of them might even be proud I'm consort. Even the ones who hate me now won't put up with having a Tellaran murdered. Kill me and there won't be a Tellaran alive who still wants peace with you. But you might be better off with the Realm at your throat." His nostrils flared. "Because if you try to hurt Alari again, you'll have *me* to deal with."

"I would *never* have permitted you to be my daughter's mate," the empress spat. "I would never have permitted you to *speak* to her."

"You aren't exactly my first pick for a mother-in-law either," he retorted. "I'd rather have a Utavian serpent. The snake would have treated Alari better!"

"Think you I have no love for my child?" she demanded. "I was harsh, overly so, but in love and regret I restored her to the succession. Against reason, against counsel of my dearest advisors I brought her to the throne and I will not have you destroy her!"

"I would *never* hurt Alari," he snarled. "And if that's what you wanted to say then I can tell you right now, we're finished talking."

He turned on his heel to walk out.

"Attend me!" Azara called.

He wasn't about to stop but her servants and her advisors rushed into the room, blocking his way. Sechon the Elder was among them, her brow creased with concern.

"My daughter's mate!"

Tedah's right. That is annoying.

He took his time turning to face her. "Yes, Imperial Majesty?"

The empress' dark eyes burned with hatred. "I welcome you to our clan," she fairly spat. "I bid you do honor to our name, Prince Consort Kyndan, Son to the *Shina' aru' Az-kye.*"

Kyndan blinked. "You—?"

"You are of the *Shina* clan. You are Az-kye." The empress bared her teeth. "Now get out!"

28

Imperial Son

Kyndan reeled out of the empress' apartments.

That was her welcome to the Imperial family?

"Consort!"

He turned at the sound of Sechon's call. "Elder."

"Your Highness—"

"Ahh!" He held up a hand. "I'm still trying to get used to 'Consort.' Let's stick to that for a while."

"As you like," she said with a nod. "Consort."

"How can I help you, Elder?"

She pressed her hand to her chest and gave a short laugh. "I was wondering if I could be of help to you, Consort." She tilted her head. "You seemed quite . . . distracted when you left Her Majesty's presence."

"Yeah," Kyndan said with a glance back that way. "That whole thing sort of took me off guard. Listen, the new Tellaran ambassador will be here soon so I have to get over that way."

"I am to be present as well for the welcome. May I walk with you, Consort?"

He inclined his head. "I'd like that."

"Surely," she said as they crossed the square, Utar discreetly behind them, "it is a good thing that Her Majesty has granted Alari's request?"

"Her request?"

"That you be welcomed properly to the clan," Sechon said. "That you be given your title and a name."

"You mean the clan name?"

"Prince Consort Kyndan, Son to the *Shina' aru' Az-kye*."

"Wait," he said. "*She* just named me 'Kyndan'?"

"Of course."

"What if she'd named me something else? Parin or Behal or something?"

"Well," Sechon said, looking perplexed. "That would be your name."

"And you'd all call me that that instead? Rather than 'Kyndan'?"

"Certainly."

"Well, hell," he managed. "I guess I should have stayed long enough to say 'thanks for not naming me Behal.'"

"But the name pleases you?" the elder asked, puzzled.

"Absolutely," he muttered. "And I think I can say with confidence that the Tellaran admiral especially will also approve of her choosing 'Kyndan.'"

"Perhaps we will all attend another naming ceremony next year?'

"Another—?" He felt his face warm. "You mean a baby."

"A new princess or prince would bring great joy to the Az-kye. An heir will help solidify Alari's rule." She looked at him seriously. "And yours, Consort."

"I didn't think you'd approve of me, Elder," Kyndan said. "Because I'm Tellaran."

Sechon sighed. "With age, you will find that people are far more alike than different. In any case," she added, her dark eyes kind, "you care very deeply for our regent."

"I love her," he said quietly.

The elder smiled. "It lifts my heart that Princess Alari has one so devoted to her." Her expression turned grave. "She has great need of you, Consort. Great need of your strength and support. Our people, too, have need of you."

"Because I'm consort," Kyndan said a little bitterly. "Because they need Alari to bear an Imperial heiress."

"We are none of us given the lives we expect." Sechon searched his face. "Think you that your role is inferior to hers? You are Ren'thar to her Lashima. It is to you that the protection of the Empire falls. Do not discount your importance, Consort. Do not discount your value to the Az-kye." She touched his arm gently. "Or to our regent."

"I haven't been a very good Az-kye mate so far," he admitted. "And I'm not a warrior. Not like your people think of them."

"Ah," she said nodding. "And what, then, should such a consort do?"

He sighed. "Get himself a new swordmaster I guess." He offered a grateful nod. "Thank you, Elder."

"Of course." She gave him a gentle smile. "I am proud to serve you, Consort. If there's anything else I can do . . ."

"I appreciate that."

He was relieved to see he'd arrived at the reception room at the eastern end of the palace before Alari and her attendants arrived.

At the doorway he had a quiet word with the Imperial majordomo, Jelara, who then announced him to the court as Prince Consort Kyndan of the *Shina'* clan. As he made his way past the bowing courtiers and the war leader he gave a quick smile to High Priestess Celara, leaning on her jeweled cane, and she smiled back.

"Mezera," Kyndan said quietly, stopping in front of the Leader of the War Council. She rose from her bow. "I want to see the logs from the rescue ship that found Princess Saria's ship. I want to see everything—visuals, reports, any sensor readings the recovery ships took as soon as it comes in. I want to see it first."

Mezera blinked, but now that he had been acknowledged by the empress as Prince Consort and Warlord she couldn't put him off. "Certainly, Your Highness."

He gave her a short nod and took up position at the door to await Alari in order to escort her inside. He had to discover if Saria's death were sabotage after all. If it was, then surely Alari too was in even greater danger than he feared.

29

ꓕꓱꓥꓛꓵꓥꓵꓥꓥꓨ
The Ambassador

Alari could plainly see the resemblance between Kyndan and his sire.

They were of a height and the shade of their eyes was similar, though the shape was different; Kyndan's were more rounded, his sire's more narrow. The Tellaran admiral's hair was bright silver, wavy like his son's, and very striking against his dark blue and white uniform. According to Kyndan the admiral had shared his same warm brown shade in his younger days and Alari suddenly imagined Kyndan with that handsome silver someday . . .

To welcome Kyndan's sire Alari ordered the official greeting of the new Tellaran representative to occur in the reception room at the east end of the Imperial palace. It had always seemed to her the most inviting of the official rooms with its soaring crystal windows, whimsical carvings of flora and spring-colored palette. In addition, the height of dais where Alari now sat enthroned, Kyndan standing at her side, was a spare two steps above the polished floor and would allow the Tellaran man to be at eye level rather than force him to look up at her while they conversed.

The sunlight from the arched windows on either side of the reception room made the red hair of the clan leader seem afire as Kinara of the Az'anti bowed beside him. Ever more restricted by the growing size of her belly, Kinara's breath came in even shallower measures now that her pregnancy had progressed.

"*Ti'antah* of the Az'anti," Alari said warmly, her hands folded over her jaha feather fan. "I am pleased to look on you again."

"Thank you, Imperial Regent," the clan leader replied. "It is an honor to be in your presence again. May I present my fa—" Kinara cleared her throat and the courtiers stirred. "The Tellaran representative, Admiral Ryndar Maere."

Alari met her mate's sire's gaze and against Imperial protocol offered a smile. "I bid you welcome here, Admiral Maere."

"The honor is mine." Ryndar's glance at her face, at the mourning makeup she wore, betrayed a flicker of distaste that made Alari's smile falter. "The Tellaran Council, its people and I, especially, are pleased to take part in these peace talks."

Alari regarded him for a moment then looked at the Az'anti clan leader. "Have the clan leaders Her Majesty named been assembled?"

Kinara blinked and Alari could feel Kyndan shift his stance beside her.

Kinara glanced at Kyndan. "I wasn't aware that was still . . ."

Alari flicked her fan ever so slightly.

"Of course, we wouldn't want to begin the talks until *that* was done," Kinara agreed rapidly. "I merely hoped today to present their representative to you."

"Hold on, so the talks won't be starting now after all?" Ryndar asked with a look between his children before settling on Alari again. "I was under the impression you were eager for these peace accords."

"I am *amiable* to the Tellarans' wish for peace, Admiral Maere," Alari said deliberately, magnanimously ignoring how he had not used any of her titles when addressing her.

"I see," Ryndar said, his voice clipped. "And just when are these talks to begin?"

Alari lifted her chin. "I expect all will be properly seen to for the talks to commence in a few months."

"A few months!" Ryndar exclaimed. "Are you *serious*?"

"If at all," Alari said sharply, feeling her face flush under her mourning makeup.

"If that's the case, young lady, what am I doing here?" Ryndar demanded, his silver eyebrows lowering into a scowl. "You *do* realize how much trouble my government—and I personally—have gone to in arranging all this for you?"

Alari blinked and a disapproving mutter ran through the court.

"Father—!" Kyndan began.

"I am sure I could not say," Alari interrupted coldly, her grip on her fan tightening. "But I will trouble you no further. You are excused from my presence!"

"Now, hold on just a—"

Kinara grabbed her sire's wrist in a tight grip and he broke off.

The Az'anti clan leader bowed quickly and her grip on her sire stayed tight until he too bowed.

Alari stood. "I will retire now."

Kyndan took his place beside her as she stepped from the dais and strode past his father and sister without a second look. Alari's maids, taken by surprise at her sudden departure, hurried after. The court bowed as Alari swept from the room, her rapid footfalls clicking sharply against the polished stone floor.

"What the hell just happened?" Kyndan demanded when they reached the hallway. "Why did you block the peace talks?"

"I did not block them," Alari said tersely.

"Then why are you still insisting on all those clan leaders?"

"Her Imperial Majesty would see this done properly. It will be done as she ordered."

"I don't think *Her Majesty* ever wanted these talks at all," Kyndan said sharply. "It looks like you don't either!"

"I was more than accommodating to their ambassador!"

"*Accommodating*? You were fucking rude!"

"*I* was rude?" she cried. "When their representative dared address the Imperial Regent as 'young lady'?"

"You know that's my father you just snubbed, right?" Kyndan asked hotly. "The same one I spent an hour convincing to come to dinner tonight so he could welcome you as his daughter-in-law!"

Alari stopped so short her attendants bumped into each other in a mad scramble not to collide with the Imperial Heiress.

"Convinced *him* to welcome *me*? As if he should not be honored to be permitted to dine with the Regent of the Az-kye Empire!"

Kyndan put his hands on his hips, looking down at her in disbelief. "I can't tell you how much I'm looking forward to Kinna's baby's arrival now. Between you and my father the nativity party *alone* is reason enough for me to put in extra sword practice."

Alari's eyes narrowed up at him. "Bid the Tellaran representative my well wishes for his journey home, my mate. And," she snapped over her shoulder as she strode away, "tell the Tellarans if they cannot present us with a mannerly ambassador there will be no peace talks at all!"

30

Jelara, the majordomo, awkwardly left with the fallout of an elaborate formal reception dinner that the guest of honor was no longer welcome to attend, explained to Kyndan that she had shown the ambassador to comfortable living quarters to await him.

"Well?" Kinara asked as soon as Kyndan joined them.

He shot his father a look. "Certainly makes me feel better a whole lot better about *my* job performance as the Tellaran representative."

"I hardly think I could have done worse," Ryndar said with an arch look at Kyndan's black warrior clothes.

"Yeah? Well, I didn't get myself thrown out of the Empire."

Kinara groaned and dropped her forehead into her hand. Aidar sighed and Tedah looked crestfallen but Ryndar was outraged.

"She did *what?*"

Kyndan folded his arms. "Threw. You. Out."

"She can't do that!" Ryndar exclaimed. The sudden silence that followed had him glancing from one face to the other. "Can she?"

"You know," Kyndan said to Tedah, "when I was an ensign I got thrown out of a bar once on Tellar. But I never met anyone who got thrown out of a whole *empire*."

"I'm glad you think this is funny, Son."

"I don't think this is funny," Kyndan flared. "I think this is a disaster. You offended her. You offended the Imperial Regent in full view of the court!"

"You think I'm to blame here?" Ryndar growled, with an angry gesture. "Little slip of a thing, no older than a cadet, practically stamping her foot at me!"

Kyndan stared. "Good thing she was wearing the Regent's cornet or you might have tried to pat her on the head when you were presented."

"This isn't my fault!"

"Who's fault do you *think* it is that she's offended?"

"Yours," Aidar said.

Kyndan's head snapped around. "What?"

"You wished to know who is at fault that your mate is offended," Aidar said seriously. "It is yours."

"*Mine?*" Kyndan exclaimed. "I didn't do anything! All I did was stand there!"

Aidar held his gaze steadily.

"Ah, fuck." Kyndan passed his hand over his eyes. "Okay," he said tightly. "Want to explain to me what I did wrong?"

"There were many transgressions."

"Like?" Kyndan prompted.

"You addressed the admiral as 'Father.'"

"I *am* his father," Ryndar said shortly.

Aidar threw the admiral an impatient glance. "You are of the Imperial family now, Consort," he said to Kyndan.

"And are not supposed to acknowledge ties to another family," Kinara said, wincing.

"Kinna caught herself," Kyndan realized. "But I didn't."

"Wait, they aren't supposed to call me 'Father'?" Ryndar demanded. "You mean to tell me that neither of my children will be publicly acknowledging me as their father?"

"Uh," Kinara held out a hand. "Aidar—!"

"It is unseemly to acknowledge relation to a Tellaran," Aidar said.

Ryndar's nostrils flared and his posture went rigid.

"Well, then," he began his voice low and furious, "I thank all you *Az-kye* for the welcome but I think I will be taking your wife's suggestion and *leaving* now."

"Father—" Kyndan began.

Kinara put her face in her hands. "Papa—!"

"Please," Ryndar fairly spat. "I wouldn't want to embarrass you."

"Believe me," Tedah said a little loudly, "*no one* would rather be somewhere else more than I would right now." He looked around at them. "But maybe we should focus on salvaging the peace talks instead?" Ryndar glared at him and Tedah raised his eyebrows. "That is your mission, Sir."

Ryndar blew his breath out of his nostrils. "All right," he said shortly, and yanked on his dress tunic. "How do we patch things up?"

Kinara sighed. "I wish Laric were here. She'd know."

"Or Lianna," Tedah said. "I can contact her."

"Uh," Kyndan said, looking at Aidar. "Jump in any time."

"First, you must apologize—"

Kyndan glanced at his father. "I don't think Alari's really in the mood—"

"—to your mate."

"Ah," Kyndan said, then after a moment asked: "Want to quickly run through what I'm apologizing for?"

"There is much," Aidar warned.

Kyndan sighed. "'Course there is."

31

ꓘꓲꓥ ꓱꓦꓕꓣꓕꓩ ꓦꓯꓵꓵꓩꓥ
The Mantle Donned

Free now of her formal garments and public mourning paint, Alari struggled to concentrate on the documents laid out before her. Even with Sechon's brief visit to offer support after the debacle with the Tellaran ambassador, her stomach churned. Alari took a quick sip of tea hoping to settle her stomach.

She did not look up when Kyndan came out onto the balcony where she worked, and feigned attention on the papers spread in front of her.

He came to stand on the opposite side of her worktable.

"You know . . ." Kyndan tilted his head to look at the parchment. "Tellarans don't use paper anymore. Just datapads."

"These are Imperial edicts," she said tersely. "They must bear the Imperial seal and one cannot place a *seal* on a *datapad*."

"Makes sense," he said, nodding.

He watched as she held back the silk sleeve of her white dressing gown and, using the sharpened reed and black ink, painted the elaborate swirls of the Regent's mark on the paper. Alari took up the carved vessel of red wax and poured a small amount then applied her seal with a firm press.

She leaned back and the scribes hurried to take one paper away and place another before her.

"You have come to ask me to reconsider receiving the Tellaran ambassador?" she asked without looking at him. "Come here to suggest I *apologize* to him?"

"Oh, hell no," Kyndan said.

She blinked and her hand paused over the parchment.

"Even after I have offended your sire with my *fucking* rudeness?" she asked, dipping her reed in the ink again.

She looked up, scowling, at his choked laugh.

"Sorry," he said, smothering a smile. "That word doesn't translate perfectly into Az-kye but trust me, it's not a word a princess should use."

"Did you deliver my message to the Tellaran ambassador?" she sniffed, signing again.

"You mean that he was no longer welcome in your Empire and not to forget his coat on the way out? Yes, I did."

She worked for a while, the reed scratching against the paper, the *ruh-ru* calls of the jaha birds rising from the park below.

"And?" she asked finally, pressing her seal to the wax harder than was necessary.

"And maybe the next Tellaran representative will have better manners." He leaned casually on the table. "But you're two for two so I wouldn't get your hopes up."

"No, I should not think to," she said shortly.

"Hey, the tea smells good. Mind if I have some?"

Exasperated, she put her reed down. "Leave us," she commanded.

The scribes and attendants hurriedly bowed and backed away.

"You have come here to complain to me that I sent your father away," she said when the last had gone. "To demand I invite him to return! Why do you not do so?"

"Actually I wanted to ask you about a tutor."

"A what?"

"I'm Prince Consort now—"

"You are?" she broke in. "Her Imperial Majesty welcomed you into our clan?"

"I'm not sure 'welcomed' is the right term . . . more like 'groused' me into it. In any case I'm of the *Shina'* clan. They're sewing the clan beading to my clothes now."

"I just . . . I did not think Her Majesty intended to do such."

"Well, she did. Just before the ceremony to greet the ambassador actually. Anyway—you don't mind, right?" he asked, already taking a cup from the serving tray. He poured himself some of the steaming tea. "I was thinking, I could use someone to get me up to speed on palace etiquette. You know, keep me from blundering like I did."

"Blundering?" she asked, shifting her weight a bit.

"I mean, I messed up pretty badly earlier—huh, this *is* good," he murmured taking another sip. "It smells a bit too spicy but it's not really."

"You did not 'mess up,'" she mumbled.

"Sure I did. I acknowledged another family group as if I were disparaging my own clan, I should have moved forward as soon as the ambassador started arguing —Come on, you can't tell me you didn't notice."

Alari looked away. "You are new to the palace. You did not even wish to be here."

"Well, now I *am* here and I might be new but that's no reason for me to continue looking like a buffoon. So," he took another quick sip of tea, "a tutor. What do you think? I would ask Laric but Kinara needs her and let's face it, the woman just hates me."

"Why are you no longer angry that I sent your father away?" Alari demanded. "Why are you no longer angry that the peace accords are delayed?"

"Well," he began, considering. "Beyond the 'young lady' comment, he really didn't put his best foot forward. And the accords are no more delayed than they were before. I understand that it's a bad plan to just reverse your mother's decisions. You want to give the impression of a completely smooth transition. But mainly because I should have known better." He met her gaze. "I embarrassed you by not stepping forward, by not speaking up when he offended you. I'm sorry."

She looked away. "He is your sire. You esteem him. I could not expect such."

"I'm Prince Consort. I'm Imperial Warlord. Hell, I'm Son to *Shina' aru' Az-kye* now. Of course you should expect it."

She swallowed. "What of your father?"

Kyndan made a dismissive wave. "It was a temporary assignment anyway. And he accomplished what he really wanted to come here for. To see how Kinara was doing and make sure I hadn't completely lost my mind."

"He was angry that we were mated," she said.

Kyndan shrugged, putting his teacup down. "He understands now."

"He does?" She had just cut him before the court. She had ordered him from Imperial territory. His son wore the clothes of an Az-kye warrior. How could he possibly understand?

"Well, sure. Now he's seen how pretty you are."

Alari blew her breath out. No one could find her "pretty" in that ghoulish makeup.

"You are joking," she said irritably and turned her back on him, tugging one of the edicts closer.

"My father asked my mother to marry him an hour after he met her. It's true," he protested at her disbelieving glance. "They met at a Fleet dance. She was actually there with someone else but my father said he took one look and that was it. He loved her."

"That is a legend, the hero's aria in an opera." She sat again. "Such does not truly happen."

"It did to me."

She froze, the reed hovering over the paper.

"The first time I saw you," Kyndan said softly. "I was counting the seconds till I could leave Az-kye, and right there in the palace hall, on your way to marry someone else . . ."

Her heart hammered and she was listening so hard she was scarcely breathing. He touched her cheek, his fingers very warm from holding the teacup. He tilted her face to meet her gaze.

"Your beautiful eyes burned right into my soul, Alari . . ."

His blue eyes shone as he leaned toward her. His lips were a hairsbreadth from hers, his breath warm and moist against her mouth. As he spoke, his hand brushed her thigh.

"And," he breathed, his fingers sliding beneath the silken dressing gown, "I loved you."

In the very instant his lips touched hers, his sensitive fingers brushed her center and the reed fell from her grasp.

Kyndan's arm went around her, his hand pressed against the small of her back to hold her in place for him as he stroked her. It was different this time, how he touched her, the way his mouth moved over hers. It was gentle, tender still, but there was an undercurrent of mastery to it that he had held back before.

In a sudden move Kyndan pushed the edicts, the reeds, and tools of Imperial authority aside and lifted her by the waist onto the table.

He undid the sash, spread the white silk of her robe wide, and freed her of her undergarment. His gaze went hot as his glance went over her, lying there naked before him and she shivered with pleasure as his hands, roughened now from his training, slid up her thighs, spreading her wider.

An almost predatory smile touched his mouth as his fingers found her center again. Her palms pressed against the wood table as he stroked her and she shut her eyes to let herself sink into the sensations of it. With quick, sure skill he brought her to the very edge of her peak. She was arching against the pleasure of it, a heartbeat from climax, but in the next moment he cupped her buttocks and pulled her toward him so that he stood with her legs held open by his powerful thighs.

Still fully dressed, he took a spare moment to free his hard shaft. He held her hip steady, and his mouth parted, his eyes going hot with pleasure as he entered her. He held her like that, his hands cupping her buttocks as he took her, the skins of his warrior clothes smooth against the inside her thighs as he thrust. It thrilled Alari in a way she never could have imagined, to see her nakedness against the skins of his warrior clothes.

The lingering fears and her need to keep some measure of control at all times, legacy of Jazan's cruel acts, crumbled away. Lying helpless beneath Kyndan she felt utterly protected. She thrilled at the power of him as he filled her, each stroke moving against the most sensitive part of her. Alari finally allowed herself to surrender, to trust, and cried out at her climax.

At her release Kyndan moved faster and deep. He bent his head, losing the rhythm for an instant, then with a cry, he thrust again and she felt him pulse within her.

He was still breathing hard from his release when he raised his head to look at her and his eyes flashed blue fire as they met hers. There was possessiveness in his gaze and in it, too, was raw power.

In those eyes she saw that, Tellaran or Az-kye, Kyndan had been made to command. Through their marriage he might have gained this mantle as a young man but had he remained with his people he would have risen to a comparable role on his own merit.

These were the eyes of a warlord.

32

An hour later Alari stretched languidly. Kyndan was warm against her back, the sheets of the bed where he had carried her for their next lovemaking in disarray around them. He brushed the hair away and he kissed the nape of her neck.

"You never answered me," he murmured.

"About what?"

His cheek came to rest against her shoulder. "A tutor, someone to teach me manners and make me all Az-kye."

"I do not want you 'all Az-kye,'" she said softly. "I want you as you are."

"I blunder all the time. I don't know palace etiquette. I smile at people. You must hate it."

She turned in his embrace. "How can you say such?"

"Because it's true. But I don't want to embarrass you." His blue eyes flashed. "And I won't endanger you anymore."

Her brow furrowed. "Think you a few smiles will do such?"

"You won't even sketch because you're worried people think you're being irresponsible."

"That is different," she said, shifting. "It is something I do, not something I am."

He gently brushed a tendril away from her forehead. "I would say being an artist is exactly what you are."

"When we were mated you wore a Tellaran's uniform. You did not care if people disapproved of your smiles, of your jokes." She searched his face. "You were happier then."

"Well, I'm Imperial Warlord now," he said, his tone firm. "And that's who I have to be so I'm going to need some help."

She looked into his blue eyes, so beloved now, and traced the curve of his cheek, the mark that Jazan had given him.

"I will help you." She brushed the warm skin of his chest with her fingertips. "I will teach you."

He smiled then. "I was hoping you'd say that."

"It will be fun." She smiled too. "Like dancing."

"Except this time you get to see where we're going and I just have to trust you aren't dancing me off a cliff."

"I would never do such," she protested.

"So," he asked, intertwining his fingers with hers. "Where do we start? I know some—no jokes, no smiling, no—"

"I would have you smile. I would have you joke."

"Warriors don't do that."

She lay in his embrace, troubled. He was right. To be a warrior meant he must have a warrior's impassivity. To be warlord he must command respect.

"I would have you smile for me," she said softly. "I would have you joke for me."

He pressed a kiss to her temple. "Yes, for you. But everyone else gets my Commander face."

Her brow furrowed. "What is that?"

His expression lost all humor and became as grim, serious, and implacable a face as she'd ever seen. At the sudden transformation, she gave a startled giggle.

He nudged her, his eyes crinkling with humor. "You weren't supposed to laugh."

"I have never seen you so! I did not even know you could."

"Oh, thanks. I'll have you know I have intimidated my share of ensigns with that look."

"It was the countenance of a fiercesome warrior," she agreed.

He raised an eyebrow. "That's my disapproval face. If that one works, then I've got half this warrior thing down."

"I am pleased you are of the clan now." She traced the scar on his cheek again. "I will be proud to look on the beading on your shoulder."

"Yeah, well." He ran his hand through his hair. "I think I can officially say your mother hates me though."

Alari sighed. "As your sire does me."

"He wants to come back when Kinna's baby's born and stay for a few weeks," Kyndan said, his voice a little strained. "Maybe he could also be invited to the palace . . . in a less official way?"

"Would he not be too offended to return?" she asked slowly. "Now that I have requested another representative?"

"He would be *relieved* to be invited and it would—it would mean a lot to me, Alari. To have you get to know my father, to have him get to know you."

"Yes," she said softly. "I will invite him."

He gave a quick smile then he shifted a bit. "Uh, there's something else. The Tellaran Council has requested that my—well, it *was* my ship—the *Dauntless*, remain in Imperial territory and the crews' visits be extended. At least until the new ambassador's ship can arrive. I think they're secretly hoping that the Az-kye will get used to seeing

Tellarans walking around the empress' city. I was planning on giving my approval. I want to know what you think."

Alari shifted on the bed, frowning a little. Why would the Tellarans wish to keep their ship in orbit? Why would they wish their people to be so visible?

"That is a decision the warlord would make with the best interests of our people in mind," she said a little stiffly.

"Look, it's not like they would be any kind of threat to the Imperial world. Not with the three warships Mezera has playing escort. A Tellaran couldn't *sneeze* up there without an Az-kye close enough to wipe her nose."

"What does the War Council leader say of this?"

"I haven't asked Mezera," he admitted. "But if I'm going to have to start asserting some authority as warlord"—he leaned up on his elbow to look at her—"I'm going to need your support."

She wet her lips, wondering if it would appear as if she favored the Tellarans too much if she allowed it. Wondering if others knew that this man, bare next to her with his sleepy blue eyes, was so dear in her heart that she would give him anything he wished.

"Of course," she murmured. "The ship may remain."

She could feel the tension run out of his body. "Mezera's an enemy in the making already," he said. "I need to watch her."

Then he pulled her close again and shook off his serious mood.

"So, Tutor," he said with his slow smile. "Where should we start?"

33

The Swordmaster

The next morning Kyndan walked listlessly around the practice arena, examining equipment he had no idea how to use. Reserved for the exclusive use of men of the Imperial family, these rooms had recently been newly equipped and made ready again.

Ready for Jazan, that is.

Awkwardly Kyndan pulled the blade from the scabbard at his back and looked at the sword in his hand. According to Nuhar he didn't even know how to hold it properly.

"I need a new swordmaster for sure." He jerked his chin at Utar. "Who taught you?"

"My father," Utar said. "Myself and my brothers all."

"Well, I can't ask mine. I wonder what it'll take to get Nuhar to come back. He doesn't look the blackmail type, maybe I should try a bribe."

He wandered over to one of the targets. Made from tree trunk with white circles painted on it and thick pegs sticking straight out like branches it was very primitive looking. With clumsy movements Kyndan crossed his sword with one of the wooden pegs. It made a dull *thunk* and did nothing more than send the target turning slowly.

Kyndan watched it slow and stop.

After a moment Utar went to the target and clasping one of the pegs, sent the target spinning. "You are to strike the circle."

Kyndan shot a look at the former warrior. He looked at the white circle appearing and disappearing as the target spun, the pegs acting as a block. He hefted his sword again. He swung and in the next instant one of the spinning pegs knocked the sword right out of his hand.

The blade went skidding across the floor.

Kyndan sighed and passed his hand over his eyes.

Silently Utar offered another to Kyndan.

"Not you too," Kyndan said with a disgusted look at the wooden child's sword. "Are you also going to tell me I can't have the grown-up version?"

"That is not what the swordmaster said."

"He said I couldn't have a warrior's sword till I was a warrior. Which, if you think about it," Kyndan grumbled, "doesn't make any godsdamned sense at all."

"He did not say such."

"Utar, I was here," Kyndan reminded. "I remember exactly what he said. Warrior's sword when I *was* a warrior. And what kind of swordmaster wouldn't show me how to hold the godsdamned thing?"

"Perhaps that is not the lesson he wished to teach you."

"What kind of sword lesson doesn't involve picking up the fucking sword?"

Utar regarded him silently.

Kyndan blew his breath out in annoyance and went to retrieve the metal blade.

"Gods, you're just like Aidar, like all the warriors I've seen just staring at me acting like a—like—" Kyndan stopped, the metal blade in his hand. "Not when I *was* warrior," he murmured. "He said when I *acted* like a warrior. That's why he walked out. Because I wasn't acting like a warrior."

Utar inclined his head.

"But he wouldn't even show me how to hold it—no, wait, he was criticizing *how* I held it." Kyndan's brow creased. "He was testing me. Seeing how far he could push me before I lost it." He gave a short laugh. "Not too far, I guess."

Just like I kept at Jazan till he lost it.

"To learn to control the sword is easy," Utar said consolingly. "To control oneself, that demands much."

"Will you teach me?" Kyndan asked suddenly.

Utar's face went pale. "I am dishonored. My name is not spoken. I am of the dead."

Kyndan nodded. "I'm not seeing a problem here."

Utar swallowed. "Master—"

Wincing, Kyndan quickly held up his hand. "I hate that more than I hate 'Your Highness.' Don't call me that again. Let's try 'Kyndan.'"

Utar stared.

"Consort?" Kyndan suggested, sighing.

"Consort," Utar began, his voice strangled, "I am of the clanless. You cannot be taught by such as I. It would be . . ."

"Unseemly?" Kyndan held his blade out. "Utar, I'm a Tellaran warlord. I don't know how to use this thing and I don't know a damned thing about being a warrior. Right now, upstairs, asleep, is the most precious thing I have ever known in my whole life. I'd die to keep her safe but as stupidly ignorant as I am right now I can't even *begin* to protect her. I need to learn and I need to learn *fast*. Look, I won't order you but I'm asking—Will you teach me?"

"To touch a blade is forbidden to me, Consort. To do so is death."

"I won't tell if you don't tell."

Utar dropped his gaze.

Kyndan sighed again. "I understand. Look, I'll find another swordmaster. Maybe Nuhar—"

"No," Utar said suddenly. "They will teach you the traditional way, it will take too long. And Nuhar's mind is not flexible enough to construct such a training as you need."

Kyndan raised his eyebrows. "You said he was one of the best. That he won the contests three times."

Utar's dark eyes flashed. "But not four."

"Fucking hell," Kyndan said. "*You* beat him?"

"Yes."

Then the former warrior deftly flipped the wooden sword and offered it to Kyndan. In the same moment his demeanor, his posture, and the very look in his eye changed. Gone was the slave and, despite his white tunic, he was now every inch a warrior.

Kyndan looked at the wooden sword. "Uh, so I still don't get a real one?"

"You must learn quickly. There is no time for errors, no time for you to heal from even the glancing cuts common to training, do you begin with a real sword," Utar said, taking the metal blade from his hand. "This practice sword is too short, too stout for you but until I procure a more suitable one, you will use this. Change." He gave a nod. "And we will begin."

Kyndan grinned and offered a Tellaran's salute. "Yes, Sir."

34

In the Footlights' Glare

Give me sword drills any day . . .

Kyndan tried not to fidget on the throne but it wasn't easy. It was a big ornate thing and, whether it was simply because it was to be used by a toughened warrior type or because no one else ever sat in it long enough to find out, damned uncomfortable. This was his first experience dining publicly as Prince Consort and he could say with certainty that he hated it.

This dinner marked the end of the official month-long mourning period for Saria. When he'd first heard about the custom, he thought it would be like a reception or sedate party that would help transition the court into a return to normal activities but that's not what it was at all.

Situated in the center of the soaring golden hall, the thrones and table were set on a raised platform that reminded Kyndan uncomfortably of a stage. Dressed again in Imperial black, Alari sat at his side at the enormous table. Not surprisingly, her throne was larger and far more ornate than his. Theirs were the only table or chairs in the place; a hundred different dishes spread before them while what seemed like half the Empire stood around staring as they ate.

"This is fun," he muttered.

Alari glanced at him. "During the First Empire the Gate of the Blessed was kept open and the common people would come to watch the Imperial family eat every meal. We are fortunate that we need only do this for the court."

He didn't serve himself, of course. Servants took a bite-sized sample of one dish or another to place on his plate. He would eat it and another servant would place a morsel from a different dish in its place. He couldn't identify half of what he had eaten. He'd lost track of which dishes he'd been served from and which he hadn't. Since the servants remained silent as they worked he wondered if they had some sort of hand signals worked out to keep track.

Kyndan scanned the room of black clad courtiers and servants with their dark eyes fixed on him. "So we eat and they just stand there and *watch* us?"

"Yes."

"And you don't find this . . . weird?"

"It is symbolic. They will give their best for our table so that we may have the strength to lead them," she explained quietly. "It is expected that we make a public display of the bounty."

Kyndan's brow creased. "Wait, how often do we have to do this?"

"Once every seven days. More during the festivals."

"Every *week*?" he murmured bleakly.

"It is not the worst tradition that could have survived." She threw him a tiny, impish smile. "During the time of the Li'thar Dynasty, when a member of the Imperial family took a mate, a bed was brought here so the court could observe the pair being bound."

His face went hot at the idea of it. "Yeah, okay, the dining would get my vote too."

"You will become accustomed to it," she assured.

"Are you?" He couldn't imagine ever getting used to this.

"Yes, but I have been doing so since I was a child."

"You did this as a *child*? I couldn't sit still for five minutes when I was a kid."

"There are some allowances made for the very young." She smiled fondly. "Once, when we were little, Saria disappeared under the table to hide near my chair. We were both giggling so that my mother laughed and even my father . . ." A shadow passed over her face. "But now it is only me."

"Us." There was a surprised stir among the courtiers when he took her hand.

Kyndan didn't even glance their way. *The hell with them.*

Her fingers intertwined with his. "Us."

After a very, very long dinner Alari rose and he with her.

"So what's this opera we are going to see?" He wasn't terribly excited about having to sit through that either but at least they would be part of the audience rather than the entertainment.

"*Ris and Letaria*," she said. "Twins, brother and sister, lost, who come to a faraway land."

"Like me and Kinara," he said. "Except we're not twins, of course."

"Ris and Letaria are separated and both come to take mates who are of warring clans."

"This has a happy ending, right?"

She offered a half-shrug. "For an opera."

Kyndan, upon being proclaimed Prince Consort, had been presented with his own retinue of black-clad servants and personal honor guard and those men accompanied him now. Between him and Alari there were a minimum of fifteen people who went with them everywhere and his personal servants wore their own sashes of honor.

Alari, Kyndan and their servants passed through the courtyard under the shade of the many blooming tashi trees from the banquet hall to the Imperial Opera House. There were other smaller theaters on the palace grounds but this one was large enough to hold a thousand guests, the curtained Imperial box situated in the very center of the tiered space.

The audience stirred and those already seated rose to bow as they entered their box. The court waited until he and Alari had taken their seats before sitting again or moving about.

Kyndan, who had never been inside, had to resist the temptation to crane his neck to look around the ancient opera house. The gold beading on his shoulder and his "Commander face" expression were starting to have effect and he didn't want to ruin it by gawking, no matter how ornate the interior. A number of the warriors here—mates or sons as well as the Imperial honor guard—met his eye with a measure of respect now before they inclined their heads to him.

Kyndan's earlier experience with the court had been seeing them scandalized by Alari choosing him as mate or the shock of Saria's death. He had never seen them excited or happy. He'd never observed alliances being formed or enemies sending cold glances to one another. The unmated among them flirted, the young women hiding giggles behind their fans, the unmated warriors' hot gazes following women they admired.

He was starting to be able to spot familiar faces. The priest of Behur was easy to spot in his blue robe. The High

Priestess of Lashima, Celara, wore bright colors as always and her jeweled cane rested against her seat. Mezera, Leader of the War Council was present as was Banne, Leader of the Council for Trade. A number of those in attendance possessed territories vast enough on the colony worlds that they spread across continents.

Jazan's mother, clan leader of the Az'rayah, gave him only the sparest of nods when their eyes met and he could hardly blame her. He flinched inwardly every time he saw the woman.

"My mate?" Alari asked when he shifted uncomfortably.

"The *Ti'antah* of the Az'rayah is here."

Alari's eyes turned that way and the clan leader's bow was just as chill to her.

"It was not to be avoided that they feel resentment," Alari murmured.

"I would say the Az'rayah clan fucking hate me." The clan leader faced forward again, her other sons and daughters around her. "There's no way to apologize for what happened, for taking her son away from her."

"Think you they grieve him?" she snorted. "I think they mourn what they lost with his defeat."

"A son in the Imperial family," he mused. "Just how much would that mean to them? I mean he would have joined your clan, just like I did."

"His position as Prince Consort would have given him great power to provide many favors to them."

"They look like they're doing okay."

"Much of the Az'rayah clan's wealth is due to trade."

"More like smuggling," he muttered, suddenly wondering if Kinara's activities as a member of the Trade Council involved smuggling too, wondering if he even wanted to know. "Am I wrong or are the Az'rayah ladies all wearing Tellaran shimmersilk? And isn't blatantly displaying smuggled goods at court kind of in poor taste?"

"Who would not wish to flaunt their forbidden Tellaran treat?"

"Yeah, but—" He broke off, his face heating. "*Funny*."

She hid her smile behind her fan as the house lights dimmed and the music began.

Kyndan, accustomed to immersive holotheaters, wasn't expecting much. He'd heard some of Az-kye music during his time here as a slave and hadn't liked any of it. But between his new fluency and the excellent performances of the troupe he was amazed to find he really enjoyed the opera and at intermission he applauded enthusiastically.

"You will make them anxious of the second act," Alari teased. "Many warlords have been patrons of the arts—they watch to see if you are pleased," she said with a nod at the closed curtain. "The singers are hopeful of your patronage."

"They were watching *me*?" he asked with a glance at the stage. "I'm glad I didn't know that. Anyway, they don't have to worry. I really liked it."

"Now they fear you will not like the end."

"So I have to clap twice as hard at the finish?"

"Or at least as hard as at intermission," she said. "We must send gifts too, to show our approval."

"What kind of gifts?"

"Sweets, little trinkets, teas to soothe their throats. If you are very moved you might present the lead with a sweetly singing araya bird but then everyone will gossip that you have fallen in love with her."

He shook his head a little. "We're bound. I can't fall in love with anyone else."

Alari busied herself with her fan. Kyndan waved the attendants away and closed the curtain of their box himself.

He sat again, facing her. "So 'bound' means not having sex with anyone else. But you could fall in love with someone other than your mate?"

"Such has happened," she said, not looking at him.

"That's why you were so upset about Nisara? Because you thought I might be in love with her?"

She sent an anxious glance at him.

"I wanted you the moment I saw you, more than I've ever wanted anything," he murmured. "I wanted to fight for you. I wanted to marry you." He cupped her cheek. "There's no one but you, Alari."

She searched his gaze and her dark eyes shone. "Truly, I could love no other more, Kyndan."

He leaned forward. "If I get caught kissing you, will it get us kicked out?"

"I would not care if it did," she murmured already tilting her face up for his kiss.

The servants and attendants had already retreated to a discreet distance but there was a shuffled consternation at the entrance of the box.

Kyndan turned, his hand automatically going to where his blaster should be. Then, cursing inwardly, he reached for the sword lying in its back scabbard beside him.

"Elder," he said, stopping short.

Sechon had a woman with her, a clan leader, by her dress, and a young man in warrior clothes. All, especially the young man, had expressions of embarrassment at having interrupted such a private moment.

"Your Hi—Consort," Sechon stammered, already stepping back. "We thought only to—We will withdraw."

"No," Kyndan said, trying to hide his chagrin and annoyance. "Please, come in." "Are you enjoying the opera, Elder?" Alari asked.

"Very much," Sechon said. "Consort, allow me to present Helia of the Az'shu and her son, Aylar."

Helia and Aylar bowed and Kyndan nodded to them. "Good to meet you."

"Helia, clan leader of the Az'shu, sits on the Council for Trade with Kinara of the Az'anti," Sechon said with an unmistakable note of pride in her voice.

Kyndan remembered then that the leader of the Council for Food had accused Sechon of favoring Trade because her daughter, Helia, was on that Council.

"I've heard good things about you," Kyndan said to Helia. The clan leader's brow furrowed and Kyndan, borrowing a phrase he'd heard Alari use, said, "I mean, you are well thought of."

Helia smiled. "It pleases me greatly to hear it so." She glanced at Aylar at her side. "My son placed well in the contests this year."

Kyndan looked at him. Probably all of eighteen, the kid was likely about a hundred times better than he was with a sword. "Congratulations."

There was a pause and he could swear Alari hid a smile.

"What will you do now, Aylar?" Alari asked.

"I have been called to the Empire's service, Regent," he replied, his face impassive but his cheeks flushed.

"In what capacity?" she asked. "Will you serve in my forces?"

"It has not been determined, Regent," Aylar said, his face still red.

There was another pause and then Sechon said, "Well, to be sure, the performance will begin again shortly."

Kyndan offered a nod to them. Helia looked a bit disappointed but the kid looked absolutely crestfallen as they left.

"Did I miss something?" he asked.

Alari smiled a bit. "I think Aylar was hoping that you might have invited him to serve you."

Kyndan blinked. "As what?"

She shrugged. "It is a great honor to be of the warlord's inner circle. It is expected you will select warriors to become your trusted companions."

Trusted companions? Hell, he knew exactly who he'd start with—Tedah and Aidar, maybe even Dael to mend fences a bit. He bet that as the Prince Consort's friends they, too, would become very powerful men—

Kyndan looked the way Aylar had gone and his stomach sank. "This is just the start, isn't it? People will be jostling to gain my friendship, to offer me flattery and gifts. Looking to me for favors and patronage and promotions. Begging me to have a word with the regent on their behalf."

She didn't answer. The music was starting again, the servants drawing back the curtains, but Kyndan's glance took in the court, their dark gazes watching them, how they watched *him*.

He thought getting the empress to accept him would be hard, learning the sword work of an Az-kye warrior daunting and taking his place as warlord the most difficult task. Now he understood what Alari meant when she'd said that they'd constantly test him.

He'd won Alari and nearly gotten killed doing it, been welcomed into the Imperial family by an empress who hated him, but as far as being consort the challenges were just beginning.

35

⌐⅄⋏ ⍵ ⍋⅄⋏ ⅄⍙⅄⋏⌐⅄⋏⋏
The Sword Unsheathed

To call it grueling would be kind. Not even during basic had Kyndan been pushed so hard physically. There was two hours of training with weighted balls, jumps, pull-ups—it seemed to go on and on. Then sprint work, then a minimum of ninety minutes of fight training.

Kyndan was trembling with fatigue at the end but it would have been a hell of a lot easier on his pride if Utar hadn't been able to do it while scarcely breaking a sweat.

"You did this *every*," Kyndan wheezed, ". . .day?"

Utar shook his head. "I do not wish to push you too hard. We will increase the difficulty when you are stronger."

Kyndan gave a short, gasping laugh—all he could manage right then.

Utar began teaching him the most basic of self-defense moves of sword work. As Kyndan would need months of intensive training before he could risk another Circle challenge with any hope of surviving, Utar coached him instead on how to avoid giving offense and how to honorably deflect any offenses given to avoid a fight entirely.

He dispensed with the usual, traditional methods of training, much of which would require Kyndan to uncover the purpose of the lesson himself. Utar was a marvel at building on the skills and strengths Kyndan already had from Tellaran sports like darshball which required fast reflexes and eye-hand coordination.

"You are far more disciplined than I gave you credit for," Utar said approvingly after Kyndan had completed an hour-long session with the target without protest.

"I was in the Fleet," Kyndan reminded, pushing his hair back *again*. Warriors wore their hair long so he was growing his out. Now just shaggy enough to annoy him by getting in his eyes, it would be years before he could tie his hair back the way they did. "That gives you focus and man, you learn quick not to complain. As long as I have some idea what the purpose of what I'm doing is, I'm fine."

"I think then you would not have lasted long with Nuhar as swordmaster," he said with a rare smile.

Kyndan gave a laugh. "From the way you describe the traditional teaching forms, I think you might be the only one who *can* teach me."

"I think this way better, quicker. I think it so for any student," Utar said, his voice betraying his excitement. "I think if my s—" he broke off, his face clouding. He busied himself returning the equipment to its proper place. "I have lost myself in this work. I forgot what I have become."

"You have a son?"

Utar's grip tightened on the bar he was holding. "I did," he said softly. "A daughter as well."

"How old are they?"

"The girl is fourteen summers, the boy only sixteen now."

"Do you ever see them?"

"I have looked on them at every opportunity," he said quietly. "Though they have not looked on me in nearly a year. They must not look on me." A smile, loving and pained, touched his face. "He has grown so tall and she looks so like her mother."

"Your mate, is she . . .?"

His dark eyes held a faraway look. "Paria died when Ulan was but ten summers, his sister eight. They had only me and I—"

"What happened?" Kyndan asked. "I mean, why were you sent away?"

Utar shut his eyes.

"Utar? What did you do?"

Utar turned away. "It is enough to say the thing cannot be undone. I will bear my shame forever but I am grateful my children have the clan to care for them."

Kyndan shook his head. "I'll never understand it. I'll never be able to accept this whole clanless thing. The way they treated me was a nightmare and I knew all I had to do was get home and I'd be free again." Kyndan faced him. "The *Dauntless* is still in orbit. I can send you to Rusco, to my father there. You'd be free."

Utar's dark eyes were sad. "You are kindly, Consort. A good man."

"Let me send you to Tellaran space," Kyndan urged. "You deserve better than this."

"Nothing pleased my son more than to see the contests," Utar murmured. "Ulan would talk of them for months before. He knew when I won, I won too his mother's heart. He was already looking to see whom he might come to fight against among those his age. He is determined to win. And Hyari is so very like her mother, her wit, her smile . . ." He shook his head. "There is nothing for me in Tellaran space." He forced a smile. "And I cannot deny you your teacher, Consort."

"I understand," Kyndan said quietly, lifting his sword for the next round. "You have to be where your heart is."

Kyndan bolted down a welcome cup of caf between the sword training and the coming meeting with the war Leader. He and Alari discussed her attending this meeting too and ultimately he decided against it. If he was going to assert himself as warlord he was going to have to do it under his own power.

The mornings he spent training, Alari spent pouring over documents and petitions and reports. Of the two she certainly had the more exhausting task; at least he got to burn off some of his nervous energy. By custom the empress and Regent, if there was one, rarely left the palace grounds except to visit the temples but he was considering arranging a few days at Kinara's house or maybe even somewhere on the other side of Az-kye. There were shadows under Alari's eyes now and, although she would let herself sleep when held safely in his arms, she never seemed rested.

No one should have to shoulder the kind of demands Alari did and the constant attempts to curry favor by advisors and courtiers alike set his teeth on edge. It made him doubly determined that she shouldn't have to do it alone.

He had no trouble getting through the palace now; the courtiers, servants and messengers parted to make way, bowing as he passed.

Fucking hell, when did I get used to that?

"Consort," the majordomo said, hurrying to catch up with him. Like him, Jelara was in her late twenties. She was prettily plump in that sensual way Az-kye women could be. Although Jelara always seemed rushed and a little out of breath, she possessed both boundless enthusiasm and seemingly inexhaustible energy. "Consort, a moment, please!"

He liked Jelara but he didn't want to be late either. "I'm on my way to a meeting with the War Council," Kyndan said, slowing his pace so she could walk beside him. "What can I do for you?"

"As you know the midsummer festival is just weeks away, Consort," Jelara said worriedly. "Ordinarily, of course, it simply would not be a question of whether or not the festivities should take place but perhaps on what scale—"

"Honored Majordomo," he broke in, not unkindly. "Your question?"

"Well, if we are to hold the midsummer festival, Consort," she said, her pretty round face troubled.

"Why wouldn't we?" Not that he knew anything about this festival. He wasn't even sure what god or goddess it honored.

Yeah, I'm going to need to study up on that too. The High Priestess Celara seems to like me okay, maybe she could tutor me a bit on their religious practices.

Jelara's voice dropped. "With Her Imperial Majesty so ill . . ."

Kyndan glanced at the majordomo. That Jelara broached this—that she was looking to *him* for guidance— was growing evidence that he was gaining acceptance, gaining respect, as warlord.

He knew there would be times that he wouldn't want to speak for the empress or Alari but in this case, he knew exactly what they'd want without asking. "Empress Azara would insist on the festival going forward, as will the regent. You should absolutely make the arrangements."

Jelara nodded, looking relieved. "I will begin the preparations. On that note, do you think you will be challenging the contests' winner this year?"

He almost missed a step. "Challenging—?"

"I just thought—" Her face flushed. "Well, it does sometimes happen that the warlord—"

"You know," he said quickly. "The contest winner, uh . . .?"

"Behen of the Li'ru," she supplied.

"Behen worked hard enough for that win," Kyndan said, trying to keep his expression serious. "I don't want to steal his thunder."

She nodded. "I think that gracious, Your Highness. Especially since he was to be presented as mate for Princess Saria but now . . . "

"Well, I'm sure he'll meet some nice girl," Kyndan said and couldn't resist raising an eyebrow at her. "You're still available, aren't you, Jelara? I mean, the royal majordomo is a pretty good catch."

She blushed and fluttered her hand in a weak, dismissive gesture. "He is years younger—"

"My mother was twelve years older than my father. She knocked him flat with one smile."

It was cute how she blinked with interest and hope. That guy, Behen, would be lucky to get her and Kyndan turned his head so she wouldn't misinterpret his amusement.

He stopped short when his gaze fell on the two women to his left bowing to him. They were dressed in court gowns, their hair and jewels done to the best advantage.

It had been nearly a year and a half since he'd seen them but he'd never forget either one.

"Your Highness," the older woman murmured, her daughter beside her.

The hall was populated as usual with clan leaders, scribes, priests and priestesses, and dozens of servants who attended to the running of the Empire, all pausing at the approach of a member of the Imperial family. It didn't take long for those present to glance up to observe that a clan leader and her heiress bowed before the Prince Consort but he did not acknowledge them.

"Narla, *Ti'antah* of the Az'quen," the majordomo murmured. "Her daughter, Unata of the Az'quen."

"I know who they are," Kyndan growled. "I know *very well* who they are."

It was not quite an acknowledgment but looking uneasy, Narla and Unata straightened.

"Consort," Unata said with a smile up at her former slave. "I trust you are well?"

Kyndan's eyes narrowed.

Her face hadn't been so warm, so welcoming when he'd been her property. He'd dropped a goblet once—it hadn't even broken—and she'd had him dragged out to the courtyard of the clanhouse and beaten. When he was shaking, retching, and hurting everywhere, she'd directed he be left there in the dirt to live or die as he would.

Narla's gaze flickered to those observing the exchange and Unata shifted uneasily.

"The warmer weather is most welcome, I find," Narla said, her face flushing. "I hope you are enjoying it, Your Highness?"

Unata looked more unnerved with every passing moment under the Consort's glare and those around them observed the exchange closely.

"There is talk that the rains will come early this year, I understand," Unata ventured.

"I want both of you out of here, *now*," he spat. "And, barring direct order of the empress, the regent, or myself, the Az'quen are never to set foot on the palace grounds again."

The women's faces went white and both cringed, seeing how many, high born and low, were present to witness their banishment.

"Jelara, make sure the Az'quen don't get lost on the way out." Kyndan gestured to two of his honor guards. "Jurar, Liat—you can help her."

Kyndan didn't look back. The majordomo and his guards would do their jobs and, while he was tempted to witness their further humiliation, he wasn't sure he could trust himself to stop there.

Just how much power *did* he have as warlord? Could he have that clanhouse, where he'd suffered so much, burned to the ground? Send *them* into slavery and let them learn firsthand the horror of it?

I could destroy their whole festering clan!

He remembered, months ago, walking this very hall with Tedah and railing against one person possessing so much power as he did now, but part of him relished it.

He stalked through the palace hallway, walking so fast the Az-kye were hurrying to clear the hall and offer their bows.

He had to force himself to focus on the work at hand when he got to the meeting. Mezera, leader of the War Council, and two of her council members were there. Ten warriors, each in charge of different warships, were also in attendance. They offered bows and his greeting to them was terse.

Clearly Mezera was unhappy with having to share military information with him at all. And her glance toward the men showed she was wondering why the warriors were present at all.

"As you can see," Mezera said somewhat stiffly, "our forces are more than adequate to repel any attack."

Kyndan looked over the display showing the deployment and pointed to one section. "You have so many ships concentrated in this one area they're practically bumping into each other. This leaves the other side of our territory barely patrolled, let alone defended."

"We face no threat from the other side of our territory."

"We'd better not because there are no ships there," he said shortly. "We need to redistribute our forces to cover all areas of our space."

Her eyes narrowed. "To do such would leave us vulnerable."

"You mean to the Tellarans," he said.

Mezera's nostrils flared. "Yes, to the Tellarans."

He'd spent a lot of time thinking about this. He was privy to a great deal of Tellaran military information and it would be a betrayal of trust to reveal it. Only if it came to open conflict would he use that information.

He also knew if Central Command made the decision to invade Az-kye space he would have to.

Let's hope they don't do anything so stupid.

"Mezera," he began evenly, "you have five warships patrolling near Az-kanzar. That's an insane number of ships to protect one outlying colony near the border."

"Not for one so close to the Sword!"

"But the Badla—*the Sword*—offers a natural buffer between our space and Tellaran territory and that area is one of the densest. Believe me, no Tellaran ship is going to be able to navigate through ionic eddies like those."

The war leader and her assistants, even the warriors, regarded him with suspicion but there was some doubt in their expressions as well. He could guess what they were thinking.

Are you a Tellaran officer or our warlord?

"Well, let me ask you this," he said. "Could any Az-kye ship make it through?"

"No," she said shortly.

"Then it's safe to assume the Tellarans can't either. I'm not saying we should leave Az-kanzar undefended. But if we redeploy the ships this way," he said, changing the display, "we will have much better coverage and we'll be able to provide any emergency assistance the outlying colonies require. If we'd had this configuration before we might have had ships close enough to assist Princess Saria's ship in time." He held her gaze. "See to it."

Her dark eyes flashed. This was the moment. If Mezera refused or demurred then he was going to have to come down hard. He really hoped she wouldn't force his hand.

"Yes," she said finally, "Warlord."

He gave a short nod then directed his attention to the men present. Behind their inscrutable gazes he could see anxiety. Clearly they were wondering why the new warlord had summoned them.

"Warriors," he said to them. "I have reviewed the service each of you has provided to the Empire. I have examined the commands you have held and investigated reports of your personal honor."

Kyndan knew enough about Az-kye body language to understand that the men were puzzled and tense but none shifted or questioned him.

"And your service has been exemplary. I have decided to divide Az-kye territory into ten military divisions," he said, changing the display to show the new military configuration. "Every division will have its own commander who will report directly to me. I have selected you ten to be Division Commanders."

There was the slightest ripple of shocked pride among them.

"It will require some reshuffling of personnel and ships but I'm confident I can rely on you. A ceremony will take place to officially name you to your new positions. At this ceremony, attended by the regent and the court, I will present each commander a sash of honor to show his new status. You," he said, "will be my most trusted officers. You will be my sword arm."

They were standing a bit straighter and he could tell they really liked that last bit. When he dismissed them, he signaled to Mezera that he wished her to remain behind for a private word.

"Do you have those records I asked for?" he asked. "From Saria's ship?"

"I shall have them to you by midday, Warlord," she said stiffly.

"I appreciate that you didn't make this meeting difficult."

She snorted. "As if I would shame myself by falling into a public power struggle. No, clearly the regent has confidence in your abilities to lead us all. And Mother will be pleased at least," Mezera grumbled. "She much disapproved of my heading the war counsel."

He frowned. "Who's your mother?"

She looked at him as if he was an idiot, and he very much felt like one right then.

"Her Eminence, High Priestess of Lashima."

He blinked. "High Priestess Celara is your mother? I didn't realize."

"It is common knowledge," she said shortly, beginning to gather her things.

High Priestess of the Goddess of Love and Compassion whose daughter led the military? Yeah, I bet that made for some awkwardness at the clan feasts.

"You've done an excellent job as war leader," he said. "My taking the position of warlord is not reflective of your work."

"How kind." She shot him a glare. "You might have said that in front of the others."

"I *will* say it, as will the regent, and the empress—if she's well enough to attend—at that same ceremony when the Division Commanders will be named. Your work will also be honored."

Her gaze met his, surprised. "I see."

"You deserve it." After a moment he gave a half-smile. "I guess you weren't about to argue that."

Mezera lifted an eyebrow. "Hardly." She finished gathering her things and gave him a nod. "You may expect those records shortly, Consort."

36

Daggers

"It actually went better than I expected," Kyndan said as he relayed the events of the meeting to Alari later that evening. "It wouldn't hurt to give Mezera some really impressive gift at the ceremony though, to smooth things over."

Alari took a sip of her tea. "I am pleased it went well."

His brow creased. "What's the matter? Something's wrong, I can tell."

With a wave she sent their attendants away, her face solemn and pale in the fading light of day.

"Kyndan," she said softly. "You banished the Az'quen from the palace."

His nostrils flared. "Damned right I did."

"What was their transgression?"

"Their transgression?" he demanded. "How about almost a year of starving me? Of no medical care and abuse? How about a couple wicked beatings, Alari? Any of those good enough to yank back their invitation to the midsummer festival party?"

She looked at him with her deep, dark eyes. "How did they offend the Imperial Consort?"

"So I'm just supposed to forget what happened? What they did to me? Pretend it didn't fucking happen?"

"My mate," she said softly. "Do you ask that they see only the warlord to whom they must bow when they look on you, you too must see only those who have rendered you the regard due the Imperial Consort."

His lip curled. "So if I want them to pretend I'm not Tellaran—"

"You are not Tellaran," she broke in, distressed. "You are Imperial Consort."

"So *they* pretend I wasn't their slave and *I* pretend I wasn't their slave?"

"Yes."

"They *beat* me, Alari!" His voice rose. "They treated their animals better! Don't you even care?"

"Think you I do not care that you were hurt?" she asked hoarsely. "Think you I do not love you, Kyndan, above all? I would do anything for you, give anything for you."

"Then make what I suffered *mean* something. End the practice of the clanless!"

Her mouth parted and he sat beside her on the chaise and took her hands in his.

"You know it's cruel, Alari, you know it's wrong! It almost happened to you. It happened to me and what's being done to these people is criminal. It has to stop—we can stop it. *You* can stop it. You're Regent. All you have to do is sign an Imperial edict and it's done."

He noticed then how her lips had gone white. He'd thought she was listening in tacit agreement but in truth he realized, he'd frightened her into silence.

"Alari?"

"Kyndan," she whispered. "Did I such, we would not survive a day."

He stared. "These people obey you in everything. The power you have is *immense*."

She shook her head. "I am the defiant Imperial daughter who took a Tellaran as mate and made him warlord. Why think you my mother made me regent, not empress? She could have abdicated the throne, become dowager empress, but she did not. I am her equal but she retains the power to counter all decisions I make."

"So we don't have her confidence after all," he said flatly. "That means we don't really have anyone's confidence."

"We will. In time. When we have shown we honor tradition. When they have become accustomed to our rule. But to defy all tradition so, to cast aside the way of things since the beginning of the clans . . .!"

He wet his lips. "But they would be *free*—"

"Do I proclaim this, take the ability of a clan leader to mete out justice from within her clan, I will take power that has belonged to the *Ti'antahs* since the beginning of the Empire. How will the *Ti'antah* rule her clan does she not have the power to punish?" Alari asked. "Think you they will simply allow me to seize their authority from them without protest? Think you they will wait idly by, content to see what other power I will take from them next?"

He had a sudden sick feeling, remembering Empress Yi'saya thrown to the rocks by her own courtiers. "No. No, they wouldn't."

"And what of the clanless you would free? Think you they could simply go home and be accepted back?"

He swallowed.

"And what would you have us do, my mate, with those who have acted against the Az-kye? The criminals, the warriors who have acted with dishonor?"

"The Tellarans have penal colonies. Prisons where criminals are punished—" He slumped back into the plush cushions of the chaise. Just the infrastructure that would be needed to make that kind of transition was massive and the cultural repercussions . . . "I didn't think this out."

"I would give you anything within my power, Kyndan." Her dark eyes were pained. "But do I do this, I would tear the Empire apart. And we would not survive it."

He passed his hand over his face. "I understand," he said, then he frowned. "With Saria gone . . . If they turned against you, who would rule?"

Her dark eyes were haunted. "The strongest would maneuver to seize the throne by manipulation and bloodshed. Each would offer power and influence to their supporters, offer her daughters as mates to their followers' sons and then seek to destroy competing clans to create a new dynasty."

Mentally he sifted through their many enemies. "Alari, if you had to pick the one who's most likely to succeed to take the throne, who would it be?"

She hesitated. "Kinara of the Az'anti."

He caught his breath. "You think Kinna would—?"

"She sits on the Council for Trade. She is reputed to be a *Cy'atta*, a Stardancer, favored by Lashima. Her star has risen high and quickly. She is lucky, she is beloved. She carries an heiress to her clan even now and her mate is much respected." Alari glanced around, although they were alone in their quarters and she pitched her voice very low. Alari put her hand on his chest. "I have told no one, not even Saria. Kyndan," she whispered, "do I tell you, you must never speak of it."

Frowning, he gave a nod.

"Your sister's popularity is dangerous. It is why my mother sought to destroy her."

"Sought to—?" He shook his head. "Alari, what are you talking about? The empress heaped honors on Kinara. Kinna said she couldn't praise her *enough*."

"The empress did not choose your sister to lead her armada against the Tellarans because she wished her to succeed. My mother intended that she be destroyed."

"But that's crazy." Kyndan's frown deepened. "Tellarans would have conquered Az-kye space."

Alari shook her head quickly. "The empress had a second force, to be commanded by Jazan, behind your sister's. If your sister failed, she would either be killed in battle or so dishonored by failure that my mother could justify destroying her."

Kyndan's eyes widened.

Alari wet her lips. "Your sister is a threat to my clan's rule, to mine. The empress did not expect her to survive that conflict. She was taken unawares when she did."

Kyndan felt his nostrils flare. "Your mother tried to murder my sister?"

"Even she cannot risk to be thought the murderer of a *Cy'atta*. But if your sister were to be dishonored or killed in battle, if by her misfortune she were proved not a favorite of Lashima—"

"Then she's fair game."

"Your sister does not understand the power she has gained, the renown she has. Were she to defy my rule—as a Stardancer, a favorite of the goddess—she may garner enough support to take the throne."

"She's my sister," he said sharply. "We're *family*. Kinna would never do anything like that!"

Alari regarded him silently.

"She wouldn't!" he insisted, his face heating. "If anything she'd come to our defense!"

Alari wet her lips. "It is possible my mother believes that as well. The empress must know too that Kinara regards you still as her brother. If the Lady of the Az'anti will not act against me because you are my mate then she is eliminated as a threat."

He stopped short. "That's why I'm still breathing, right? Why she hasn't just had me dragged off and killed?" he asked angrily. "If the empress gets rid of me you'd get an Az-kye mate but then Kinara would seek revenge and become a real danger to you. It's too risky unless Azara takes me and Kinna out at the same time but with that Stardancer thing she's not confident she can."

Alari dropped her gaze. "It is possible."

He gave a short humorless laugh. "There're godsdamned daggers at our throats and I'm here asking you to turn the Empire upside down by outlawing clanlessness."

"My mate." She took his hand tenderly. "To bring you happiness I would do anything, but—"

"I understand." He sighed, pulling her into his embrace. "I really do. I didn't really stop and think about how much chaos it would cause. I want it so I just assumed everyone would want it. It's just not that simple, is it?"

"No," she said quietly and closed her eyes, her cheek resting against his shoulder. "It is not."

37

The Innocent

Kyndan left Alari sleeping and pulled on a robe, wrapping it around himself as he padded through their empty quarters. As soon as he opened the door Utar straightened. No matter how early he rose he found the former warrior awaiting him in the hall. He'd good-naturedly accused the man of sleeping out here though Utar denied it.

Alari's attendants took a step forward and he waved them back.

"No," he murmured. "Let her sleep a while longer."

It was the second night in a row she'd been woken by a terrifying nightmare. Her screams brought the attendants running and he held her as she sobbed of trying to reach Saria and failing only to watch her sister be pulled into open space.

"Caf?" the former warrior asked quietly.

"Please," Kyndan returned. "I'll meet you downstairs."

He eased the door shut and went down the hall to his dressing room. Alari had her own; her wardrobe as regent would take up the house on Rusco where he'd grown up. He made a habit of bathing after his morning workout but he had to dress in warrior black to get from their quarters to the practice arena. He sat down on the bench and yawned again, trying to rub out the exhaustion from his eyes.

Alari was thinner now, her lovely dark eyes shadowed with fatigue, and he was really starting to worry. She worked constantly and rebuffed any suggestion that she rest or unwind or play, as if an hour's inattention to the Empire's running would have a mob pushing their way into their quarters, ready to throw them from the top of the falls. Only in lovemaking and for a little while afterwards, when she lay cradled in his arms, did she relax at all.

Maybe when I've finished taking the reins from Mezera she'll start to feel safe again. Once I'm truly warlord she'll know I can protect her.

Kyndan leaned down to fasten his boots, hoping the caf would be ready when he got there. He could sure use it.

A light's flash caught his eye. Up on the shelf of his dressing room, placed neatly next to his dress uniform, the indicator on his comm unit flashed again.

Kyndan frowned. No one should be trying to reach him on that thing.

He stood and in one smooth movement grabbed the unit and thumbed the control. "Maere."

"Kyndan." His father sounded relieved, the transmission crackling with static. "I've been hailing you for twenty hours!"

"What's going on?" Kyndan asked. "Where are you? I'm barely getting you."

"I'm just at the edge of the Badlands. I've boosted the signal as best as I can."

Kyndan's frown deepened. There was still a Tellaran ship in orbit. "Why didn't you contact me through the *Dauntless* relays?"

"I couldn't risk anyone to intercepting this. Look, I don't have much time, Kyn. A civilian ship entered Az-kye space two days ago."

"*What*? What the hell were they doing here?"

"Private charter. Apparently they took it for granted that the peace treaty would be signed and decided to cross the border."

Kyndan passed his hand over his face. "Did they exchange fire?"

"No, thank the gods. They managed to get out a distress signal before they were captured."

Kyndan went still and felt a knot form in his stomach. "Father, why are you contacting me?"

"Kyndan, they've been captured by the Az-kye! You know what that means."

He knew very well what that meant.

Kyndan shut his eyes. "You shouldn't have contacted me. There's nothing I can do."

"Kyndan, they're civilians!" Even light years away, even through the static, he could hear the shock and horror in his father's voice. "Most of them are just university kids! You can help them. Godsdamn it, you have to *help* them."

"There's nothing I can do!" Kyndan hissed.

"Listen, Kyn, I can't send the *Dauntless* and I can't go in after them. We'd be violating the non-aggression agreement. You're the only one who can help these people."

He'd just asserted his authority as warlord. What kind of reaction would he get if he turned around and used it to help Tellarans?

"These people are *harmless*," Ryndar continued. "An archeologist and eight of her students plus a civilian transport crew stupid enough to take the job."

His father couldn't see him, at this distance the transmission was audio only, but he shook his head. "I'm sorry. I really am. Have the Tellaran Council make an appeal to the Empire. Send it through official channels."

"There are no official channels! They haven't even agreed to let the talks *begin*! They're under no obligation to send those people home. These people aren't spies, they aren't commandoes. We're talking about fourteen civilians, our own people, enslaved!"

Kyndan wet his lips, gripping the comm unit tightly in his hand.

"Commander, you are still an officer in the Tellaran fleet." His father's voice went hard. "You took a vow to protect these people. I am *ordering* you to get them out of there!"

He'd resigned—no matter what status his father had entered into the official record. He was Imperial Warlord, a member of the Az-kye Imperial family; it wasn't as if the Fleet could court-martial him if he disobeyed an order. He didn't—*couldn't*—show loyalty to the Tellarans, not even his own father.

Godsdamn it, I can't!

But he couldn't get the words out.

If he and Kinara tried to purchase those Tellarans and send them home, it might take years, might even prove impossible, and in the meantime those people would have no rights, no recourse against possibly horrific treatment. Kinara had been able to gather those Tellarans to return them—to return *him*—to Tellaran space and freedom only because she held an Imperial writ from the empress for the period of her command.

He *couldn't* go to Alari with this. Not after the talk they'd had about clanlessness, not after he understood how carefully she treaded, how precarious a balance she held.

But those students wouldn't be much older than Kinna had been when he'd left on his first Fleet rotation, the same age as some of his crew when he'd watched them captured, beaten.

Utar was his friend and he couldn't do a damned thing to free him either.

Kyndan's heart was hammering so hard he felt dizzy and suddenly he was back in that cage, back with his stomach so empty it hurt, having his eye blackened because some fucking Az-kye thought he wasn't moving fast enough.

There were so, so many enslaved, so many suffering, that he couldn't help, maybe not for years and years.

But . . . these very few . . .

"*Commander!*" his father's barked.

"Yes, Sir!" he snapped off automatically, his voice rough.

He drew a deep, steadying breath. His father hadn't been stupid about this. The comm signal they were using now was a military encrypt, and there would be no signal relayed through the *Dauntless* to get picked up by the Az-kye escort ships.

If the warship was still near the Badlands, if the Tellarans were held by a single Az-kye crew, there might be a way to do this quietly.

"Give me all the information you've got, Father," he said hoarsely. "I'll get them home."

38

ᗁᎱᏟᎧ ᎧᎱ
Beloved

Kyndan put the datapad showing the records from Saria's ship and the vessels that answered the distress call on his carved wood desk and sat back, his tea long since gone cold beside him. His stomach was still knotted from what he'd done that morning, of using his authority as warlord to get the Tellarans released, to command the Az-kye crew's silence. He'd thrown himself into this work hoping to assuage some of that guilt, to make up for it by devoting himself entirely to his responsibilities to the Az-kye.

The air was thick with the scent of flowers from enclosed park below and the dark polished paneling of his private sitting room smelled faintly of tashi tree oil polish. Kyndan rubbed his tired eyes and drew in a long slow breath, wondering if it were too late in the day for some caf.

Why is doing the right thing making me feel so fucking sick?

But there was no "right" anymore really; his life no longer had the simple clean lines of right and wrong. Good and bad. Az-kye and Tellaran.

And maybe would never again.

As soon as the war leader submitted the records from Saria's ship, from the vessels that answered the distress call for his review he'd holed up in his private study. This, at least, he could do for Alari and he threw himself into the work hoping to give his heart, and possibly hers, some peace.

"My mate?"

He looked up and gave a smile to see Alari in the doorway. The sun was setting now, and she was only just returning to their quarters.

"Are you well?" she asked, her brow creased.

"I'm fine."

He had a fierce headache and a gut full of guilt, but after the loss of her sister, her mother's illness, and the strain of becoming regent, the last thing she needed was to be worrying over him.

She looked questioningly at the datapad he'd tossed onto the desk. "What troubles you so?"

He glanced at the maids accompanying her. "Leave us and shut the door behind you."

The leather-padded chair creaked as Kyndan stood and he came around the desk to join her, not sure if what he had to tell her was good news or bad. "I was looking over the data from the destruction of Saria's ship."

She went still, as if she were bracing herself. "What have you found?"

"Nothing," he admitted tightly. "I've been over every bit of data that the rescue ship took. The logs they recovered from her vessel, the readings of the ships that were sent to recover the wreckage. Everything. And I can't find a festering thing that's suspicious. Everything points to the navigation system going down, then they wind up off course near the Badlands and before they set out on the correct heading they get hit by an ionic front."

"It was an accident then, after all," Alari said thickly.

He scrubbed his face. "Yeah, an accident."

"Did you—do you know—?"

"The part of the ship where Saria's quarters were located got hit pretty hard. She died quickly." He didn't know that for sure, of course. He could provide enough data to show that part of the ship was very badly damaged though if she asked. And it would give Alari the only comfort he could offer. He cupped her cheek. "I'm sure she didn't suffer."

She swallowed. "Meithea was merciful in that at least."

She stepped into his embrace, her cheek against his shoulder. When he was introduced, he had a few blistering words for the Az-kye Goddess of the Dead for taking Saria away from her sister like this. As a Tellaran, Bathea would guide him to his peace in the spirit world but he could probably talk her into a quick stop to speak his mind to Meithea.

Damn it, I just keep feeling like I missed something . . .

His comset signaled and sighing he reluctantly let her go. "Yes?"

"Your Highness, Kinara is laboring for the child." Aidar's voice, tight with anxiety, filled the room. "She wished you to know."

"That's great!" he enthused then a rush of worry hit him. All their enemies, all the dangers . . . "Isn't it? Is Kinna okay?"

"The healer says the child is strong," Aidar said. "As is my mate. The healer says there is no reason to worry. That we should none of us worry."

Kyndan and Alari exchanged a smile at the sound of just how *not* worried the expectant father sounded.

"We'll meet you at the medcenter," Kyndan said.

"My mate will bear the child at our clanhouse."

"What?" Kyndan stopped short. "*Why?*"

"She wishes it so."

"Damn it," he muttered. Why was she always doing these stupidly stubborn things? He ran his hand through his hair. "All right, we'll be there as soon as we can."

There was a pause.

"Perhaps," Alari said quietly, "it would be best not to burden the Az'anti with an Imperial visit this night, my mate."

"This is *Kinna*, this is my little sister," he said sharply. "I'm going. If it were Saria, you'd be there, wouldn't you?"

Sadness filled her dark eyes.

"Gods, I'm sorry," he said instantly, catching her hand. "That was absolutely—I'm sorry."

She nodded and if Kyndan expected Aidar to disagree, to insist that yes, of course he should come, he was very disappointed.

In fact, his brother-in-law wasn't saying anything at all.

He wet his lips. "Aidar, I know we've had our differences but I need you to be completely honest with me here—What does Kinna want?"

Aidar was silent for a moment. "I think were you Kyndan Maere still then your presence would be a comfort to her," he said slowly. "Perhaps though, Your Highness, it is best for her if you allow us to welcome you at another time."

Alari's fingers intertwined with his.

His throat was tight. In some part of his mind Kinna wasn't a grown woman. She was still a trembling eight-year-old girl with tear-filled blue eyes and he was her big brother, two kids left with a father so stunned by his wife's death he could barely function. For that whole first year Kyndan woke Kinna for school and made her breakfast, made her clean her teeth before bed, checked her homework. His own grief was pushed aside because she needed him to take care of her.

He wanted to be nearby in case she needed him, or needed anything. He wanted to be in the waiting area like any other uncle, ready for the medtech to come and tell him the good news.

But he wasn't like any other uncle now.

Kyndan let his breath out slowly. "If she changes her mind, if she wants me at any time, I'll be there. In fact, I'm going to have a litter at the ready to get me there fast. And the Az'anti will be excused from any 'greeting' nonsense. You contact me if—just keep me informed how things are going, okay?"

"Yes, Your Highness."

"Okay," Kyndan mumbled and ended the call. He gave Alari a rueful smile. "It's going to be a long night."

"Longer for the Lady of the Az'anti, I think," she said, with a small smile.

He gave a short laugh. "Yeah."

"I know you are worried. Distressed that you cannot be there."

"Well, I'm a lot closer than I would have been on the *Sertarian*," he joked, then swallowed. "Aidar'll take good care of her; he'll make sure she gets the best care she can. And I'll get to see Kinna and the baby in a day or so."

She looked at his hand in hers. "I have something for you. Perhaps my gift to distract you."

"Princess." His gaze ran over her. "You have my full attention."

She laughed and shook her head. "Wait here."

"Oh." He raised his eyebrows. "Uh, okay."

Alari slipped out and he went to the balcony of his study. The moons had risen but the palace was still a hub of activity. In the park below he could see that workers were still laboring to prepare for the festival of Azis.

He looked to the west, toward the Az'anti clanhouse. He couldn't see it from here of course, but tonight Kinara would have her baby and the Az'anti would have its new heiress.

A year ago I hated this planet and almost everyone on it. Now not only is it my world, it's a world I'm responsible to protect and defend.

Alari came back carrying a parchment, her dark eyes shining.

And she makes it home.

"What's this?" he asked as she laid the paper on his desk.

She pulled aside the protective parchment and his breath caught.

"It is a gift for you," she said, blushing. "I hope it pleases you."

His eyes went over the sketch; the swaying blooms of trees in the enclosed Imperial park, the fountain at the very center with its spray creating a feeling of movement against a cloudless sky.

"Oh, Alari," he murmured, spreading the drawing over the table. "It's beautiful."

"Does it please you?" she asked. "Truly?"

"I love it." He shook his head, smiling. "When did you even have time to do this?"

She gave a shy shrug. "A little here and there."

"You couldn't have given me anything better."

Her blush deepened.

"What is it?" he asked, catching her against him and very curious now.

"I thought," she mumbled, "perhaps we too could try for a baby, my mate."

He burst out laughing and she gave him a hurt look.

"You do not wish for a child, Kyndan?"

"Oh, believe me," he said, grinning, "I'm ready and willing to do my part." Then his sobered a little. "I wasn't sure if you were ready. I know everyone's been pressuring you."

She looked surprised. "How did you know it so?"

"Are you kidding? If everyone is asking *me* when we're going to be providing an heiress they must be *hounding* you."

"They wish security for our line, they long for the safety of a heiress. But that is not why I wish for a child now." Her mouth curved into a tender smile. "I want something of us, of how I feel for you, to add to the wonder of the universe, to make it that much more beautiful."

Kyndan's eyes stung. A daughter of theirs would rule this vast empire. If they had only boys, the eldest's mate would rule. Any child they created would link them forever throughout time, generations of their progeny—of an Az-kye princess and a Tellaran commoner—would shape this section of the galaxy.

He knew that, of course. But what flashed through his mind was holding a chubby hand for the first steps, tucking a toddler into bed with a story, tickling and giggles and carrying their child on his shoulders.

A child with eyes as dark and beautiful as Alari's.

"Kyndan?" She searched his face. "What is it?"

"I want to be worthy of this. Of you. Of our child." He swallowed hard. "I'm not sure I am."

She traced the curve of his cheek. "I am sure."

Her velvety gaze was lit from within and his heart swelled with gratitude to whatever deity let him be part of her life.

He didn't trust his voice but he managed to nod.

She smiled. "I think that is only the second time I have seen you without words, my mate."

He gave a short, shaky laugh. "I'm sure there were more than two times."

She took his hand, drawing him to their bedchamber. "Well, two where you still clothed."

"Let me," he said softly, then started with the pins that held her dark hair; gently he eased them out, smiling when her glossy hair fell free down her back.

"You know," he said lightly, starting on the shoulder closures of her beaded and embroidered overdress, "I think the toughest thing for me about you being regent is the ten million layers of clothing you have to wear. We both know I'm not a patient man."

She sighed in relief as he eased the heavy layer away.

"I am to represent Lashima of the Night Sky," she reminded. "Though I much wish she were more like the Tellaran's goddess of Love, Arrena, and more often went about naked instead."

He gave a short laugh. "Yeah, but goddesses don't get cold," he reminded, helping her out of the next layers. Alari raised her arms so he could lift the underdress. He tossed it aside and hooked his fingers at her final tiny undergarments to slide them down to her ankles.

Kyndan knelt there, looking up at her, awed as always, at the sight of his princess. "But Arrena can't be more beautiful than you."

"Flatterer," she said and held her arms out to him.

"No," he said seriously and stood. "There is no one, nothing, that compares to you."

"I love you, Kyndan," she whispered. "I could love no other more."

He brushed a tendril away from her cheek then cupped her face to kiss her. She let him deepen the kiss then tugged at his clothing. His hand went the fastenings of his warrior clothing, yanking it free.

When he was bare his fingers lightly traced her cheek. "I want her to look like you."

She touched his chest. "I want him to have your courage."

He swung her into his arms, smiling at her startled, delighted cry, and carried her to the bed. He kissed her forehead, her eyes, her cheeks, brushed her mouth with his as he settled protectively over her.

He was gentle with her, this precious one, taking his time to rouse her, till her cheeks were flushed and her mouth reddened. He watched her face as he moved inside her, watched her intent inward focus as she found her pleasure, and when he couldn't hold back his climax any longer he brought his mouth to hers in the most tender of kisses.

39

Outflanked

The afternoon light warmed the reception room and
Kyndan shifted his weight beside Alari's chair listening
with half an ear as the Priestess of Azis enthusiastically
outlined plans for the coming festival. Alari's seat, while
ornate, was nothing compared to the one in the throne room.
She also wore a more casual gown and conducted today's
meeting without her cornet as regent. Court business was
finally winding to an end and he could hardly wait.

He had a new niece to visit.

The call had come in just before dawn. Kinara had
given birth to—according to a jubilant Aidar—an absolutely
beautiful baby girl they had named Aris.

Showing up for the labor would have been an Az-kye
social blunder but now that the new heiress had made her
appearance it was perfectly acceptable to make their visit to
the clanhouse to present gifts.

He shifted his weight again and Alari sent him an
amused glance. She knew how eager he was for the day's
business to conclude so they could leave. The honor guards,
attendants, and the ornate litter Alari would travel in—as
warlord it was more appropriate that he walk at her side—
were standing by ready for their departure.

"And," the priestess concluded, "with your permission,
Majesty, the final ceremony will take place in the
southernmost park of the Imperial grounds."

"This is a fine plan to honor Azis," Alari said kindly. "I
am sure that we will *all* enjoy this year's festival."

Alari looked at him and he gave a very, very faint smile. That morning he had sent a very *generous*—in his opinion—message inviting the Az'quen to the palace for the festival.

The clan leader of the Az'quen had instantly accepted and sent absolutely gushing well wishes for the Imperial family's health, well-being, future rule, and on and on. Kyndan reminded himself that he just had to be polite to them. He didn't have to *like* them and it meant so much to Alari.

The high priestess beamed and bowed, her attendants, all dressed as brightly as she, bowed as they left.

"I understand that the Az'anti have welcomed a new heiress," Sechon murmured as the next—and hopefully last—order of business was being readied.

"Yes," he said brightly. "A girl, Aris."

The elder gave him a smile. "I hope to visit and offer a gift to the future clan leader in the next few days."

"I hear she's the most beautiful baby ever born on Az-kye."

Sechon's dark eyes were lit with humor. "Ah, well, I shall be sure to claim it so as well when I look on her."

He winked. "She can hold the title until the Imperial Heiress makes her appearance."

The elder caught her breath, her glance going to Alari. "May we thank Lashima that—"

Kyndan cleared his throat. "Not yet. But hopefully soon."

The elder touched his arm, her smile warm. "It will be welcome news indeed, Your Highness."

He barely kept himself from grinning back, imagining a little princess or prince with Alari's dark eyes running through the palace.

"The War Council," the majordomo announced.

Kyndan's brow creased as the women hurried forward. There were five women on the Council and as warlord of course he'd met them all. They'd all seemed to take the news that the Council would soon be dismissed, well, except, of course, for Mezera.

Today, though, they looked positively grim.

Damn it, what now?

Kinara would be expecting them pretty soon and, while it had been agreed formalities would be kept to an absolute minimum, she'd just had a baby. The last thing he wanted was for their visit to be more trying for her. Showing up late because Mezera was scrambling to cling to power as war leader was not something he was going to tolerate.

"Honored Council," he began shortly. As warlord it was his prerogative to speak to them first. "We were just concluding for the day. Is this urgent?"

"This matter is both urgent and grave," Mezera said to Alari.

His eyes narrowed at the omission of his title and the fact that she hadn't addressed him. Alari straightened in her chair, she hadn't missed Mezera's slight either.

"Well?" he demanded. "What is it?"

Mezera kept her gaze on Alari. "We beg you to hear us, Regent."

His face heated with annoyance. Mezera knew very well whom she should be addressing here.

"I'll take the Council to one of the reception rooms so you can finish up here," he said to Alari. Kyndan took a step forward and addressed the War Council. "Come on. Anything you have, you can give it to me there."

"Regent, we are here to safeguard the Empire itself!" Mezera cried. "We will speak only to you."

"We don't have time for your maneuvering today, Mezera," Kyndan snapped. "You're well aware that the Council for War is to be dismissed tomorrow so any information you have, you present to me."

"I have nothing to present to *you*," she snarled.

His nostrils flared. "Then you are excused from our presence!"

"Of course you wish me gone," Mezera spat, her dark eyes glittering. "Of course you wished the War Council dismissed. How much easier then to conceal your actions, Tellaran! Regent, we have proof that this man—" She pointed at him. "This *false* consort is guilty of treason against you!"

40

The Fall

"What the hell are you talking about?" Kyndan demanded.

"Treason," Mezera repeated. "You are an honorless pretender, an agent of the Tellarans sent to destroy us!"

The sword in his back scabbard was proving an awful temptation and Kyndan clenched his fist to keep from drawing it. "I don't know what you think these lies are going to get you, Mezera, but if you're smart you'll stop this right now."

"Lies?" she cried. "*You* are the one who lies, Traitor!"

"You are nothing but a power-hungry schemer," Kyndan snarled. "And if you think you're going to hold on being war leader like this you're dead wrong."

The majordomo, Jelara, was wringing her hands at the turn the audience had taken. The courtiers, clan leaders and their mates in attendance were murmuring amongst themselves.

"Regent," the elder said urgently. "Perhaps it would be best if we should adjourn and—"

"I have proof!" Mezera cried to Alari then the war leader narrowed her eyes at him. "You once led a Tellaran attack against the Az-kye."

"He was a Tellaran officer then," Alari said tightly. "He has already told me of this, War Leader."

"Then tell me, *Consort*," Mezera made his title sound like an obscenity. "Do you take orders from the Tellarans still?"

"No," Kyndan said impatiently. "Of course not."

"He is our warlord," Alari said, standing.

"So he has sworn, but he lies." In response Mezera waved one of her assistants forward. "We intercepted this transmission. It took days to break the encryption. Listen and you will know I speak true!"

The recording began, audio only, the words in Tellaran.

Kyndan felt himself blanch.

"Is that your voice, Consort?" Mezera asked.

Oh, gods. "Yes, but—"

"We do not know what they say," Sechon put in quickly, stepping to his side. "We cannot judge what we do not understand."

"No," Kyndan began. "Hold on. Alari—"

She met his gaze, her dark eyes confused, questioning.

Afraid.

"Translate it," Alari said hoarsely. "Let me hear for myself what they say."

Kyndan swallowed hard as the datastreamer translated the recording into Az-kye.

"—*Commander, you are still an officer in the Tellaran fleet. And I am ordering you to get those people out of there! Commander!*"

"*Yes, Sir!*" A pause. "*Give me all the information you've got. I'll get them home —*"

The room was silent when the recording finally ended.

Alari's gaze met Kyndan's. "You are not a Tellaran officer. You resigned. You told me you had resigned."

He wet his lips. "I did."

"But he calls you 'Commander.'" Alari gestured at the datastreamer. "He says you are an officer still."

Kyndan shut his eyes briefly. "He didn't—When we met he didn't want to accept my resignation. I told him but—he placed me on inactive duty. Gods, Alari, the Fleet is *everything* to my father. I think it was just his crazy way of trying to save my career."

"You lied to me," she breathed, then her voice rose. "You said you had resigned!"

"I *did* resign!"

"Did you follow his orders?" she demanded.

He shook his head. "Alari—"

"Did you?" When he didn't answer she looked at the war leader. "Did he?"

"This traitor ordered the *Oshur* to return the Tellarans to their ship. He ordered that they be permitted to return to Tellaran space." Mezera's nostrils flared. "He ordered the crew of the *Oshur* to conceal this fact and to purge all references of this from their records."

"They were Tellaran civilians!" Kyndan said sharply. "Their only mistake was trusting that peace was at hand— that *I* had done the job my people had sent me here to do. They were godsdamned academics, Alari! An archeologist and a bunch of students who wanted to take a look at ruins on your side of the Badlands!"

The elder put out her hand. "Perhaps, Your Majesty, if it was an act of compassion only—"

"There's more," Mezera spat. "He concealed evidence about Princess Saria's death."

Kyndan's eyes snapped to her. "That's a fucking lie!"

"Saria's death was an accident." Alari shook her head. "There was a storm—"

"And who told you such?" the war leader demanded.

Her gaze went to Kyndan. "You said there was no evidence—"

"Of course there was not!" The war leader threw a glare at him. "He erased it!"

"I didn't *erase* anything!" Kyndan met Alari's wide gaze and softened his voice. "Look, it's true that I helped those people. I spared them years—maybe a *lifetime*—of the worst hell I can imagine. They would be clanless, slaves, and if there's anyone I could save from that misery . . ." He swallowed hard. "Alari, if the Tellarans had broken the nonaggression pact, if they had sent a ship to attack the Az-kye, it would have been different. Those would have been soldiers who knew the risks but these people were innocents. I admit I helped them but before the gods I swear I didn't hide anything else from you. I told you everything I know about Saria's death!"

Alari took a step back. "How? How would it have been possible for him to tamper with them?"

"The consort demanded that he see the records first."

"Yes." Kyndan threw his hand out in frustration. "To find out if Saria's ship had been sabotaged!"

"Imperial Regent," Mezera said urgently. "The data submitted by your consort to the war council is different than the original data sent to him. The records he returned to the Council to support his findings about Princess Saria's death were altered."

Alari's eyes met his and Kyndan shook his head sharply. "That's not true! I returned them just as I got them."

"Altered how?" Alari asked.

Mezera held up a datapad. "Here is the original *unaltered* data."

Wordlessly Alari took the pad from her and looked at the display.

"Regent, you can see it here, from the sensor log of Princess Saria's ship." Mezera pointed to the screen. "A Tellaran energy signature."

"What?" Kyndan rounded on her. "There was no Tellaran ship there!"

"The energy pattern is unmistakable," Mezera retorted. "Az-kye vessels use a single caliber containment design, only *Tellaran* ships use a triple containment design."

"That's not—Let me see." Kyndan took the datapad from Alari and his brow furrowed. "This isn't possible. This *wasn't* in the data I reviewed." He shook his head. "This isn't even large enough to be a cruiser, it's smaller—"

"Then the Tellarans have new, smaller ships that are equally deadly!" Mezera interrupted.

"They don't!" Kyndan objected but he read in their faces that they didn't believe him.

Alari sought his gaze and he shook his head again.

"Alari, I swear to you, there was no Tellaran ship in the records I saw!"

She searched his face for a moment. "The data showing the Tellaran ship," she said finally. "Could it have been altered instead? The ship added when it was not there at all?"

"No," one of the other council members said. "This data was recompiled from the original sensor recordings. We each," she continued, gesturing to her fellows, "came to the same conclusion."

"Very convenient that you decided to recompile them," Kyndan said glaring, "the day before the Council was to be dismissed."

Mezera narrowed her eyes at him. "It was not *convenient*," she hissed. "I discovered by accident that the data showed a discrepancy—that the records you returned were *shorter* than the originals." She looked back at Alari. "The Tellaran signature appears to have been hidden by the storm's disruptions. It appears only for a brief period in the ship's sensor log."

"What are you saying?" Alari whispered.

"Your Majesty," Mezera began urgently. "This man is a traitor. He is still an officer of the Tellaran Fleet. He used his power as Imperial Warlord to act against the interests and security of the Az-kye. He erased evidence that implicates the Tellarans in the destruction of the First Daughter's vessel. We can only assume he did so because it was not a storm that destroyed your sister's ship, that Princess Saria was murdered by the Tellarans."

Alari blanched. "No."

He didn't care that they were all staring at him in shocked horror. No one mattered but her.

"It's not true!" he said roughly. "I didn't have anything to do with Saria's death. I didn't hide anything about it from you. I don't know why there's a Tellaran ship there but there *has* to be an explanation." He wet his lips. "Let me contact Central Command. Let me—"

"You said you had resigned." Alari's hand went to the high headrest as if she needed the throne's support to remain upright. "You used power I gave you as warlord to—I believed you had become Az-kye. I did not want to see. . .You concealed your true loyalties, your true goals, Nisara and—and Saria—" Tears shone in her eyes. "My little sister. . ."

"I didn't—"

She shook her head. "I trusted you."

"Alari, listen to me! I—"

"I *loved* you!" Alari's shout echoed through the throne room.

"No, you have to listen to me! You have to *believe*—!"

"I cannot have one at my side who bears no loyalty to the Az-kye, whose true loyalties have been concealed!" Her grip on the throne tightened, her knuckles showing white. "I cannot have such as a consort. We must be unbound."

"No," Kyndan whispered hoarsely, then his voice rose. "No! I love you, Alari. I would never, never hurt you."

Alari drew herself up and every inch of her form shone with the pride and strength of the hundred generations of Az-kye rulers in her blood.

"You would have no Tellaran endure the pain of being clanless?" she demanded coldly. "I now grant your request."

He held his hands out to her. "Alari, gods, please —!"

"Kyndan Maere," she continued, her voice ringing with icy command, "you—and every other Tellaran—are banished from Imperial space. I will allow your people three days to reach safety then the border will be closed. From that day on any Tellaran found in Imperial territory will be put to death and if *any* Tellaran vessel enters our space again"—Alari's dark eyes burned—"it will be an act of war."

41

ᖴᐧᘔᕽᑎᐧᓬᕽ
Pariah

Alari's honor guard had their blades at his throat before he'd taken two steps after her. Her advisors and the courtiers followed as she swept from the room and the disgusted looks they gave him made it clear he had no allies here.

The guard's eyes, men who only this morning had met his eye with respectful regard, were black ice. Looking past their swords Kyndan saw only one whose face revealed shock and grief.

"Elder!" Kyndan cried.

Sechon stopped and turned to face him, her posture stiff.

"Mezera is lying!" He shook his head. "I didn't do this. I didn't betray Alari!"

Her gaze remained steady, but unyielding to one who she thought a traitor to her beloved regent, to the Az-kye.

"Whatever you believe of me," he said hoarsely, "believe that I love Alari."

Sechon's mouth was still tight, but there was hesitation in her eyes.

"Tell her for me—that I told her the truth, that I loved her from the very first moment I saw her." Kyndan swallowed hard. "Tell her that I always will."

The elder searched his face, then she gave a scant nod.

"And please . . ." Kyndan wet his lips. "Take care of her for me."

Now she did soften and wordlessly Sechon inclined her head. Then she too turned away.

They took his sword and, blades at his back to get him moving, ordered him into the hall.

Kyndan's jaw was so tight it hurt.

Mezera faked the data. Somehow she added a Tellaran energy signature. But it was the comm call that really damned me. She must have been watching me, waiting for something she could use against me—

"Cons—Commander!"

"Your Eminence," he said. Even the guards at his back stopped respectfully as High Priestess Celera made her way to him, leaning heavily on her jeweled cane. From the opposite direction one of lesser priestesses of Lashima came at a run.

He reached out a hand to steady Celara, her white hair a bit windblown, her aged face flushed from her hurry. She waved the priestess forward to offer him a wooden box.

"What's this?" he asked.

The young priestess opened the lid. Within, supported by a pillow of fine cloth, was a small, stoppered bottle. It looked very old and instinctively the scent that rose from it made his gorge rise.

Kyndan recoiled with sudden, horrified understanding. "I don't want it!"

"Commander, you and Princess Alari must be unbound," High Priestess Celera said hurriedly. "The empress has sent me to you."

He pulled up short. "The empress? How could she know already? She wasn't even *in* the audience chamber!"

"Please, there is little time for me to tell you all you need know!" Celara gestured toward the case. "To be unbound you will—"

He remembered how Lianna once argued—successfully—with High Priestess Celara to keep Tedah.

"Since when does the empress get to make Lashima's decisions for her?" Kyndan interrupted. "She'd put it in my heart, wouldn't She? If I were meant to be unbound Lashima would decide. Not the fucking *empress*!"

"Commander, please, I would spare you the agony of being bound to one no longer bound to you—"

"Do you know what they've done? They *lied* to her!"

"Commander—"

His fists clenched, his eyes stinging. "They *took* her from me!"

Celara put her hand on his arm, her dark gaze calm, compassionate.

"No one speaks for the Goddess but Lashima herself," she said quietly. "Not even I, though I have served her these many years. Only you and She truly know what is in your heart."

"I was told no one could be unbound. They said you would never do it," he said, his tone accusing. "Damn it, I don't want this!"

"In all my time serving the Goddess I have never agreed to do so." High Priestess Celara closed her eyes briefly. "Now I have no choice."

"Please." He blinked against the tears blurring his vision. "I love her."

"I believe you," Celara said softly.

He swallowed, his heartbeat picked up with sudden hope. "Will you help me?"

"I am trying to, Commander." She nodded to the bottle. "It will be painful, but do not underestimate the suffering if you do not do this. I would not have grief and longing drive you mad." High Priestess Celara touched his cheek gently. "Trust that the Goddess will not abandon you."

What did I expect? Of course she's talking spiritual matters, she's a priestess.

"What happens . . . what will I feel when it's done?"

"Peace," she promised. "Your heart and mind will be clear again."

"I don't want them clear," he said hoarsely. "I want to stay just as I am. I want her just as she is."

"Commander," Celara urged. "There is little time."

Numbly he took the box. She finished the instructions for an unbinding that he didn't want, then laid her hand on his head—he had to bend down so she could reach—to give Lashima's blessing.

The guards pushed him into the courtyard and Utar met him there with the bag he'd brought from Rusco. A quick check when he put the wooden box in it showed his Tellaran uniforms neatly packed inside.

"I was proud to serve you, Kyndan Maere."

"I don't know how Mezera managed to pull this off but this is not over, not by a fucking long shot," he snarled, slinging the bag over his shoulder. "I'm going to get back here, I'm going to get her back."

Utar regarded him silently and Kyndan realized he must sound like he was raving. The guards still had their swords at the ready but they were a half-dozen paces away.

"Come with me," Kyndan urged, pitching his voice low so the guards wouldn't hear. "You'll be free in Tellaran space. Just as I promised."

"No." Utar's glance slid away. "I cannot."

"You might never see them again," Kyndan said. "Your children. They wouldn't look at you if you did."

"But do I look upon them, I will see them safe and living in honor. And know all I have suffered worthwhile."

"There's no godsdamn way it could be worth—" The breath rushed out of Kyndan's lungs. "This is for *them*? You became clanless for their sake? Why?"

The former warrior regarded him with dark, pained eyes.

"You want to tell me but you can't, can you?" Kyndan breathed. "You can't tell anyone because if you do . . . gods, your children will be cast out too."

Kyndan wet his lips. They were bringing the shuttle to return him to the *Dauntless*, still in orbit around Az-kye. He had a minute, maybe less, to figure this out. Utar couldn't tell him but the warrior *wanted* him to know.

"All right, you were cast out but they wanted you to keep silent even after you were dishonored, so they threatened your kids. That means what you know can still hurt them. Something really bad that you saw or heard—"

There was the tiniest of flickers in those dark eyes.

"You overheard something, something that your clan leader had to shut you up about and quick. But clan leaders are powerful, so who does Helia of the Az'shu fear so much she'd cast out a warrior who didn't deserve it?"

The shuttle was landing; something Kinna had once said about having to lead the Az-kye forces—

"The empress," Kyndan said. "Because the empress can destroy a clan."

The shuttle doors opened, and the warriors moved in, pushing him that way.

"Utar!" he cried. "What did you hear?"

Utar turned his face away, then, so low he could scarcely hear it, the disgraced warrior said, "I am sorry, Kyndan Maere."

42

Six hours later Kyndan sat in the command chair of the *Dauntless*, the blue and green of the Az-kye homeworld spinning below as the last of the shuttles docked.

It was a mad scramble to locate and get everyone on board. They were going to have to push the *Dauntless'* engines to the breaking point to make it across Imperial territory and back to Tellaran space in the thirty hours of safe passage they had left. As it was they'd be lucky not to wind up on the wrong side of the Badlands and target practice for the Az-kye ships. With the new weaponry they might be able to fend off one warship, maybe two, but Kyndan was willing to bet there would be a bunch on hand to make sure the disgraced Consort left Imperial space.

The bridge lift doors opened and Kyndan's brow furrowed.

"Nisara? What are you doing here?"

Nisara came to attention. "Permission to come aboard, Sir."

He gave her a searching look. "I thought you were going to remain on the Imperial world and become Dael's mate, become Az-kye."

Her face tightened. "That isn't the plan any longer."

Guilt tightened his throat. The lengths the Az-Kye were going to in order to get rid of him were hurting a lot of people.

It was ultimately going to hurt them all—Tellaran *and* Az-kye.

"I'm sorry," he said quietly.

Her eyes showed pain for a moment, then she gave a short nod.

"Permission granted," Kyndan said.

Nisara took up her position at the helm and from her movements he could see she was as grateful to have something to do as he was.

His eyes were drawn again to the image of Az-kye on the screen. He was aware of the movements of the bridge crew around him, the reports coming in, Nisara running her final checks before breaking orbit.

Even now he considered trying to stay behind, though it would be insanity. Kinara had offered to hide him, to find some way to conceal him within her clan, but he wasn't about to put his little sister and her new baby in any more danger than they were already in.

His gaze narrowed on the image of the planet, trying to plan, trying to think this out.

He hadn't altered those records, which meant someone else there *had*. Someone who didn't know a festering thing about Tellaran engines because they chose to add a signature that could only belong to a smaller ship, not a Fleet cruiser—the signature read like a civilian freighter. But it *couldn't* have been real. There was no way in hell a Tellaran freighter could go up against an Az-kye warship and survive.

He had to force himself to nod when Nisara asked permission to get underway.

He could almost feel Alari, alone in their chambers, kneeling on the hard floor, her heart hurting so much that death seemed easier . . .

Think, godsdamn it! Think!

If a ship with that small a signature had attacked an Az-kye warship—especially one deemed worthy to transport Princess Saria, Heiress to the Empire—they wouldn't have had the firepower to *dent* her ship's plating, let alone destroy the vessel. A ship that size would have been blown to dust in seconds by the warship's pulse cannons.

The *Dauntless* broke orbit and sped away from the Imperial world. Clenching his fist, Kyndan forced himself to focus past the sick, tearing feeling in his chest, past the agonizing terror he might never see her again.

Someone added that ship to make the Tellarans look guilty, to make me look like a traitor.

The question is who. I certainly made my share of enemies.

That palace was a nest of vipers.

And someone had just forced him to leave Alari in the middle of it.

43

↗⅄ᖚ⅃ЄꓩꓫↃↃꓩ↗ꓫↃↃ
Discernment

An heiress must attend to her duties, not her wants.

Or so her mother had reminded her. But still Alari delayed. She brushed aside the urging of her advisors, her mother's demands, the compassionate coaxing of the high priestess to be unbound immediately.

After three days without him she could hardly eat or sleep, after six she no longer cared to and the longing for him grew with every heartbeat . . .

But that was all she had left of him. The traitor. The false mate.

It shamed her to love him still.

She hoped desperately that she might have gotten with child. Something of him, something perhaps that she could use to force them to allow him back. Surely they would not risk the strain on her body to have her unbound if she were carrying an heiress. They would not risk her health to have her separated from her bound mate for the length of the pregnancy.

That hope proved foolish and on the tenth day after Kyndan's banishment the healers assured her she was not with child after all.

Alari looked at the sky, the same blue as his eyes, as she circled the Imperial park alone. She could stand to have none with her as she walked, round and round, knowing the court whispered that she neglected her duties to pine for him.

He was in Tellaran space now; her warships had reported the moment he left Imperial territory.

By her own order it would be his death to return.

Her mother was relieved to have his treason at last revealed, pleased to have him gone. Far too ill to rise from her bed she had priests of Ren'thar bring the ancient book that cataloged the names of all those within their clan so she could witness for herself Kyndan's name being struck from the record.

Mezera, the war leader, was almost strutting in her triumph, and Alari felt such hatred for the woman that made it hard even to look at her. One good thing about being forced to take another for mate would mean Mezera would be removed from her position of power, denied the fruits of her cruel ambition.

Alari knew they would press her to choose another consort as soon as she was unbound. Already names were being mentioned by clan leaders eager to push their sons forward for her consideration. The thought of it brought such dread she could not even speak to it.

Only the High Priestess Celara, who visited daily with her young attendant bearing the box that Alari refused, and Sechon showed any consideration for the depth of her pain.

Utar, too, watched her with grieved eyes. No other clanless had ever served in the Imperial house but she kept him as an attendant, finding comfort in his silent presence.

Over tea the previous evening Sechon had relayed Kyndan's last message to her. The china rattled in her hand at his words and Alari handed the teacup to her maid and rose, leaving the room without a word.

Had he loved me then? Had he, but simply not enough to choose me over his people?

Alari closed her eyes against exhaustion.

I cannot bear to let him go but I cannot rule like this.
And my people are all I have to live for now.

An hour ago the High Priest of Behur and healers confided that none of their remedies had made any inroad against the empress' illness. There were no medicines or treatments left to try.

It was full summer now, the Imperial gardens ablaze with blooms. The rains would start in a few short months and there was no question her mother would not live to see them.

There is no other choice. And there is no more time.

She paused at the path's edge. The gardener, his fingers knotted with age, stood and bowed at her approach.

At her feet were sprays of flowers, one color among dozens of the blooms and flowering trees in the park.

"Gardener?"

"Yes, Imperial Majesty?"

"That flower," Alari said with a nod at the bloom. "What is it called?"

"Lovers' blush, Your Majesty."

She reached down and plucked a bloom to examine the delicate petals, the sweet fresh scent; the pale pink color that matched exactly the gown Kyndan had purchased for her.

Alari let the flower fall to the stone path.

"Take it and all its like from the palace garden and burn them," she said. "I do not wish to look on it again."

The gardener bowed again and Alari walked, alone, into the palace.

"How do you feel?"

Kyndan lay looking listlessly at the ceiling of his quarters. He couldn't even summon the energy to answer Nisara's question.

At that moment he honestly didn't care if he never spoke again.

They'd crossed into Tellaran space yesterday. Somehow he knew he could tolerate the separation—not that it would be pleasant—if he knew it were temporary but the idea that he would feel this way forever, unchanging, when he would never see her again broke him apart. The *Dauntless* was still two days out from Rusco and he was ready to claw open the hull of the ship to get back to her.

Nisara got him to his quarters. Between rages and the sobs shaking his chest she got out of him where he'd stashed the box Celara had given him.

The high priestess talked about unbinding as if it were a relief, as if it freed one from heartache. Maybe it was a welcome end for an ill-suited pair.

Kyndan knew now that to be unbound from one you loved was agony.

"Like hell," he rasped finally.

"You look it."

Ordinarily he'd smirk, throw out a crack of his own, but he couldn't dredge up the motivation.

She sighed. "Was it bad?"

"You can't imagine." Tears stung his eyes again. "I thought I'd lost her before, now I've really lost her. I can't feel her anymore."

Nisara's frowned. "*Feel* her? Wait, is being bound some kind of telepathic connection?"

"I don't know." He closed his eyes again. "I don't know anything anymore."

He could hear Nisara moving around the cabin. After the palace this really did look the size of a snouse's nest and his chest felt emptier than eternity itself.

"Here." She held a drink pack to his face, the straw already pointed to his mouth. "You must be dying of thirst."

He looked at it dully.

"Come on, Kyn," she urged. "It's going to get better from here. I'm sure of it."

He wasn't, but he let her put the straw in his mouth. He took a pull on the straw, the jinja juice hitting the dry tissues at the back of his throat. It hurt to swallow.

It hurt to live.

"Am I still in command?" he asked when he'd finished the juice.

"Yup." She pushed the empty pack into the trash receptacle. "You've been in here, reading reports or whatever it is you command-types do."

"You shouldn't have done that. Covered for me."

"Yeah, you know." Nisara folded her arms. "I seem to remember someone saving my life during the last Az-kye–Tellaran confrontation. Coming back when the ship was about to blow to hell and carrying me over to the *Sundragon*." She pursed her lips. "Probably shouldn't have done that either, Kyn."

His body ached everywhere. High Priestess Celara hadn't said anything about that either but at least his mind was finally starting to clear.

"Why are you here?" he asked.

Nisara frowned. "Because we're friends. Because you needed me."

"No." He managed to wave his hand a little. "Why didn't you stay on Az-kye with Dael? Why didn't you get married?"

Her face clouded. "He wanted to but Cenon—his sister—was afraid to bring me into the clan. Afraid of the backlash. Az-kye aren't supposed to notice blue eyes or blond hair once you become part of the clan but . . ."

"Alari and I changed that didn't we?" he asked. "Suddenly here was an Az-kye married to a Tellaran, one in a Tellaran uniform, and no one could pretend not to see it."

He rubbed his hand over his eyes. "Kinna was sure she was going to be all right, but—"

"She's been there for a while and she's the Az'anti clan leader. She'll be okay."

"I know Aidar will do everything he can," he swallowed, "to protect her and the baby."

I've got to get back somehow.

"I couldn't ask Dael to—Anyway, Dael and Cenon had it out. It got pretty ugly, vicious even." Nisara gave a bitter snort. "I'm sure you know how sisters can be when they're determined."

Kyndan froze. "What did you say?"

"Nothing against Kinara—" Nisara stammered. "It's just, you know, sometimes sisters are hard to deal with."

Sisters . . .

The empress looking at him with hate from her sickbed, Alari in her white mourning gown, the erased Tellaran ship, the self-hatred in the Jazan's eyes . . .

And it all fell into place.

"Oh, fucking hell," Kyndan whispered.

There was far more going on within the walls of the Imperial palace then he'd ever imagined.

"*That's* why." Kyndan shut his eyes. "That's why he did it."

Gods, this wasn't about getting rid of me at all.
Alari!

Every muscle screamed in protest as Kyndan pushed himself up to sitting.

"Why *who* did *what*?" Nisara asked.

Sweat broke out on his brow and he had to take a few breaths through clenched teeth before he could speak. "Tell the bridge to reverse course and head for the Badlands."

"The Badlands?" Nisara frowned. "Why do you want to go there?"

"Because that's where Princess Saria was murdered." Kyndan gripped the cot, his stomach roiling. "Change course then get me a priority signal to the Tellaran Council."

"Sir?" Nisara's sudden formality showed she was worried that he'd lost it completely. "May I ask why you want to speak to the Council?"

"Because I think they might be interested to know"— Kyndan's jaw hardened and he pushed himself to his feet— "that I'm about to conquer the Az-kye Empire."

44

Dusk

Alari shifted on her bed. Her whole body hurt, her chest cracked open to an emptiness that seemed to stretch into forever.

The high priestess wiped her sweat from her brow with a cool, damp cloth. "How do you feel, Your Highness?"

"Torn," Alari rasped. "As if I will never again be whole."

My heart is his, and his heart is Tellaran . . .

His treason was so clear now. So irrefutable. But she was unprepared for the depth of grief, the scalding agony of losing even this last hopeless link to him.

"To long for him and feel nothing but emptiness in return was torment. I thought now that I am unbound it would be better," Alari said, unable to keep the accusation from her voice. "I thought the pain would be less."

"It will be bearable," High Priestess Celara said.

"Someone else's pain always seems bearable," Alari said bitterly.

"The memories will fade, child." Celara patted her hand. "You will forget."

Alari turned her face toward the window.

"As long as I can see the sky," Alari whispered hoarsely, thinking how today it was just the shade of his eyes when he made one of his jokes, "I will never forget."

They brought her food that seemed tasteless and iced juices that proved bitter on her tongue. Her maids helped her to the bath, exchanging glances as Alari sat in the tub, listlessly letting her tears fall into the water.

It was late afternoon when they coaxed her from the bath.

"No," she said when she saw the black dressing gown her maid was carrying. The attendants were startled. It was the first time she had spoken in hours. "Bring me the white."

"Your Majesty," Tilanna began nervously. "No period of mourning has been declared."

"Do not tell me whether or not I may mourn," Alari said brittlely. "Bring me the white!"

The maids blinked at her harsh tone but they obeyed. Wrapped in a dressing gown of pure white Alari sat with a cup of spiced tea untouched on the low table before her, staring sightlessly over the empress' city.

He had come for her when she was in disgrace, a cast-off princess with no hope to inherit. He had made her laugh, taught her to dance, and brought her to the heights of sexual pleasure with no chance that she should ever make him consort, to give him such immense power.

But she had thought he loved her then.

Was it only that I became regent? Was the opportunity to rule through me simply too tempting?

There was a ripple of consternation in the next room then Tilanna hurried out.

"Your Majesty, your advisors—it is urgent."

Alari shut her eyes. Could they not even for the space of an evening, when it hurt even to draw breath, leave her in peace?

She looked to her maid to order them sent away when Mezera and Sechon hurried in.

They were both pale, their eyes wide with alarm.

"What is it?" Alari asked, frowning. "What do you here?"

"Your Majesty," Mezera began, and Alari saw that she was trembling. "Our outposts, all of them, from Az-kanzar to Az-litha, have gone dark."

Alari glanced between them. "What do you mean 'gone dark'?"

"We cannot raise them," Sechon said. "We cannot raise any forces beyond the home system."

Alari shook her head a little. "A communications problem?"

"There was one last sensor relay before the station on the third moon went dark." Mezera's lips were white. "The relay showed Tellaran ships—an entire Armada closing on the Imperial homeworld."

"It is not possible," Alari managed. "It is *not*. How could they possibly broach our defenses so completely?"

But she knew.

Alari's horrified gaze went to the sky. The sun had nearly set; the stars were just now beginning to appear as the last of the light faded from Az-kye's sky.

"Kyndan . . ."

45

Return

Dressed in Imperial black, attended by her advisors, Her Majesty, Regent of the Az-kye Alari, sat on the throne, her hands folded serenely around her jaha fan, awaiting the conquerors of her empire.

Communications were out. The Tellarans' use of the override codes rendered the Empire helpless and even the most powerful of Az-kye warships drifted away like a child's discarded toy from the invaders' ships. The codes entrusted to the Imperial Consort had been changed upon his disgrace but he had clearly obtained the new ones. The Tellarans took the homeworld and the empress' city with ease; there had been virtually no resistance possible.

And Az-kye swords were no match for Tellaran blasters.

Warriors were hit in groups with wide-beams; some fell before they had even drawn their blades. With no defenses left and the invaders closing in, there was no escape.

There was nothing to do now but wait.

Alari would be the last Az-kye ruler but she would not shame those who sat upon this throne before her by hiding.

The empress too waited here. She had been carried in and sat propped up with pillows, her face ashen. Her eyes were deeply shadowed but there was pride still in the tilt of her chin.

A fearful murmur ran through the courtiers as the sound of blaster fire came from outside.

"Have they broken through the Gate of the Blessed?" Alari asked calmly.

"They have, Your Majesty," the majordomo reported, her voice trembling.

Alari concentrated on keeping her breath so slow and steady that even the jaha feathers on her fan did not stir.

"The warriors in the courtyard have fallen, Imperial Regent," Jelara cried from the window.

She considered ordering her warriors to cease any resistance at all but now, in the final moments of the Empire's twilight, Alari could not deny them honorable deaths.

They would be the fortunate ones.

Her guards, assembled around the dais, tensed at the sound of blaster fire in the hall. As one, their swords cleared the scabbards at their backs to defend her as the doors to the throne room burst open.

Alari's face twitched to watch her guards, honorable warriors all, fall to Tellaran blasters before they had taken a single step.

He led them, these invaders of her home, these conquerors of her people, but then again, she knew he would.

Kyndan wore the dark grey combat uniform of a Tellaran commander and his hair had been cut back to the short length favored by Tellaran warriors. Two dozen Tellarans, all armed with pulse rifles held at the ready, came into the throne room with him.

Kyndan's own hand blaster was leveled at the courtiers but his glance first snapped to her and a look of pleased satisfaction crossed his face.

"Secure the room!"

At his sharp order the Tellarans fanned out, moving the courtiers back, keeping their weapons trained on the prisoners.

Apparently convinced his men would meet no further resistance here, Kyndan raised his weapon to the ready position. Stepping over her fallen guard he crossed to the bottom of the dais to look up at her.

"Gods, I can't tell you how happy I am to see you, Alari," he said, a smile curving his mouth. "But I *am* going to have to ask you to get down off the throne."

"I do not take orders from you, Tellaran," she said coldly. "If you would have me from this throne you will have to tear me from it."

His smile widened. "I bet you five—no, make it *ten* creds—I'll have you off that thing in a couple minutes."

He holstered his blaster and, to Alari's surprise and alarm, approached the empress.

"I'm glad to see you, Your Majesty," he said.

"Alive, you mean." The empress' gaze narrowed. "So that I may witness our defeat at your hands, Tellaran?"

He smirked. "That's one reason, yeah."

Two Tellarans came to the door and Kyndan jerked his chin at them. "Well?"

"The palace is secure, Sir."

"Go make sure it stays that way."

"Yes, Sir!"

"This him?" another Tellaran asked, his hand clasping Utar's upper arm as he brought the former warrior in. "He's the only one I've seen in white."

Kyndan gave a nod. "That's him. How're you, Utar? Did they treat you okay while I was gone?"

The former warrior looked at him with horrified eyes as the Tellaran released his arm. "You—you have done such, Con—Kyndan Maere?" he asked, taking in the warriors lying at Kyndan's feet.

"Oh," Kyndan said. "Right. Let's get these guys out of here. Wouldn't want them to wake up and try to kill me. In fact," he said with a wave at the courtiers, "while you're at it, clear them out of here too. Not them," he said to the Tellarans with a nod toward where Mezera, Sechon, and the High Priestess of Lashima stood at the sides of the dais. "They stay here."

"Wake up?" Alari blurted. "You have not killed them?"

"I haven't killed anyone," Kyndan said, looking a little offended. "I knocked out the sensor grids and transmitted the emergency shutdown codes. Your ships are stalled but the crews are unharmed. The hand weapons my people are using are set on stun."

To her astonishment the guards' chests still rose and fell.

"Why—" Alari began as the Tellarans started to drag her guards out. "Why have you not?"

"I didn't come here to hurt you, Alari," he said seriously. "I came here to save you."

"Save me?" Her brow creased. "Save me from what?"

"Your Eminence," Kyndan said genially to the High Priestess of Lashima. "It's nice to see you again. And," he continued as the last of the courtiers and Tellarans left, "I see the war leader is here, doing her usual excellent work."

Mezera's face flushed. "How were you able to so easily breach our defenses?"

"I had the shutdown codes," he reminded.

"I ordered them changed," the war leader insisted. "I am sure they were."

"Yeah, but I know the algorithms that you use to generate your security codes. With that information breaking the new codes was easy. Elder," he said to Sechon, inclining his head, "I trust you're well? You know," he added, putting his hands on his hips, and nodding round at them all, "I can't begin to tell you how *very* happy I am to be back at the palace again."

"Save me from *what*?" Alari repeated sharply. "Tellaran! I have addressed you!"

"Sorry, 'fraid you'll have to forgive me my good mood." Kyndan threw her a smug look as he crossed the room to the throne room door. "I'm about to win myself ten creds. Although it has been my great pleasure," he said as she clasped his hand and entered the room, "to escort Princess Saria home."

46

The Masked One

"Saria?" Alari breathed.

She shook her head a little but it *was* Saria smiling as Kyndan led her into the room. In the months since her disappearance, she had become a bit thinner, her eyes a touch sadder and more mature, but it was absolutely, unmistakably, her sister.

Alari rose, dimly aware of the others in the throne room who made their own exclamations of amazement, of her mother's cry. Alari dropped the ancient fan, careless that it clattered to the floor, and lifted the skirts of her heavy court gown to race down the dais steps.

"Saria!" she cried, running across the throne room to throw her arms around her sister.

"Alari," Saria said, hugging her back.

"I cannot believe it! I cannot!" Alari drew back to look at her, her hands on either side of Saria's face. "It is you!" She shook her head, laughing a little even as her vision blurred with tears. "It is you! But—how? Where have you been?"

Saria smiled sadly. "Tellaran space. The area they call the Badlands."

"You have been the Tellarans' prisoner all this time?" Alari demanded, with a glare at Kyndan.

He held up his hands. "Oh, now hold on! Tellarans *rescued* her! That Tellaran ship in the recording really was there. Answering the distress call."

"Je—" A shadow crossed Saria's face. "The captain of that vessel rescued me."

"But, why did you not come home? Why did you not contact us?"

Saria hesitated. "I longed to. But to do so would have been . . . difficult."

"The Badland territories aren't exactly home to the most upstanding of Tellaran citizens." Kyndan shifted his weight. "In fact, one of them even nailed me with a blaster bolt when I went to get Saria."

Before Alari could stop herself her glance went over him worriedly. He caught her look and she flushed.

The empress reached her hand toward her daughters. Saria's smile turned toward Azara then her face blanched.

"Mother—! Your Majesty is ill?" Saria cried, hurrying to her to clasp her hand. "Where are the healers? They must be brought immediately!"

The war leader caught her eye and shook her head gravely.

"There's something I have to do now and I'm sorry," Kyndan said, throwing Alari a troubled look. "I really am. But it's all part of the same puzzle."

"Puzzle?" Alari's brow creased. "What do you mean 'puzzle'?"

"Your Majesty," he said, addressing the empress again. "I owe you an apology. I was pretty damned rude to you but I was working under a false belief that made me—well, I sure didn't like you much." His face was grim. "I thought you'd sanctioned Jazan's assaults on Alari but that's not what happened at all."

The empress reared up and Saria's shocked eyes met Alari's.

"*Assaults*—?" Some color came back to Empress Azara's sunken cheeks and her nostrils flared. "Jazan *never*—"

Feeling the eyes of the others in the room too Alari's face heated and she dropped her gaze.

"Your Majesty?" The elder asked, horrified. "Is it true?"

"But . . . Jazan was an Az-kye warrior," the war leader exclaimed. "To do such a thing would cost him all honor, shame his clan beyond redemption."

Alari lifted pained eyes to him. How could he humiliate her further like this? To make so public what she'd suffered?

"I'm sorry," he said again. "But believe me, there's no other way to trace it all back."

"Alari," Saria murmured. "Oh, Sister! That is why you so feared him."

"Is it true?" the empress demanded. "Did Jazan—?"

"You know it so," Alari broke in sharply. "I sought an audience with Your Majesty the next morning. I begged you to release me from my betrothal the first time it happened."

"Yes! But you did never say—Dear gods," the empress cried. "Alari, was *that* why?"

Even now it hurt, even now the feeling of betrayal burned in her chest. "You told me as heiress there were things I must endure."

Azara shook her head. "I did not mean—I thought only that you were anxious of being mated, of the responsibilities to come. Jazan showed only the finest of manners to me. Truly I did not know . . ." The empress' expression collapsed and Alari saw the sheen of tears in her mother's eyes. "I should have known. It is my place to know. Oh, my sweet girl, I am so sorry. I am sorry I did not understand. That I did not hear what you were trying to tell me."

Alari searched her mother's eyes and the genuine sorrow and guilt she saw there healed some of that hurt.

"I don't think Jazan actually wanted to force Alari," Kyndan said. "He was told to."

"Told to?" High Priestess Celara exclaimed.

"Who would tell him to act with such dishonor?" the empress asked, outraged. "And why would he obey?"

"You know, my sister scolded me when I showed up at her clanhouse with Alari because the Az-kye follow strict social rules. They obey their empress. They have to obey the clan leader. They're sworn to obey all their social superiors. Isn't that right?"

Alari's brow furrowed. "The clan leader of the Az'rayah ordered her son to rape me?"

"No. That was orchestrated by the one planning our destruction all along. The one ready to murder everyone in the way to seize the throne. Our enemy from the very beginning," he said.

Kyndan moved protectively to Alari's side and met the dark eyes of the usurper. "You."

47

Revealed

The elder blinked. "Commander, how can you even *think*—"

"Despite what convention says about the clans, Sechon," Kyndan interrupted, "family bonds are very strong among the Az-kye and Jazan was your son's son."

"Well, yes, I told you so myself," Sechon acknowledged, bewildered. "And it is hardly a secret!"

"No, but your orders to him were." Kyndan's face went hard. "You knew Alari wanted to end the betrothal with Jazan. She told me she'd confided her doubts to High Priestess Celara and to one of her mother's advisors—you. Jazan wanted the warlord's power more than anything and this opportunity was too good to pass up, for both of you. You told Jazan the only chance he had left to become warlord was to get Alari pregnant and that's what you told him to do—even if he had to force her."

"What?" the empress rasped.

"Alari once told me it's expected that an Imperial Daughter will bear children with only one man even if, over her lifetime, she has more than one mate," Kyndan continued. "I mean, half-sisters each with a different father's clan interested in seeing them take the throne has been the perfect recipe for civil war in the past, right? And, as you yourself said, Elder, the Az-kye don't like change. If Alari became pregnant through his assaults, the pressure on her to take Jazan as bound mate—to bear children only with him—would have been enormous. He did what you ordered but in his heart it cost him his honor. I saw that guilt, that self-hatred, for myself in the Circle."

"You think I would have told him to do such?" Sechon looked at Alari wide-eyed. "My dear child, have I not always been your friend?"

"Well, Jazan's dead so we can't ask him but there was someone who, very unintentionally, overheard that conversation. Utar was a warrior of the Az'shu clan—your daughter Helia's clan. He heard what Jazan was going to do, what *you* ordered him to do—"

"Your slave is your witness?" the war leader broke in with a disdainful look.

"That's *how* he became a slave," Kyndan returned impatiently and looked at his servant. "Because you did what an honorable warrior would do, you told Helia, the clan leader, what you heard."

"It did no good." Utar's face was drawn and he met Alari's gaze. "I failed you, Your Majesty. I knew what was to come. I should have protected you. I should have found a way and I cannot ask your forgiveness. I cannot ever forgive myself."

Alari's eyes stung but she could not rail against him, this man who had endured clanlessness simply for seeking to prevent Jazan's crimes.

"Helia had to silence him quickly," Kyndan said. "She had to keep what was happening from the empress and she knew no one would listen to a warrior who had been cast out of his clan. Of course, just in case, she warned that if he ever talked, his children would be cast out as well." Kyndan looked at Utar. "That's what you were trying to tell me the day I was banished. I thought you meant that the empress was responsible but you meant the empress would destroy them if she knew."

Utar swallowed and gave a nod.

"You said that Sechon tried to kill Princess Saria," High Priestess Celara reminded, looking deeply distressed. "Have you proof of that as well?"

"Oh, I have proof all right." Kyndan's gaze narrowed on the elder. "I was banished on the charge I altered the records to hide that Tellarans murdered Princess Saria. And those records were altered—by *you*, Sechon. You were there when I asked Mezera for the sensor logs and in that moment I gave you the perfect opportunity to get rid of me. You diverted the records and altered them. I sent what *I* got—the altered copy with the ship's energy echo erased—to Mezera with my findings," he said with a nod to the war leader, who regarded him round-eyed. "And I can't blame you for accusing me of treason, Mezera. I looked guilty as hell. But a treasonous consort was the perfect distraction to keep you—and anyone else—from discovering that *Sechon* was the one responsible for the sabotage of Princess Saria's ship."

"Why would I harm Princess Saria?" Sechon demanded. "She is like my own daughter!"

"She's actually your grand-niece, isn't she? *You* were once Second Imperial Daughter and High Priestess Celara was Third," Kyndan said with a glance at that lady, frowning as she leaned on her jeweled cane. "Taking a place on the Council of Elders means you're out of the running, Sechon, but through you, as Second, your eldest daughter, Helia, has the best claim to the throne."

"But Empress Azara has two daughters," High Priestess Celara said with a frown. "The succession is assured."

"Oh, but it's a lot less assured with only *one* heiress. The original plan was that Alari was going to Az-litha, not

Saria—remember? Plans were already in the works to make Alari regent because of her mother's illness." Kyndan met the elder's gaze. "I doubt you were going to tell Jazan that you intended to murder his new mate. I'll bet too that when the time came you would see to it that Jazan wasn't on-board that ship. You needed him as warlord and even with Alari dead Jazan would still hold that right, remaining in full control of the military until the new First Daughter—Saria—took a mate. Isn't that right, Mezera?"

"Yes," Mezera said, with a frown at Sechon. "And you were very careful to remind me I was to hand over control to Jazan two days after he and Alari were mated, Elder."

"Well, yes! I wished the transition to go smoothly for Alari's mate." Sechon looked at Kyndan. "As I did for you, if you recall, Commander."

Kyndan snorted. "You know, at first I must have seemed like a gift from the gods to you, Elder. Alari's disgraced by marrying me, out of the succession for sure with a Tellaran mate, and there's no warlord to deal with. Even better, now there's only Saria left, only *one* unmated daughter in your way." He regarded Alari. "You've never been off Az-kye."

She frowned. "No. I was First and not permitted to go until I took a mate."

He looked at Saria. "But you were."

Saria blinked. "But I wanted to go!"

"I'm sure you did," Kyndan said. "And you might even have thought it was your idea to ask but I'm pretty sure it wasn't."

"No, I—" Saria frowned and she sought the elder's gaze. "No. *You* came to me the morning after Alari and Kyndan left the palace and suggested I might go in her stead. That if I asked, Her Majesty would allow it."

"Sechon said that I should," the empress added slowly. "That it would do well for Saria to undertake her duties early if she was to become regent."

"And just like that, Sechon arranged for Saria to take her sister's place on the sabotaged ship. Now," Kyndan held up a hand. "Things went off course a bit when Alari was made regent instead of Helia after Saria disappeared. The empress herself told me she had been counseled not to restore Alari's claim to the throne." He glanced at the empress. "By Sechon, right?"

The empress stared at Sechon. "You did counsel me so."

"Sister?" High Priestess Celara asked, her frown deepening.

"It was I who begged Alari to become regent!" the elder exclaimed impatiently. "You were there yourselves!"

"And by doing so," Kyndan agreed sardonically, "you convinced everyone, including me, that you genuinely wanted Alari to take the throne."

"Of course I did! She is my regent."

"Right." Kyndan's nostrils flared. "So the empress is dying, Saria is dead, and Alari is shamed by her disgraced Tellaran consort, harried by rumors that her rule is cursed, rumors I'm sure you helped along. Not *quite* enough to push Alari off the throne—not yet. But with me banished by her own command, Alari is unmated and without a child of her own. Finally, your daughter Helia is within striking distance of the crown."

"This is absurd!" Sechon spat. "I have devoted my life to the service of the Empire."

"Fuck, yeah." Kyndan folded his arms. "Because your daughter, Helia, was supposed to rule it."

"Think you I could have managed such a wide-reaching plot?" Sechon asked. "It would be impossible!"

"Alone, sure. But Jazan's clan was already in your pocket. *You* suggested the empress add all those clan leaders when I arrived for the peace talks, to delay open trade and keep their smuggling business going. Besides, Helia wanted Alari's crown for herself as much as you wanted it for her." Kyndan smirked. "Oh, don't worry, the Az'anti were proud to come to the aid of their regent and the Empress Azara. Helia is being held *very* securely at my sister's clanhouse as we speak."

Sechon's lips thinned.

"So Alari's rule is very shaky. She has to depend on you—her mother's most trusted advisor. With Saria dead and me gone, you can finally maneuver Helia into being named to the succession, you know, just until Alari takes a new mate, has a child of her own. Not that you were ever going to let her live that long. And when Alari succumbs to the same mysterious illness her mother did, *her* heiress— your daughter—Helia would have been crowned empress." Kyndan's jaw clenched. "When I rescued Princess Saria, I also tracked down and captured the Tellaran smugglers you've been working with. Those smugglers have been providing you with qulcyne, a Tellaran poisonous compound that Az-kye healers would almost certainly mistake for an organic illness—one impossible to treat with Az-kye medicine."

"*Poison?*" Alari rounded on Sechon. "You poisoned my mother?"

"She's been poisoning *both* of you," Kyndan said tightly. "Certainly couldn't have you conceiving with me. This would keep you from getting with child too—until it killed you. Easy enough to explain away why you might feel ill, Alari, what with the strain of losing your sister, becoming regent, having your consort betray you. But you would have started getting much sicker as soon as your mother succumbed and you were crowned empress."

"How could she have poisoned us?" the empress asked. "Our food is prepared in the palace kitchens or by our own attendants. Are they all her creatures?"

"The tea," Alari breathed. "She gifts tea to so many—she even sent some when we were at the Az'anti clanhouse." She frowned. "Could it be? She often drank it with me."

"But didn't share the antidote chaser," he said. "It's a slow poison. She wanted both of you to look sick, to give the healers plenty of time to make their best efforts to curb suspicion. And as for proof, that compound will be in both your bloodstreams and in tea she gave you."

"But"—Alari sought his gaze—"Kyndan, you drank it too."

He gave a nod. "That's why she *had* to get rid of me quickly. Mother and daughter suffering the same mysterious symptoms? That could happen. The empress *and* both of us? No, that's way too suspicious." He threw Sechon a cold smile. "You blundered there, Elder. I usually drink caf. I even had my father send more from the *Sundragon* when he came to Az-kye. I didn't drink enough of the tea to get sick. I might never have caught on—if you hadn't forced me away from Alari."

"You were my mother's own sister!" the empress cried. "I thought you my friend!"

"Yeah, I thought she was my friend too, Your Majesty. An Az-kye who could see me as an honorable man, even though I was Tellaran." Kyndan's smile was bitter. "You played me very well, Elder."

Sechon gave a faint smile. "Not well enough, it seems." She glanced at Saria. "That Tellaran ship . . .was something I did not anticipate."

"Yeah, those Tellarans are always fucking things up, aren't they?" Kyndan glanced to where other Tellarans bearing equipment had quietly gathered in the doorway. "Rescuing people you need dead."

Alari looked at her sister, whom Sechon intended to kill. Her mother who had suffered so greatly by the elder's hand, the world and empire beyond that he had conquered though not with bloodthirsty cruelty. Perhaps he would be merciful to her people . . .

She swallowed. "Commander—"

"If this is about the ten creds, you can get it to me later. Over here!" He waved to the Tellarans in the doorway. "Your Majesty, these men are medtechs I've brought to treat you. I give you my word, they will do their best to heal the damage that poison has done."

"It is not too late then?" the empress asked shakily. "I might yet live?"

One of the men already had a medscanner out and was checking the readings. "Before we start any kind of treatment I'd like to have her moved to someplace a little"—he took in the soaring throne room with wide eyes—"uh . . . quieter."

The empress hesitated. "What of my people?"

Kyndan glanced at Alari. "I didn't save the Az-kye from Sechon to see them destroyed."

Azara glanced at the elder, at the medtechs and her daughters. "I did not believe a Tellaran could ever show himself worthy . . . I was mistaken; you are indeed the equal of a warrior, Kyndan Maere."

He inclined his head. "Well, I'm sorry for believing what I did about you too. I'm glad it wasn't true."

"Sir—" one of the medtechs prompted.

"Right." Kyndan stepped back as servants were summoned to carry the empress. He gave permission for Mezera, Saria and the high priestess to accompany her.

The elder clasped her hands before her. "Had I known what you would bring us to, Alari, I would have thrown you to the rocks myself." Sechon's lip curled. "Imperial Regent Alari, last ruler of the Az-kye. She who let a great people be crushed beneath the boot of barbarian conquerors. Generations will curse your name."

"Hey, do me a favor, Utar." Kyndan scooped up one of the swords Alari's honor guard had dropped when stunned and tossed it to him. The warrior caught it deftly. "Get *her*"—with a dark look at Sechon—"out of my sight for a little while."

"Elder?" Utar indicated the door. With a final cold look, Sechon swept past them.

Kyndan turned toward her and Alari lifted her chin. The silence of the soaring space echoed around them as they two, Tellaran and Az-kye, faced each other before the empty throne of a conquered Empire.

48

"So, you have made me your slave after all," Alari said at last.

"Hardly," Kyndan scoffed. "You're Regent of the Az-kye Empire."

Alari sent a meaningful look at the wall of windows behind the throne, at the night sky above. "Your battleships surround my world, Commander. Sechon is right. I am a defeated ruler."

He threw a dismissive glance that way. "Once I'm sure the situation is stabilized here those battleships will be on their way back to Tellaran space."

Alari blinked. "You have conquered us."

"I did what I vowed to do in Lashima's temple. I protected my mate."

Alari searched his face. "I do not understand."

"You would never have listened to me if I'd tried to warn you from Tellaran space and for Sechon to pull this off at all she had to have help. That meant you were here, surrounded by enemies and dependent on your worst enemy of all. You needed me, and the only way I could come back to the Imperial world was pry myself a way in with a Tellaran armada."

"Why would the Tellarans withdraw?" she demanded. "We are defeated."

Kyndan gave a short laugh. "Not defeated, more like stunned by a sucker punch. My lockout isn't going to last forever and that'll leave all those Tellaran ships smack in the middle of Imperial territory and surrounded by very, very angry Az-kye. Believe me, getting those cruisers here is a hell of a lot easier than *keeping* them here. It would cost oceans of Tellaran blood to hold this territory—if it even proved possible, which I doubt. But the Tellarans are getting something even better for their efforts." Kyndan's mouth quirked upward. "Soon the whole Empire will know exactly who just saved their collective butts from the traitors to the throne. There's a lot to be said for the value of Az-kye obligation."

"So now we are in the Tellarans' debt," Alari said, her voice sharp.

Kyndan folded his arms. "Yup."

"What will you have of us then?" Alari asked tightly. "Our servitude?"

"Well, those peace accords I was originally sent here to get, for one. I convinced the Council that saving the rightful heirs and getting a treaty pushed through quickly would be a whole festering lot smarter than fighting a war against the pretenders. And they're eager to open trade, of course."

"'*They*' are?"

Kyndan raised his eyebrows. "In case you missed it, I just saved your throne. The empress just *apologized* to me. Restored my name, praised my honor, declared me as worthy as any warrior . . . for fuck's sake, Alari, weren't you paying attention *at all*?"

"But you—you said you wanted me *off* the throne."

"Well, hell, yeah." In a swift move he caught her against him and gave her a quick smile. "How else am I gonna kiss you?"

She saw a flash of blue eyes then his mouth was on hers, hot and demanding. She softened against him instantly, her arms going around his neck to return his kiss.

When he broke away a little breathless, she searched his eyes.

"I released you from our vows," she said thickly, tears suddenly stinging her eyes as she drew away a little. "I was unbound. I thought—Were you not, Kyndan?"

His face clouded. "Yes," he said fiercely. "And the worst of it was that Sechon's manipulations *took* you from me and there wasn't a godsdamned thing I could do to stop it. I didn't even realize what Sechon had done till I was out of Az-kye space. I left you *alone*, surrounded by enemies and completely unprotected because I was too blinded by worrying about being Az-kye or Tellaran. What I should have been concerned with was being the mate I promised to be, the one you deserved."

He touched his forehead to hers. "The mate I will be now. If you'll have me, Alari."

Tears blurred her vision. "Of course I will have you."

"I miss what we had. I miss being bound to you but being unbound never changed how I feel, not for an instant." Kyndan's fingers whispered over the skin of her cheek. "I love you, Alari. All that matters to me is that we're together."

"I love you too." She closed her eyes briefly. "I never stopped loving you. Being unbound was torment."

His smile was rueful. "I know we can't get back what we had. I know it won't be the same, Alari, but we can still be married the Tellaran way."

Alari's brow creased. "Then you do not wish to be mated the Az-kye way?"

"Mated the—?" Kyndan went still. "Wait, you mean it's possible for us to be bound again?"

"Of course," Alari said, surprised.

His blue eyes were riveted. "Bound . . . the same way?"

She could not help but laugh at his intent expression. "Yes, Kyndan."

On no one, Az-kye or Tellaran, had she ever seen a grin as wide as the one that now spread across Kyndan's face.

"Oh, Princess," he said huskily, pulling her close again. "What are we waiting for?"

The peace accord celebrations rivaled even the festival of Ren'thar. The air was turning cooler but one would have thought it springtime for the excitement on the Imperial world.

In the eastern park of the palace grounds, pavilions were set up, bright with streamers, their colors mingling in the breeze as Alari watched the guests, both Tellaran and Az-kye, stroll the grounds.

"It is going very well," Saria said, coming to join her. She looked over Alari's lilac dress and shook her head. "I did not think to ever see you in colors."

"Nor I you," Alari said with a nod at Saria's crimson gown. "You may be the only First Daughter who has dressed so since the Xar dynasty."

"Yes, well I have your mate to thank for that," Saria said, smiling. "But we all have much to thank your mate for."

Alari's gaze went to where the empress stood talking with the Tellaran ambassador. "Do you think she was disappointed?"

"When Kyndan named his reward? I think our mother would have your heart happy." Saria giggled. "But I do think the court as equally scandalized by the new wearing of colors as they were to hear their former regent would now be a Tellaran artist."

"I will still be Az-kye," Alari reminded. "And the Dethara Academy is one of the finest schools of art in Tellaran space."

Saria took her hand as she had when they were girls. "I will miss you."

"I will come home to visit as often as I can," Alari said. "And I will be the artist I longed to be."

"You are still Second," Saria reminded.

Alari laughed and put her hand over her heart. "And I do beg you, Sister—choose a mate soon so I may be just an Imperial Daughter!"

But Saria was not smiling now. Alari followed her eyes to see a warrior, his gaze hot on her sister for a moment before he turned away to speak to an older man.

"Do you know that warrior?" Alari asked.

"No." Saria let go of her hand. "I do not."

Frowning, Alari took a step to follow her sister when Kyndan caught her from behind.

He kissed her temple, and she smiled over her shoulder at her mate, looking handsome in his blue and white dress uniform.

"Best Tellaran–Az-kye party in history," he said approvingly, his cheek against hers.

She laughed. "*First* Tellaran–Az-kye party in history."

"My father just told the Niman ambassador that he thinks Aris'll be talking any day now," Kyndan said.

Ryndar Maere had hardly relinquished his granddaughter since his arrival. Kinara and even Aidar watched with warm amusement as he doted on the baby. The admiral proudly displayed Aris, who took in everything with her father's dark eyes and her mother's smile, to visiting dignitaries and clan leaders alike.

"She is but four months old!" Alari protested.

"Yeah, of course the ambassador got her job by knowing how to be diplomatic. She was nice enough not to contradict him."

As the Tellaran dignitary moved off, the empress nodded in their direction.

Kyndan caught her hand. "Looks like your mother wants to talk to us."

The empress, now restored to health, looked twenty years younger and her eyes on Kyndan were genuinely warm. "I was just discussing the possibility of Princess Saria making a state visit to Tellaran space."

Alari smiled. "Mother, that is a wonderful idea."

"Now that the Tellarans are our allies," the empress said, "it is important that we learn as much about each other as we can."

"Maybe you should make a visit too," Kyndan said. "No reason the Imperial Daughters should have all the fun."

The empress blinked. "I did not—" but then she smiled. "Yes, perhaps I should."

"Imperial Majesty," Kyndan said suddenly. "Is it my imagination or are you wearing *blue*?"

"It is dark blue," Azara said a little defensively. "I thought—well, if the Imperial Daughters have decided to honor the Goddess Azis by the wearing of bright color perhaps I too . . ."

"It's very becoming," Kyndan said seriously. His glance went to Utar standing nearby, dressed again in warrior black. The empress had also granted Kyndan's request and issued an Imperial edict to empower the owner of any clanless to free them. Kyndan had freed Utar before the seal had time to cool. "I bet I'm not the only one who thinks so."

Utar flushed but surprisingly the empress did too.

Alari hid her smile. *Apparently we are not only ones who have noticed those admiring glances.*

"You know, Tellarans make a fabric called shimmersilk," Kyndan said. "I had my father bring some for Alari. Perhaps you would honor me by accepting a bolt as well? Maybe in an emerald green?"

Still pink-cheeked, the empress inclined her head graciously. She also suddenly found a pressing need to speak with the Apovian representative.

"You shouldn't tease her like that," Alari said, smiling.

"I was teasing *him*," Kyndan corrected, watching Utar hurry in the opposite direction to join his son and daughter by the fountain. "You'd think a warrior who took the famous Nuhar apart in the contests would have enough courage to ask a woman to dinner."

"He would be asking the empress to dinner."

"Okay, so we just need to get *her* to ask *him*." He raised an eyebrow. "You don't disapprove, do you?"

"You mean of royalty taking a once clanless man as mate?" she asked mock-scandalized. "Can you imagine?"

"Almost as bad as being mated to a Tellaran."

"You know there will be many more such pairings to come," she said, with a nod at the Tellarans and the Az-kye mixing, the lingering glances and flirtations.

"You know, I don't know if I mentioned this," Kyndan murmured into her ear, "but the only thing better than getting bound to you once, Alari, was getting bound to you *twice*."

"I think you might have done," she said with a laugh.

He pulled her close and touched his forehead to hers, his blue eyes shining. "Then have I mentioned today how much I love you, Princess?"

"And I love you," she said, lifting her face for his kiss. "My brave, wonderful Tellaran warrior."

Also by
Ariel MacArran...

Futuristic Romance
Available Now!

Kinara's quest for revenge goes horribly wrong when she crosses into Az-kye space. Defeated and enslaved Kinara offers herself to Aidar, the Az-kye commander, in exchange for her crew's protection. But this warrior wants much more than just her submission, he wants her to give herself completely . . .

STARDANCER
An excerpt follows

STARDANCER
©2013 Ariel MacArran

Tall and heavily muscled, the passing warriors were indeed an intimidating bunch. Between the arrogance of their strides, the dark skins they wore and the obvious scars of battle-hardened men, they seemed to be spoiling for a fight.

They might be strong, but she bet if something blocked their way they would probably hammer at it for hours with a sword rather than simply walk around it.

The thought made Kinara smile.

"That warrior pleases you?"

"Huh?" she said, jolted out of her thoughts to find a warrior looking back at her intently as they passed.

"Perhaps pleases you enough to share a bed with him."

She looked at Aidar to see that he was genuinely annoyed. "No, I was just thinking."

"And looking you on other warriors."

"Is there something wrong with looking? I'm curious about your people too."

"Do you look so boldly on them, they will think you wish them to join with you."

Kinara immediately dropped her eyes. She didn't want any of these warriors thinking she was making offers, and she didn't want any trouble right now either. She watched her feet and she looked at the walls. She tried to make a mental map of the ship so she could get back to her crew if an opportunity for escape came up.

They went down a passage she hadn't seen yet, but the curve of the floor was so steep she knew they were going down another level. Aidar nodded to the warriors at the door. One of the warriors stepped forward to follow them inside and the other opened the door.

The sight that greeted her was appalling. Her crew was here, dressed as she in plain white smocks, but if Barin's slave quarters were bad, these were atrocious.

They were herded together like animals, and there was not so much as a heating unit or a blanket here. Cold lights placed high on the walls gave a sickly greenish light and the room was freezing. Kinara suddenly realized that they were huddled together mainly for warmth.

Tears stung her eyes at the enthusiastic greeting they gave her. They looked so frightened, and so young. Tedah rushed forward and and pulled her into his arms.

He was dirty and the growth of his beard scratched her cheek as he hugged her.

"I'm so sorry," she whispered. "I'm sorry about all of this."

"Kinna, I thought they'd- no, never mind. You're all right." He cupped her face, and briefly kissed her. "You're all right."

"Tedah, is everyone-?" This was her fault, all of it, and the shame she felt wouldn't let her finish.

"We're all right," he soothed. "We haven't been hurt and everyone else is here."

All right for now. But in a place like this they wouldn't be all right for long.

She let go of Tedah, motioning him to stay behind.

She stood before Aidar.

"My lord—" It took a moment before she could lift her eyes. "My lord, please, my people are not used to this treatment. They will sicken and die in this cold. Please, some blankets and heating unit—"

His disbelief was evident. "They will not die. Even Tellarans cannot be so weak."

"They will. Look at them."

His dark eyes ran over them with a mixture of contempt and calculation.

"Please, some comfort for them would-"

His lip curled. "Think you I care for the comfort of slaves? Come, if looking on them upsets you so, we will leave."

She put her hand on his arm.

"Please, Ad- my lord," she said, her voice low and her eyes downcast. "I would—" She swallowed. "I would be grateful."

He looked at her face, glanced at her body. "And in your gratitude, *Cy'atta*, what do you offer?"

She wet her lips. "You wanted to bed me. You wanted me willing. That is what I offer."

Stay informed at www.arielmacarran.com

Historical Romance
by Ariel MacArran

Available Now

Fleeing charges of witchcraft at the English court, Lady Isabella Beaufort agrees to a marriage arranged by her cousin, Queen Joan of Scotland. Deep in the Highlands, Isabella is captured by Colyne MacKimzie, an enemy to the king and a man set on claiming a rich ransom for her return.

Even as she is drawn irresistibly to Colyne, Isabella's visions show her terrifying images of him. Colyne knows giving into his desire for this beautiful, haunted woman invites his swift destruction just as he knows he will risk anything to have . . .

Another Man's Bride
An excerpt follows

Another Man's Bride

She might have been alone in the world, Isabella thought, as the silence deepened around her. She could neither see nor hear the others from her place by the well. There was no sound but the faint stirring of the cloths as they moved in the breeze and Isabella stood for a long time, watching them.

Offer a prayer for herself? What could she pray for? A swift end to her imprisonment? That she find her betrothed pleasing, and he, her? She had all the wealth she could wish for. Provided her husband did not squander it or deny her pin money, she should never fear hunger or cold.

Nothing she could think of seemed right somehow.

An end to her visions?

The visions retreated to haunt her nightmares but she knew they would return. She might have escaped her enemies at Bella Court by fleeing to this frozen country but they would follow her to the ends of the world.

She dipped the cloth in the water, surprisingly warm despite the frigid weather.

Isabella thought of the French girl she had seen in Rouen, the girl they called La Purcell, twisting and screaming in the flames.

Her hands were shaking as she tied the cloth to the tree.

"Please," she whispered.

Isabella looked at her tied cloth, hanging on the branch in this sacred place. She bent her head and heard a sound behind her. Seeing who it was, she quickly fanned her hair to hide her face.

"What is it, lass?" Colyne asked softly.

She kept her head turned away and her hand covered her mouth.

"Are ye longin' for home then?"

She did not reply and he continued, his voice rough, "Ye're nae afeared of me, are ye? I'd never hurt ye."

Her eyes closed when she felt him touch her hair, sliding his fingers through the strands. Just that simple touch was enough to break through her fragile self control and very gently he gathered her in his embrace as she sobbed. His body was warm, a refuge in a world of loneliness, and she clung to him. He rocked her, murmuring soothing words softened with a Scottish burr.

Isabella lifted her face as he pressed a kiss to her temple. His eyes searched her face for an instant, and then he caught her chin gently, tilting his head to bring his mouth to hers.

She clung to him as he explored, reaching up to his powerful shoulders, catching the silky strands of his brilliant hair between her fingers. His hands were under her cape now. This kiss was gentler yet hungrier than the last.

He broke away suddenly, breathing hard, his forehead against hers.

Had she done something wrong? Timidly she tilted her head to bring her mouth to his again but he would not let her. He squeezed his eyes shut, and with his hands firmly at her waist, pushed her away.

Shocked by the chill Isabella scrambled to pull her cloak closed against the cold. He was looking down at her, his mouth tight and drawn now.

"Ye're not for me."

Of course, Isabella thought. *Alisoun.*

And Douglas.

"No," she agreed hoarsely.

"Dinna fear." He took a step back, his mouth tight. "I'll nae lay a hand on ye again, lady."

With that he was gone, leaving her alone and bereft in the cold, a thousand heartfelt prayers fluttering in the tree beside her.

Stay informed at www.arielmacarran.com

Also by

Ariel MacArran...

Futuristic Romance
Available Now

Discovery means death but Arissa risks everything to save
Fleet officer Jolar's life. Repaying this telepath means
saving her from execution but Jolar will do whatever it
takes to clear his debt to her. The only thing he absolutely
cannot let himself do is fall in love with her . . .

The Seer
An excerpt follows

The Seer
©2014 Ariel MacArran

Jolar reached into his pocket and pulled out an ID scanner. "Come here."

Arissa recoiled instinctively. "What's that for? You already have my scan."

"Here's the first rule if you want to live, Arissa. You do *what* I tell you *when* I tell you," he bit out. "Come *here*."

She took a few reluctant steps closer, watching him warily.

He held the scanner up near her eye and caught her chin before she could turn away. "Don't flinch. It's a simple ID scan. People do it everyday, several times a day. It doesn't hurt and no one is afraid of them."

Arissa willed herself not to move as he flashed the red light in her eye.

He glanced at the reading. He turned the scanner so she could see the display.

She blinked. It was her face, her as she was now, not a little girl's face. No black stripe above her image reading 'deceased'.

"*Legan*, Arissa?" she breathed. "What is this?"

"That's your new name. Hope you like it, though doesn't much matter if you don't."

"My new—?" The breath rushed out of her lungs. "I have an ID? Will it—Will that show on all the scanners?"

"Oh, yes. System wide, absolutely authentic and official."

An ID, a real one, a non-telepath one? The possibilities, the safety, the *freedom* of it made her dizzy.

"You did that?" Arissa managed.

"No, I called in every favor and debt owed me to *make* that happen. I just burned through every bit of influence I've built up in the last ten years – goodwill that was intended to land me Zartan's seat on the Tellaran Council after I retire from the Fleet." Jolar's eyes were blue ice. "I expect to be well paid in return."

"Oh." She wet her lips and glanced at the cot. A real ID in return for letting him have her? She couldn't afford to refuse, it didn't even occur to her to try. "You want—I mean, here or—?"

He burst out laughing and Arissa's face went hot.

"You couldn't fuck me enough to pay for this!" Jolar sobered. "No, that's not what I want from you. There's something on Sertar I have to do. Something important. Having a woman with me is actually a liability—unless she has a unique talent to bring to the table. *Your* talent."

She searched his face. "You need a telepath."

"Want one," he corrected. "I don't need one. Which means you do as you're told or your best hope is that Doctor de'Sar gets her longed-for opportunity to study one of you. Are we clear?"

Arissa swallowed. "Yes."

He held up the scanner. "This is a solid ID—unless something happens to me. Make sure *nothing* happens to me. Still clear?"

Her cheeks were burning. "Don't kill you in your sleep. Got it."

His sense was as cold as his eyes now. "Don't misunderstand me. If I think for a moment you've betrayed me, I'll put that blaster bolt in your head myself."

He was such a jumble of emotion she couldn't sort it all but just the words hurt. She blinked away the sudden sting of tears. "Sorry. I was—I was joking."

He locked gazes with her. "Don't joke like that again."

She dropped her eyes.

"All right," he said finally. "You're going to shower and change. I have clothes for you. They might not fit perfectly or be what you like, but put them on anyway. Fix yourself up as best you can in twenty minutes."

Arissa frowned. "Why?"

"Because that's how much time I'm giving you," he said impatiently, turning away.

She pushed the curls out of her face. "Whatever you say, Commander."

His sudden anger hit her so hard she gasped.

"Don't *ever* call me that again," he snarled. "Understand?"

She shook her head. "I don't—I mean, I thought—well, isn't that what you are?"

He gave her a narrow look. "Are you fucking with me? Or have you forgotten I know you're a Seer?"

Arissa seethed. "Are you expecting me to read your every thought? Because it doesn't work like that. I *told* you. And if you want me to help you, you're going to have to tell *me* what you need me to do."

He huffed a sigh. "Fine. Part of our cover story is I never rose above Lieutenant. I left the fleet five years ago when we moved to Aylor. Can you remember that? Because it's time to go."

She frowned. "We? Our cover story?"

"Yes, *we*. I'm Jolar Legan." He nodded toward the open door of the cell. "Your husband."

Acknowledgments

Many thanks to my amazing editor, Erin McCabe, for her work on *The Consort*! She has a keen eye, wonderful ideas and a great sense of humor. Working with her is a privilege and a joy!

Thanks again to my cover designer Steven James Catizone for making my vision for the book a reality. I am so grateful for the beautiful covers!

Thank you to my friends who supported and encouraged me and, most of all, to my family.

About
Ariel MacArran

Ariel MacArran has had a lifelong love of books, stories and writing. Nothing makes her happier than the opportunity to give back some of the magic of being swept up into a story that other writers have given her. Ariel lives in Charleston, South Carolina.

Ariel loves hearing from readers! Please visit her website:

www.arielmacarran.com

www.ingramcontent.com/pod-product-compliance
Lightning Source LLC
Chambersburg PA
CBHW020824180626
46814CB00001B/93